Michele Giuttari is former head of the Florence Police Force (1995-2003), where he was responsible for reopening the Monster of Florence case and jailing several key Mafia figures. He is now a special advisor to the interior minister in Rome, with a remit to monitor Mafia activity.

DEATH
UNDER A
TUSCAN SUN

MICHELE GIUTTARI

Translated by Isabelle Kaufeler

Little, Brown

LITTLE, BROWN

First published in Great Britain in 2015 by Little, Brown

3 5 7 9 10 8 6 4 2

A CIP catalogue record for this book
is available from the British Library.

Hardback ISBN 978-1-4087-0600-8
Trade Paperback ISBN 978-0-4087-0601-5

Typeset in Horley OS by M Rules
Printed and bound in Great Britain by
Clays Ltd, St Ives plc

Papers used by Little, Brown are from well-managed forests
and other responsible sources.

MIX
Paper from
responsible sources
FSC® C104740

Little, Brown
An imprint of
Little, Brown Book Group
100 Victoria Embankment
London EC4Y 0DY

An Hachette UK Company
www.hachette.co.uk

www.littlebrown.co.uk

For Christa

For me, justice for the individual, be he the humblest,
is everything. All else comes after.

Gandhi

PROLOGUE

Morning, Saturday 30 October 2004, Florence

Darkness.

Her eyes would not open.

She tried to say something, but in vain. It was as if her eyes and mouth were sealed.

Her mind was full of blurry fragments of memories. Confused voices. Indistinct noises. Distant echoes. Harsh blows that ripped through the air, followed by endless silences.

And then that sharp, scorching pain, obliterating everything else.

After a while she thought she heard a voice and a shiver ran down her back. She tried to get up, but she couldn't feel her own body. She tried to speak again but only managed a few muffled syllables.

The wait was infinite.

When she finally opened an eye, a single strip of colourless, ashy light burst into view.

Her mind was a dense web of memories, impossible to unravel.

She closed her eye again and the darkness overcame her once more.

4.20 p.m.

She re-emerged from oblivion with a horrific headache and pain in every part of her body. Her breathing was laboured, her stomach was in knots and she felt extremely sick.

She tried to open her eyes again and this time she succeeded.

She saw a man sitting on a metal chair, one leg crossed over the other, his fingers tapping rapidly at the keypad of a mobile phone. She recognised his face immediately.

Her breathing sped up and her eyes grew damp.

With an annoying bleep, the machinery to her left registered the increase in her heart rate, which was now pumping way too fast.

'But . . . ?'

'Don't speak,' murmured the man, getting up from the chair. He came closer and stroked her arm without the drip in it. He stared at her and she noticed that two dark circles had appeared below his beautiful black eyes that were normally so lively. She let her gaze move past his head to work out where she was: it couldn't be anywhere but a hospital room. The pale green walls and the smell of disinfectant in the air left no room for doubt.

'But . . . where a—'

'You mustn't tire yourself. You need to stay calm, this will all be over soon,' he interrupted her again.

She looked at him for a long moment. 'What happened to me?' she asked.

He didn't respond.

'How long have I been here?'

'More than twenty-four hours,' the man told her, without taking his hand off her arm, his eyes fixed on hers and a gentle smile on his face. 'Don't you remember anything?'

She seemed to be thinking. New details were surfacing in her mind. The raid, the shots, the burning in her shoulder . . . She concentrated harder, staring at the ceiling as she tried not to succumb to panic, but she couldn't visualise anything beyond the odd blurry image.

It was as if, after a certain point, the darkness had swallowed up everything else in that damaging silence.

Looking at the man once more, she asked, 'But will it really all be over soon?'

'Yes.'

'I want to know what happened.'

'I will tell you.'

'Why not now?

'It's not the right time for that. You need to concentrate on getting back on your feet.'

'They shot me, didn't they?'

It was her first lucid moment.

'Yes, that's right.'

She felt the sharp pain in her shoulder and her head: she knew it, knew she was about to return to the darkness. She looked around again and scrutinised the room, lit by the pallid glow from the neon strip-light, in search of further answers. As if those green walls could talk. The other two beds were empty. It was just her. She lowered her gaze to the bedcovers and read the letters *S.M.A.*

'I'll come back and see you again,' the man murmured to her as he said goodbye, and in that moment she thought she saw a guilty expression on his face.

She wanted to shout after him that it was nobody's fault, but he had already gone.

That night her doubts kept her awake for a long time.

There was only one thing she was sure of: for her, nothing would be how it was before.

She breathed deeply, gritting her teeth, and found the inner strength to confront the thoughts that were terrifying her. She dived into that languid flow, letting herself be carried along by the river of memories. And she saw.

She relived every single event, right from the beginning, as if in a film. Every sequence brought to life forgotten, tension-laden freeze-frames from the preceding weeks. She gradually felt such a fierce rage grow inside her that it took her breath away. She felt the blood pulsing in her neck and she began to gasp, especially when she relived the final scenes, scenes she would never be able to erase and which would torture her for who knew how long.

She clenched her fists as green lines worked their way across the monitor beside the bed. And in her heart she prayed to God to let her live.

She was only twenty-six.

PART ONE

AN OUTSTANDING DEBT

1

Monday 27 September 2004, Pisa

The three weeks in the infirmary had seemed an eternity to Daniele De Robertis. They had treated a gunshot wound to his right wrist, the hand with which he'd been holding the gun during his shoot-out with the police.

He had been in that cell with its rusty bunk for three days now. It was a narrow space, a little under ten feet square, a squalid hole where he felt in constant danger. If nothing else, he was alone. Many would have considered this a privilege, but that thought did not even occur to him. It would never have crossed his mind that someone might show him any favouritism.

He suddenly felt as if he were suffocating, as if his life was coming to an end.

Gripped by panic, he looked around him: even the grimy walls, their original colour no longer identifiable, made him breathless. And then there were the unbearable odours of urine and sweat stagnating in the air. They had insinuated themselves into his nostrils and he couldn't get rid of them.

But there was something else tormenting him. *Those* terrible memories, which had returned several times to rob him of his sleep the last three nights; deep, indelible traumas, distant yet ever-present because they were seared into his memory. They hadn't left him for a moment, not even when day began to dawn.

He was still short of breath. And he was irritated by everything going on outside the four walls of his cell, too: the coughing fits, the cacophony of noise, the stink from the kitchens, the invisible subterranean world inhabited by horrible insects that seemed to want to attack him by night, to torture him and suck the remaining life out of him. He even thought he saw an army of enormous cockroaches emerge from the corners, crawling up the side of the bed and clambering all over his body.

This place is sucking out my soul, he thought. It's worse than death.

Being in prison made him feel like a man without a future at the age of thirty-six.

The pain was spreading through his bones now, worse than ever. He could feel his nerves twisting, and he had to bite his lip to stop himself crying out.

Stretched out on the thin, sticky mattress, he tried to regain control while he still had some energy left. He glanced at the window, on the other side of a solid metal grille, and saw dust motes floating in front of him and a glimpse of the clear blue sky. Nothing else. But he imagined the outline of the hills undulating in the light of the sun, and, beyond them, the mountainside where he had spent his childhood and adolescence. The place where, through a vile twist of fate, all hope of a normal life had been brought to an end when he was not much more than a boy. It was there that he had been first a defenceless target, then a killer with scores to settle, until finally he was hunted down like prey, with no means of escape.

His entire existence had been caught up in the circle of his own evil, a spiral from which it was impossible to escape.

There were so many questions in his head.

Too many thoughts.

He looked away from the view of the world outside and returned his gaze to those four walls. In addition to the damp patches, they were covered in graffiti, although much of the writing was indecipherable. Some were bold slogans, carved with the most unlikely objects by those who had been there before him, perhaps to combat the boredom and the sadness, perhaps to leave one last trace of themselves.

One seemed to shout louder than the others: FREEDOM COMMANDS A HIGH PRICE, FIND THE COURAGE TO PAY IT!

He was reflecting on those words when the sound of approaching footsteps made him turn towards the door.

'Hey, De Robertis! You've got a visitor,' announced the guard in a strong Calabrian accent. In his right hand was a bunch of keys that were fixed to his uniform belt with a long chain.

He got up reluctantly from the bed, put on his laceless tennis shoes and shuffled out without changing, still wearing the black tracksuit he'd slept in.

His face sported a three-week-old beard and he looked like someone else, someone completely anonymous, no different to everyone else in that place. Even his hair, which he was always dyeing different colours, and which, combined with his six-foot-plus athletic physique, used to catch the eye of the most beautiful women, had been shaved off.

His hard, icy gaze was but a distant memory. His eyes, which could be grey, or sometimes green or blue, depending on the situation, were hollow and expressionless now. They no longer had that cold, ruthless look that told of another life comprising too many dark days and too much suffering for such a young man.

Until that point nobody had come to see him, and deep down he would never have expected a visit. The only person he had left lived in Paris and was dependent on an electric wheelchair to get around. She was a rich heiress in her seventies who had invested her capital in real estate in France and Italy. A noble-hearted woman, she had become his guardian a long time ago and had then gone on to adopt him.

No, it couldn't be her.

2

A man of about sixty was waiting for him in the interview room of Don Bosco Prison, which was named for the patron saint of young boys. His short hair was peppered with grey and his sideburns were completely white. A thin, Zorro-like moustache adorned his face, which was tanned from hours spent sitting in the sun, and he had light-coloured eyes. He was six foot tall, a fine figure of a man, elegant and distinguished in a dark suit from a high-end tailor, rendered more serious by an extremely shiny black leather briefcase.

'Go and sit at the table,' the guard ordered his prisoner, pushing him forward with a hand on his right shoulder.

Daniele De Robertis obeyed in silence, stopping in front of the lone metal table whose legs were screwed to the floor. There were only two scratched grey plastic chairs. The bare, cold room was small and the same indefinable colour as his cell. On the ceiling the blades of a fan that had seen better days turned lazily, stirring up dust and dead mosquitoes, and a crude neon striplight gave off a constant buzzing noise. The only ornament was a sign declaring NO SMOKING. The unmistakable odours of sweat and damp hung in the air.

The building was so decrepit it was falling to pieces. The plaster was crumbling, a section of the changing rooms had been closed for some time due to water leaking in and some of the rooms were out of use due to the risk of the ceiling collapsing.

The man put his briefcase on the table and walked towards him. He held out his right hand and introduced himself with a confident air.

'I'm Amedeo Russo, a lawyer with offices in Florence and Rome.'

Daniele De Robertis briefly shook his hand and said, 'I don't understand. I haven't requested a lawyer.'

The other man gave a shrug. 'I know, but I've been nominated by the Prosecutor's Department of the Florentine Republic. You need to be questioned as soon as possible and the law requires the presence of a lawyer.'

De Robertis felt an overwhelming sense of oppression at the prospect of having to face interrogations, proceedings, courtrooms, photographers, journalists and, most of all, the public, who would doubtless be loath to miss the opportunity to stare at him and treat him like some animal in a zoo. And then there were the TV stations. One of the channels would broadcast the entire proceedings live, hoping for indiscretion on the part of the prosecution, the lawyers and the witnesses at the end of each hearing.

The very thought of it made him wish he hadn't survived the firefight. That police officer should have aimed for his heart, not his wrist.

The guard gave him a gentle push to make him sit down, then turned to the lawyer, who was also taking his seat, and said, 'Let me know when you've finished. I'll be right outside the door. You've got half an hour maximum, though.' Then he left, so they could have their conversation in private.

Seen from behind, his uniform shirt was stuck to his back with sweat. He closed the door with an annoying metallic noise and positioned himself in front of the spyhole to keep an eye on whatever went on inside the room.

The prisoner began to study the lawyer more carefully. His hands were long, slender and well cared for, like a pianist's; his eyes were small and moved constantly, as if ready to notice the smallest thing, and his face showed no sign of sagging in spite of his age. He vaguely reminded De Robertis of some actor, but he wasn't sure which one.

'I hope you're satisfied with your cell,' began Russo. 'I knew they'd want to lock you up in the maximum-security wing as soon as you were out of the infirmary, but you're all right where you are for now,' he said, running a hand through his hair.

Lost in his own thoughts, De Robertis was barely listening. He sat hunched over, his muscles tense, his expression unreadable, almost uncertain, and he didn't blink at all. The lawyer's face seemed so familiar.

Suddenly he realised: yes, he had seen him before. The memories fell into place.

He was one of those lawyers who paraded their clients under the spotlights to increase their own notoriety. He had seen him on TV several years ago on a news broadcast. His expression triumphant, the lawyer had been filmed alongside a client who'd just been acquitted of serious charges. It had been a professional triumph; no one who'd followed the case had seen it coming. He could even remember the client. He was a criminal called Fiorenzo Muti, and De Robertis knew a thing or two about his past.

Amedeo Russo, meanwhile, had turned his attention to his briefcase. With two hollow clicks he released the metal clasps to open it.

'I'll speak frankly,' Russo began, looking De Robertis in the eye. 'Yours is an extremely difficult case. I've read the police statements, particularly the one listing all the crimes you've been charged with: double homicide, kidnapping, sexual assault, rape – in effect, a fair chunk of the penal code.'

He paused, waiting for the prisoner's response. But his wait was in vain. There was silence but for the whirring of the fan and the whine of the electric light.

Daniele De Robertis was like a marble statue. Not a grimace crossed his face. Nothing at all.

The lawyer took two packets of cigarettes out of the briefcase and put them on the table in clear view. Then he took out a folder containing various sheets of paper, picked some up in his right hand and waved them in the air. 'This is the police report. It's very detailed and among the attachments is the arrest report with all the allegations. It's an open-and-shut case.'

There was another pause while he waited for questions. But he was disappointed once again, so he shook his head and continued speaking, 'We have only one path open to us: to plead insanity. It's the only way of avoiding a life sentence ... ' And he explained that, because of the need for a psychiatric evaluation, the trial would have to be delayed. Only once that was complete would the doctors be able to declare his inability to stand trial. 'The timetable for proceedings against you will come to a standstill,' he concluded.

After a few seconds of silence, the accused finally spoke. And he did so in a resolute tone. 'No. I don't want to be declared mad. Because I'm not.'

The lawyer burst out laughing, showing off the work he'd had done to his teeth. They were dazzling, whiter than white. He knew how to take care of himself. For a long moment he drummed the fingers of his left hand on the tabletop.

'It's the only way to avoid life imprisonment, don't you understand?' he asked, raising his voice slightly. Just enough for his words to reach the ears of the guard, who became more watchful, practically pushing his head through the spyhole like a huge guard dog, eager to leap forward and start snapping.

Inside the room, silence fell once more.

The two men continued to stare at one another. The lawyer

was still gripping the police report in his hand. It was all De Robertis could do to control his temper; he would have tipped the table over on top of Russo or hurled it against the wall if it hadn't been fixed to the floor.

He took a breath and then began to speak again. 'I don't want to be shut up in a high-security mental hospital,' he said in a monotone.

'So do you want to plead guilty to all charges?'

'No.'

'Well then, do you want to collaborate?'

'No.'

Silence again.

'I won't say anything. Justice *must* run its course, but I won't answer a single question,' he explained in his usual cold manner.

The lawyer started shifting in his seat. He'd defended many important criminals in his career but never had he faced such a complete lack of cooperation. He went over to the door and asked the guard for a bottle of water while he pondered what to do next.

'I'll get them to bring one right away, Signor Russo.'

So he came and sat back down, still pondering how he could regain control of the conversation.

He didn't want to give up.

As he waited, he wondered for the first time why the Prosecutor had nominated him since he wasn't even on the list of state lawyers provided by the Council of Lawyers. He knew that there were exceptions; every once in a while the Prosecutor or Deputy Prosecutor on duty would ignore the list altogether and choose a lawyer of his or her own liking. An expedient in 'unusual' cases.

But was this an 'unusual' case?

He would soon find out.

*

'You have to trust me. You can speak freely and tell me your version of events and anything that might prove useful for the defence, even any dark secrets that are on your conscience.'

The lawyer had drunk a glass of water in one gulp and now he started speaking again in a professional tone, which he was trying to make as convincing as possible. He refilled the glass and drained it.

'You have to put your trust in me,' he continued. 'I'm your lawyer and I will act in your interest. But you shouldn't talk to journalists or any police officers who might show up wanting to chat about the investigation, and, since you have dual nationality, you shouldn't speak to officials from the French Embassy. Don't speak to any of them. And don't reply to any letters, especially the ones from people who are fascinated by violent crime.'

He was referring to the floods of letters murderers received. Some correspondents were driven by a fascination with evil, others by a desire to vanquish boredom, loneliness and suffering. Along with the insults and invitations to repent, there were letters of support, of admiration, if not outright declarations of love. In some cases this led to weddings conducted through the prison bars or once the prisoner was released. The news was full of such stories.

'I don't know what to do with your advice, Signor Russo. I won't speak to anyone, least of all you . . . ' replied the prisoner. He paused, his eyes fixed on the lawyer, who seemed to have frozen. 'Unless *you* tell me something,' he continued, leaning forward for the first time, both hands on the table. Now his eyes shone with a new light.

'Me? *Me* tell you something?'

'Yes, *you* tell me something.'

'And what do you want to know about *me*?'

'If you want me to tell you my "dark secrets", you'll have to tell me *your* secrets first,' replied De Robertis, leaning even further towards the lawyer.

Amedeo Russo frowned. 'Secrets? What secrets? I don't understand.'

De Robertis could smell fear in the air. Once again his instinct had proven correct.

The lawyer closed his briefcase with trembling hands. The veins in his forehead had swollen. In almost thirty years of honourable work he had never found himself facing such a bizarre request, or felt himself compelled to allow such a reversal of the client–lawyer roles.

'I have no idea what you are referring to.'

'To the sex parties . . . To that client of yours – Fiorenzo Muti, the one you made so famous on television, and not just in Italy. Have I made myself clear? Or do I need to be more explicit?'

The lawyer stared at him open-mouthed, as still as if a dagger had pierced his heart. Then he sprang to his feet. 'I've no idea what you're talking about . . . This is absurd . . . You really are insane! The most sensible thing would be for you to be locked up in a high-security psychiatric hospital. I'll send a report to the Chief Prosecutor, Luca Fiore, immediately.' And he gestured to the prison officer that the meeting was over.

'OK. We've understood each other,' replied De Robertis with a disdainful look. 'Go ahead and report. And you can keep your cigarettes – I don't smoke. I have one last thing to tell you. Trust me: the moment has come for *your* secrets to come to light. They could be a kind of life insurance.'

Reeling from the impact of these words the lawyer hurried from the room, grim-faced. He missed Daniele De Robertis's parting shot: 'Go fuck yourself, you and that Prosecutor Fiore who sent you here!'

Drops of sweat shone on Amedeo Russo's forehead as he made his way through the corridors. It was blackmail. Foul blackmail.

The moment has come for your secrets to come to light. They could be a kind of life insurance.

He walked rapidly out of the prison and made his way towards the car park to collect his car. His hands were shaking as he took a packet of cigarettes out of his jacket pocket and lit one. From the whirlpool of thoughts that flooded his mind, two floated to the surface:

Who was Daniele De Robertis – nicknamed 'Genius', according to the paperwork – really?

And why had Prosecutor Fiore nominated him in particular as the public defence lawyer?

3

That night Daniele De Robertis woke up with a start, and for a few moments he couldn't work out where he was. Instinctively he ran his hand over his clothes and realised he was dripping wet, but not due to the muggy heat, which still continued even though it was now the end of September. No. He had had one of his nightmares. The worst one.

The fat old man's sweaty hand had slipped inside his underpants to touch his genitals. If you say a word, I'll kill you. Terrified by the arm around his neck, he hadn't made a sound. Then, pushing him down with his face pressed into the pillow, that monster had brutally raped him. Afterwards, sitting on the toilet, he had discovered he was bleeding . . .

Even though he wasn't completely conscious, he began trembling as moments from his adolescence flashed before him.

They came one by one, snapshot after snapshot, the experiences that had followed that first time. They were as vivid as if they had happened only yesterday.

The den of sin, the dark room in the former convent between Dicomano and San Godenzo where the 'prophet' Bartolotti, officially the owner of a large agricultural estate and dairy which was inherited by his son upon his death, took care of underprivileged young people who had been abandoned or had no parents.

There were other men at that place, all of them absolute beasts.

They always kept their heads covered by a hood with two holes at eye level. He had been aware of the assaults on the other boys and girls. Young girls were forced to parade in low-cut T-shirts to show off their little nipples and hot pants with waistlines so low their sexes were visible. Then they'd be stripped completely naked.

Paedophiles, the prophet's perverted accomplices. Men with misshapen bodies, some of them high-ranking officials or occupying prestigious roles in their day-to-day lives.

He felt himself suffocating again, but this time it wasn't due to the putrid air in his cell. He had been holding his breath without realising it. Only when his left arm touched the floor did the heat of the cement bring him back to reality. He sat up and pressed his hands to his eyes to stem the flow of tears.

The images of the den disappeared, along with the figures of the hooded men who had abused him and so many other innocent young children. Thanks to his 'research', he had managed to track one of them down.

He felt another rush of anger.

So much hatred. Such thirst for revenge.

And he thought again of the mission he had set himself:

Kill, kill, kill.

He looked out through the single window and saw nothing but the dark of the night. Then he let himself fall back on the mattress. The pain spreading through his body had become the only undeniable sign of his existence. The pain that had turned him into a monster, too.

A smile suddenly crossed his face. He closed his eyes and the flow of memories drifted to more recent events: the scene of his injury and capture. Then it stopped. Next he went over the visit from the lawyer, Amedeo Russo, and the words he'd said to make him understand that this wasn't over, that the game was still on and he was prepared to keep playing right until the very last moment to complete his vendetta.

He told himself that the meeting had been a stroke of luck. Yes, luck – because luck was almost always the fruit of someone else's mistake. It certainly wasn't the hand of destiny: Daniele De Robertis didn't believe in destiny, it was merely a matter of choices. And only the truly difficult ones mattered.

But who had made the mistake? Amedeo Russo? Or the person who had sent him?

He turned towards the wall to his right and reread the sentence that had struck him: FREEDOM COMMANDS A HIGH PRICE, FIND THE COURAGE TO PAY IT!

He was not short of courage. In fact, he had courage to spare, and he'd shown it.

He took a deep breath, realising the time had come to regain full control of his own existence, to make some difficult choices. Because the hunt, *his* hunt, needed to continue. He needed to move on to the final piece of the puzzle, the piece his capture had prevented him from putting in place.

He would kill anyone who got in his way. Anyone.

He could relax now, curl up under the worn, stained sheet, and surrender to sleep.

He was Genius and he couldn't forget it.

It was a restless night for the lawyer, Russo, too. The Valium he'd swallowed half an hour before going to bed hadn't worked. He'd woken abruptly and now sat leaning against his headboard, out of breath, his heart pounding.

Consumed by fear.

After the visit to the prison at Pisa he hadn't done anything else all day except replay the prisoner's words. Even in the peace of his own home, they had resonated in his head like a pneumatic drill.

To the sex parties . . . To that client of yours – Fiorenzo Muti, the one you made so famous on television, and not just in Italy. Have I made myself clear? Or do I need to be more explicit?

And then that piece of advice as he was leaving the room: *The moment has come for your secrets to come to light. They could be a kind of life insurance.*

Millions of fears, possibilities and half-truths crowded his mind. He got up to catch his breath without even switching on the light and, barefoot, he stood leaning against the wall in the passage, careful not to wake his wife, who had been sleeping in a separate room for almost five years now.

Did De Robertis know anything specific, or was he just bluffing like an expert poker player, trotting out the gossip that made the rounds of the drawing rooms from time to time?

But even if that were the case – why?

He returned to his room in a cold sweat. The alarm clock on the night stand read 2:25. He closed his eyes for a long moment to breathe deeply and concentrate. Inhale, exhale, inhale, exhale.

In the course of his life, he had endured a number of difficult moments but he couldn't remember anything quite like this. And yet experience had taught him that there was always a solution. While he tried to slow the pounding of his heart, he repeated over and over, as if to convince himself, that there must be one this time, too.

He lay down on the bed, but after a moment he realised that he wasn't ready yet. He got up again and tiptoed to his office. His ideas had slowly clarified: he couldn't hesitate, he didn't have the option of waiting for tomorrow, because time would be one more enemy, and he couldn't have that.

He took up pen and paper. Then he began to write.

4

Tuesday 28 September

A gentle light was spreading through Daniele De Robertis's cell.

It was almost seven in the morning and his pistol was pressed against the temple of the man facing him. When he suddenly opened his eyes he had the impression that his hand was still grasping the imaginary weapon.

He had dreamed about the scene of the murder so vividly and in such detail that it had seemed real and blazed itself on to his mind. It was very strange: recently his dreams had been vanishing completely when he woke up, leaving him with a painful empty feeling in his stomach. But this time it was different.

In reality, he thought, perhaps I wouldn't have used the pistol, but a long, well-sharpened knife so as to leave fewer traces. The wounds would've been anonymous. A good forensics expert would have been able to reconstruct the dynamics of the execution if he considered the bloodstains too. But nothing more. Science, on its own, wouldn't have solved anything.

A bullet, on the other hand, could be traced back to the gun from which it had been fired and, with all probability, to compromising people and places.

His eyes open and his head against the wall, he imagined

slashing the Great Beast's neck, slitting his jugular with a neat semicircular cut. Quick. Precise.

He saw his hand slice through the air, already preparing for the first strike.

He saw the spurts of blood gushing like a fountain, slowly lessening in intensity until the heart stopped beating.

He saw himself finally happy after avenging Leonardo, his twin brother, killed on the Great Beast's direct orders.

A sadistic smile appeared on his lips as he imagined a more satisfying murder. He would have done it in such a way that everyone would have thought that the Great Beast had died during an auto-erotic game. He would be lying on his back on the bed, his eyes closed and his head turned to one side on a pillow. There would be a scarf around his neck, one end attached to the headboard in a kind of slipknot, the other by his right hand. It should look like an accidental death, but really it would be a challenge to the investigators, those investigators who had lacked the ability, and perhaps not only that, to investigate those above suspicion and capture Leonardo's killer.

A shiver ran over his skin. He tried to relax his muscles, which were as tense as violin strings, and got up. It was time to set these thoughts aside and prepare himself for the usual routine: breakfast, yard time, shower, head to the infirmary to join the huge queue of prisoners waiting for their dose of tranquilisers or other drugs.

That routine could yet be interrupted by dramatic events: a suicide, a brawl, a suspicious fall down the stairs, someone trying to suffocate themselves by swallowing a solid object.

It was life in prison, but it wouldn't be his life for much longer. He was sure of it now.

5

Association

It was a few minutes after eleven in the morning and Daniele De Robertis was in one of the three walkways. Among the safest places in the world. In theory.

Under a sun that was already scorching, all he could hear was whispering; for the most part the words were incomprehensible, sometimes accompanied by rapid hand gestures, perhaps to emphasise what was being said, or perhaps a form of coded communication.

Daniele De Robertis was leaning with his back against the wall, his right hand up by his forehead like a visor to shade himself from the sun's rays. He was staring at a man wearing a crumpled red tracksuit emblazoned with the name of a well-known car company. Tall and well built with a thick beard, he was a guy who would never pass unnoticed: and yet until today, he hadn't noticed him. Something about that prisoner disturbed him.

And, furthermore, it looked as though he was heading his way. *What the fuck . . .*

Instinct told him that something ugly was about to happen. He didn't like the guy's bulldog face, the way he walked or his body language one bit. He thought back to the meeting with

Russo, the words he had said to him and the reaction he could have set in motion.

And he looked up instinctively, ready to confront the brute.

Meanwhile, on the opposite side of the walkway a scuffle broke out that drowned the strange murmur that had been drifting from that direction only a moment before. A shout. Noises. Swearing. A frenetic crescendo of sounds.

A dozen men, almost all North Africans – drug dealers, muggers, thieves, all still waiting to stand trial – were laying into each other, while the only guard on duty was some distance away, too far away, and didn't seem aware that anything was happening.

De Robertis stayed where he was, his eyes fixed on the bearded man. But the guy wasn't interested in him. In fact, he turned quickly to his right to approach a young man standing less than two metres away, who must have been the intended target. Within two seconds the young man collapsed to the ground.

The man in the red tracksuit had dealt him a blow to the stomach and now something slender and pointed, a kind of awl, was flashing in the air. He would deliver the coup de grâce in no time.

De Robertis decided to act.

With a leap through the air and a sweep of his arm, he blocked the attacker's arm mid-strike and the man turned to him, incredulous. Their eyes met and a shiver ran down the bearded man's spine: never in his life had he seen eyes like the ones looking back at him. Not in any of the various prisons where he'd been held. Not even in the faces of his worst enemies. They were icy, devoid of emotion. Inhuman. Even more inhuman than his own. He tried to defend himself with his knee, but it was an unfortunate move.

Daniele De Robertis knew what he was doing. With a strange smile fixed on his face, he dodged, threw himself on the man with a howl like an animal and head-butted him in the face. The bearded man lost his balance and the weapon slipped out of his hand and clattered to the floor. He touched his bloody nose as De Robertis kicked him ruthlessly in the privates. Crying out in anger and pain, he crumpled to the ground.

De Robertis straddled him and held the awl to his throat. When he tried to move, De Robertis pressed the point against his skin to show he wasn't messing around, he was willing to kill him there and then, in front of all those people who were apparently indifferent to what was happening.

In the meantime, the guard had set off the alarm and the deafening sound of the sirens drowned out the shouting.

'Who the fuck are you?' the bearded man asked him in a small voice, as the veins in his neck dilated in fear.

'I'm Genius,' the other man murmured in reply. 'Remember that name, if you survive,' he added, keeping the weapon against his throat.

The bearded man stopped struggling.

At that moment, some of the guards grabbed De Robertis by the shoulders. They hit him repeatedly on the head and shoulders with their truncheons until he passed out, ignoring the boy's shouts.

Then everything went black.

When he next opened his eyes, he found himself in bed in the infirmary.

He immediately recognised the doctor who had treated his wrist wound. He also noticed the commander of the prison guards, a short, fat man not far off retirement. He looked a bit like a traditional Chianti bottle, and this was the nickname that his staff – and not just them – used to make fun of him behind his back.

'Look at you, tough guy!' said the commander, gesturing towards De Robertis's battered face with a smile that distorted his harelip further. Then he praised him for having saved the boy's life. He didn't apologise for his men's behaviour, though.

De Robertis returned the smile: it was the first time he had risked his life for not entirely personal ends. He wanted to ask who the bearded man was, but he quickly reconsidered. He didn't give a damn about him; he was water under the bridge.

'I want to rest,' he said, closing his eyes.

'Sweet dreams,' replied the commander, moving over to the patient in the neighbouring bed, the boy who'd been attacked. He had been fortunate. As luck would have it, the wound to his abdomen had missed his vital organs.

The son of a Sicilian Mafia boss, he was in prison waiting to stand trial for involvement in a number of crimes, including murder, extortion rackets and money laundering.

His father, an icon of the Cosa Nostra, had been captured a few months earlier after over twenty years as a fugitive. He was a favoured fugitive – even favoured, according to some, by certain commissioners who hoped he would provide them with valuable information about rival Mafia clans in exchange. It was an example of that give and take the police sometimes allowed in the interest of the state, without crossing the line between the legal and the illegal. A balance that only the most experienced investigators were able to maintain. In this case, it was a give and take that was shining a light on the role of investigators suspected of having embarked on an all-out negotiation with the Mafia in an attempt to stem the trail of blood that began with the Mafia bombing campaign in Florence, Rome and Milan in 1993. The commissioners' mandate may have come from a political éminence grise who had remained behind the scenes. It wouldn't have been the first time.

'I'll have to question you later, once you've had your medication,' the commander told him.

The young man gave him a questioning look.

'Don't worry. They'll take you to my office on a stretcher. We can talk in peace there.'

'I don't know anything, Commander. What can I tell you? I

don't know that man and I've no idea why he attacked me. He must be crazy.'

'We'll talk about it in my office,' the commander replied, shaking his head.

That night Daniele De Robertis had another dream. It was a good one, but with an ending that left a bitter taste in his mouth.

The Great Beast was hanging upside down from that wrought-iron gate. He had stripped him completely naked first, then tied his hands behind his back and bound his ankles. Afterwards he had looked right into his face, normally so well cared for, now deformed and unrecognisable.

'Now I'll tell you what I'm going to do to you. You want to know, don't you? I'm going to pull out all your hair, even your pubic hair. Then I'm going to chop off your penis with this scalpel. You see this scalpel here – I'm to chop off your penis with it and then I'll stuff it in your mouth. They'll find you like this, right underneath the frieze of those three goddamned crossed roses. Your symbol, you damned Beast. But first you have to tell me everything you know. Now talk, you bastard!'

The other man seemed to be moving his eyelids slightly, trying to open his mouth to tell him the location of the hiding place.

Talk!

Talk!

Nothing. The dream had vanished, just when it was getting good.

6

As he woke up, Daniele De Robertis realised that, although slightly blurry, he could still see the image of the Great Beast hanging by his ankles. His lips were opening, perhaps trying to answer him. He looked around and spotted the guard standing at the other end of the room. In the neighbouring bed he recognised the boy whose life he had saved the day before: he studied him more closely and he seemed even younger, perhaps still a minor.

'My name's Gino,' the boy said in a weak but clear voice. 'You risked your life for me without knowing me. Thank you.'

Daniele shook his head as if to say that he really didn't owe him anything, that he would have done the same for anyone in that situation.

The young man waited for him to say something in reply, but not a word left his mouth. He couldn't be sure that the guards hadn't hidden a bug to record their conversations. And he also knew well that in prison, 'even the walls have ears'.

The young man didn't give up. 'My father, Salvino Lo Cascio, is in your debt. He already knows everything he *ought* to know.' He spoke without hesitation, as if he were confident he wasn't being bugged. And, glancing at the guard every so often, he told him that a new war between the clans had just broken out in Palermo.

'At this point no one knows how many have died,' he said, explaining that by attacking him they had tried to strike at his father. As the only son, he would take over as boss when the time came. 'As late as possible, though,' he clarified.

He continued his tale, claiming that someone had 'become cocky', taking advantage of the many arrests, including his father's, and the information given to the police by the turncoats, who had started out as 'brown nosers' and were now taking advantage of the laws on guilty pleas and collaborators to get out of a tight spot and obtain benefits from the state.

'But the turncoats will always be turncoats and our *family* will strike when they least expect it, even if they're under police protection. My father's authority is as strong as ever,' he added in the firm tone of a hardened criminal.

Daniele De Robertis was looking him right in the eye. The speech he had made was worthy of the heir of a top-level Mafia boss.

'I can see you're feeling better from the way you've been talking,' hissed the guard, coming over to them.

The young man fell silent.

At first De Robertis just nodded, then he asked to go back to his cell.

'You'll have to see the doctor first; you need his authorisation to leave the infirmary.'

'When's he coming?'

'He's with the governor. They've got important things to discuss,' replied the guard. 'But you'll both be back on your feet again in a few days. You were lucky,' he said, before moving away.

Gino Lo Cascio remained silent.

There was nothing more for him to say.

Friday 1 October

This time there wasn't a brawl, but an all-out riot.

The prisoners had been complaining for some time about the terrible living conditions caused by overcrowding, which forced up to six men to share a cell intended for no more than two inmates. In practice, despite having a capacity of just over two hundred inmates, the prison at Pisa currently held in excess of four hundred. Not even complaints from SAPPE, the prison officers' union, which had protested against the crowded conditions and lack of security on more than one occasion, had achieved anything.

The Minister had noted their concerns and left it at that. The truth was, funds to construct new buildings and take on more staff simply weren't available. Even a series of cases brought before the European Court of Human Rights at Strasbourg by prisoners had come to nothing: the government continued to turn a deaf ear.

Protests had broken out at a number of Italian prisons the previous month. The inmates had refused to leave their cells and had shouted 'Amnesty!' through the bars. It was a solution that some political parties were considering on the grounds that, although it wouldn't solve the problem, it might improve the situation.

Then on 1 October, things escalated.

There was no holding back, the inmates ran amok. They burned mattresses, sheets and blankets. There was shouting in the corridors and loud bangs were heard, along with a constant clanging as prisoners drummed on the bars and gates with any object that came to hand. It was total chaos. The most violent inmates took members of staff hostage to make sure the authorities got the message that they were serious this time and they weren't going to be messed around.

First to be seized was the commander, 'Chianti bottle', who

had put himself forward as a mediator. Despised for his hard-line methods, he was led to a cell by some inmates who'd covered their faces with dusters and sheets; after tearing off his uniform, they started beating him up.

Extensive negotiations followed, initially conducted in person by the governor, a man in his forties who had never had to deal with such an explosive situation before. On several occasions the police special forces were on the verge of intervening to re-establish order. Guaranteeing the hostages' safety would be down to Enrico Bartolini, the deputy prosecutor on duty, but, unprepared to deal with an emergency of that magnitude, he, too, was playing a waiting game.

Eventually a civil servant from the Ministry of Justice arrived from the capital to take charge of the negotiations. The prisoners met with him to set out their demands and by late evening the prison was back to normal and the hostages had been released. The commander emerged from the cell where he had been held with a nasty black eye and a bloody harelip. The inmates were subjected to careful searches and questioning: no mean feat, especially since the few CCTV cameras that were still working had been turned off. Most of them had been broken for ages and funds had not yet been allocated to pay for repairs.

However, the state had to uphold the law. Those responsible had to be identified and punished in an exemplary fashion. The corridors and cells were searched from top to bottom for weapons, blunt instruments or proof, especially any external correspondence.

In one of the cells the officers found a surprise they would not easily forget.

Following the spots of blood, which grew bigger and bigger, they found themselves confronted with the body of an inmate whose right hand had been cut off. But that wasn't all.

He had been dismembered like an animal in an abattoir and

his heart had been torn out. It was found in the games room, between two rackets on the ping-pong table. A young officer covered his mouth with a handkerchief at the sight. He was about to vomit but he collapsed in a dead faint before he had the chance.

The body belonged to Pino Esposito, the bearded attacker of Salvino Lo Cascio's son. Originally from Colombia, he was a Camorra associate who'd been imprisoned for large-scale cocaine trafficking. Considered a complete son of a bitch even in the circles he moved in, Pino Esposito had been born to kill. But he had failed when it came to Lo Cascio and he'd been unable to save himself from his punishment, which had been decreed by the Cosa Nostra. There was no right of appeal.

At this point the authorities realised that the riot had been staged purely to punish Esposito and make it clear to those who had sent him that although Salvino Lo Cascio might be in prison, he was still a powerful man, powerful enough to lay down the law, both inside and outside the prison system. It was also confirmation that, unlike some of the other bosses, he had renounced neither cruelty nor the desire for revenge, two *qualities* he'd displayed since the start of his career. He was an old-school boss who disdained the methods of the new generation of Mafiosi, businessmen who infiltrated their way to the heart of the country's financial and economic systems. The new Mafiosi, with their polished, shiny shoes, were light years away from the older generation who, with caps on their heads and shotguns slung over their shoulders, had brought Italy to its knees from their base in Corleone.

The news spread through the prison in the blink of an eye.

The oldest inmates, the lifers, remembered a similar incident that had taken place at Badu'e Carros Prison near Nuoro on Sardinia in 1981.

On 17 August some of the prisoners had stabbed and eviscerated Francis 'Angel Face' Turatello, a criminal who had operated in Lombardy, and Milan in particular, during the seventies. The leader of a bloodthirsty gang of ex-cons from Catania, he had controlled illegal gambling dens and prostitution in the area. He had also committed a number of armed robberies and kidnappings with the cooperation of the Marsigliesi clan. His murder had caused a sensation, mostly due to the violence his killers had inflicted on the body: the mess they had made of him suggested that the victim must have committed an unforgivable crime and that the order to kill him had undoubtedly come from the Nuova Camorra Organizzata, an emergent Mafia organisation that was trying to assert its supremacy.

Daniele De Robertis considered the distance that separated him from the Mafiosi. What made them powerful was their internal structure, the *family*: he remembered the emphasis Gino Lo Cascio had put on that word during their conversation in the infirmary. He, on the other hand, was alone. All by himself. He had no one he could count on. Even his lone accomplice, Angelica, with whom he had made a blood pact during their adolescence, had ended up betraying him. She had fallen in love and lost her head over a woman. And now she was under house arrest at a secure location, thus avoiding imprisonment. He felt a surge of anger at the thought.

Damned bitch! he thought to himself.

He started to question everything. He was convinced he had made the wrong alliances. The Mafia would have been more loyal than that perverted lesbian Angelica. However, he had never shared their interests: he had never been a drug or arms trafficker, nor had he ever been involved in extortion or money laundering.

He belonged to a different world.

The Mafiosi aspired to money and power, even venturing

into politics, although without drawing more attention to themselves than necessary. He, on the other hand, had always been driven by hatred and the need to carry out his vendetta against the person who had made his life a kind of hell and who had wanted his brother Leonardo dead.

He would never be stopped.

7

Thursday 7 October

Once again it was Association time in the three walkways.

And, once again, there was only one officer on duty rather than the three who were scheduled. Only one guard to supervise almost one hundred and fifty inmates. Not all of them were authorised to leave their cells, and there were also those like Gino Lo Cascio who, given the option, preferred to stay in their cells. Since he'd been stabbed, he had limited his contact with the outside world to a minimum.

However, a single guard was not enough. And the delay in raising the alarm on 28 September had shown that.

Daniele De Robertis had been doing exercises and press-ups in his cell for several days. Exercises to build up and strengthen his muscles, the way he used to do when he had a rock-hard physique.

He exchanged a quick glance with another inmate, a Sicilian waiting to stand trial for the murder and attempted murder of a couple from Palermo living in Tuscany. He was skinny and slightly smaller than De Robertis with pale eyes, an olive complexion and arms covered in tattoos. He adored chocolate and kept a toothpick between his teeth when his supplies ran out.

Perhaps due to this habit, or perhaps because of his weedy build, everyone called him 'U Stecchinu, The Toothpick.

Lo Cascio had introduced him to De Robertis as one of his father's most trusted men. At that moment De Robertis had put two and two together: Pasquale Schimizzi, 'U Stecchinu, who he tended to think of as 'the blond', could well be the one who'd butchered Esposito.

The boss had recruited him from the streets of the Brancaccio area of Palermo when he was barely sixteen years old. Back then he'd been one of those boys with no future, prepared to do anything in order to become a 'real man'. After the usual string of minor crimes, all that remained was the decisive step: starting to kill without compassion, without looking anyone in the face.

It was blood that sealed a man's entry into the 'honourable society', as the Sicilian Mafia was once known. Only blood could mark the start of a new life and a bond that became stronger every day, murder after murder.

This was the path taken by Pasquale Schimizzi, who had soon become a man of honour and unquestionable integrity, as loyal as a dog to its master. And now the prison was his new home, so much so that the free world had become nothing more than a junction between release on the grounds of insufficient evidence and the next conditional sentence.

His eyes were pale blue, a different shade from De Robertis's, but equally cold. Their cells were in the same area and this had allowed them to meet during the afternoon association period, when prisoners could move around the communal areas and socialise. This was when they had come up with their plan.

Now there was nothing to do but carry it out.

De Robertis re-examined every single walkway and for a moment he half-closed his eyes, imagining another smell, unlike the ones in his cell.

The smell of freedom.

After a few minutes he felt the blond's gaze on him. He checked that nobody was watching, then turned to face him. He saw him make a show of checking his watch. It was a coded message.

FREEDOM COMMANDS A HIGH PRICE, FIND THE COURAGE TO PAY IT!

It was time to seize the moment.

And he didn't need to be told twice.

They began to move in perfect synchronisation.

Without a flicker of emotion, they made their way along the other passages and across internal courtyards. They reached a hidden corner of the garden where there was a ladder that had been used for some repair work a couple of days earlier and abandoned. This was what allowed them to scale the walls. Once outside, they held up a silver Mercedes SUV, the first vehicle that came along. They threatened the woman driver, forced her out and hijacked the vehicle.

'U Stecchinu got behind the wheel and the car roared away, leaving burnt rubber on the asphalt.

The woman was rescued by passing motorists, who dialled 113 to raise the alarm. Someone also rang the 118 operator, who sent an ambulance to take the poor woman to the Santa Chiara Hospital.

A full-scale manhunt got under way, with roadblocks at the toll booths along the A11 autostrada and main roads throughout the area. Officers from the Pisan *Squadra Mobile* and Carabinieri also checked every supermarket in the area in case the two fugitives decided to turn to armed robbery for cash. Soon two helicopters, one belonging to the State Police, the other to the Carabinieri, joined the search, hovering in the sky like vultures, ready to swoop down on their prey.

But there was no trace of the fugitives. Nor of the SUV. De Robertis and Schimizzi seemed to have vanished into thin air.

After a journey along B roads, which 'U Stecchinu knew like the back of his hand, they had reached a safe place to wait until the police dropped their guard. Only then could they set the riskier and more difficult second phase of their plan in motion.

For Daniele De Robertis it would be one more step towards his final objective.

8

It didn't take long for news of the escape to reach Florence. At Police Headquarters, with its handsome eighteenth-century portico on the Via Zara, just a stone's throw from the city centre, the impact was akin to an earthquake.

'But how is this possible?' was the question on everyone's lips in the offices and along the long corridors on the first floor, where the *Squadra Mobile* was based, and even in the rooms that once played host to guests of a different kind: the insane, held in the famous Bonifazio Hospital, the first modern psychiatric unit.

After the initial incredulity, some officers were overcome with anger. 'We work our arses off to catch him, we risk our lives, we sacrifice ourselves and our families, and then they let him escape. What the fuck are we working for?'

Chief Superintendent Michele Ferrara was in his office, sitting at his desk poring over documents when his colleague from the Operations Room told him what had happened. The paperwork was routine: a few reports on domestic break-ins, a couple of incidents involving pickpockets targeting tourists in the historic town centre. Two arrests, both habitual offenders. The files would be sent to the Prosecutor's Department that same day and, in all likelihood, they would be freed immediately after the conviction. It was another depressing aspect of police work. They caught them and the judges convicted them only to set them free again. Fortunately this wasn't always the case, but it happened all too often.

Ferrara sat still for a long moment, trying to assimilate the news. Then he picked up the phone and rang the governor of the prison at Pisa. He wanted to know more about it, to understand how that escape had been allowed to happened in broad daylight, right under everyone's noses. A complete fiasco.

He didn't find out much. Only a few details about the Sicilian fugitive. A name that meant nothing to him. At the end of the short conversation he decided to take action, so he summoned his closest colleagues.

Within five minutes they were all sitting around the rectangular conference table in front of his desk. There was Gianni Ascalchi, with his usual gruff expression, Francesco Rizzo, Ferrara's deputy, Teresa Micalizi, the newest member of the *Squadra Mobile*, and Inspector Riccardo Venturi, the team's memory bank and an IT expert.

The Chief Superintendent brought them up to date, recounting the limited information he had gleaned from the prison governor.

'In addition to Daniele De Robertis, a Mafioso named Pasquale Schimizzi is also on the run. He's a Cosa Nostra killer, thirty-two years of age, and he comes from Palermo,' he summarised.

They all made notes.

'Venturi, run a search on this Schimizzi,' ordered Ferrara. They could hear the urgency in his voice; if he wasn't caught, it would only be a matter of time before Daniele De Robertis killed again. 'I want all the patrols sent out, checking De Robertis's regular haunts. We can't rule out the possibility that he might return to the mountains or San Gimignano.'

They all nodded in agreement. None of them would ever forget the events of 28 August – the 'night of horror' as it had been dubbed in the media – when De Robertis brutally murdered the former senator, Enrico Costanza, and his butler, gouging out the former's eyes.

After the murders, De Robertis had kidnapped and assaulted a woman called Guendalina Volpi, the ex-con lover of his former schoolfriend and accomplice, Angelica Fossi. Hostage in tow, he had attempted to hide out in the mountains, but the police had tracked him down and captured him.

Led by Ferrara, a team of officers had searched the killer's den in the Mugello area between Dicomano and San Godenzo. They had seized some highly significant material; in particular, a diary with an aged leather cover emblazoned with the words 'EVIL GENIUS'. A number of well-known names featured in the diary, including ex-senator Enrico Costanza. Some names cropped up again and again, most notably Sir George Holley, also referred to as the 'Great Beast'. De Robertis had even sketched a plan of Holley's villa, which was located in the countryside between San Gimignano and Certaldo.

Chief Superintendent Ferrara had gone directly to the villa, only to discover that Holley had boarded a private jet and departed within hours of De Robertis's capture.

Coincidence? Perhaps. But Ferrara didn't believe in coincidences.

There had been holes in the story that needed to be filled in, but their attempts to find out more about Sir George Holley, and to establish how his path had come to cross that of De Robertis, had hit a brick wall. A formal request to the Prosecutor's Department for permission to carry out a comprehensive search of Holley's villa had been denied. As a result, all his secrets remained hidden in the darkness, behind that black wrought-iron gate with its frieze of three enormous, entwined black roses – an image that had haunted Ferrara ever since.

He was convinced that the Englishman was implicated in two other cases that were currently under investigation: the murders of Inspector Antonio 'Serpico' Sergi and Fabio Biondi.

A few weeks ago Sergi had been found dead in the waters of Lake Bracciano. The autopsy had revealed that it wasn't an accident or sudden illness, as first thought, but homicide. Damage to the hyoid bone was consistent with the victim having been strangled.

The investigation, conducted by the Prosecutor's Department in Civitavecchia, under whose authority Lake Bracciano fell, had delved into every aspect of the inspector's private and professional life. Officers had meticulously eliminated various possible motives, including gambling, debt and involvement in actual or potentially illegal activities involving informants. They had also scrutinised Sergi's second home at Lake Bracciano, around 160 square feet of floor space with a small amount of land. It turned out that Sergi had bought the place almost ten years earlier for sixty million lira, taking out a loan to cover 50 per cent of the asking price. But there was nothing to suggest that he was corrupt. No apparent secrets. No double life. The investigation seemed destined to peter out . . .

. . . Until Chief Superintendent Ferrara found out that Sergi had been working undercover for the Secret Service, trying to infiltrate a shady international criminal organisation known as the Black Rose.

The second victim, Fabio Biondi, was an IT expert who'd been hired by the *Squadra Mobile* in strictest secrecy to recover images from a video Daniele De Robertis had left at the scene of Senator Costanza's murder. The killer had taped a message over a previous recording, which showed a woman being sacrificially murdered in a deconsecrated chapel in Sesto Fiorentino. The victim had been identified as Madalena Miranda Da Silva, owner of a private club known as The Madalena.

Before Biondi could deliver the results of his analysis, he was killed in a fire at his apartment. It turned out to be arson. Investigators found a dossier entitled 'The Black Rose' in his safe. All the documents within the folder were labelled 'Secret'.

It later turned out that Sergi and Biondi had been in contact: their respective mobile phone records showed several recent calls between them.

To Ferrara, those two unsolved murders were like a wound that would not heal. And now, with Daniele De Robertis once more at large, the wound was opening up again – and it seemed more painful than ever.

Determined to prevent another killing spree, Ferrara stood before a detailed ordnance survey map of the Florentine area that hung from his office wall, assigning tasks and briefing his officers. He concluded the meeting by drawing up five teams and placing them under the direction of his deputy, Francesco Rizzo.

Rizzo, an officer of average height and a stocky build, was a man of few words, but utterly dependable. He had worked with Ferrara for many years and they'd reached the stage where a simple exchange of glances communicated volumes. A perfect understanding existed between them.

After dismissing his officers, the Chief Superintendent sat alone in his office, reflecting on the events of the summer. Sergi had been one of his best men, even saving his life on one occasion. He was certain that the undercover investigation into the Black Rose had led to Sergi's death. And though he couldn't prove it, he believed that the Englishman De Robertis called the 'Great Beast' was not only a member of that organisation but possibly the driving force behind it. How else would he have managed to stay one step ahead of the police, fleeing the country as they were on their way to question him? How else could he have thwarted the investigation at every stage?

Now new questions were buzzing round inside Ferrara's head.

Where was the man at the heart of the Black Rose at this moment? In Tuscany, or abroad, perhaps in England?

And why was Interpol unwilling to cooperate?

He had assumed that the English authorities would be in a position to supply crucial information, but Interpol had yet to grant them authorisation to act. Routine inquiries about Sir George Holley had received no response whatsoever.

Was it a simple case of bureaucratic inefficiency, or were there other, more sinister reasons for the dealy?

Of course, paperwork was forever causing delays to investigations, especially when inquiries extended beyond national borders, but intuition told him that this particular delay was laden with hidden meanings.

He was annoyed with himself for not having put more pressure on Interpol or the Prosecutor's Department, but he'd been too distracted by the other files piled up on his desk. It seemed as long as the world kept turning, criminals would never stop – and he would forever be trying to catch up.

9

It was almost nine in the evening when Ferrara walked through his front door. Aside from being a stone's throw from the Ponte Vecchio, the small loft apartment where he lived with his wife, Petra, boasted a roof terrace that was, by Florentine standards, large. And it had another advantage over most buildings in the area: it offered a panoramic view of the Arno and the distant hills beyond. Petra had built a small temperature-controlled wood-and-glass greenhouse up there, and the terrace was dominated by the fragrance of rosemary, lavender and jasmine. Along with the kitchen, this was her territory.

'Home at last!' Ferrara sighed to himself as his key turned in the lock. He was immediately swept into a long, affectionate embrace by his wife, who had registered the tension on his face. She refrained from asking any questions; she didn't want to seem too curious about her husband's work, and, besides, she knew it would be pointless. He'd always gone out of his way to shield her from the evil that he had to deal with on a daily basis.

But Petra could guess what was worrying him. She had heard the news of the Pisa jailbreak on the radio, and knew that one of the two escapees was the killer who'd caused her husband so many sleepless nights this past summer.

She held her tongue until they were having dinner in the peace of the kitchen.

'You can't keep living like this, Michele. You're not a boy any more. We all change, you have to adapt, and this is a country that needs young men,' she told him.

It wasn't the first time they'd had this discussion.

'Come on, Petra, don't start! You know very well that I haven't reached retirement age yet,' was all he said. He would have liked to go on to say that, while he agreed that people did change, some things, like the strength of his vocation and his need to unmask the guilty parties, would never change.

It had taken many forms over the years, but that desire for justice had remained intact within him, and it had always gone hand in hand with his love of the whole process of investigation, something that had got under his skin a long time ago and never left him.

They sat in silence for a while, and gradually her face relaxed into a calmer expression. Then she continued, a slight smile on her lips: 'Why don't we go and see my parents? You could relax at their place in the forest at Baden Baden, go on long walks and breathe clean air instead of all this smog.'

Petra, who had lived in Germany until her marriage, had been amazed by the pollution in the centre of Florence, much of it generated by the huge number of mopeds on the streets. She was always saying that it would make them both ill.

Ferrara shook his head but didn't reply. He knew all too well that organising a period of leave, even a short one, was practically impossible in his job. On those few occasions when they did manage to arrange a little trip, some last-minute work commitment would inevitably prevent him from going. Rather than continue the discussion, he retired to the living room.

It was a spacious room, divided into two separate areas. On one side were leather sofas, armchairs and a desk, where he would sometimes spend entire nights working on his cases. On the other was a long, narrow eighteenth-century table that occasionally served as a worktop or a breakfast table, especially if they

47

had guests and the weather wasn't nice enough to be out on the terrace. On the walls were an assortment of pictures, many of which had belonged to Petra's family. There were also lots of framed photographs arranged on the various tables. This was another of his wife's passions. There were portraits of them both, always together, taken at the happiest moments of their lives, as well as photos of family and friends. There were so few of the latter that you could count them on one hand – and perhaps still have a finger or two to spare.

He slumped into a leather armchair and put his feet up on the pouffe. This was his favourite position for shrugging off the tension after a hard day at work. All he needed now was a glass of Alpestre, an aromatic liqueur made according to a mid-nineteenth-century recipe using 320 different kinds of herb. It was the perfect digestif after a heavy dinner, and the meal Petra had prepared hadn't exactly been light: tagliolini pasta with porcini mushrooms, followed by another of his favourites, sardine gratin made with fish bought fresh that morning from San Lorenzo market, served with raw Tropea red onions.

Ferrara took his first sip of the liqueur and turned on the TV. On Rai Uno a veteran presenter was engaged in a political debate with his studio guests. The usual hot air from the same old regulars. He snorted, turned off the television and switched on the CD player. Seventies music filled the room. Although opera had been his passion ever since his friend Massimo Verga had introduced him to it, he'd always loved pop songs that took him back to a time when his life had been free of trouble and stress.

Soon he was luxuriating in the dulcet tones of Fabrizio De André. The lyrics were pure poetry. It was exactly what he needed after Genius's escape. The nickname seemed grotesque, belonging as it did to one of the most savage murderers he had ever had to deal with. He shuddered at the memory of what Genius had done to Senator Costanza; that had been the first time he'd ever seen a corpse with the eyes gouged out and the image had imprinted itself on his brain.

He shook the thoughts from his head. There was no point dwelling on the past. He needed to think about the immediate future. What would Genius's next move be if he wasn't caught within the next few hours?

Where would he go?

Would he be alone or with an accomplice?

Would he attempt to track down and kill Sir George Holley?

With these thoughts percolating in his head, Ferrara finished his drink and went to bed. Experience told him he needed to grab some sleep while he could, because once the investigation got fully under way he'd be locked in a race against time.

There would be no time for rest tomorrow.

10

Dawn was still a long way off.

Menacing thunderclaps had been rumbling in the distance for almost an hour. The long-awaited break in the weather was finally drawing near: soon the rain would come, like a blessing.

It was the ideal night for the two fugitives to break cover and abandon their hideout.

The old barn was surrounded by grass that stood almost a metre high. The doorway and windows were barred with wooden planks. Inside, the plaster was crumbling and the entire structure showed signs of wear and decay. It was obvious no one had been near the place in years. At one time the Tuscan countryside had been teeming with derelict buildings like this, but now they were a rarity; most had been bought up by American or British tourists who renovated them and turned them into holiday homes.

Apart from the two fugitives, there hadn't been a sign of life all day. The only sounds were the buzzing of insects and the chirruping of birds. Their presence, their words, seemed incongruous in the silence of that deserted countryside, abandoned by God.

Isolation had given them the opportunity to become better acquainted than they had been in prison. But Genius had remained uncommunicative. What was the point in talking?

There was no way his companion could understand the pain he harboured, or the hatred that had exploded inside him back in July when he'd learned that his twin brother had been murdered. The Black Rose had sent a sniper to shoot him, as if he were some rabid dog that needed to be put down. How could Pasquale understand that? He had grown up in a world that was a million miles from the one Daniele had known.

But now the moment had come for them to move on. Someone was waiting for them a dozen or so miles away, ready to lead them on the next stage of their escape plan. It had all been organised down to the last detail by Salvino Lo Cascio's *family*.

They made their way along minor roads, deserted at that time of night, until they reached a point just over a mile outside the city of Vinci, birthplace of Leonardo, one of the greatest geniuses of all time.

They turned on to a dirt road flanked by olive trees and followed it for about three-quarters of a mile. The last section took them up a gentle incline, with cypresses growing on either side of the road. They came to a wrought-iron gate that had been left wide open, drove through it and crossed a large yard full of car parts: chassis, bonnets, bumpers and wheels of all makes and sizes.

The SUV stopped outside a cement barn, the pebbly ground crunching under the wheels. A short, muscular man in his fifties with a dark complexion was waiting for them, sitting in front of the door in an old leather armchair, doing a crossword by the light of a lamp hanging from the ceiling. He was the sort of man you would never want to get on the wrong side of.

As soon as he saw them climbing out of the car, he stood up and went to meet them with a smile on his face.

'I knew you'd make it, Pasquale,' he said, embracing him and kissing him on both cheeks. 'And you must be Genius,' he added, shaking his hand. 'I'm Filippo. You have shown courage and we are all grateful to you.'

De Robertis stepped forward and embraced him.

Pasquale had told him that they were going to meet a 'man of honour' who owned a junkyard. There they would receive all the help they needed and the SUV would be destroyed. No trace of their visit would remain.

'Everything's ready,' Filippo confirmed, getting straight down to business. He led them into the barn, where the lights were on in readiness for their arrival but there were no other signs of life. Machinery for breaking down cars was arranged along one side of the barn with a line of new or nearly new cars parked end to end down the other side. Almost all of them had powerful engines.

'Take that one. There are documents in the glovebox and it's got a full tank of petrol. You can abandon it if necessary – they'll never trace it, certainly not back to me,' he said, indicating a BMW 6 Series with tinted windows and paintwork as black as ink. 'But first, go through to my office out the back and change. I've set out some clothes in lots of different sizes,' he added, gesturing to the door.

The two men put on Ermenegildo Zegna suits and Ferragamo shoes. They looked like two executives – bankers, perhaps.

Genius found everything he needed in the small bathroom and was finally able shave his beard off. Looking in the mirror, he noticed a gleam in his eyes. The evil that was growing inside him was clearly visible now.

Outside, the storm had broken and the rain was getting heavier from one flash of lightning to the next. It was the perfect night. Luck was still with them.

They said their farewells with more embraces and kisses on the cheek and got into the car. Pasquale revved the engine while the car was still in neutral and a plume of grey smoke came out of the exhaust pipe. The roar of the engine was incredible, an explosion of sheer power. Then he put the car into first, put his foot down and they set off into the storm, water drumming against the windscreen, wipers going at top speed. The cypresses at the roadside were practically bent double from the force of the wind and a flash of lightning struck the hill opposite with a great rumbling noise as they drove through the gate.

The car vanished into the night along the deserted roads, the built-in sat nav telling them which route to follow.

Next stop: Milan.

Now the game was really on. Genius could feel pulses of energy flowing through his body. After the weeks stagnating in prison, he'd come alive again. Here, on the outside, he had purpose, a goal that made it worth living.

He remained deep in thought for most of the journey. Only once he'd managed to come up with a strategy for his hunt did he decide to confide in Pasquale and thus assure himself of gaining the final piece of the puzzle.

Yes, I need *family* too, he thought to himself, and it was all he could do to stop himself laughing out loud.

11

Friday 18 October

Chief Superintendent Ferrara was listening to the radio while he showered and shaved, paying particular attention to the news about the escape from Don Bosco Prison and the fruitless search efforts.

Then he went out on to the terrace before breakfast. It had stopped raining barely an hour before and the tiles were still wet. The sky was a mass of grey clouds and it looked as though it might still be raining in the distance. Below him, the Ponte Vecchio was deserted. Built in the fourteenth century on three solid arches at the narrowest point of the Arno, it was still the true heart of the city. Once home to grocers and butchers and now to gold and silver smiths, it was the public face of Florence, representing the best the city had to offer. Poverty and decay didn't exist there. It wasn't enough, being the cradle of the Renaissance, with a precious legacy of literary, artistic and scientific endeavour; Florence needed to appear wealthy in the eyes of the rest of the world.

He looked up towards the Piazzale Michelangelo, a favourite tourist destination all year round due to its extraordinary views across the city. This was another of Florence's public faces, the city gleaming like a newly finished canvas below.

He went back into the house and sat down at the table. The welcoming aroma of coffee filled the air. Petra had made breakfast. Rich and abundant as always, it was often the only meal that husband and wife ate together. But this morning his thoughts continued to be preoccupied by the escape. Petra's plans for a trip to Germany, first broached the night before, were an unwelcome distraction.

'My parents would be so happy if we went, even if it was only for a few days,' she told him.

'We'll go as soon as possible,' was his only reply.

A frown that spoke volumes appeared on Petra's face. She was aware that that 'as soon as possible' meant 'who knows when' or perhaps 'never'. It was always the same old story. His work commitments came first. She would have liked to remind him that we're only given one family and that she hadn't married the police force, but she didn't. This wasn't the moment.

Michele ate a couple of slices of Tuscan bread slathered in butter and a thick layer of blueberry jam, and drank a cup of coffee with just a drop of cold milk. Then he got up, went over to his wife and kissed her on the lips.

'Will you be back for lunch?' she asked him.

'I'll let you know. It'll depend on how things go when I get to the office.'

'Mm, I can only guess . . . ' she sighed.

When he stepped out of the front door his driver, Giancarlo Perrotta, a young officer from Naples, was waiting next to a pool car, the standard-issue dark-coloured Alfa Romeo 156, scanning the street for potential threats. His dark, collar-length hair shone with gel. As soon as Ferrara climbed in, he leapt into the driver's seat and turned the ignition.

Within minutes they had arrived at Headquarters, where the Chief Superintendent found the usual blizzard of paperwork on his desk. The morning papers with the news from the last twenty-four hours. The memos from the Ministry and other regional headquarters. Reports from his staff for him to review before they were sent to the judicial authorities . . .

Ferrara moved it all to one side and concentrated on the newspapers. Organised as ever, his secretary, Nestore Fanti, had left them by the computer table for him.

He was about to leaf through the first one when Fanti came in.

'Can I get you a coffee, chief?' he asked.

'Yes, please, and make it a good one, eh?'

'Of course, chief.'

Fanti withdrew into his own office to fiddle about blending various brands of coffee. The exact mix was a secret he would never share with anyone – and perhaps he had other secrets, too. Almost six foot three, worryingly thin with hollow cheeks, blue eyes and bristly blond hair, the forty-something-year-old Fanti was an impenetrable mystery. In all the years he'd been working there, none of his colleagues had succeeded in discovering a single detail of his private life. Nobody had ever heard him talk about his family, or make even a passing reference to his day-to-day life. Never a mention of a film, a television programme or a politician. Nothing. He simply got on with his job, and was devotedly loyal to his boss. And that was more than enough.

Ferrara lingered over *La Nazione* for some time while he waited for his coffee.

The article on De Robertis was on the front page, under the headline A JOKE OF AN ESCAPE with the subtitle *Still No Trace Of The Two Dangerous Criminals.*

To one side was a panoramic photo of the prison with a Carabinieri patrol car parked in front of the vehicle entrance.

After a reconstruction of the various phases of the escape, the journalist reported a brief statement by the governor of the facility. He took responsibility for the failings in the security systems and asserted with absolute confidence that the two fugitives would be recaptured soon and taken to a high-security facility to complete their current sentences and the additional ones the judges were bound to hand down.

At the end, in the last few lines, it said that Police Headquarters and the Commander of the Pisan Carabinieri had declined to comment.

Ferrara's gaze fell on a neighbouring article, entitled WAS THE ESCAPE TOO EASY?

A disturbing question.

The article – a vitriolic attack on the prison authorities – had been written by Luigi Frasca, a young roving reporter who was blazing a stellar trail at the Tuscan daily. Why wasn't the infrared security system working? Were they too short of money to pay for its upkeep? Or had it been deactivated by someone on the prison staff, either accidentally or to facilitate the escape?

The parting shot read, 'We hope that, this time, whoever made the mistake will pay for it'.

'Look what happens when you try to save on security,' Ferrara thought to himself, as he folded the paper. It looked as though the prison governor was living on borrowed time – and probably he wasn't the only one who'd be looking for a job before long.

That morning's coffee proved even better than usual. There was no doubt that his secretary's talents were approaching mastery. Fanti had tiptoed in so as not to disturb Ferrara's reading, carefully placed the coffee cup on the desk and disappeared like a ghost.

But this delicacy would be the only positive point in the day. Ferrara's mood got worse and worse as hours went by without anyone catching so much as a glimpse of the two fugitives. There was something else bothering him too: Petra's insistence that they needed to take a holiday, to go off to Germany so that he could unwind. For years she'd been urging him to put his family first instead of his job. But he'd always resisted, even when he'd had problems with his superiors and the Chief Prosecutor and when he'd been injured in the shoot-out with Leonardo Berghoff in Bavaria.

After several hours, while his umpteenth cigar slowly smouldered out in the ashtray, he summoned Rizzo to his smoke-filled office. He told him to prepare a new request for a search warrant for Sir George Holley's villa at San Gimignano as a matter of urgency.

'It's time everyone faced up to their responsibilities,' he told Rizzo afterwards. 'Even the Prosecutor's Department. And it's important to have evidence on file, documenting our initiatives and the inertia from above and on the part of the deputy prosecutor in charge of the investigation. Enough is enough!'

Rizzo was of the same mind.

As his deputy left the office, Ferrara told himself that the time had come to force the Prosecutor's Department to fulfil its obligations. In his heart, though, he knew that this was uncharted territory, full of mines waiting to explode. And, most probably, they, the State's humble servants, would be the only ones to take the hit.

12

Milan

'So this is the famous club . . . ' Daniele De Robertis thought to himself as he sat in a luxurious lounge on the ground floor. Pasquale had spoken to him about it as *their* club in the heart of Milan, a stone's throw from the prestigious Via Montenapoleone.

He observed the room's rich furnishings, the marble floor, the door with its extraordinary sculpting and the antique prints on the walls. Three beautiful young women crossed the room; he noticed that they walked like the models he'd seen gracefully strutting the runways when he'd accompanied his adoptive mother to fashion shows in Paris.

A shiver ran through him – it was a sensation he thought he'd long forgotten.

At that moment Pasquale entered the room. At his side was a girl with her hair tied at the back of her neck; it was dark, in stark contrast to the pale skin of her face. She wore a Versace dress with a slit up one side which gave her figure a certain harmony. Her nipples were visible beneath the extremely thin layer of fabric. The high-heeled shoes she was wearing added at least four inches to her height.

'This is Bambi,' Pasquale told him with a smile that lit up his face, as if to underline that he was a man of his word who kept his promises.

Daniele shook her hand as they were introduced. Her fingers were soft, her nails polished to perfection. Looking into her pale blue eyes, he was sure she couldn't be older than eighteen. An exquisite fragrance reached his nose; it had to be a very expensive perfume.

'Bambi will show you upstairs,' Pasquale added. 'I've got something to take care of – something for you. We'll see each other later, but in the meantime, enjoy yourself!'

The young woman took him by the hand and led him to one of the rooms. It was like a suite in a luxury hotel, with frosted windows, marble floors and Persian rugs. Hidden speakers played a French song that he couldn't quite identify. He spotted some small bags of white powder on a round table by a stuccoed pillar. It was cocaine, no doubt of the highest quality. This was sheer luxury – exactly what he needed after being in that cesspit of a prison.

The girl started to take his clothes off; with practised movements she ran her fingers down his back and across his thighs and genitals. Clearly accustomed to satisfying demanding clients, she was prepared to offer sensations he had forgotten existed and had never experienced with that bitch, Angelica.

Suddenly overcome by a strange, fastidious feeling, he got up and gestured to her to move away from him. No, he wasn't ready. He didn't feel free of his nightmares, even in here. It was as if he were split in two: he was here in the room, but somewhere else, too. The touch of the woman's hands had awakened images in his memory of a past he couldn't erase. Picking up one of the little bags from the table, he went into the bathroom without saying a word.

When he came out after a quarter of an hour or perhaps more, he found Bambi stretched out on the silk sheets. She was naked and appeared to be feeling the effects of the drugs. Her outfit, the shoes and hold-up stockings were scattered on the floor. He lay down next to her and she turned to him with a smile then began delicately touching his body, which was now ready for pleasure. One finger slipped into his anus and another between his lips. Finally aroused, De Robertis let himself go. It was an hour of frenetic sex, just the way he liked it. The girl didn't put up any resistance and did everything he wanted and more to fulfil his every desire. Presumably she was anxious to please whoever had given her the job.

Later, in the apartment opposite Police Headquarters in the Via Fatebenefratelli where he was a guest, Pasquale told him about the decision he and the other members had made at the club. They would help him carry out the rest of his plan, which he had decided share with Pasquale during the journey to Milan.

'You won't be alone any more. The *family* is with you,' he told him.

A token of the old boss's infinite gratitude.

And then there was another goal to achieve: making everyone aware of Genius's qualities. A bold and courageous man, a potential 'man of honour' who could prove useful to the *family*.

That night, before he went to sleep, Daniele De Robertis oiled the parts of the pistol Pasquale had given him. It was a powerful and lethal semi-automatic, a Beretta 92 Parabellum with a fifteen-round magazine. Its registration number had been filed off.

He arranged the pieces side by side on a piece of newspaper, then, once they were dry, he put the gun back together. Then he went to stand in front of the mirror, looked at himself and pulled the trigger. There was a dull noise and he felt the recoil of the weapon run up his arm.

He put it back in the underarm holster. It was made of soft leather and had already seen enough use to smell of sweat, but he didn't care. It was ideal for the job he had in mind: it was very comfortable and could be easily concealed.

He looked at the clock: 2.25 a.m.

The countdown was about to begin.

13

Friday 15 October

There was still no news of the fugitives. Nothing from the Prosecutor's Department either. The search warrant for Sir George Holley's villa had still not been granted. Deputy Prosecutor Luigi Vinci had not been in touch with the Chief Superintendent.

No progress whatsoever.

The Operations Room at Headquarters had received quite a few phone calls in the first few days, the majority of them anonymous, claiming that the wanted men had been seen somewhere in the city or at various locations in the provinces of Pisa and Florence. However, they had all turned out to be completely false, perhaps the work of the usual conspiracy theorists, or perhaps people acting in good faith but deceived by the strong resemblance between the person in question and the photos of the fugitives that had been published in the local papers and shown on regional TV. Then, as always, interest in the investigation had dwindled, the phone calls had grown fewer and the press had moved on to other matters. The news was stale. The media would only pick up on the story again in the event of a capture.

That Friday the Chief Superintendent needed to get to grips

with a new investigation. A riot had broken out in the early hours of the morning at a Roma encampment on the northern outskirts of the city. Two rival clans had been facing off and, as was often the case, things had got out of hand. A young man had been killed by a direct stab wound to the heart.

This, too, could happen in Florence.

It wasn't the first time the police had had to intervene in matters amongst the caravans. Usually when they went in it was to carry out searches for stolen goods. In fact, there was a separate group within the community that dealt almost exclusively in bag-snatching and muggings. But from time to time the police also went to deal with brawls and accidental deaths, mostly from fires caused by unsafe illegal connections to the mains electricity. The sight of the spider's web of overhead wires running from shack to shack carrying electricity stolen from the network intended to power the public street lights was impressive. It was a scene worthy of the Third World, not 'noble' Florence.

When the Chief Superintendent arrived at the office, the corridor was full of people who'd been brought in for questioning. But nobody seemed prepared to collaborate and help them solve the crime. Not even the family of the victim. On the contrary, they seemed intent on obstructing the investigation. So there wasn't a single witness. No evidence. No weapon. Someone must have taken the trouble to make it disappear.

It was the law of *omertà*. The law of the Roma, who resolved every disagreement, with or without violence, in accordance with the orders of their respective clan chiefs. These men were bosses in the truest sense. Despite their living arrangements, they travelled in powerful cars, almost always Mercedes, and wore heavy gold necklaces and rings adorned with precious stones.

Ferrara could still vividly remember an incident a couple of years earlier when a six-year-old girl had been burned to death after fire broke out in the shack where she lived. Her relatives had been unable to get her out before the whole thing burned to the ground.

At the time there had been discussions at Commune level about finding an alternative solution to that camp, to assign social housing to the Roma, given that they had been living in Florence for such a long time. Aware that the public had been moved by the death of the little girl, the Mayor had declared that incidents of that type were an insult to the city.

But the camp was still there, and here was another crime.

Ferrara read the reports filed by the first patrol on the scene. Then he skimmed through the transcripts of the interviews. He shook his head as he turned the pages: nothing useful. He took a cigar out of his leather case, lit it and took his first puff. It was his second of the morning. As the smoke curled up towards the ceiling, he looked at the shapes that formed and reformed, trying to spot some kind of pattern.

It wouldn't be long before opposition parties would start ranting about the lack of order, claiming the Mayor was at fault for being too generous to the Roma, squandering public money on state education for the children, who were taken to school each morning on one of the Commune's school buses.

Soon their anger would turn on the police, too. He was willing to bet on it. The politicians would look for a scapegoat, as they always did.

In the meantime, gypsies had begun to gather outside Police Headquarters to show their support for those being held inside. A man tried to come in, demanding to speak to the Commissioner, but he was forcibly ejected. He tried to fight back, but fell to the pavement in the scuffle. The tension was tangible, electric.

'Look how they treat us. They've beaten him up!' cried a woman with a newborn in her arms.

It was the spark.

Some ran to help the man, who was struggling to stand up. He wasn't hurt, but the dice had been cast. They threw themselves against the doors while police officers struggled to close them. The protesters started to shout, 'Open up! Let them go and catch the killer! We want justice, justice, justice!'

The front doors held and the Roma began to move away in search of another target. They didn't find one. Officers from the riot police, experienced in maintaining public order, had been stationed at all the entrances. That same division of riot police had come to international attention during the G8 summit at Genoa in 2001 when, without provocation, officers had set upon a group of protesters staying in one of the Diaz schools. Then they had come up with false evidence against the young protesters, accusing them of making Molotov cocktails that they had actually brought in themselves. Had the officers responsible been acting on their own initiative or simply following orders? Either way, the ensuing controversy had done nothing to contribute to the honour of the police force and would not be easily forgotten.

After a lively discussion amongst themselves, the gypsies remained waiting on the pavement. Every so often they would shout and swear at the police officers.

Ferrara summoned Inspector Riccardo Venturi to put him in charge of the case. They needed to get moving and have answers ready for the Commissioner. Right on cue, Ferrara's mobile began to ring: it was the man himself. Ferrara took a deep breath, certain that he wouldn't enjoy what he was about to hear.

The Commissioner was calling from the Prosecutor's Department, where they were about to start an Extraordinary Meeting on public order and safety, presided over by the Prefect and attended by representatives of all the forces of law and order and the Chief Prosecutor.

All those bureaucrats in the same room could not be good news. Chief Superintendent Ferrara was sure of it.

*

That evening, as he was getting ready to head home, Ferrara had a visit from Venturi. He seemed tired and he slumped into the seat on the other side of the desk like a dead weight.

'What's up?'

'You can see it for yourself, chief. I haven't eaten, my back's killing me and my head feels like it's about to explode. And all that for nothing.'

Apparently nobody at the Roma camp had been willing to speak. No one had seen or heard a thing. A thorough search hadn't turned up a single weapon, although they had found a number of gold items, which had been passed on to the theft team to run the necessary checks. It was an expensive procedure, and almost always a pointless one: the jewellery usually belonged to tourists who had already left Italy.

'We haven't seen the end of this, chief. There are bound to be reprisals, but there's no way of knowing who the targets will be. You can feel the tension in the air at the camp,' he concluded wearily.

This was nothing new. The Roma were highly organised, with their own law code, but the Inspector's last words gave Ferrara pause for thought. The last thing they needed was another death. If this turned into a full-blown war between clans, a blood feud, it would alarm the local Florentine population. They needed to intervene, and soon. And the Commissioner's terse phone call left no room for confusion: 'Our jobs are on the line,' he had said before hanging up.

'Venturi, summon the clan leaders to the office tomorrow so we can have a little chat. Let's try to make them understand where we're coming from.'

'First thing, chief.'

As he closed his office door behind him and set off for home, Ferrara realised that he hadn't managed to give even a minute to his other cases. This was how it had been back when he was based in Calabria and had to contend with the 'Ndrangheta.

Each murder was immediately followed by another, and there wasn't even time to fill in the victim's details on the paperwork before they were called to the scene of another crime.

The realities of Calabria and Florence were distant and different, but the fatigue he felt and the physical and mental endurance required of him were the same. It was all part of an investigator's job.

14

Saturday 16 October

When the Chief Superintendent arrived at Headquarters that morning he found a man walking nervously backwards and forwards in the corridor. He was short and muscular with a dark complexion and wore a shirt unbuttoned at the neck to reveal a hairy chest and a heavy gold chain from which hung a crucifix that was also made of solid gold. He was probably around seventy.

'You sent a patrol car to bring me in, Chief Superintendent, but what do you want from me?' he asked as soon as he saw Ferrara.

'Please, take a seat.' Ferrara waved him into his office.

The man sat down on one of the two black chairs in front of the desk, choosing the one nearer the door. He seemed calm, as if he had nothing to hide.

At that moment Inspector Venturi appeared. 'Chief, allow me to introduce the victim's uncle. This is Signor Markovic.'

'Yes, I'm his uncle,' the man confirmed. 'They killed my nephew. He was like a son to me. I was the one who brought him up.'

'Vendettas and blood feuds are for barbarians. Times have changed,' said Ferrara, getting straight to the point. He knew that the man sitting in front of him was not merely the victim's uncle but one of the heads of the Roma camp.

'Times don't change for us,' the man replied.

'That shouldn't be the case. You live in this society and you ought to respect its rules, the same as the rest of us. There can be no exceptions.'

'But we're not like everyone else. You police, and even the judges, treat us badly. You don't trust us. You're prejudiced. You come and search the camp every other day, as if we were the cause of every single problem in the city.'

The Chief Superintendent paused to consider this. He took a half-smoked cigar out of the packet and put it between his lips without lighting it. The mention of prejudices had reminded him of a survey published in one of the national daily papers: the majority of those interviewed considered all Roma to be nothing but a bunch of gypsies who made a living from their wits and petty crime, were closed to wider society, who were not like them, and who exploited minors.

'You need to trust us and not try to administer your own justice. You ought to speak out, Signor Markovic, tell us what you know to ensure that your nephew's killer is brought to justice. You must know who it was. And don't tell me that you know nothing,' replied Ferrara, articulating each word and skirting around the issue of prejudice.

Venturi nodded vigorously.

Markovic got to his feet, took his crucifix in his hand and waved it at them, shouting, 'I'll speak before God alone. You find the killer, it's your job. It's what you're paid for.'

'Take him away!' Ferrara ordered the inspector. There was no point prolonging the conversation. The look in the man's eyes said it all: they could go fuck themselves, he would never tell them what he knew.

Before he could leave the room, Ferrara called after him: 'One more death, Markovic, and you can say goodbye to Florence.

And that goes for all of you!' he finished, thumping his fist on desk.

The man gave no sign that he'd heard, storming out without a backward glance.

It was impossible to start a dialogue with the Roma, to find the middle ground. It had always been that way. Ferrara had been well aware of this, nonetheless he had wanted to make the effort and, more importantly, to inform the inhabitants of the camp, Markovic's enemies included, that further crimes would not be tolerated, that life in that camp would be far from easy, that the police would do everything in their power to obstruct their sordid business activities. Even if it meant stationing a permanent watch there and keeping them under round-the-clock surveillance.

Ferrara listened to the footsteps fading along the corridor, then went over to the window. A couple of minutes later he saw Markovic leave the building. He was immediately surrounded by a group of women and young girls from the camp. It was almost as if they were trying to protect him. Ferrara watched as they hurled inaudible insults at the police officer who had escorted Markovic out. This man was their king, to whom they had sworn eternal loyalty. Slowly they made their way towards the nearby Piazza della Libertà, where – Ferrara would be willing to bet on it – their Mercedes would be waiting to whisk them back to the camp.

Returning to his desk, Ferrara glanced at the wall where he displayed the awards he had won in the course of his career. As always, his eyes lingered on the certificate that had come with a 150,000 lira reward from the Head of the State Police during his posting to Calabria back in the eighties. He'd been given the award after capturing a criminal who'd tried to blow up a shop by lighting the fuse on a stick of dynamite – Ferrara and his driver were nearly blown sky-high. All that remained of that day was that piece of paper in a clip frame which shouted out to the whole world how little the Head of the State Police valued his life.

Things had changed a lot since then. In the nineties, awards had been given out like sweets, often for operations where there was almost no risk to the officers' lives and all the intel had been provided by informants, so there was none of that 'creativity' that a real police operation would have required.

From bad to worse, thought Ferrara with a bitter smile.

15

Sunday 17 October

Chief Superintendent Ferrara arrived at the office later than usual the next day. Since he'd been appointed head of the *Squadra Mobile* there had been few Sundays or bank holidays when he hadn't popped into the office to see how investigations were going and get an update on the latest news.

It was almost eleven and he'd barely set foot in the building when he saw Venturi bouncing along the corridor towards him with a satisfied expression on his face. Clearly there had been a breakthrough of some kind.

'Chief, the murder's been solved!' Venturi beamed. He went on to explain that half an hour earlier the killer, accompanied by a lawyer, had come to turn himself in. 'I called you at home, but your wife told me you'd just left.'

'Has he confessed?'

'Yes.'

'Any incriminating evidence? Something that links him directly to the murder?'

'The murder weapon. A five-inch-long switchblade with a mother-of-pearl handle, complete with traces of dried blood. He brought it with him and handed it over wrapped in a piece of newspaper.'

'Send it to Forensics for blood and fingerprint analysis.'

'Right away, chief.'

'What do we know about the suspect?'

'He doesn't have ID, but he claims he's under sixteen. By the look of him, I'd say he's younger still.'

'Put in a request for an anthropometric expert to establish his age,' Ferrara ordered. When young gypsies were arrested they invariably claimed to be younger than they were in an effort to be tried in a juvenile court.

'He says he fled to one of the travelling Roma camps after the crime,' Venturi added.

'But is he telling the truth?' mused Ferrara. He wouldn't have put it past Markovic to offer up a scapegoat, the first poor bugger he came across, in order to get the police off their backs.

The Inspector excused himself so that he could make a start on the paperwork for the Prosecutor's Department. Whatever doubts his boss might harbour, Venturi was happy to have avoided an investigator's greatest frustration: an unsolved case.

Ferrara was about to continue to his office when two officers appeared, accompanied by a young man in handcuffs. One of them was waving a finger in the prisoner's face: 'You have to stop stealing tourists' wallets . . . '

The young man merely sneered at him in silence. He was then told to take a seat in the corridor. One of the officers remained standing guard while the other went into an office to fill out the paperwork.

Such scenes were becoming more and more common. The two officers would have to appear in court for his trial, spending hours and hours waiting to testify. Then they would wait for the verdict. Even if the defendant was found guilty, chances were he'd get off with a small fine or a light sentence which would be suspended. A complete waste of a day.

That was how justice worked, leaving police officers feeling bitter and depriving the public of confidence in the law's ability to protect them.

'That's why it's known as imperfect justice,' Ferrara thought to himself as he started to flick through the newspapers. After a gap of several days, *Il Tirreno*, printed in Livorno, had turned its attention back to the escape from Don Bosco Prison with a brief article, no doubt prompted by someone leaking the findings of the internal investigation being carried out by the regional superintendent of the penitentiary administration.

The unsigned article read:

> Although there is no concrete information likely to lead to the capture of the two fugitives, the investigation may be at a turning point.
>
> It is rumoured that a prison guard is to be arrested in the coming hours as a result of evidence that would appear to implicate him as an accomplice. Of course, in this case it is important to establish whether he was bribed or coerced into cooperating. Whatever the case, we are sure that one officer's betrayal will not discredit all the other staff who carry out a challenging job in a difficult environment.

Eager to find out more, Ferrara ordered Rizzo to go to Pisa the next day to see what he could glean from the Prosecutor's Department. Perhaps this prison officer would provide them with information that would lead to Genius's capture.

Then he moved on to the inside pages, which featured some articles about the murder at the Roma camp. *La Nazione* published an interview with a Florentine member of parliament, Orazio Dentice, who blamed the police for their failure to control the situation, and the *Squadra Mobile* in particular: 'Ultimately the blame must fall squarely on their leader, Michele Ferrara, who seems intent on chasing shadows.'

Chasing shadows? What the hell was that supposed to mean? Ferrara could only conclude that Dentice bore some personal grudge. Why else would he have been singled out for censure?

And why would Dentice have chosen to overlook the many cases where the *Squadra Mobile* had been actively involved in bringing dangerous criminals to justice?

Ferrara knew Dentice only by name. *La Nazione* had interviewed him in the past, but he'd never been so critical of a public institution before, and especially not of an individual civil servant. It was completely out of character. Which suggested that the murder of the Roma boy was merely a pretext, and some other agenda lay behind the attack. Ferrara cut out the article and filed it away in one of his desk drawers.

Ferrara set off for home that evening hopeful that, with a bloody feud between the Roma averted, peace had been restored. He should have known better.

The fight against evil is never over.

PART TWO

A STRANGE CRIME SCENE

16

Monday 18 October, *Borgo Bellavista gated community*

It was a little piece of earthly paradise a few miles from the centre of Florence. A place where the grey of the *palazzi*, discoloured by pollution, gave way to the green of the countryside. Where everything was clean and pleasant, not a trace of decay in sight. The olive groves were well tended. The cars were immaculately polished. The people were rich and stuck up – the women in particular; it was obvious just from the way they dressed and walked that they thought themselves better than anyone else.

And there was another attraction: the breathtaking panorama from the terrace. It was an enviable view, especially when lit up at night: the city of Florence with Brunelleschi's cupola towering over everything. Looking upon it from that oasis of peace and tranquillity, you felt you were a million miles from the stresses of city life.

From this day on, all that would remain was the breathtaking panorama.

This was no longer a place of peace and tranquillity. As he stood on the terrace, Ferrara's mind was besieged by questions for which he had no answer.

He'd received the call from the duty officer shortly after half past seven that morning: a body had been found, along with a woman who'd been seriously injured. Both had yet to be identified.

When the Alfa 156 – driven, as ever, by Officer Giancarlo Perrotta – arrived at the big wrought-iron double gates they were standing wide open. With the gravel crunching beneath them like broken bones, they pulled into one of the designated parking spaces. The Chief Superintendent jumped out of the car, slamming the door behind him. Pausing to run a hand through his longish, salt-and-pepper hair to tidy it, he made his way towards one of the houses. Like the others it had been recently remodelled, though it retained the features that typified Tuscan style: a combination of natural stone, terracotta tiles, sandstone columns and wrought-iron gates. The wood and earthy colours were perfectly in tune with the surrounding countryside and would have contributed to the calm ambience of the place had it not been for the police activity surrounding the house.

Two uniformed officers were sitting on a low stone wall. As soon as they saw the head of the *Squadra Mobile* they got up and saluted, bringing their right hands up to the visors of their caps and clicking their heels. Ferrara spotted another uniformed officer by a bush on the other side of the building. He had his back to him, so Ferrara couldn't see his face.

He greeted them and continued towards the main entrance. As he approached, Gianni Ascalchi appeared on the threshold wearing his usual gruff expression. Ascalchi was the duty officer; he'd arrived on the scene ten minutes earlier with a patrol car, having already spoken to the flying squad to gather the preliminary information. As was often the case in these situations, it was fairly confused.

A Roman by birth, Ascalchi had been working in Florence long enough to have acquired an in-depth knowledge of the city's criminal underworld. Short and thickset, his crooked chin made him resemble a young Totò, the comic actor.

'Hi, Gianni!' called Ferrara as he went over.

Ascalchi returned his greeting and stared for a moment at the cigar between his lips. Then he told him about the body in the swimming pool and the woman who'd been found with gunshot wounds. 'The ambulance had been and gone before I arrived. She's at the hospital at Careggi now,' he explained.

'Is anyone else from the *Squadra Mobile* here?'

Ascalchi shook his head. 'Only an officer from the flying squad.'

Ferrara pulled out his mobile and called Teresa Micalizi. She might be the youngest member of his team, but her talent had got her noticed and won Ferrara's favour. He told her to head to the hospital and find out whether the woman had said anything to the medical staff or paramedics. If they were lucky, she might have mentioned a name or some detail that would help the investigation. Then, as soon as the doctors would allow, she should question the woman. Witnesses were generally at their most reliable in the immediate aftermath.

Finishing the call, Ferrara turned once more to Ascalchi. 'Who are the victims?'

'We're not sure yet, but we're keeping in touch with the Operations Room,' he replied, pointing to the earpiece in his right ear. 'The house belongs to the Russo family, though,' he added.

'Which Russos?'

'The lawyer.'

'The famous one?'

'Looks like it.'

'Let's get going.'

Ascalchi set off into the garden, followed by Ferrara. A helicopter hovered overhead for a moment before moving away towards the woods. After a few metres they reached the start of a path that led to the swimming pool and a couple of steps brought them to a dog, a German Shepherd with long, black fur.

He was lying next to a storage shed with his head on his paws and a melancholy expression, as if he understood that something had happened. As the two men approached he lifted his head for a moment and stared at them with his big, shining eyes. Then he dropped his muzzle again without barking. He was a puppy, too young to be fierce.

Ferrara noticed that his bowl was empty. He looked around and spotted a rubber hose attached to a faucet. He turned the tap so water flowed into the bowl. The dog got to his feet and drank noisily.

There were hand-painted terracotta pots overflowing with flowers at regular intervals around the pool. A human figure was bobbing face down in the blue water, the arms at right angles from the body. It appeared to be a man.

Just then they head the rumble of a motor and, a few seconds later, the dull thud of doors slamming, followed by the sound of feet on cobblestones. Turning towards the path, Ferrara saw the Forensics specialist Piero Franceschini and Deputy Prosecutor Luigi Vinci, with a uniformed officer leading the way.

Franceschini was in his forties and at the pinnacle of his career. Tall and lean with straight, blond, mid-length hair, he had a slightly clumsy gait. He was a protégé of the Director of the Institute of Forensics. He was wearing a new brown suit that was at least a size too big, but at first glance he still appeared elegant, if a little awkward.

'Damn! A body in water – that complicates things,' the pathologist exclaimed as soon as he reached Ferrara. He greeted him with a wave while Vinci reached out to shake his hand.

The Chief Superintendent told them that it might be Amedeo Russo, the lawyer.

'Haven't we confirmed the identity yet?' asked the Deputy Prosecutor.

'The body's face down and we'll need to get it out of the pool to confirm the identity, but you're in charge,' replied Ferrara.

Then he moved aside to let Franceschini work under the gaze of the Deputy Prosecutor, who raised his phone to his ear a few seconds later. Now that they were here it would finally be possible to retrieve the body and confirm both the identity and whether there were any indications of violence.

As Ferrara looked up from the pool he caught sight of Officer Pino Ricci from the *Squadra Mobile* waving his arms frantically in an attempt to attract his attention. He was about fifty metres away from the swimming pool, standing beside a metal fence that ran along the perimeter of the gated community.

After ordering Ascalchi to stay where he was to observe the pathologist's work and to contact the Operations Room to find out if there was any news on the injured woman's condition, Ferrara went over to him.

Ricci was a street cop. He and the late Inspector Antonio Sergi had been partners; two big, tough guys, they'd made a formidable pair, with a combined weight of almost thirty-eight stone. The death of his friend death had taken its toll on Ricci. He would never forget the sight of Sergi's corpse stretched out on the ground after being removed from the waters of Lake Bracciano. When he'd shouldered the coffin alongside his colleagues on the day of the funeral, he'd sworn that he would do everything in his power to capture the people who'd killed his friend.

'What is it, Pino?'

'Look there, chief!' Pino, clearly excited, pointed at the two-metre high chain-link fence in front of him.

Someone had cut a hole big enough for a man to fit through, obviously with the intention of entering the property. There were no other houses on the far side of the fence, just agricultural land planted with olive trees – small ones, not like the tall, bushy trees Ferrara remembered from his home in Sicily and his time in Calabria. In the distance were woods, the green beginning to turn to autumn reds and golds now. It was an ideal place to enter the property without being seen.

The Chief Superintendent looked around, slowly turning his head.

'There's something else, too,' Ricci continued.

'What?'

'Come with me.'

They reached the area between the fence and the swimming pool, next to the path where the grass was sparser.

There were footprints.

The Chief Superintendent studied them carefully. Two sets of prints, different sizes, apparently fresh; they were heading in the direction of the swimming pool. He was silent for a few seconds, and all that could be heard were the sounds of the countryside.

'Have you checked the other side of the fence, Pino?' he asked.

'Not yet.'

'Do it. There might be other prints. If there are, we'll need to find out where they lead. But first, call one of the Forensics technicians to come and make casts of these,' Ferrara ordered. It wouldn't be long before the crime scene was swarming with people and he didn't want them trampling over the prints.

'Right away, chief.'

'Keep me informed – I'm going back to Vinci.'

As he made his way back, he saw a wide-hipped woman come out of one of the neighbouring houses. She looked at him, curious, and he waved for her to wait and then hurried across to join her.

The woman, a Filipina, listened to his questions and then replied in imperfect Italian that she worked as a maid for the Corti family. She pointed out the second house on the left as you entered the compound.

'Where are you going?' asked the Chief Superintendent.

'To the pharmacy. I need to get some pills for my mistress. She's in a real state. They were friends.'

'Did you see or hear anything?'

The woman shook her head vigorously. 'No. I've only just arrived. I don't live here.'

'Thank you anyway. Don't let me keep you any longer.'

The Filipina set off along the path to leave the compound and the Chief Superintendent continued on his way towards the swimming pool. During the short walk he couldn't think of anything but the hole in the fence. Although he knew it was too early to say for sure, his mind was coming up with an initial hypothesis.

This might be a classic case of a burglary gone wrong.

17

Gangs specialising in burglary had been targeting isolated villas and farmhouses in the hills around Florence for several months. They almost always struck in the late evening or at night when householders were asleep. On several occasions they had left injured victims behind them, and there had been a couple of rapes too, but, as yet, there had been no fatalities. No prints had been found at the crime scenes and no traces of DNA or fibres either. This scrupulous attention to detail had led the police to conclude the gang were professionals, capable of dealing with unexpected situations.

The investigation had been made more complicated by the lack of witnesses. Traumatised by their ordeal, the victims insisted they'd seen nothing. They were probably too afraid to pass on whatever they had seen for fear of reprisals. That left the police with only one witness: a woman in her forties who'd been raped. She said four men had attacked her, all with their faces covered by balaclavas, and the one who had raped her had seemed quite young, even if she'd only been able to see his eyes. They were light, the way northerners' eyes tended to be.

The investigators thought it might be a gang from Eastern Europe. There was no concrete evidence to support the idea as yet, but it was as likely a hypothesis as any. After the collapse of the Soviet Union, a significant number of Russians had bought property in Tuscany; money was no object to them, and they always paid in cash. Along with these nouveaux riches had come gangs of criminals. According to restricted files compiled by the Secret Service, they were violent and devoid of scruples. It was a repeat of the situation that had arisen in the nineties when asylum seekers fleeing the former Yugoslavia began to arrive. Bandits and hardened criminals mingled with the genuine refugees and it wasn't long before they made their presence felt in every field of criminal activity ranging from child exploitation, prostitution, drug trafficking and extortion to old-fashioned robbery. They too had shown themselves capable of incredible savagery.

If the perpetrators in this case were Eastern Europeans, the Chief Superintendent knew they'd have a hard time catching them. Unlike home-grown armed robbers, they didn't have a fixed abode and they didn't follow any pattern. There was no way of predicting what their next move would be.

Ferrara told himself that it was time to set the hypotheses aside. Even though his intuition often proved correct or stimulated a train of thought that contributed to the solution of a case, it was time to focus on hard proof.

He made his way to the swimming pool where two officers had stripped down to their underwear and got into the water. Under Franceschini's supervision, they were using their arms to create gentle waves so that the body would drift towards the shallow end. Then, under the pathologist's attentive gaze, they carefully lifted it out and laid it face up on the tiled poolside.

Ferrara went over to take a closer look before Franceschini began his examination. The dead man still retained some of his good looks, although he would soon lose them for ever. His glassy, staring eyes were fixed on the grey sky. A Rolex glinted on his left wrist.

It was indeed Amedeo Russo, the famous lawyer.

A cloud of mosquitoes and wasps started to buzz around the body while a uniformed officer brandished a piece of paper in an attempt to fend them off. One of his colleagues had turned pale and looked like he might faint. Perhaps it was the first time he'd seen a murder victim at close quarters. Ferrara gave him a quick look of understanding. It took time and experience to be able to control your emotions when faced with death.

A photographer from the Forensics team began taking a series of shots of the body. Vinci was busy talking on his phone, so Ferrara stepped away from the poolside and waved for Ascalchi to give him the latest news from the Operations Room. They'd identified the injured woman as Elisa Rotondi, Amedeo Russo's fifty-two-year-old wife. She'd suffered two gunshot wounds and her condition was critical.

'They're still operating on her,' Ascalci added. 'Let's hope she makes it.'

Ferrara pulled out his mobile and called the office. When his secretary, prompt as ever, answered on the first ring, he told him to send more officers to the scene to conduct a fingertip search of the house and interview the neighbours.

'Who shall I send, chief?'

'Everyone available, Fanti.' He needed to use every resource at his disposal; if they didn't come up with anything useful in the first twenty-four, or at worst forty-eight, hours, chances were the trail would grow cold and the investigation would turn into a cold case.

The pathologist was standing beside Vinci, waiting for him to finish his call. He'd completed the external examination of the body and had conclusively ruled out the possibility of accidental death. The corpse presented with a violent injury to the head caused by a blunt object like a baseball bat or hammer; there was nothing to indicate the use of a firearm.

Sounding rather like a teacher, Franceschini explained that he was not yet in a position to declare a definite cause of death.

'When will you conduct the autopsy?' asked the Deputy Prosecutor.

'First thing this afternoon. I've got another three corpses waiting for me. Three young men who died in a road accident after a night out at the disco. The crime takes precedence, though. I'll let you know the official cause of death this evening, Deputy Prosecutor Vinci.'

'Good. Send me a preliminary report.'

'And send a copy to my office, too,' said the Chief Superintendent.

Franceschini nodded. Then he added that there was no external indication that the victim had tried to defend himself, but he would check under the fingernails for fragments of skin or other substances.

'What about the time of death?' asked Ferrara.

'Somewhere between two and four this morning,' said Franceschini. He checked his watch and put his instruments away, then swiped the back of his hand across his forehead. 'My work here is done,' he said, waving goodbye to those present and starting to amble away.

'Wait a moment,' Vinci stopped him. 'Where are you going? You came in my car – hold on while I finish here and I'll be right with you.' And after formally authorising the removal of the body and reminding Ferrara to make sure the investigation extended to the room where the woman was shot, he hurried to join the pathologist.

Two paramedics who had been standing by for Vinci to give the go-ahead hurried to the poolside and began to load the body on to a trolley.

The Chief Superintendent watched in silence as the body was transported to the mortuary van. Its destination was the morgue at the university's Institute of Forensic Medicine.

Though the precise method was as yet unknown, it was definitely a murder. So, once again, they were on the hunt for one or more killers.

After a closer look at the body, he had rejected his original theory that it could have been a break-in or an armed robbery gone wrong. Robbers would surely have taken the gold Rolex from the victim's wrist.

And why would robbers have shot the wife? Could she have tried to stop him giving them something? But in that case, would *two* shots really have been necessary?

Ferrara's train of thought was interrupted by the sight of the Filipina returning through the entrance to the compound. He watched her until she went into one of the houses.

'I'm just going over there a moment,' he told Ascalchi, nodding towards the house in question.

'Who lives there?'

'Friends of the Russos.'

'What about the other crime scene?'

'Forensics are in there at the moment – I'll go afterwards. You can keep an eye on things for now – and make sure that the victims' family have been informed. Nobody's turned up here yet.'

'OK, chief.'

On his way towards the house, Ferrara sent officers to begin searching the area around the swimming pool and on the far side of the fence:

'Inspect the entire area, including over there, under the trees. Pino Ricci's already there.'

The door was ajar.

Ferrara rang the doorbell. He waited for a few moments, then the Filipina appeared.

'I'd like to speak with Signor and Signora Corti.'

'Please come in.'

He followed the woman down a corridor that smelled of coffee. Then she went into a living room, furnished in a modern style with paintings on the wall and lots of plants. Inside were a man and a woman, both in their fifties.

He was tall and seemed to have a dark complexion, although

he might just have been very tanned. He was wearing jeans, a dark zip-up jacket and a pair of moccasins, and was standing in front of the window with a glass of orange juice in his right hand.

The woman had chestnut hair and very pale skin. She was enchanting, at least at first glance. She looked up from staring at her own legs as if emerging from a dream. Her eyes were red where she'd been crying. A Neapolitan coffee pot and two cups were arranged on a side table. Behind her was a large painting of a jockey on a black horse approaching a jump.

The Cortis seemed surprised when they saw him in the doorway. The maid silently left the room.

'I'm Chief Superintendent Ferrara, Head of the *Squadra Mobile*, and I need to ask you some questions. I understand you were friends of the Russos,' he said.

The wife started sobbing and her husband went over and put a gentle hand on her shoulder.

'Calm down, darling,' he murmured, bending down beside her. 'Yes, we were friends,' he said, turning towards Ferrara. 'We were guests at their house last night.'

In response to Ferrara's questions he revealed that their names were Antonello Corti and Rosanna Tommasi, both were fifty-two years of age, and they'd been living at their current address for over ten years, having bought the place soon after the gated community had been renovated. He added that he and Amedeo Russo had been partners in a law firm in the Via dei Tornabuoni.

After making some notes, Ferrara turned to look at the woman. Even overcome by sadness, she seemed younger than Corti.

Silence had fallen in the room.

Corti looked from Ferrara to his wife, then his gaze drifted to the window that overlooked the swimming pool, as if curious to see what the police were doing. Suddenly he turned back to Ferrara. 'What about the nightwatchman?' he asked, breaking the silence. 'Chief Superintendent, how can it be that the security guard didn't realise what was happening? How can he have failed to notice?'

'The security guard?'

'Yes. We pay him, and handsomely, too, so we can live in peace.' And he explained that the residents had a contract with a security company who were supposed to ensure that a night-watchman was on duty.

Ferrara made a note of the company. It was one he knew. The owner was a former police officer who'd worked under him for several years until he passed retirement age. Ferrara remembered him as being overweight with a chubby face adorned by a care-fully groomed moustache. At work he'd acted as if he was glued to his desk, spending his days filling out the necessary forms for reports of theft by an identified suspect which were then sent to the Prosecutor's Department once a month. He was, in essence, a bureaucrat. When he left, Ferrara had given the same job to a newly qualified officer.

'Does your wife work?' asked Ferrara.

'No, she's a housewife,' replied Corti, who had stood up and returned to the window.

The woman confirmed this with a slight movement of her head.

Having come to the conclusion that there was no point trying to talk to the wife at this stage, Ferrara turned to the husband and asked, 'Can you tell me how you spent yesterday evening at the Russos'?'

The man told him that they had dined at their friends' house, as they often did at the weekend. After dinner, while their wives chatted in the lounge, he and his colleague had watched a boxing match on TV and then discussed some of the cases they were working on.

'You see, this is the good thing about living near one another, Chief Superintendent. When necessary, we could discuss our work outside the office.'

'How late did you stay at the Russos'?'

'It was probably one, quarter past one, when we got home.'

'Did you hear any strange noises during the night ... any shouting?'

'No, nothing at all. We would have called the police if we had. I dialled 113 as soon as I found poor Amedeo in the swimming pool.'

'You were the one who found the body?'

'Yes. I gave my details to the officer who took the call.'

Then he went on to explain that he'd got up early that morning, as usual, and after drinking a double espresso, he'd put on a tracksuit and gone for a jog. He'd started off down the path to the swimming pool but then turned left towards the small gate that led towards the woods. As soon as he'd spotted the body floating in the water he'd run back home to call the police.

'I recognised him immediately. It was Amedeo.'

'What time did you go out?'

'Seven, maybe quarter past seven.'

'How many families live in the compound?'

'Another three, in addition to us and the Russos. Two houses are still unoccupied, perhaps because the company managing the properties has set a very high asking price.' He gave Ferrara the names of the other residents: a famous shoe designer, a businessman and a fashion stylist. The latter was living alone following a divorce.

'What were relations like between these neighbours and the Russos?'

'Normal, but they didn't socialise together. We only really spent time with the Russos and they only really spent time with us.'

Ferrara glanced up from his writing for a moment and thought he saw a sort of grimace on the woman's face following her husband's last words.

'You don't meet socially?'

'No.'

Ferrara closed his notebook and stood up. As he said goodbye he told them that he would almost certainly need to speak with them again. 'You can contact me on these numbers,' he said, giving them a business card. 'Call me if you remember anything that could be useful . . . anything at all that could help us in our investigation.'

'I'll call you at once if anything comes to mind. I want to help you catch whoever's responsible,' replied the man. 'The security service owes us an explanation, Chief Superintendent. Where the hell was the nightwatchman?' he spluttered indignantly as he shook Ferrara's hand.

'We'll be questioning them,' was Ferrara's brief reply as he left, asking himself whether those two – the wife in particular – might be hiding something.

He'd forgotten to ask Corti if he'd been the one who found the injured woman. With a shake of the head he made a mental note to ask him at the earliest opportunity.

He couldn't help wondering about the way the woman had grimaced. Did she know something about the relations between the Russos and their neighbours?

The Chief Superintendent was struck by another detail. The man hadn't once mentioned the possibility of a break-in or a robbery. Why not? At this stage it seemed the most plausible explanation, especially if you hadn't been inside the house to see whether anything had been disturbed.

Perhaps the Cortis knew more than they were letting on.

18

It was almost eleven and the gated community was coming to life as reinforcements started to arrive. Soon the little square was crammed with police vehicles.

The Forensics team were ready to turn the house inside out in their search for evidence, in accordance with the principle espoused by Edmond Locard, the famous forensics expert and director of the first-ever police laboratory at Lyon. Locard theorised that when the author of a crime comes into contact with an object or another person in the process of committing the crime, though it may be tiny or difficult to find, they always leave a trace of themselves behind.

Francesco Rizzo had been on his way to Pisa, intending to carry out Ferrara's order to liaise with the authorities there about the jailbreak, but when news of Russo's murder came through he'd told the driver to turn round.

Once he'd been brought up to speed, Ferrara put him in charge of the investigation. Then he gave Ascalchi the task of conducting door-to-door inquiries.

'We need to gather detailed information about the victims: their lives, their habits, who they spent time with, their professional interests. We can't exclude the possibility that the motive stemmed from some aspect of the victims' lives,' he reminded them.

'I know exactly what you're thinking, chief.'

'And what's that?'

'That once the motive's been identified, you're halfway there.'

Ferrara nodded, distracted. It had just struck him how strange it was that none of the residents had come out to see what was going on. Perhaps they preferred to hole themselves up at home, or perhaps they were busy, or even out at work. 'I'm going to go and examine the other crime scene,' he said.

'Forensics have finished their examination, chief, and Officer Perrotta is waiting for you by the front door. I've shown him the room.'

'Thanks.'

Ferrara put on the plastic overshoes and the gloves his colleague handed him then followed him into the house.

They went through the living room, the kitchen and a utility room before reaching a corridor with a wooden staircase. They climbed the stairs to the first floor.

Perrotta slowed down as they came to the first door, but Ferrara carried on past him. He wanted to get a general idea of the layout of the house. He saw the two bedrooms, some distance from one another, then went back to the first room. And, taking a preliminary glance at the entrance, he saw the bloodstains.

It was the second crime scene.

He crossed the threshold.

19

Carregi Hospital

That morning Teresa Micalizi was wearing a pair of worn black jeans, a white T-shirt and a jacket made of soft, black leather.

She was accompanied by Officer Alessandra Belli, a young blonde in her early twenties who'd been working with the IT team for several months. Her current ambitions included graduating with a degree in law and passing the assessment to become a police superintendent.

The two policewomen went straight to the reception desk where Teresa inquired after Signora Elisa Rotondi. They then made their way through a maze of corridors to the emergency surgery ward and the office reserved for the doctor on call, but it was empty.

'Can I help you?' asked the head nurse. She was wearing a white coat and on her feet were white clogs. Sleek black hair framed her slightly podgy face, and the name badge on her coat read 'Luciana'.

Teresa introduced herself, showing the nurse her police ID. When she asked for news of the victim, the nurse told her that the patient had suffered two gunshot wounds and had undergone surgery to remove the bullets from her body.

'Where are the bullets?'

'We gave them to the officer on duty at the hospital's police post. It's procedure.'

'Has the patient said anything yet?' asked Teresa.

'No, I'm sorry. She was in no state to communicate.'

'I don't mean a conversation. Perhaps she's murmured a name, or a few words that might help us in our investigation.'

'Nothing. I wish I could help you, but she was in no state to speak.'

'Could your colleagues who're monitoring her have heard something?'

'I don't think so, and if you saw her you'd understand why. As a matter of fact, we've all been keeping an eye on Room 11.'

'Is her condition that serious?'

The nurse nodded. Then she explained that the patient's blood pressure was unstable and her chest wound was still bleeding. They would be taking her back into surgery soon. 'Her vital signs are not looking good, I'm afraid. The next few hours will be crucial,' she concluded.

A red light over a nearby doorway came on, claiming the woman's attention. 'Please excuse me, they're calling me,' she apologised and ran off.

The two policewomen set off down the corridor in search of Room 11.

Teresa knocked gently on the door with her knuckles.

There was no reply.

She turned the handle and opened the door far enough to glance inside. The blinds were down and the room was in shadow. It seemed empty, not a plant or a chair in sight. She could see a figure with a partially bandaged head in the bed. Teresa hesitated on the threshold, scanning the corridor for medical staff while debating how far she dared go.

'Stay here, Ale,' she ordered the officer and slipped into the room, moving through the half-darkness toward the bed. The body seemed very small, encircled as it was by monitors, tubes and wires. The right-hand side of the head was hidden by heavy dressings, while the left-hand side, lit by the glow of the machines, was uncovered. As the nurse had said, it was obvious that the woman couldn't have spoken and was unlikely to have regained consciousness. She lifted the sheet a little and imagined the incisions in the woman's chest, which was still orange from the Betadine that had been used to disinfect the area. The wounds were covered by bandages. She gently replaced the sheet.

'I'm a police officer,' she murmured, bending over the patient.

The unbandaged eye blinked. The pupil seemed to focus on her for a moment, but there was no reply. Then it rolled back and the eye closed again.

Teresa gently stroked the woman's cheek. 'We need your help.'

The eye opened and closed again, an automatic, involuntary movement.

Teresa took her hand and stroked it. 'What were your attackers like?' she asked in a soft voice. ·

The other woman didn't react.

'Who shot you?'

'Move away from her,' a man's icy voice ordered from behind her.

Teresa turned calmly. A man in his thirties had appeared in the doorway. Officer Belli was trying in vain to push him back out into the corridor. He was tall with black, slicked-back hair and a strikingly pale face.

'Let go of her hand and move away from her,' he shouted.

He couldn't be a doctor. He was wearing a dark tailored suit, not a white coat.

Teresa gently laid the woman's hand on the bed. 'I'm sorry. I'm from the police and I came to see whether she'd woken up. Could you tell me who you are, sir?'

'I'm her son. Leave her alone. You didn't protect her and now you've come to cause trouble here, too. Go away or I'll call the head doctor.'

His voice was seething with resentment and his pale eyes were bloodshot. It wasn't hard to understand why. His father had been killed and his mother seriously injured.

As Teresa left the room, followed by her colleague, the man started shouting again behind them: 'Find those responsible. Find whoever killed my father and left my mother in this state. I want to know who did it. It's my right!'

Teresa didn't reply. She couldn't.

At that moment a uniformed officer appeared. He was the one who should have been keeping watch over the victim. As soon as he saw Teresa he started guiltily, as if he'd been caught committing some terrible crime. He tried to explain himself, saying he'd only been gone a couple of minutes, just long enough to go to the toilet and buy a coffee.

'Don't worry. Nothing happened,' she replied. 'The son's inside,' she added, before walking away with Officer Belli.

The two policewomen made their way to the nurses' station, Alessandra full of apologies after failing to stop the man at the door.

'Of course, it would have been different if that other officer had been there as well,' she said.

'Don't worry about it, Ale. He was out of his senses and we have to understand his point of view. He's their son and he's distraught. Think about the hell he must be going through . . . '

The young officer shook her head. She hadn't stopped to consider the victim's point of view. Once again Teresa had shown her ability to empathise with those who are suffering.

Luciana wasn't at the nurses' station. They waited patiently and after a few minutes they saw her come out of one of the rooms.

Teresa went towards her and asked whether she'd spoken to her colleagues.

'Yes, I did.'

'Any news?'

'No, unfortunately not. They all say the same thing: the patient hasn't made a sound, nor shown any signs of consciousness. I'm sorry. I wish I could be more optimistic.'

'Thank you for checking, anyway.'

As they said goodbye, Teresa gave the nurse her business card. 'Please, call me if she shows any signs of improvement, no matter what time it is.'

'We can only hope for a miracle. But in that event, you can be sure I'll be in touch.'

They went back along the corridor to the entrance and stopped in front of a vending machine to buy two cups of coffee. It was bitter and boiling hot.

'Ugh, it's disgusting!' exclaimed Alessandra.

Teresa nodded. 'It's really awful. I don't understand why the coffee at Headquarters is fine and this is so bad. They're identical machines and the price is the same. Who knows!'

Then they set off for the ambulance bay, hoping to find the paramedics who had attended the woman. As they turned the corner, Officer Belli spotted a closed door with a sign saying STATE POLICE above it. 'Superintendent, the bullets!'

'Well done – I'd almost forgotten them.'

They knocked, but there was no reply. They were about to leave when they met a uniformed policeman, the officer on duty.

'I'm on my own and I have to go from one ward to another,' he told them, almost trying to justify his absence. 'The Commissioner refuses to hear a word on the subject of reinforcements and it's only me and a colleague based here. One of us works the morning and the other the afternoon.'

'Do you have the bullets extracted from Signora Russo's body?' Teresa asked him, ignoring his complaints.

'I had them.'

'And where are they now?'

'I rang the Prosecutor's Department and they told me to send them to Forensics. I sent them via courier.'

The two policewomen thanked him and said goodbye. They'd found out from the ambulance headquarters that the injured woman hadn't said a single word during the journey. 'She was in a bad state and had lost a lot of blood,' explained one of the paramedics who'd attended her.

Finally, walking quickly, they made their way to the exit. They went to their car, a white Fiat Punto, which was parked in the space reserved for police vehicles. Alessandra Belli got into the driver's seat and they set off for Headquarters.

Nothing useful gained.

20

Borgo Bellavista

The search would go on for some time yet because, in addition to discovering useful prints or traces, the police wanted to understand the interests, habits, lifestyle and friendships of the people who lived in the house.

The technicians from Forensics were now busy with the injured woman's bedroom. It was a pleasant room with period furniture: a double bed, a large wardrobe, a dressing table with a looking glass and a small desk.

Based on the position of the bloodstains, they had been able to reconstruct what had happened. The woman had been sitting up in bed watching television when the first shot hit her. She had then dragged herself towards the door, where she had been hit by the second shot. Both the bullet casings were for a 7.65 calibre gun.

The Chief Superintendent had studied the scene carefully, aware how important it was to interpret a place and plot the victim's initial position and subsequent movements. The Forensics team's photos didn't always do justice to the space where a crime had taken place.

And then there was the blood. He had been particularly struck by the splashes of blood on the shining parquet and the door.

These clearly indicated that, after being wounded in her bed, the woman had tried to move away and call for help. In fact, there were several bloody handprints at various points on the floor, which had been circled in white chalk by the technicians.

He went into the study, which was very untidy in comparison with the other rooms. All the drawers of the desk and other furniture were open, the books and papers were in a jumble and the paintings had been taken off the walls and laid on the floor. The red light on the answerphone was flashing and the display indicated that there were seven messages. Six from the couple's son and one from someone who hadn't left a message. There was just a rustling sound, nothing else, but even this detail had to be kept in mind.

Ferrara called Rizzo over and asked him whether any mobile phones had been found during the search. His colleague nodded. They had found one charging, but there was no SIM card inside it. He suggested that the attackers might have taken it. A reasonable hypothesis, which Ferrara shared. Given all the information it contained, the presence of a SIM card would have saved the investigators hours, if not days.

'There's no way we can tell whether anything's missing in all this chaos,' observed Rizzo, as his eyes travelled over the floor.

'They were probably looking for something,' Ferrara was thinking aloud. 'Money? Valuables? Documents? Something else? We need to make an inventory of everything with the help of a family member. On that note, have they been informed?'

'Yes, chief. Ascalchi arranged it with the officer in the Operations Room. The son, Donato, is a lawyer. He's coming back from Rome, where the Russos have another law firm, and the victim's brother will also be joining us. He's a university law lecturer and lives in Livorno.'

'Good, Francesco. What about the other rooms?'

Rizzo gave him all the details. The front door, which was made of solid wood, was intact and also featured a spyhole. The attackers hadn't forced it open. 'Perhaps they were known to the victim,' he commented.

Then he continued explaining how they had conducted a thorough search of the rooms, emptying every item of furniture and examining the contents one by one, even taking all the books down from the shelves. Many of them were legal tomes. They'd looked behind all the antique paintings in the living room. The bin under the kitchen sink had been empty except for a plastic bag containing the remains of their supper. There had been a scrap of paper with a shopping list attached to the fridge door: cheese, ham, milk, mineral water . . . FOR NELA, the maid, had been written at the top in red felt-tip. The laundry basket in the bathroom had only contained a few items of women's clothing. There was nothing strange in the medicine cabinet, just plasters, bandages, antiseptic, aspirin and a bottle of Valium that someone had already opened.

They had been particularly careful in their inspection of the two wardrobes. One was in the husband's bedroom and the other in the wife's. They had examined each item of clothing one at a time, if only in the hope of finding a note or a telephone number that had been forgotten in one of the pockets, but again their search had drawn a blank.

'Now we've only got the cellar left to search,' he said at last.

'OK, keep me posted.'

The Chief Superintendent went outside. He wanted to light a cigar and mull over two theories that had formed in his mind while Rizzo was talking.

First: the attackers must have found what they were looking for in the office, which was why they hadn't bothered going into Amedeo Russo's bedroom. But in that case, why go into his wife's room? And why shoot her twice, as if they wanted to be sure of having killed her? Was it purely to get rid of a witness?

Second: the criminals had been disturbed by someone or

something – the security guard, maybe – before they'd managed to search the husband's room.

Pure conjecture, to be set aside for the moment, because he needed to be sure of all the facts first. Only then would he be in a position to put all this chaos in order. They would have to examine the various pieces of evidence that had been gathered, discarding what was irrelevant and focusing on what was important. But how would they be able to distinguish between the two?

Ferrara had confidence in his method: one thing would lead to another, and so on until all the links in the chain had been connected.

One thing was undeniable, though, even at this early stage: the anomaly between the two crime scenes.

As he'd walked through the house, he'd formed the impression that what he was seeing didn't fit with the theory of a robbery gone wrong.

He was about to discover that this wasn't merely intuition on his part.

21

The cellar

They had left the cellar until last in accordance with standard procedure.

Unless there was evidence to suggest it was of immediate primary interest, the cellar, along with the garage, was always searched after the rest of the building had been examined.

The police got a surprise when they went in.

It wasn't at all how they had imagined it would be. Most cellars smell of stagnant air and mildew; here there was nothing but the bitter odour of cigarettes. The lawyer must have been a heavy smoker. They'd been expecting a storage space for random bits and pieces; instead they found a luxurious refuge.

It was a single room of about 230 foot square with no windows and only the one door. What's more it was a bulletproof door, a detail that struck them as odd. The front door wasn't bulletproof, yet the cellar door was. The walls were covered with rich chestnut panelling. Spotlights on the ceiling lit the surface of an antique desk with an Apple computer on it, along with a mobile phone attached to a charger and a crystal ashtray overflowing with cigarette butts. There was a squashed cushion on the armchair. It looked as though the lawyer spent a lot of time down here. A landline telephone, a laser printer and a fax machine were neatly arranged on a small mahogany table. There were a couple of large black leather sofas, a standard-sized flat-screen television and a bookshelf crammed with books and files.

It was Russo's second office. A strictly private one.

The police officers combed it from top to bottom.

They examined the computer, which didn't have a single password, and the mobile phone, making a note of the most recent calls made and received, and the names in the phonebook.

While the bookshelf was being inspected, Rizzo focused on the desk drawers. Evidently they held no secrets, for they were all open, although they did have locks fitted. Or perhaps Russo considered this room to be so secure he didn't bother to lock anything.

At first glance, everything appeared normal. The drawers mostly contained receipts and extracts from bank accounts, documents for that year's tax return, each sheet labelled and carefully organised, like the work of an excellent secretary.

Before putting everything back in its place, Rizzo removed the drawers from the desk one at a time, just to be certain. He found the A4 envelope, attached with sticky tape, under the last one. Careful not to touch it, he reached for his mobile and dialled Ferrara's number. Realising there was no mobile coverage in the cellar, he sent an officer to go and fetch him.

As soon as he joined Rizzo, Ferrara pulled on some gloves and detached the envelope. It was glued shut. He turned it over but didn't see any writing on either side. An anonymous envelope. But why had it been so well hidden? What did it contain? It felt as if it held documents.

'We'll get Forensics to open it,' he decided. 'And we'll seize everything here, Francesco. I'm going back to the office.'

'What about the envelope?'

'I'll take it with me. I'm going to see Gianni Fuschi later.' Fuschi was the head of the Tuscan Regional Forensics Centre.

It was now afternoon and Ferrara was tired. He glanced around before getting into the Alfa 156. The gated compound appeared uninhabited apart from the police presence. He couldn't see a single sign of life behind the windows of the houses.

He turned and looked beyond the fence. It still seemed a peaceful, almost silent, place. An uncontaminated paradise. But those who lived there would know different. Their lives had changed overnight, and who knew how long the change would last. Perhaps for ever.

The gravel crunched under the wheels as the driver turned the car towards the exit. There was a moment of confusion by the gate. A small group of people had gathered there, most of them photographers, snapping pictures in the hope it might earn them some money. Perhaps a few fans of the macabre, too; they tended to turn up outside crime scenes like this. But there were also a couple of journalists and cameramen jostling one another for the best position. One had even climbed the perimeter wall.

Ferrara knew almost all of them by now, including Cosimo Presti. Short and shabbily dressed, Presti considered himself an expert when it came to investigations. He liked to tell people he was an old school hack who knew the Florentine scene like the back of his hand. In reality, he was an alcoholic who'd been fired from his last job a couple of years earlier and now worked freelance for a handful of euros an article. He was almost pitiful.

The Chief Superintendent glanced at him and thought he saw a malevolent sneer on Presti's face.

'Put your foot down!' he ordered Perrotta, as a reporter prepared to shout a question.

The news would soon spread throughout the city. With no official statements forthcoming from the investigators, the media would turn their attention to the residents of the gated community, seizing on anything that would allow them to cobble together an article, most of which would be pure invention. It was the way things had always been.

Once the car was past Fiesole and beginning the winding descent, the city appeared spread out before them. The cloak of pollution around it was easily visible.

Soon its lights would come on one by one, ready for a new night.

And another mystery.

22

Forensics, Piazza dell'Indipendenza

It was a short journey from Headquarters to the Piazza della Indipendenza, where the Tuscan Regional Forensics Centre was based, no more than ten minutes at normal walking speed, so Ferrara decided to go on foot. As he walked, he puffed on his cigar, a cloud of smoke trailing behind him. Officer Perrotta followed him at a distance, not letting him out of his sight for a moment. The Chief Superintendent didn't think anyone was likely to follow him, but he was always on his guard.

Arriving outside the front doors, he stopped to read the stone sign with the office's name. Stubbing out his cigar, he went in, shaking his head. Perrotta took up position outside the building to await his return.

'Don't you ever go on holiday, my dear ... ' Gianni Fuschi was about to add *'Gatto'*, the nickname that many police officers used to refer to the Chief Superintendent, but, noticing a particularly melancholy expression on his colleague's face, he stopped himself just in time. It was a friendly nickname, a tribute to Ferrara's cunning and his slightly feline eyes, but sensing that this wasn't the moment for levity, the head of Forensics held his tongue.

Ferrara had found Fuschi in the ballistics lab. He was wearing a white coat and looked more like a university professor than a man who divided his days between scientific techniques, computers, tests, optical comparators and microscopes.

'You don't either, if I'm not mistaken,' replied Ferrara.

'And how am I supposed to leave the office? You lot are always filling my lab with thousands of pieces of evidence,' the other man fired back. 'Well, let's see what you've brought me this time,' he added, spotting the file in Ferrara's hand.

'Just this, Gianni,' said Ferrara, sliding the folder on to the table. 'It contains an envelope found at the victim's house. It was hidden beneath one of the desk drawers.'

'Mmm ... that seems fishy. Take a seat while I check it for fingerprints.'

Ferrara slumped into a swivel chair while Fuschi went into another room. Ten minutes later he returned, still wearing a pair of latex gloves. 'There aren't any usable prints,' he said. 'Whoever touched it must have been very careful.'

'OK. Open it, Gianni,' murmured Ferrara with an anxious expression. Fuschi didn't need telling twice.

Inside the envelope was one of those cheap photo albums you can buy in supermarkets. On the cover was a panoramic photo of Florence with the sun like a ball of fire on the horizon. A single word was written beneath it in black marker:

PORTRAITS

It contained 7 × 5 inch colour photographs, which had been inserted into plastic wallets.

Fuschi pushed the album and a pair of gloves towards Ferrara: 'Put these on and take a look.'

The first thing Ferrara did was flick through the album and count the photos. There were nine in total; the last six wallets were empty. Then he started again, examining them more carefully one at a time.

The first showed a woman's body on a bedroom floor. A number of knife wounds were visible on the body. She was naked except for a pair of knee-high socks and a blouse. A round queen-sized bed, its edges decorated with fabric, was also visible.

The second was a close-up of the same victim. She seemed to stare into the lens, her right cheek pressed against the floor. A vivid trickle of blood ran from her neck to the ground.

Ferrara studied the photo for a long time. That face seemed somehow familiar.

He moved on to the next one and his fears were confirmed.

Yes, he remembered the body in the next portrait perfectly. It was another naked woman and there was a large knife wound in the left-hand side of her neck. She'd been killed in her modest apartment in the city's historic centre, which was where she saw her clients. She was a prostitute who used to work on the street corners near her home at night. Her name had slipped his mind for the moment, but he could remember the investigation, which he'd worked on personally. As was the case in too many of the investigations his team carried out, the killer had not been identified.

The fourth picture showed a close-up of the prostitute's face. A classic death portrait.

He continued leafing through the album, stopping at the fifth image. It was another body, a woman once again. She, too, was naked, lying on the floor near a bed with her legs spread wide and her tongue hanging out of her mouth.

Another shock for Ferrara.

He remembered that crime scene, too. The third victim was also a prostitute, who had worked from a sports car in her youth. In more recent years she had taken men back to her home.

'What is it, Michele?' asked Fuschi, noticing that the Chief Superintendent seemed shocked.

'I know these cases,' he replied numbly, and carried on looking through the photographs.

The remaining shots showed eight men, hooded and wrapped in long grey robes. They were standing in front of what looked to be an altar, surrounded by chalices and black candles.

In one of the photos a woman was stretched out on the altar. Dark-skinned and completely naked, her eyes were staring upwards. Something that Ferrara couldn't quite identify was protruding from her vagina. Her arms were attached to two cornerstones and her feet had been tied with string or leather cord.

Another shot focused on two hooded men: one was holding up an inverted crucifix; the other clutched a dagger with a serpent-shaped handle in his left hand, while his right hand held a chalice to his lips so he could drink from it. The girl's body lay between them, marked with clearly discernible bloodstains.

The next image was a close-up of the crucifix showing Christ's headless body.

As if to complete the review, the final photo was a shot of the poor woman's face. She was a young dark-skinned woman.

There was no longer any doubt: this was some kind of rite. Almost certainly a satanic one.

Ferrara felt a tension in his stomach. Only a few months earlier he'd investigated the murder of a woman named Madalena, who'd managed a private club in the centre of Florence; her charred remains had been found in a deconsecrated chapel in the hills of Sesto Fiorentino.

Without batting an eyelid he closed the album and handed it back to Fuschi, who placed it in a plastic evidence bag.

'There could be prints on the photos, Michele. Whoever put them in the plastic wallets might have left some.'

'Check it out. And then make me copies and enlargements, especially of the pictures of the woman on the altar. Perhaps we'll be able work out what that is protruding from her vagina. Make sure you give us back the originals as well as the copies tomorrow, though.'

'OK. I'll send you the report with the results of all the tests, too.'

Ferrara thanked him and said goodbye, but his colleague called him back as he was leaving the room.

'What is it, Gianni?'

'I received two 7.65 calibre bullets from the hospital. I'll run a search for them on the database tomorrow and let you know what I come up with.'

'Perfect.'

Ferrara thought over these new developments as he made his way back to the office.

Why had Russo, a lawyer, been in possession of those photos?

Could he have been involved in the crimes?

Who was behind those murders?

Even if Russo had nothing to do with the incidents himself, he might have been blackmailing those responsible.

But how had he got hold of the pictures?

These were all questions without answers, but they led him to think that lurking behind the death of Amedeo Russo and the attempted murder of his wife they would find unspeakable truths – and they wouldn't be easy to face.

23

Police activity continued at a frenetic pace throughout that evening and on through the night.

The area around the compound was searched with a fine-tooth comb. House by house. Courtyard by courtyard. Street by street. Even the famous caves at Maiano, which had been mined since the nineteenth century for the 'pietra fiesolana' stone used in various local monuments, like the stairs and other architectural features of the National Central Library on the Piazza dei Cavalleggeri. The terrain was rich in woodland and gorges, one of which contained caves that were often visited by young couples looking for some privacy, along with peeping toms and drug addicts.

But no one had noticed anything unusual, or they weren't willing to talk about it if they had.

Nothing. A dead end.

At the office, Inspector Venturi was examining the material they'd seized. He was extremely skilled when it came to paper evidence, but this evening he was focusing his attention on Russo's computer and the contents of his inbox, which seemed mostly work-related. There were, however, a few emails that caught his eye. They'd been sent by a woman whose nickname was Veri.

For his part, Ascalchi, along with Pino Ricci, had spoken to almost all the residents of the compound, but he hadn't discovered anything useful. No one had seen anything suspicious that night, or over the preceding days. This may have been the truth, but it was also possible that they just didn't want to get involved or that they were afraid of collaborating with the police, as was often the case with investigations regarding a high-profile victim.

The only person they hadn't managed to speak to was the fashion stylist. She was probably abroad, but nobody had been able to tell them where she was or when she would be returning to Italy.

All the residents seemed nervous at the prospect of living in the compound after what had happened to the Russos. There wasn't any sense of community or willingness to cooperate with the police to catch those responsible. Judging by some of the responses to his questions, Ascalchi got the feeling the victims hadn't been on the best of terms with their neighbours.

He had succeeded in identifying the two security guards, having found their identity passes in the cabin by the main gate. He tracked one of them down, only to discover he couldn't provide any useful information. The other, a Sardinian by the name of Italo Ortu, had been on duty but had just taken ten days of annual leave to go hunting at home.

Rizzo questioned Nela, the Russos' maid, in his office. Originally from Moldavia, her residency paperwork was in order and she was red-eyed and obviously distressed when she came into the room.

'I hope my mistress pulls through! I can't believe it. She was such a good woman,' she sobbed.

She explained that she'd been taken on by the Russos at the start of the year, and that she lived with her sister, who was studying architecture at the university.

'Can you tell me what you did yesterday evening?' Rizzo asked her.

The young woman told him that she'd served dinner, tidied

up the kitchen and then left at around eleven. She confirmed that the Cortis had been there, but she didn't mention noticing anything suspicious, either that evening or during the preceding days.

There was one detail that struck Rizzo as peculiar, though. On Sunday, shortly before the guests arrived, the telephone had rung. The lawyer's wife had answered, but there was nobody there.

'What time was it?'

'It must have been around seven, maybe quarter to seven.'

'Did your mistress make any comment?'

'No, not in front of me.'

'Were there any other silent calls in the preceding days?'

'No.'

Rizzo had her sign the statement and a car took her home. The studio apartment she shared with her sister was near the Camerata Hospital in San Domenico, on the road that led to Fiesole.

When Nela told her sister about being questioned, her sister said she'd been right not to mention the unfamiliar red car she had noticed near the compound on the afternoon in question. There was nobody in the car except the driver and, when she'd looked at him, he'd turned away and driven off with a squeal of tyres. It hadn't seemed particularly suspicious at the time, though. He might simply have taken a wrong turning.

'Yes, I was right not to mention it. It probably had nothing to do with it in any case, and if I had mentioned it they'd have only asked more questions and kept me there for hours.'

'And then they'd have wanted to call on you at home, make you attend the hearing, the trial, give evidence, the journalists . . . ' Her sister shuddered at the thought.

24

Lake Garda

They saw him come out of the restaurant in Sirmione, where he'd been living under a false identity for several months. He was accompanied by a tall brunette with long hair who couldn't have been more than thirty. The couple were joking and laughing together as they made their way to a metallic grey Audi A4. She stumbled a few steps from the passenger door, but the man caught her arm and held her upright. Then he stroked her hair. They set off and, after exactly a quarter of an hour, they pulled into the parking space belonging to the terraced cottage with a view over the lake.

Pasquale Schimizzi and Daniele De Robertis had followed them in a white Ford Fiesta.

'Not yet,' said Pasquale, seeing that the man was about to open the door. They watched them get out of the car and, still joking, make their way inside.

'But he's old enough to be her father!' exclaimed Daniele.

'He's almost seventy, but the shameless fool still feels young. He sold out for a reduced sentence and a life of secrecy organised by the state. That's the law when it comes to Mafia informers: a new identity, a one-off payment of fifty thousand euros, a monthly stipend and a secret relocation. It's a secret from everyone else, but not from us,' he explained, a smile playing on his lips.

Daniele would have like to find out more, but he didn't ask. He looked at his watch. It was five to ten in the evening. The evening of his 'baptism'.

Half an hour later they surprised the couple in bed.

They were naked and a half-empty bottle of champagne and two crystal glasses stood on the bedside table. The images of a pornographic film were still flickering on the television screen.

The two accomplices had entered the house silently using duplicate keys. Pasquale took care of the woman, who started whimpering. He shut her up, pointing his pistol, complete with silencer, at her head. Daniele, meanwhile, threw himself on the man, just as they had planned. He yanked his head off the pillow so hard his back arched. His right hand held a hunting knife which he used to make the first deep cut in his neck. The man's eyes suddenly opened wide and a jumble of incoherent words spilled from his mouth. Then further knife blows severed the muscles in his neck. The blood from his artery sprayed over the wall and soaked the sheets, trickling down his arms and chest. It wasn't enough: with two long slices Daniele cut off his head and, finally, his tongue, which he placed in one of the champagne glasses. A punishment and at the same time an unmistakable warning from Cosa Nostra to anyone else who might break the blood pact.

The woman had been kneeling in a corner with her back to the wall, pleading with Pasquale not to hurt her, telling him that she wouldn't say anything to anyone, least of all the police.

He laughed in her face. 'That's true. You won't tell a soul.' The first shot from his gun blew her head off.

Milan

Three hours later De Robertis and Pasquale met with Filippo, who'd travelled from Vinci, and Salvino Lo Cascio's brother-in-law, Cosimo Buda, who was acting as the *family's* representative, in the usual Milanese apartment near Police Headquarters.

Pasquale Schimizzi had studied Daniele De Robertis carefully. He'd seen proof of his friend's courage, his reserve, his cold-bloodedness, his patience in biding his time to take revenge and his discretion when confronted with things he didn't know: all necessary qualities for admission into the *family*. And that was why he had supported his membership.

The moment for the solemn oath, preceded by the traditional *puncitura* rite, had arrived.

Cosimo Buda, the oldest man present, pricked De Robertis's index finger with a golden needle so the blood came out on to a holy picture the initiate was holding in his hands. Pasquale set the picture alight and De Robertis stared at the image burning in his hands while he pronounced the words of the rite: 'I swear to be faithful to Cosa Nostra. If I should turn traitor, my flesh shall burn as this picture burns.'

Then Buda read the 'commandments', putting greater emphasis on the most important: never enter into family relationships with men of the state like carabinieri or police officers; always show complete obedience to the clan heads; and never turn traitor, because 'You can join Cosa Nostra, but you cannot leave until you're dead.'

And so Daniele De Robertis became a member of the *family*. From that moment on he would no longer be alone.

25

Tuesday 19 October

Chief Superintendent Ferrara slept badly that night. He'd never been one of those police officers who leave everything at the door when they get home. The cases that got under his skin only left him in peace once he was sure he had captured the person responsible. The real person responsible.

He'd reviewed the photos several times during the last few hours, and the words of Silvia De Luca, the expert on esotericism Venturi had introduced him to after Madalena's murder at the deconsecrated chapel, had come to mind. She had explained that there were faithful servants of Satan in Florence who worshipped him through black masses and magical rites that took place on prearranged occasions, for example on the night of a full moon. The participants engaged in sexual relations and made sacrifices to evil in the belief that this would increase their strength and they would become 'supermen'.

He had heard his wife get up at about six thirty and had watched her through half-closed eyes as she tiptoed out of the bedroom. Then he'd listened in silence to her muffled steps between the corridor and the kitchen, but he'd stayed in bed, exhausted and with his head overflowing with thoughts. Then, shortly after seven, Petra had appeared at the door in a tracksuit, her blonde hair tied back in a short ponytail.

'Breakfast's ready,' she'd told him.

Ferrara dragged himself to the bathroom and saw his puffy eyes and tense face looking back at him in the mirror. He had the impression that he'd aged at least fifty years overnight. He stepped under the shower and stood motionless, allowing the scalding water to wash over him as he thought of the naked body in the swimming pool and heard the buzzing of the flies and wasps in his ears.

He dried himself, hurriedly put on a pale grey suit and went into the kitchen.

Everything he might want was on the table: butter, bread, jam, ham and cheese. There was a wonderful smell of coffee in the air, the perfect thing to energise him.

The news from the last twenty-four hours was running continuously on the TV. It repeated every fifteen minutes from six until the news bulletin at eight.

A panoramic view of the city filled the screen, the Ponte Vecchio in the background. The subtitle read: *Brutal Crime In Florence.*

There was a shot of the Borgo Bellavista from above, then, for a moment, a view of the Russos' house. The journalist, the Tuscany correspondent, began to speak. He was a tall, stocky, middle-aged man, perhaps too stocky recently, who always wore a turquoise jacket, either lightweight or heavy-duty, depending on the season.

'A well-known lawyer has been killed at the gated community's swimming pool and his wife is in critical condition at Careggi Hospital, where she has already undergone two delicate surgical procedures to treat gunshot wounds, having been shot at least twice. Investigators maintain that it is the work of a criminal gang of Eastern European origin that has been operating in the Florentine hills for some time, but we'll know more after midday when a news

conference will be held at the Prosecutor's Department, hosted by the Chief Prosecutor in person.'

When the image of the umpteenth bombing campaign against the NATO forces in Afghanistan came on to the screen, Ferrara turned off the television.

He didn't know anything about a press conference. And at the Prosecutor's Department, no less! Statements were normally made from Headquarters, and only to accredited journalists. It was standard practice, had been for years. Perhaps in this case the Prosecutor wanted to get the media on his side to gain as much control as possible over the news. A strange initiative, but it seemed even stranger, given that the Prosecutor's Department had never previously engaged with the media on a suspected case of robbery gone wrong.

He ate a quick breakfast, a piece of bread with butter and jam and a cup of milky coffee. Petra's protests were in vain.

'You're bound to have a long, tiring day. Eat something else! Shall I make you a couple of fried eggs?'

'No, Petra, I need to go. I'm late.'

He kissed her goodbye and went out into the light of a new morning.

He told the driver he fancied a walk, perhaps just to be able to relax a bit before immersing himself in work, or perhaps to think some more about the news of the press conference.

He walked along the Lungarno for a while, always within view of Officer Perrotta. He stopped to look at the seemingly motionless waters of the river. Then he carried on along the pavement, which was bathed in sunlight and still silent, just as it always was at that time of day.

With its squares, monuments and proudly flaunted art, Florence seemed immaculate and distanced from Evil.

But nothing was ever what it seemed.

Chief Superintendent Ferrara was convinced that some force of devastating evil was at large in the dark heart of the city. He reviewed the information available for the umpteenth time: satanic rites, murders, blackmail and human sacrifices. He saw the naked body of the girl once again, sacrificed on the altar of a forgotten deity; the hooded man brandishing the serpent-handled dagger in the air and then drinking from a chalice; the acolyte holding the crucifix in the air.

The number of missing people was increasing daily, most of them women and of all ages. But now they were receiving less and less attention.

There weren't many people on the street at that hour. A few shop assistants; the odd schoolboy, late for school, and racing through the streets; a few delivery men towing trolleys overflowing with copies of the free newspaper to leave in café doorways, and some street sweepers washing the streets to further beautify the cheerful face of Florence.

The city that continued to enchant millions and millions of tourists, the majority of whom would never have imagined the mysteries buried beneath its gilded façade.

26

Headquarters

There were more cars than usual in the courtyard that served as a car park.

When Ferrara arrived at the first floor it was all he could do to get down the corridor. Every seat was occupied, men were crammed in with their backs pressed against the wall. Fatigue and dismay were evident on their faces. It was a sample selection of the city's criminal lowlife: housebreakers, junkies, pushers, alcoholics and pimps.

The officers were taking their details then directing them to rooms to complete the formalities. Some were responding to questions. Others maintained a provocative silence.

Ferrara looked at them as he passed through; he recognised a couple of ex-cons. One of them got up and, accompanied by a uniformed officer, headed towards the office belonging to Luigi Ciuffi, Head of Narcotics. Ferrara had recently brought Ciuffi in on the investigation into the murder of former senator Enrico Costanza, in whose villa a large quantity of drugs had been found.

The ex-con was called Felice Contini. He was in his forties and strikingly thin with gelled, dyed brown hair and a narrow face marked by deep lines. He was chewing gum with his mouth wide open.

'What a pleasure to see you again, Chief Superintendent,' he said when Ferrara entered the room.

'It's been a while,' Ferrara replied with an ironic smile.

'All right, you want to know about the murder, right? As I've already told your colleagues who came to pick me up last night, there are certain things I don't do. I'd help you if I could, but I don't know anything about this. It's out of my league,' the man continued in a confident tone, looking now at Ferrara, now at Ciuffi.

'You made me a promise,' said the Head of Narcotics.

'Felice Contini keeps his promises.'

'When?'

'The opportunity hasn't come up.'

There was a brief silence.

'We'd be grateful if you could keep an ear open, tell us if anything's being said, if anything's going on,' Ferrara continued.

'If I hear anything, I know who to contact,' he replied, meeting Ferrara's eye. 'But you've got to believe me, I didn't have anything to do with this crime. I only do smaller jobs—'

'Scams,' clarified Ciuffi.

And paedophilia, thought Ferrara to himself, well aware of the man's proclivities. Paedophiles never changed. No matter how many times you arrested them or threatened them, it would only be a matter of time before they'd be at it again.

'Call it what you want, but I've got to make a living. And it's better than pushing drugs and killing people, don't you think?'

'What about possession of a firearm? Where does that fit in? And that other more serious offence. Have you forgotten that Ciuffi already got you out of a tight spot once?' Ferrara reminded him.

'That firearm business is ancient history, and it cost me three years in the slammer. But it was only one time. And I know what you mean by "the other more serious offence", Chief Superintendent. I haven't forgotten, I know I owe a debt.'

'Well then, sniff about and see whether anyone's bought themselves a 7.65 calibre pistol on the black market in the last few days. You hang out with the non-EU dealers, muggers and extortionists and all that charming crowd anyway, so you won't need to make much of an effort.'

'They'd never tell me, Chief Superintendent. There are rumours going round that there are grasses about who'll tip you and the Carabinieri off. Florence has become a difficult place, it's not how it used to be. Everything's changed now, especially with the Albanians and the Romanians. If I make a wrong move, one of these mornings you'll find me laid out on the cobbles at the end of a blind alley or in a rubbish bag. Those guys don't mess around.'

'At least try!' snapped Ferrara.

There was a pause.

'Keep talking with my colleague,' Ferrara urged him, breaking the silence. 'You've got options open to you. Show a bit of goodwill and we'll pay you back when the time comes.' He turned towards the door.

'Good morning, Fanti.'

The secretary leapt to his feet as if on a spring, almost dropping the plastic cup of coffee he was holding. Some drops fell on to the paper napkin. He'd been sitting behind his desk wearing his usual inscrutable on-duty expression, his fingers tapping briskly at the computer keyboard. One glance at his boss told Fanti that this was not going to be a good day. He returned Ferrara's greeting.

'Any news?'

'Nothing important, chief. The flying squad carried out a raid last night and they're in the process of identifying the people they brought in. The local immigration office is helping them check the documents of any non-EU nationals.'

'Yes, I saw.'

'I've left the papers in the usual place, chief.'

'What are you working on?'

'I'm inputting staff overtime. With the hours from yesterday, we've exceeded our monthly allowance.'

Ferrara walked into his office shaking his head, leaving Fanti tapping away at the keyboard with the air of a man who has too much to bear. Just one more small cog in the investigative machine.

The daily papers were first on the agenda. Ferrara knew there wouldn't be any pleasant surprises on that front.

MASSACRE IN THE HILLS screamed the front page of *La Nazione*. LAWYER AND WIFE BRUTALLY MURDERED.

That pretty much summed it up. The gun aimed at the poor victim's head. Her eyes wide with fear. The tears running down her cheeks. The sobs. The tears. The shouts. And then the shots. Quick. Sharp. The tears stop falling. Her face is now blank in death.

Ferrara started reading the article:

... Signora Russo was cold-bloodedly shot in her bedroom in the hills by one or more individuals. The body of her husband, the famous lawyer Amedeo Russo, was found in the swimming pool, where he drowned following a blow to the head.

He was distracted from his reading by the telephone. The caller ID display showed the Commissioner's number.

'Come to my office.' No preamble; the order was delivered in an authoritative tone.

'Right away,' he answered, and hurried to the second floor. The secretary announced his arrival and he went straight in.

Filippo Adinolfi gestured to a chair and placed the newspaper he'd been waving in his other hand on the desk. Before Ferrara even had a chance to sit down the Commissioner launched into a tirade: 'They've been brutally murdered! A massacre! Two dead. And us? What are we doing about it?'

He was even redder in the face than usual and the veins on his forehead had begun to pulse. It was clear that, along with *La Nazione*, he counted Signora Russo as dead, in spite of the machines that kept her alive.

Ferrara observed him in silence for a long moment, telling himself that the heart attack was just biding its time and that one of these days there'd be no saving him.

'Well, what have you got to tell me? What are your men doing?' Adinolfi demanded, then lapsed into a coughing fit that lasted several seconds.

Ferrara told him about the examination of the crime scene and the search, the discovery of the album containing the photographs and the first fruitless results of their interrogations.

'They've been brutally murdered!' repeated Adinolfi, as if he hadn't heard a word Ferrara had said. 'We need to catch these Eastern European criminals as soon as possible, otherwise we'll have more deaths to deal with. Other wealthy families will be *brutally* murdered,' he continued, staring Ferrara in the eye.

'We're working on it, Commissioner. I've got all my men on the case. But it might not be an Eastern European gang. The photo album, which was very well hidden, suggests otherwise.'

'Why are you making so much of these photos, Chief Superintendent? Russo was a lawyer and he had access to documents pertaining to legal cases. There will be existing copies in the tribunal's files, cases that he was involved in or that he was following.'

Adinolfi's theory was credible in as much as Russo had worked on a number of murder cases. But that didn't explain why he kept the photos so well hidden. If he'd obtained them legitimately, there would have been no need. No, it didn't make sense. And what about the images of the sacrificial rite? Were these too part of a case file? Ferrara tried to remember, but he couldn't come up with any investigations of that nature. There was no point raising these misgivings with the Commissioner, though: he'd only work himself up into an even worse temper at being contradicted. Besides, the last thing Ferrara needed was to get himself bogged down in a pointless argument with his superior just then, so he bit his tongue.

'Get to work and see this case is solved quickly. The public need to see we're taking action, otherwise the fear level will increase, and our life will become intolerable. We had a nasty moment a few days ago with the trouble at the Roma camp. Did you read the interview with Orazio Dentice on Sunday? His attack on the police, and you in particular? You can expect more of the same if you don't deliver results.'

'We'll do our best, Commissioner.'

Adinolfi leaned back in his leather chair. 'Bring me your findings and keep me constantly updated. I want to be informed of your every move.' Then he waved a hand in dismissal.

Ferrara felt himself flushing with anger. It was always the same old tune: a quick result was all that mattered. So far as the Commissioner was concerned, any arrest would do, even if it were an innocent scapegoat who would end up being acquitted. Anything to get the media off their backs and satisfy the Ministry's insatiable hunger for arrests that would boost its crime statistics, make it appear cases were being solved.

Restraining his anger, he replied, 'I'll get right on it, sir,' He hoped that the Commissioner wouldn't put a spanner in the works as he had so often done in the past.

He'd made it as far as the door when he was called back.

'Yes, sir?'

Adinolfi told him that the Minister was setting up a parliamentary inquiry into the security situation at the Roma camp. 'I'll send details to you in the morning so you can prepare our response,' he concluded.

'I'll get on to it straight away,' Ferrara assured him. He didn't bother asking which politician had demanded an inquiry; it had to be the Honourable Orazio Dentice.

Ferrara was in a rage as he made his way back to his office. He'd seen several commissioners come and go in the course of his career, but none of them had ever exhibited such authoritarian behaviour or used that tone of voice in their dealings with him. And it wouldn't be long before the other high-and-mighties started breathing down his neck. The Chief of Police, for one. He was another political animal, always wanting instant results so he could trumpet about them to the Minister for the Interior and make himself look good. Then there was the Chief Prosecutor. And the Mayor. And who knew how many others.

Back at his desk, Ferrara resolved that he would not let himself be swayed by external pressure. The investigation must be allowed to follow its natural course; he wouldn't force the flow for the sake of politicians and their precious statistics.

After reading the initial autopsy report on the body of Amedeo Russo and the Forensics report on the crime scenes, he summoned his men.

It was time to plan the next stage of the investigation.

Once everyone was present, Ferrara closed both his office door and the one that linked his office with his secretary's room.

'Fanti, I don't want to be disturbed under any circumstances,' he ordered. 'By anybody,' he added, as his secretary sprang from his seat and hurried out to take up sentry duty in the corridor.

'May I have your attention, please,' Ferrara asked, turning back to his team. He noticed that no one was looking their best, the inevitable consequence of staying up all night on the hunt for evidence.

Ascalchi and Venturi, who'd been whispering to each other, fell silent. Everyone's eyes were on him. He waited ten seconds or so, then opened the report folders and started to bring them up to date.

First, he briefed them on the contents of the envelope seized from the cellar, then on the results of the autopsy and the Forensics tests.

Franceschini had found no scratches on the lawyer's hands, nor fragments of skin under his nails. So there was nothing to suggest that Russo had tried to defend himself before being struck on the back of the head. He must have been taken by surprise.

In the hours leading up to the attack, the lawyer had eaten a substantial fish-based meal, washed down with plenty of white wine – the blood tests had shown a fairly high alcohol content. Based on analysis of the body's temperature, the degree of rigor mortis and the presence of hypostasis, time of death had been narrowed down to some time between two and four o'clock on the morning of 18 October 2004.

'The report does not specify the type of weapon used,' Ferrara went on. That came as no surprise: they all knew that Franceschini always confined himself to recording the technical facts concisely and precisely in his reports, never venturing his own personal impressions or assessments. Unlike his colleague Francesco Leone, who would attach a note detailing considerations that might help them reconstruct the dynamic of the crime. But then, Leone was a one-of-a-kind pathologist, revered by colleagues for his experience and intuition; he gave the bodies of crime victims a voice, allowed them to tell what had happened.

Rather than linger over the autopsy results, Ferrara moved straight on to the initial Forensics results from the crime scene.

The fingertip search of the garden and surrounding area hadn't turned up anything new. The shoe prints, which corresponded to a size 8 and a size 9½, were the only traces found. So at least two people had entered the property by stealth. From the depth of the prints it was possible to deduce that one of the two must have been toward the larger end of average build for a male, while the other, the owner of the size 9½ prints, seemed to be more heavily built. The sole pattern matched a brand of trainer that was widely available. The Forensics technicians had preserved the prints using a chalk-and-water compound which had been blended to achieve maximum absorbency, then poured carefully into the prints. The shoe size and the weight estimate would be an essential tool when it came to identifying potential suspects.

The entire area beyond the fence had been inspected. The woods offered several pathways for the escape, but no further footprints had been identified, most likely because the attackers had walked on the grass and leaf-litter, which had been recently trampled.

'Various soil samples have been taken, which might prove useful,' Ferrara continued. The house, on the other hand, had yielded no fibres or traces of DNA that might lead them to the killers. 'Obviously there were fingerprints, so we'll need to supply Forensics with the prints of anyone who had reason to visit the house, for elimination purposes.' He only hoped there'd be some prints left over after the elimination process, prints that belonged to the killers.

'They still need to complete the analysis of the two bullets and the casings,' he said in conclusion. Then he set about assigning various tasks to his team.

Inspector Venturi would continue going through all the material they'd seized. He would also take charge of the research into Satanism in Florence.

After the funeral, Teresa Micalizi would question Amedeo Russo's son and brother.

Rizzo would collate the information they'd collected on the residents of the gated community, and contact their network of informers to gather any intelligence they might have relating to vendettas against the couple, their financial dealings or any other possible motives for murder. He would also review the case files on the prostitutes killed in the nineties.

Ciuffi would contact his informers for any news on Eastern

European gangs. They couldn't neglect the possibility that this was connected to the series of burglaries that had been carried out in recent months, no matter how unlikely it might seem at this stage. Ciuffi was also to keep up the pressure on Contini and make sure the paedophile delivered on his promise to help them.

Then it was Ascalchi's turn. He was assigned the task of investigating the security guards. On the night of the crime, three patrols had been carried out: at ten past midnight, at one forty-five and at ten to four. The last two had been conducted by Italo Ortu, who'd been almost half an hour late.

'Have you checked his record?' Ferrara asked.

'It's clean.'

'Have you spoken to the owner of the company?'

'Yes. He insists that his employees are honest and highly capable individuals.'

'Have you been given a copy of the contract?' Ferrara asked.

'Yes, here,' said Ascalchi, handing him a standard form with all the information filled in. The Russos had hired them in July.

Strange, Ferrara thought to himself. They had been living there for about ten years, but they'd only felt the need to employ security since the summer. Could there have been some reason the lawyer no longer felt safe? Was it due to the spate of robberies in the area?

'We need to track down Italo Ortu. Check the passenger lists for flights and voyages to Sardinia,' Ferrara instructed Ascalchi.

'Yes, chief.'

'Any questions? Anything to add?' the Chief Superintendent asked.

They all shook their heads.

'Then let's get to work.'

Meeting adjourned.

27

RUSSO AND CORTI LEGAL PRACTICE

The writing was sculpted on to the sandstone of a building on the Via dei Tornabuoni, right in the middle of the city's historic centre.

Ferrara stared at it for a moment while he stood aside to make way for a couple who were exiting the building. From the few words he managed to catch, it seemed they were talking about the Russo murder.

The Chief Superintendent was keen to observe every detail of the offices: the secretaries, the clerks, the furnishings and any clients who might be in the waiting room.

He wanted to know more about the lawyer: the Russos slept in separate bedrooms, so the involvement of a jealous lover or a rejected ex seemed unlikely, but not impossible. An alternative hypothesis involved a client so disappointed by the defence offered in court that they had turned to murder.

Ferrara climbed the stairs to the first floor and had barely pressed the buzzer when the door clicked open. He found himself facing a long horseshoe-shaped desk, behind which were seated two secretaries. One was tapping away at a keyboard at lightning speed and the other was talking on the telephone and making notes. The first, an attractive young woman of about thirty, came towards him with a smile, asking whether he had an appointment. Her long dark hair was tied back in a severe chignon at the base of her neck.

Ferrara replied that he didn't and introduced himself. The other woman continued her conversation.

'I need to speak with Signor Corti.'

'He's in a meeting.'

'Could you let him know I'm here? It's urgent.'

She looked at him for a couple of seconds with her big, grey eyes. Ferrara realised she was weighing up whether to interrupt the meeting.

'Please wait a moment. Make yourself comfortable in the waiting room, it's the first door on the left.' Then she walked away, her hips swaying in her blue skirt.

Ferrara took a seat in the empty waiting room. The ceiling was decorated with religious imagery. After a couple of minutes Corti appeared wearing an immaculate dark suit, a white shirt and a coordinating tie with a pattern made up of tiny flowers. Ferrara almost didn't recognise him as the man he'd met the day before.

'Would you mind waiting a few minutes, Chief Superintendent?' Corti asked, adopting an artificial tone. 'I need to finish a meeting with some colleagues.'

'Of course, but could I take a look at Signor Russo's office while I'm waiting?'

'The Deputy Prosecutor, Signor Vinci, came yesterday evening. He's already looked at everything. He took some of poor Amedeo's files away,' replied Corti.

'I'm aware of that,' said Ferrara. It was clear that Corti was reluctant to grant his request, but he wasn't about to back down.

'Please go ahead, Chief Superintendent.' Corti, now visibly annoyed, gave up the battle.

'Thank you. Could you ask one of your staff to accompany me?'

Corti summoned the secretary with the chignon. 'Lucrezia,

show the Chief Superintendent to Signor Russo's office,' he told her.

'Of course. This way . . . '

The spotless white blinds were down and the office was completely in shadow. The secretary switched on the light. Ferrara looked around and felt as though he had entered a different world. There were soft leather sofas, paintings by famous artists on the walls and an enormous desk with nothing on it except the telephone, a silver pen holder and a couple of framed photos. He sat down in the chair and continued survey his surroundings, as if memorising the objects around him.

The secretary stood by the door, following his every movement.

Ferrara's gaze settled on the photographs. One of them showed the Russos at a coastal resort, it looked like Forte dei Marmi. They were quite young in the photo and perhaps not yet married. They seemed very happy and she was beautiful. The other showed a young boy of about fourteen wearing sports kit and a scowl. It had to be their son.

Ferrara opened drawers and cupboards, still not sure what he was looking for. There might be documents concerning the firm that could reveal a motive, perhaps professional jealousy. Corti and the victim had been partners, but there was no doubt that Russo had a higher profile and an enviable CV. A simple theory with a weak motive, but at this stage of an investigation nothing could be discounted. Corti didn't strike him as a murderer, but you could never tell.

Or perhaps he would find a note or a letter from a disappointed lover.

But then how could the hole in the fencing be explained? Unless the lover had hired professionals to do their dirty work. Having dealt the victim a blow to the head, did they then shoot his wife because she'd seen too much?

Ferrara found this highly improbable.

His thoughts returned to the photo album. Could Amedeo Russo have been in possession of other compromising images? And, if so, where would he have kept them?

'They searched everything yesterday, Chief Superintendent,' the secretary told him when he started going through the contents of the drawers. 'I had to come from home to open the office and witness the search. The Deputy Prosecutor had a police officer with him who examined the computer while he searched the office. It was the middle of the night by the time I got out of here.'

'I know,' was all Ferrara said in reply as he continued his search. But he didn't find anything interesting. He put the drawers back and asked the woman a few questions about the firm. If her account was anything to go by, the business was run in an exemplary fashion and the victim was a paragon of virtue, dedicated to his job and his family and beloved by all.

'I've been working here for almost ten years and I can assure you that Signor Russo was an exceptional man, extremely erudite and a first-rate lawyer. I was very fond of him and I owe him a great deal. He was like a father to me, we had a special understanding.'

There was sadness in the woman's eyes as she said this.

'What about his wife?' Ferrara asked.

Lucrezia stopped to consider this, as if trying to find the right words.

'She was very beautiful, but I didn't know her personally and she never came to the office. She won the Miss Versilia contest when she was seventeen. I've often heard them on the phone, and Signor Russo's tone was always the same: affectionate.'

'Then why did they sleep in separate beds?' was the question that had wormed its way into Ferrara's thoughts. This secretary certainly wouldn't be the person to provide him with an answer. He wouldn't learn anything from her that would be useful to the investigation.

He'd seen it time and time again: when someone was murdered, everybody, especially the victim's friends and acquaintances, exaggerated their good points. Even if they knew that person had a darker side, they wouldn't mention it.

He was on the verge of giving up and returning to Headquarters when Corti appeared.

'I'm sorry to have kept you waiting, but the meeting took longer than planned,' he said. Then without even looking at her, he dismissed the secretary with a nod. She left the room silently, closing the door behind her.

Ferrara studied Corti for a moment, trying to read him, but before he could formulate his first question the lawyer impatiently cut into his thoughts.

'How can I help you, Chief Superintendent?'

'I forgot to ask you something yesterday.'

The lawyer's face betrayed a hint of nervousness. 'Ask away!'

'Were you present when Signora Russo was found wounded?'

'Yes. I meant to tell you. After seeing Amedeo in the swimming pool, I went along the path to the Russos' house. The door was ajar. I shouted several times but no one answered, so I went inside, calling Elisa's name ... When there was still no answer, I went up to the first floor. Her bedroom door was wide open and I saw her stretched out on the floor. She wasn't moving and my first thought was that she was dead. I ran home and called the emergency services.'

'Did you touch anything?'

'No. I know how you have to behave in these situations.'

'Did you go over to your friend to check whether she was still alive?'

'No. I didn't want to contaminate the area. There was so much blood.'

There were a few moments of silence.

Ferrara was perplexed: surely one's first instinct would be to try to help the woman instead of worrying about the crime scene.

'Tell me about your colleague. Did he have any personal or professional problems?'

'No.'

'Any misunderstandings with clients?

'Absolutely not.'

'With his family?'

'Misunderstandings? No, none whatsoever. They were a very close couple, neither of them had lovers or kept secrets from each other, I'm sure of it.'

'Do you happen to know why they slept in separate bedrooms?'

'No. We weren't close enough to exchange that sort of confidence, Chief Superintendent.'

'Had you noticed any change in him recently?'

'No, he was the same as always. Calm and absorbed in his work.'

Ferrara saw that it would be pointless to carry on. He would have liked to ask him about the photos, but decided that would be premature. They needed to dig a bit deeper first.

But he did ask him one more question before leaving. 'What do you know about your colleague's cases?'

'They'll eventually be transferred to me. Amedeo and I had signed a contract stipulating that, in the event of any impediment or the death of either partner, their cases would be transferred to the other.'

'With the clients' consent, of course,' Ferrara observed.

'Naturally. It will be down to me to let them know what's happened and offer them the choice.'

Ferrara said goodbye at that point.

As he was making his way to the door, Lucrezia, the secretary, gave him a friendly smile, which he returned. He was sure they would see one another again – and next time it would be at Headquarters.

He left the offices with a thousand thoughts whirling in his head. Corti had worked with Russo for years, they were partners. They lived minutes away from one another and they spent a lot of time together outside work. It was hard to believe that they'd never exchanged even the smallest confidence. But assuming it was true, how could Corti be so sure that there were no marital problems or secret lovers? This alone was enough to disprove at least part of what Russo's business partner had told him.

There was no doubt about it, Antonello Corti would have to go back on the list of suspects. The fact that he would inherit Russo's clients and thus boost his income would be motive enough for some people. But where did the wife come into it?

Ferrara looked at his watch. It was 11.02 a.m.

He decided to stop by the Prosecutor's Department to confront Deputy Prosecutor Vinci. He wanted to understand his intentions and how seriously he was taking the case. Then he would ask him to issue some warrants for the investigation.

PART THREE

OBSTACLES

28

11.09 a.m., the Prosecutor's Department

The driver parked the Alfa 156 in the space reserved for the Criminal Investigation Department outside the door to the Prosecutor's Department, which was in a dead-end side street off the Piazza della Repubblica.

'Wait for me here, Perrotta!' Ferrara ordered, striding past the Snai betting kiosk, where several old men were arguing about football while others queued to try their luck at the scratch cards. As always, the moment he opened the door and entered the building, a sense of loss descended upon him. It had been that way ever since his friend Anna Giulietti, the former deputy prosecutor, had been killed in a Mafia attack on 8 October 2001. Three years had gone by, but for Ferrara the pain was still as raw as the first day.

It didn't help that he bore an intense dislike for Luca Fiore. The man was like no other prosecutor Ferrara had ever come across: since his appointment, Fiore had never once attended a hearing, not even to support a colleague in a particularly complex case. The only time he put on his formal robes was to attend the speech on the state of justice at the opening of the legal year. For that ceremonial occasion he would make sure he had a front-row seat, posing for photographers in his ermine cloak.

Ferrara rang the bell, but there was no reply. He was about to turn round and head for the secretary's office when he heard Vinci's voice behind him. 'Speak of the devil! I was just about to call you.'

Ferrara returned the greeting and shook his hand.

'Take a seat!' the Deputy Prosecutor offered, letting Ferrara lead the way. He was wearing a dark grey merino-wool suit, a white shirt and a striped grey tie of pure silk.

Luigi Vinci had worked in Florence for the last ten years. He was nearing fifty, of average height and dark complexion, he played tennis to stay in shape, he could be found at a private club at Poggio Imperiale twice a week, and on Sundays he went jogging in the Parco delle Cascine. That summed up all Ferrara knew about him.

So far as his professional life went, Vinci had acquired a reputation as a slacker and a coward, so much so that the officers of the *Squadra Mobile* had taken to calling him 'No-balls'. Whenever a dossier went missing or a case got stalled because the paperwork hadn't been signed off, they'd assume it must be lying in a corner of the Deputy Prosecutor's office.

Ferrara dropped into the only empty seat in front of the government-issue desk. He missed the beautiful Art Nouveau chestnut desk that Anna Giulietti had inherited from her notary grandfather and brought to the office to make it less anonymous.

The other chair was piled high with dusty-smelling files, perhaps too many for a single deputy prosecutor, especially one involved in complex cases such as the murders that had occurred over the summer, some of which had an international dimension.

There was a black gown on a coat rack in the corner.

'Signora Elisa Russo has died.' The Deputy Prosecutor's tone was curt. 'She passed away this morning while undergoing another surgical procedure.'

Now there were two murders.

'I had a lot of paperwork removed from Russo's law firm yesterday evening, Chief Superintendent,' Vinci continued.

'Anything new?'

'Nothing. At least, not so far.'

Vinci explained that he was having the documents checked by experts from the Fraud team, who often collaborated on financial investigations. So far they'd found no incongruities. Russo and his office seemed clean. The firm wasn't in debt, and neither partner had any financial problems. The accounts seemed immaculate. So far, no suspects had emerged from their client list. In sum, a portrait of perfect respectability.

'The Fraud team have yet to complete their checks on the firm's clients, in particular the ones who were found guilty and are currently in prison, and those who've served their sentences and been released. It's a long list, but I'm inclined to rule out the possibility of a vendetta on the part of someone convicted due to an inadequate defence by Russo,' Vinci added.

Ferrara nodded in agreement. He doubted they'd find anything useful, but he knew it was important to formally rule out the possibility.

'I much prefer the theory that it was a robbery gone wrong,' Vinci continued. 'We need to catch the Eastern European gang that's causing all these problems, Chief Superintendent. If we don't act soon, we'll find ourselves with more deaths on our hands. These criminals kill just for the hell of it. The Chief Prosecutor has called a press conference – it's due to start in a few minutes. He's going to appeal for the citizens of Florence to come forward with information. Perhaps someone will have something of interest to tell us.'

'There might be another possibility,' Ferrara ventured, annoyed that this was the first he'd officially heard of the press conference.

'Go on then, tell me,' said Vinci, feigning interest in this alternative point of view.

Ferrara told him about the envelope with the photo album and the nine colour photographs.

A long silence fell. It was interminable. Deathly.

Ferrara tried to catch Vinci's eye, but the other man turned his head towards the window which looked out over the Piazza della Repubblica. Ferrara saw him check the clock with a restless expression, as if this were a waste of time.

'Any leads?' he asked, glancing back at Ferrara.

'Nothing specific, but we want to begin some surveillance—'

'What would that entail?' Vinci interrupted.

'Tapping a number of telephone—'

'Which ones?'

'Well, those at the law firm, and then . . .'

This time he stopped himself. He had been on the verge of saying that he wanted to launch an investigation into Satanism in Florence, prying once again into the world of those above suspicion – something that they had already brushed against in the course of their investigation a few months ago. But he didn't.

'In your dreams!'

'What's the problem?'

'The firm's clean, Chief Superintendent. And do you have any idea how many phone lines we're talking about? They have so many clients your men would be constantly tied up trying to monitor them. It's a complete waste of energy, especially in this period of austerity. Only a few days ago the Minister for Justice sent us yet another letter instructing us to limit our interceptions because of the high costs,' the Deputy Prosecutor objected.

The strictures imposed by the Minister didn't come as news to Ferrara. As a result of a cost-cutting initiative several years ago, the task of carrying out interceptions had passed from the government to private contractors. Those private companies now charged exhorbitant prices for their services, but that wasn't the only reason Ferrara was opposed to the privatisation: his primary objection was that the confidentiality of tapped conversations could not be guaranteed.

The atmosphere in the room had become hostile: Ferrara let himself slump in his seat as if he'd given up. He was convinced he'd been right not to expand upon his other theory.

Then the telephone rang. Vinci answered it and, after a couple of seconds, replied with a terse, 'I'm on my way.' Ordering Ferrara to stay put until he returned, he got up and left the room, straightening the knot in his tie as he went.

Luca Fiore had summoned him.

Vinci came back barely five minutes later, his expression grim.

'You went to Russo's law firm this morning, Chief Superintendent, to scrutinise documents in his office. On whose authorisation?' he began in a shaking voice. 'The Prosecutor is incandescent with rage. He says it's not the first time that you've acted without consulting anyone. In fact, he tells me he's given you strict instructions not to take personal initiatives in the course of investigations.'

Ferrara looked him up and down indignantly. 'I haven't scrutinised anything. I went to have a quick word with Signor Corti and one of the secretaries – a woman called Lucrezia.' Despite his attempt to justify his actions, he knew that things were going badly for him. You needed to have a deputy prosecutor present to carry out a search of a law firm's offices; it wasn't something that could be delegated to the police, nor something that could be carried out without a warrant. And, in any case, kid-glove treatment was necessary: lawyers, and particularly those at Russo's level, formed a powerful caste. You couldn't go rummaging through their offices without strong evidence, and even then you were supposed to give advance notice to the president of the council of the local bar association.

'The boss will have to write an official letter of apology – and I wouldn't rule out the possibility of his opening disciplinary proceedings against you,' said Vinci. He left these words to hang in the air for a few seconds before carrying on. 'But let's get back to our case, Chief Superintendent. What's your plan of action?' he asked. 'And try to be concise – the media are already starting to arrive for the press conference and I need to be present when it gets under way.'

'The murder of the wife doesn't fit with the robbery theory. It was more like an execution, an act of hatred or revenge,' Ferrara replied.

'What do you mean it doesn't fit? They were afraid of leaving a witness, Chief Superintendent. The poor thing obviously saw something.'

'But it's one thing to be tried for robbery and quite another for murder,' Ferrara objected.

'When you're dealing with heartless, bloodthirsty criminals, decision-making processes often depart from logic. We know all too well that those Eastern Europeans are trigger-happy.'

Ferrara wasn't prepared to back down. 'But she was in her bedroom, while her husband was killed outside. She wouldn't have been able to see anything, the swimming pool is some distance from the house. Besides, all the witnesses from the robberies at the other villas have mentioned that the robbers were wearing balaclavas or masks to cover their faces,' he replied, his voice calm but his jaw clenched.

There was absolute silence while Vinci put on a show of considering this.

'I'll have to discuss it with my boss, Chief Superintendent,' he said eventually. 'Prosecutor Fiore is following this case personally. He and Russo were on friendly terms, although they hadn't seen much of each other for a while. He told me that Russo didn't lead a double life – he wouldn't have had time for one – so we can dismiss any possibility of it being a crime of passion ... That's what you were referring to when you mentioned revenge, wasn't it? Don't let your imagination run away with you: there's no lover at the bottom of this!'

It was like a punch in the stomach for Ferrara. He had clashed with Fiore in the past over the latter's tendency to show favour to certain suspects, and every time he'd come out the loser. Even though it was completely inappropriate for a chief prosecutor to behave that way, there was nothing Ferrara could do about it. Fiore and his deputies gave the orders and the police were supposed to follow them. In his opinion, it should be the police who dictated the course and pace of an investigation; they should be the motor driving the whole thing forward. Instead they were forced to apply for official approval from the Prosecutor's Department at every stage. It was an intolerable state of affairs.

Struggling to control the rage simmering inside him, Ferrara asked, 'When will you let me know?'

'The moment Chief Prosecutor Fiore makes his decision,' said Vinci, with a condescending smirk.

Ferrara got up and, as they shook hands, he heard Vinci say, 'Get down to work and capture this gang'.

Ferrara nodded, not trusting himself to speak.

'On that note, Chief Superintendent ... '

'Yes?'

'Who do you plan to put in charge of the case?'

'The whole team are involved at the moment.'

'What about later on? Why not give it to Superintendent Micalizi – she seems on the ball and motivated.'

'We'll see.'

Ferrara was well aware that Vinci had his eye on Teresa. He'd invited her to go jogging with him on more than one occasion, and he'd let slip the odd remark that betrayed his interest, right from the day she joined the team: 'I'm pleased to see that the *Squadra Mobile* has received reinforcements. And finally there's an officer of the fairer sex on the team. Welcome!'

Ferrara could only force a smile and turn away, his mind already adjusting to harsh reality.

Once again, someone was trying to obstruct him, trying to throw a spanner in the works.

29

Russo didn't lead a double life.

There's no lover at the bottom of this!

He wouldn't have had time for one.

Vinci's words resounded in his head as he made his way down the stairs of the Prosecutor's Department. If Fiore hadn't seen the victim for a while, how could he know what he got up to in private?

And why had the Prosecutor spontaneously brought up the topic of a 'double life' with Vinci? Was it merely to exclude the possibility of the lawyer having a lover? Or was 'double life' intended to encompass illegal activity linked to his profession as well?

It was a catch-22: Ferrara was convinced the motive would only be found by delving into Amedeo Russo's professional and private lives. Focusing on appearances would get them nowhere. In the majority of cases, victims know their murderers, giving lie to the easy reassurance that evil comes from outside. A husband kills his wife. A junkie kills his dealer. A Mafioso kills his enemy from another *family* and so on.

When he emerged from the building, Perrotta was leaning against the door of the pool car enjoying a cigarette. Ferrara told him that he wanted to make his way back to the office on foot: he needed some air, the chance to stretch his legs and reorganise the ideas that were tangled up in his mind, to have a decent coffee and smoke half a Tuscan cigar.

He crossed the Piazza della Repubblica, which was packed with tourists, many of them Japanese, taking photos with the latest model digital cameras and next generation mobile phones. Then he began walking along the Via Roma, turning right when he reached the first side street. He was almost at Caffè Robiglio when he was surprised by a familiar voice behind him.

'Good morning, Chief Superintendent.'

He spun round.

It was Father Giulio Torre, the expert on the esoteric he'd met through his friend, the bookseller Massimo Verga. He'd also consulted him during the recent investigations into the murder of the former senator Enrico Costanza, in the hope the priest could explain the significance of the victim's eyes being gouged out.

'It was a punishment, and at the same time a message to those able to understand it,' Father Torre had told him. He'd gone on to explain that, historically, the Masons had considered the eye a symbol of enlightenment, the means by which the darkest secrets could be understood. Thus, through his actions, the killer had sought to exclude Costanza from the ranks of the enlightened.

'Good morning to you, too, Father. Can I offer you a coffee?'

'I'd be delighted to accept.'

The place was crowded with customers, almost all of them Florentines. Cakes, petits fours and pastries were displayed along the long counter. They looked like the jewels in shop windows on the Ponte Vecchio.

Father Torre couldn't resist and ordered a croissant overflowing with fresh cream to go with his coffee. No sooner had it been placed in front of him than he fell upon it with ill-disguised greed. Ferrara, on the other hand, stuck to a simple jam-filled croissant.

They made small talk while they drank their coffee: a double espresso for Ferrara and a strong, black coffee with a teaspoon of fresh cream for the priest.

On leaving the café, they shook hands and exchanged a few pleasantries before parting, then Ferrara glanced at his watch. 'You'll have to excuse me, Father Torre, but I've got a complicated case waiting for me.'

'I'll bet it's the murder of the lawyer, Russo.'

Ferrara nodded and turned to leave, deep in thought. After a few steps he spun on his heel and called after the departing priest. 'Father Torre!'

Bemused, the other man walked towards him.

'Father, we may end up needing your valuable insights again.'

'I'm always at your service, Chief Superintendent. Just let me know when I can be of use.'

'I'll call you myself.'

The priest nodded and they said goodbye once more, then Ferrara set off in the direciton of Headquarters.

The crowd queuing to go inside the Baptistery of Saint John was taking up so much of the piazza that he had to use his elbows to clear a path. Enchanted by its beauty, the tourists were busy taking selfies and posing for pictures with the beautiful bronze panels of the doors in the background, depicting scenes from the life of the city's patron saint. The portrait artists were at work along one side of the square and more tourists were clustered around the Column of Saint Zenobius in front of the north gate, reading guidebooks and listening to a guide describing how Saint Zenobius's body was transported from the Church of San Lorenzo to the Church of Santa Reparata, which is now under the Cathedral of Santa Maria del Fiore. Just as it passed the Baptistery, the coffin brushed a wizened elm tree and the tree suddenly burst into bloom. A miracle. And Zenobius became a saint without undergoing any form of martyrdom. Eight centuries later, a marble column had been erected on the very same spot to commemorate the event.

That was the way Florence was. Beautiful, splendid and rich in history, fantasy and legends.

Or at least, that was the face it showed to tourists.

Not the evil one.

It was shortly after one by the time Ferrara reached Headquarters and found the ballistics report from Forensics on his desk.

The 7.65 calibre bullets, which had been recovered during the surgical procedure on Elisa Russo, were so deformed that it was impossible to determine the furrows and grooves of the weapon's barrel, so they would be no use in tracing the make and model of the pistol from which they'd been fired.

There was no match for the casings on the database of weapons used in previous crimes. So the pistol was clean.

Then he opened another envelope.

It contained the photographs from the album, both the originals and the copies, including the enlargements, and a copy of Fuschi's report. They'd lifted fingerprints belonging to Amedeo Russo. He was the only one who'd touched the album.

By examining one of the enlargements, Fuschi had been able to identify the object that was projecting from the vagina of the young woman stretched out on the altar: a small crucifix with an inverted Christ.

Ferrara shivered. It was madness, pure madness.

He was about to set the report aside when his phone rang.

'Hello?'

'Hi, Michele.' It was Lorenzo Braschi, the Head of the Pisan *Squadra Mobile*.

'Hi, Lorenzo, what's up?'

'I'm calling you about that lawyer, Russo. I've got some information you might find useful . . . '

His colleague went on to tell him that he'd had a visit from a prison officer earlier that morning. Having read about Russo's

murder in *La Nazione*, the man had come to report that he'd
been present when the lawyer paid a visit to Daniele De Robertis
in Don Bosco Prison a few days before the latter's escape.

'Was Russo his lawyer?'

'Yes, he'd been nominated by your Chief Prosecutor.'

'Fiore?'

'That's the one. The prison officer mentioned something you
might find useful . . .' Ferrara heard the rustle of papers at the
other end of the line. Then his colleague resumed: 'As the lawyer
was leaving the interview room, the officer, who was standing
guard, heard the prisoner say "Your secrets will come to light"
or something along those lines. He was absolutely certain he used
the words "your secrets", though.'

'Did he make a statement?'

'Of course. I've got it here in front of me. And I've done
something else, too.'

'Go on.'

'I've sent one of my inspectors to the prison to check the visitor log. I've also had a photocopy made of the page where
Russo's name is listed, along with the date and the time he
arrived and left.'

'When was the visit?'

'Monday 27 September.'

Ferrara's heart skipped a beat. 'Can you send me a copy of the
statement and the page from the visitor log?'

'I'll send you photocopies. The originals are for my
Prosecutor, but I expect he'll send them on to Florence in due
course.'

'Have you checked for other visits Daniele De Robertis
received while he was in prison?'

'Yes. According to the log, Russo was his only visitor. Even
during the three weeks he spent recovering in the infirmary, he
didn't see anyone.'

'Thanks for the information, Lorenzo.'

'Good luck.'

'And to you.'

After hanging up, Ferrara dialled his deputy's number and summoned him to his office. Perhaps there was a glimmer of light at the end of the tunnel.

But once again Fiore was involved.

Was it really just a coincidence?

'We need to start with the facts, Francesco. Then we'll move on to the analysis and decide which leads to follow.'

Ferrara had finished bringing Rizzo up to date on his conversation with Vinci and the phone call from their colleague in Pisa. He had, for the moment at least, omitted the Deputy Prosecutor's warning that a disciplinary case might be brought against him; he didn't want to worry Rizzo.

Ferrara could see that Rizzo's mind was hard at work, analysing every detail in an effort to find answers to the three key questions: who stood to gain from these murders? Why now? And what were Russo's 'secrets'?

Their next step was to devise a strategy that would allow them to act discreetly, without bowing to the influence of the Prosecutor's Department and, in particular, Luca Fiore. The Chief Prosecutor was like a ticking time bomb, ready to explode at any moment, and the authority he wielded made him all the more dangerous.

Ferrara had always been convinced that in order to reach the truth it was necessary to use the facts as a starting point and never to lose sight of them as an investigation progressed. He therefore began to recap the information in their possession, subdividing it into five sections.

1. The attackers – two men, based on the sizes of the shoes and the depth of the prints – had entered the Russo property by stealth between the hours of two and four in the morning. It was clearly a premeditated act because the criminals had brought the

tools necessary to cut through the metal fence and the blunt object they'd used to hit the victim.

2. According to the scientific reports, Amedeo Russo had died of acute asphyxiation due to drowning. There was, however, some doubt as to whether the victim had fallen into the water following the blow, or whether his attackers had thrown him into the swimming pool having rendered him unconscious.

3. The wife had been attacked in her bedroom, the killers most probably surprising her as she was watching television. They had shot her twice to make sure she was dead. This too raised further questions: Had she been shot before or after her husband's murder? And, perhaps more importantly: why had they killed her?

4. The criminals searched the study. Therefore they must have known, or at least had a strong suspicion, where to focus their search. In fact, that was the only room that had been left in a mess. In addition, the mobile phone that had been left charging on the desk was missing its SIM card. Had they been the ones who'd taken it? Had they found what they were looking for?

'We need to carry out an inventory to establish whether anything's missing,' he told Rizzo. 'And then contact the telephone company – have them send the relevant call records for the Russos' telephone numbers.'

Rizzo raised one objection to his boss's summary: 'They might have found the object they used as a weapon in the house.'

Ferrara nodded. 'All the more reason we should make that inventory our number one priority. And make sure you coordinate with Teresa; I've put her in charge of questioning Russo's son and brother after the funeral.'

Then he moved on to the fifth and final point: the colour photographs in the much-discussed album. It was another objective fact, perhaps a crucial detail that could somehow be linked directly to the crime. Were those photos, as Vinci had suggested, part of a legal dossier relating to a case Russo was following? Or were they actually linked to the 'secrets' Daniele De Robertis had referred to?

If they could find the answer to these questions, they woud be in a position to arrive at a credible theory regarding the motive.

'We need to examine the dossiers for the cases Russo worked on,' Ferrara told Rizzo. 'The motive, or even the killer's name, might be written on one of those pages.'

Rizzo frowned. 'We'll need authorisation from the Deputy Prosecutor.'

'Only if the cases are still covered by the statute of confidentiality. For now, let's start with the archived cases.'

'I'll make arrangements for the files to be sent up. In the meantime, I'll keep ploughing through the files on murders of prostitutes.'

30

The questions kept buzzing around in Ferrara's head.

What had De Robertis meant by Russo's 'secrets'?

Was the timing of this meeting between the serial killer and the lawyer merely a coincidence?

Could De Robertis have been the one who'd killed Russo and his wife?

Ferrara realised there was a piece missing from the mosaic: who could his accomplice have been? His fellow fugitive?

He asked Rizzo to contact Police Headquarters in Palermo and request the usual information on Pasquale Schimizzi, the man De Robertis had escaped with. 'We can't rule him out, Francesco. As you know, people make all kinds of friends in prison. Strange alliances are formed that would have been unthinkable on the outside.'

Rizzo nodded.

'And another thing. Are you still able to ask favours from that friend of your wife's at the phone company.'

'Yes.'

'Is she reliable?'

'One hundred per cent.'

'Great! See if she'll give you records of mobile phones using the network around Maiano on the night of the crime on an unofficial basis – and Russo's records, too, or at least the calls made and received in the last few days. Somehow I don't think the Prosecutor's Department are going to give us authorisation to make an official request.'

'I'll have a go.'

Then Ferrara asked whether the confidential sources had come up with anything, but it came as no surprise when Rizzo said there had been no information and no clues.

'They've assured me they'll get to work, though,' he concluded with a disappointed frown.

Ferrara didn't comment. He knew that while the public face of Florence seemed to be all about dressing up and parading for all the world to see, there existed a private face that was hidden away behind closed doors. Florentines were prone to curl up as tight as a hedgehog if they thought that their privacy was about to be violated. And this was particularly true among those who had the most to hide.

Ferrara turned on the TV to catch the regional news, his mind still mulling over Russo's 'secrets' and the album with its nine photographs, but when images relating to the double murder appeared on the screen, he turned the volume up and got ready to listen.

Both the news anchor and the two journalists seemed sceptical about the likelihood of a swift solution to the case. Nor did they omit to share their strong doubts about the abilities of the police investigating the crime, in particular the *Squadra Mobile*.

Next they aired some interviews with the residents of the Borgo Bellavista gated community. They, too, complained about the police, accusing them of failing to provide a sufficient level of security. One portly woman, shopping bag in hand, had been interviewed at the bus stop. She seemed genuinely worried as she told the reporter that nobody felt safe any more, not even in their own home.

'Fear' was the word that kept being repeated. Fear: the

people's true state of mind, Ferrara thought. It would be the police's job to assuage that feeling, but, for the moment, they appeared to be powerless.

The next segment covered the press conference at the Prosecutor's Department. They must have put it together in a hurry, given the short amount of time available to them.

Luca Fiore had been filmed sitting behind his desk. Vinci was sitting beside him, a painting of a knight in armour visible in the background. Ferrara noticed that neither Fiore nor the cleaning woman had taken it upon themselves to straighten the painting. Ferrara had observed that the painting was lopsided a long time ago, but it clearly wasn't noticeable to those who were in the office on a daily basis. Or perhaps the Prosecutor liked it better that way.

As the journalist delivered his report, only a snippet of Fiore's speech was heard: 'We'll catch these evil Eastern gangsters.'

Irritated, Ferrara pressed a button on the remote and the screen turned black. Just the mention of the Prosecutor's name was enough to make him angry.

'Let's get to work,' he told his deputy.

'What about the other security guard?' Rizzo asked.

'Ascalchi and Ricci have gone to Sardinia to track him down. We need to concentrate on finding Daniele De Robertis.'

Rizzo nodded and made to leave the room, but Ferrara called him back.

'Is there something else, Michele?'

Ferrara told him about Vinci's latest request: that Teresa Micalizi should be put in charge of the investigation.

'He must want to get her into bed!' Rizzo laughed. 'Guys like him seem to lose their heads when they see a young female police officer or junior lawyer. It's as if they'd never set eyes on a woman before.'

Ferrara shook his head. He was thinking of all the relationships, many of them extramarital, which occurred between deputy prosecutors and young auditors and policewomen. Some of those illicit affairs had torn entire families apart.

Then Rizzo said, 'Perhaps it wouldn't be such a bad thing, Michele. Let's keep him happy. We'll make him think that Teresa will be the official liaison for our team. Maybe "No-balls" will soften up a bit for her.'

Ferrara gave it a moment's thought, saw the sense in what his deputy suggested and gave his full agreement.

Alone once more, Ferrara switched on his computer and ran a Google search with Luca Fiore's name as the subject. He didn't want to miss a single piece of news relating to the Prosecutor. He wanted to be aware of his every statement on TV, in the local press and on any blogs.

Nothing would slip past him.

When Ferrara got home it was already the middle of the night. It had been a long hard day, yet he felt he'd achieved nothing.

Before opening the big door to the entrance hall he paused, still under Perrotta's watchful gaze, to look around. The only people he saw were a couple of young tourists arguing loudly with no regard for people trying to sleep. He could also hear drunken laments drifting from the Lungarno degli Acciaioli, the voices hoarse from all that wailing.

A Carabinieri squad car shot past, sirens blaring and lights flashing, with another car right behind it. There'd been a stabbing in a pub in the Santo Spirito district on the far side of the river, probably a row between drunks that got out of control. Such callouts were almost a matter of routine in that popular, lively quarter, which in recent years had also become a haunt of dealers and junkies.

The night was still young, and the party was in full swing not only in the bars and discos but in exclusive private clubs and the homes of the nobility and the haute bourgeoisie: the most secret and mysterious side of Florence, whose roots stretched back into medieval and renaissance history, rich in crime and dark intrigues.

Ferrara hurried up the stairs, opened his front door and slipped inside without making a sound.

After switching on a small table lamp he went into to the bathroom to take a long shower. While the warm water flowed over his shoulders, which were aching from frustration, he heard Luigi Vinci's threat echoing in his ears. His career, marked by so many successive triumphs during his time in Calabria and Naples, seemed to be stalling in Florence, and might end up compromised forever.

His thoughts returned to the problems he'd been having these last few months with the police hierarchy, and even the upper echelons in Rome. He'd never regretted turning down the transfers he'd been offered, even though he'd been offered equally or even more prestigious positions. 'Would I have been better off accepting?' he asked himself as he got out of the shower and grabbed a towel to wrap around his waist.

But he'd stayed, because he had unfinished business: getting to the bottom of Florence's dark secrets. If he were to abandon that quest, give up these investigations into the lives of the untouchables, the elite who were above suspicion, and concentrate on appeasing his superiors – the Prosecutor, the Commissioner and the Chief of Police – his life would be much easier. He would have more time to enjoy himself and be with his family.

'Just leave it. You've got a family to provide for,' he told himself again as he stared in the mirror. His face looked tired and the lines either side of his mouth seemed deeper than usual. Sadness and disappointment. He had not long turned fifty-five, but he'd never felt that old until recently. Too much pressure, too much stress. Although he loved his job, the investigations and conflicts with his bosses were taking their toll.

For the first time he asked himself whether the path he'd chosen to follow had precluded other possibilities, including career opportunities. It had been a mistake to assume there would be time to change his mind. There hadn't been, and now he was left to bitterly weigh up his debts in that thankless balance.

Then a small voice whispered to him: 'No, you should continue. You owe it to all those who believe in the state, in Justice with a capital "J", not the kind delivered by Luca Fiore, that low-life, ball-less womaniser!'

He huffed, took a deep breath and told himself that the time for reflection was over. He'd be better off going to sleep.

On the way to the bedroom he stopped for a few seconds to look at the framed photographs of him and Petra, happy moments caught on camera and printed for posterity. Amazing experiences, shared with his wife, the person he loved most in the world. Those things nobody would ever be able to take away from him.

It was life. Their life.

He shook his head, telling himself no, he hadn't chosen the wrong job. No, he had no regrets. Even if he had the power to turn back time, he would make exactly the same choices.

In the bedroom he found Petra asleep, the lamp on the bedside table switched on as usual. She never switched it off when she was alone, and often not even when she was with him. It was a simple habit that Ferrara no longer noticed.

He slipped into bed, trying not to wake her.

As soon as she felt him next to her, she opened her eyes and smiled. 'What time is it?' she asked, turning towards him.

Her voice was tinged with concern, as it always was when her husband returned home in the middle of the night. She knew what a minefield her husband's work could be, and she was unable to control her anxiety, even after so many years of living together.

'It's almost two. But don't worry, Petra.'

'What time do you have to get up?'

'At seven,' he replied, and kissed her on the lips. 'Go to sleep, sweetheart.' He pulled her head on to his shoulder, slipped his hand under the covers, searching for hers, and stayed like that. Awake, with his mind whirling like mad.

Petra had trouble getting back to sleep, too. Her eyes remained wide open for some time as she thought about what she would have liked to tell him. Eventually, though, she convinced herself that it still wasn't the right moment.

31

The night of Wednesday 19 to Thursday 20 October, Milan

The recurring nightmares that had long tormented his nights had disappeared. But from time to time, especially when he was half asleep, the image of the Great Beast, the only face he could see clearly, would appear.

'Damn you and may you rot in hell,' he would shout at him, before delivering the coup de grâce. Then he would spit on his bloody body.

It was just after one in the morning and Daniele De Robertis was in Milan in a private room at the *family*'s club.

'Salvino Lo Cascio extends his compliments and can't wait to meet you personally,' Pasquale told him, coming into the room.

Since their escape, Pasquale had not only had confirmation of his companion's courage, he'd learned something he hadn't known before: Daniele De Robertis was highly resourceful and hungry for revenge. The *family* had need of those qualities; they had recently come to an agreement with the Colombian drug cartels to create a monopoly over the cocaine trade in Italy, thus supplanting the 'Ndrangheta.

'The Calabrian bosses are already nervous and there will be repercussions,' he told De Robertis. 'But we won't be taken by surprise. There are foot soldiers arriving from Palermo, and not just from there. These young men are absolutely loyal.'

'What about my business?'

'Don't worry, we've thought of that, too. You won't be on your own,' Pasquale added in a murmur. 'When we start a job, we see it through. We can go over the plan now ... '

They discussed it for a good hour.

When they finished, Pasquale assured him that it would be child's play and uncorked a bottle of champagne. After they'd clinked glasses, he left the room, promising him a pleasant surprise.

And half an hour later, De Robertis found himself lying under black silk sheets in the arms of a young girl from Venice. She was breathtakingly beautiful.

Eleonora – although who knows if that was her real name – couldn't have been more than eighteen. She had an extremely pale complexion, thick blonde hair and long, slender legs. She was one of the many girls who use their pussy to pay for their studies. She'd already stripped him completely naked, flashing a confident and lively smile.

After a while, De Robertis put his hands around her neck so spontaneously that it seemed like a natural gesture. It was actually one of his favourite erotic games: to reach orgasm as the woman began showing the first signs of asphyxiation. He felt Eleonora's body go rigid, a film of sweat forming on her skin, while her shining eyes stared at him with a questioning look and her lungs struggled for air. Then he let her go while she was still gasping to catch her breath.

On another occasion he would probably have killed her during sex. It had happened several times in Paris, where he had been introduced to the world of sadomasochism by a stinking rich plastic surgeon he'd met through a bridge circle. It was a world that had allowed him to discover the techniques of the Marquis de Sade, which awakened an arousal in him he would never have thought possible, given that every experience he'd had with the opposite sex until that point had been a complete disaster. He'd killed without feeling any remorse; his victims were almost always young prostitutes, and the colder he managed to be, the more strongly he felt the sexual pleasure explode inside him. It had been during that period that he had finally begun to feel like a man, and, in fact, a monster. He was no longer the boy mocked by his peers for his small penis.

But there, in the club, he needed to control his arousal.

He leapt up from the bed and used the next few seconds to rein in his instincts. He filled a glass of water and handed it to Eleonora, who was beginning to recover. But the fear was still visible in her eyes, even if her heart rate was returning to normal.

He told her to get dressed and slipped a thousand euros into her clutch bag as they said goodbye.

32

Wednesday 20 October

Ferrara summoned Teresa Micalizi first thing that morning.

The policewoman took a seat and gave him an inquiring look. She was wondering whether she might have done something wrong.

As if reading her mind, Ferrara assured her, 'It's nothing bad, Teresa, don't worry.' Then he went on to explain that he and Rizzo had decided to make her their liaison officer with the Prosecutor's Department for the Russo case.

'I'll make the decision official later on with a written declaration to Deputy Prosecutor Vinci. He's the one who expressly asked for you.'

There was a pause while Teresa stared at him, waiting. Ferrara lit a cigar and inhaled several times before placing it in the ashtray.

'But, chief—' she started to protest.

Ferrara interrupted her. 'This is my decision, Teresa.'

'OK.'

'Go and see Vinci and run through the investigations with him. Listen to his what he has planned and warn him that you'll be sending him a request for warrants in the near future.'

'I'll get over there right away.'

'Thanks, Teresa. And remember: stay on the ball. You've got what it takes and you'll go far.'

A slight smile appeared on the policewoman's face.

She left the Chief Superintendent's office with those last words bouncing around in her head. Inevitably her thoughts turned to her father, a police marshal who'd been killed by robbers during a bank robbery only a few steps from the Galleria Vittorio Emanuele in Milan, the city where he had served and where she had gone to school.

He would have been proud of her.

33

Oristano, Sardinia

Italo Ortu was short, thin and swarthy, and his lean face sported a two-day-old beard. But the most striking thing about him was his gaze. His sunken eyes were like two burning embers. He also had a large Adam's apple. He was wearing threadbare jeans and a dark woollen jumper.

They had traced him an aunt's house in Bauladu, a community of around seven thousand people in the province of Oristano. It was the address the man had given to the security company when he applied for work as a nightwatchman. According to the checks Ascalchi had carried out, his name had appeared on the passenger list for the Florence–Olbia flight on 18 October 2004. The same day the body had been found.

Now he sat in front of them in a small room at Police Headquarters, a new ten-storey building erected after the town had become the provincial seat in 1974.

Italo Ortu was hunched forward in his seat, his gaze lowered and tension etched into his face. He looked up from time to time to glance timidly at the police officers, waiting for someone to start talking.

Ascalchi got up and went to sit on the edge of the desk. He kept one foot on the floor and let the other dangle in front of the witness. He stared at him for a few moments, then asked the first question, just to get things started and get a feel for his reactions. 'Well now, Signor Ortu, how's the hunting going?'

The man, who had appeared to be staring blankly at the floor at the policeman's feet, raised his head slightly and replied, 'I'm making plans with some friends.'

'And where will you go?'

'To Arzana.'

Ascalchi knew that this was in the heart of the Ogliastra, which stretched from the seashore up to the highest peaks of the Gennargentu, the island's main mountain range. It had once served as a den for bands of fugitives and regularly made the headlines back in the seventies and eighties in relation to abductions and kidnappings for ransom. Almost all the victims were wealthy businessmen, landowners or entrepreneurs, often imprisoned as an act of revenge by the poor towards the well-off. It was one of the cruellest crimes, which played on the pain suffered by the victims' families.

'Who are these friends of yours?'

Ortu maintained a lengthy silence, then asked. 'What's with all the questions?'

'You just worry about answering them!' Ascalchi raised his voice, letting him know who was in charge. 'We are in a police station and you are being questioned,' he added, to remind him that he'd been brought there in connection with a police investigation.

Silence fell once more.

An expectant silence on the policeman's part.

An unnerving silence for the man being questioned. Beads of sweat formed on his forehead and ran down into his eyes. He knew that he was in trouble.

But why didn't he want to give them the names?

If everything were in order, there'd have been nothing to fear. He would have spat out the names and confirmed the reason for his presence in Sardinia.

'Now, tell me! Who are these friends of yours?' Ascalchi demanded, leaning forward so that he filled the witness's field of vision.

It was one of the interview techniques he'd learnt during his years in the job. Leaning forward invaded the other person's space, underlining your desire to get answers, while leaning back suggested you'd heard what you wanted to hear.

'You don't need to worry, Signor Ortu. You're being questioned as a person who may have information of interest to our investigation. You're not accused of anything – at least not at the moment. I would remind you, however, that our legal code anticipates and provides punishment for perverting the course of justice,' he continued, explaining that the penalty comprised imprisonment for up to four years.

The man gave them two names.

'Where do they live?'

'I don't know exactly. I meet them in the piazza at Arzana.'

'What?! You go hunting with friends but you don't know where they live?' Ascalchi shouted, having moved behind the desk to make a note of the names. Afterwards he sprang up and rushed out of the room in a temper, closing the door behind him. Ricci stayed where he was to keep an eye on the witness. He'd done nothing the entire time but observe the man, almost as if he wanted to take his measure.

Italo Ortu needed to stew in that small, ground-floor room with its lone window and a single neon light on the ceiling. Experience had shown that, in situations like this, time helped break down impasses, especially in cases where a witness feared that revealing the true version of events would turn out badly for them.

Ascalchi came back into the room after almost half an hour, but the time he had spent sitting under Ricci's stare seemed much longer to Italo Ortu.

'Ortuuuu! That's enough!' exclaimed the police officer, slamming his palm on to the desktop, which reverberated like a pistol shot. 'You talk nothing but crap and you're digging yourself into deeper and deeper shit with your own hands,' he continued, waving a piece of paper in the air. His voice had gone up an octave. And his expression was that of a tiger about to pounce on its prey.

A shiver ran down Ortu's back. Ascalchi was pacing back and forth across the room, his face livid. He did this whenever he was angry, and it made witnesses nervous. Then he went and sat down behind the desk, leaned back and took a deep breath before launching into a barrage of questions.

'Why do you want to make things so difficult for me? What do you think, that we came to Sardinia so you could piss us around? If that's the case, you're sorely mistaken.'

Ascalchi felt an icy rage building inside him. He couldn't stand being conned and in this case he had even less tolerance, given that Italo Ortu was a security guard who had sworn in front of the Prefect to observe the law faithfully and to carry out his duties conscientiously and diligently with respect to the rights of citizens. A solemn oath that had sealed a bond of loyalty between him and the state.

Ascalchi had a strong desire to incriminate him and have his licence revoked. He wasn't worthy of it.

'I don't want to piss anyone ar—' the witness began, then stopped again.

'You're digging yourself in deep, Italo,' shouted the police officer, switching to the man's first name without realising it. 'Listen carefully to what I'm about to tell you. The Carabinieri have tracked down one of your friends and he didn't even know that you were in Sardinia. And I'm sure that the other will say the same thing when he's questioned on his return from work.'

As he said the last few words, Ascalchi leant forward again, drawing close to Ortu's face. They were separated by less than eight inches.

After a brief pause he resumed: 'When I inform the Prefect, he'll revoke your licence to work as a security guard. You can bet you'll lose your job and, in these straitened times, it'll be difficult for you to find another.'

'No, not that, please. Not my job.'

'Talk, then. Tell me the truth. Where were you on the night the lawyer, Amedeo Russo, was killed? What did you do? What did you see? I don't want to ask you again, and I've had enough of your fairy stories! Fairy stories are for telling to children, not police officers.'

There was another long heavy silence.

Ortu's eyes were like two chinks of light in a dark night. His lips were drawn tight in the expression of someone who's deciding whether or not to confess a sin to the priest.

'Italo, you have to talk!' intervened Ricci, clearing his throat and moving to stand beside the witness as he did so. He put a hand gently on his shoulder, leant one hip against the desk and added, 'If you tell the truth, we can help you. We're men of the law, and when we say we'll do something, we do it.'

As he said this he was thinking, 'Spit it out, you're nothing but a bloody fool.'

'OK, I'll tell you what I know.'

'Great! Start talking, then,' Ricci invited him, without removing his hand from his shoulder.

'Listen, Marshal, the truth is that I've been scared,' Ortu began, turning to Ascalchi. 'I guessed the reason you were here straight away.'

'I'm not a marshal, I'm a police superintendent.'

'I'm sorry,' the man stuttered, and added, 'I'm still scared, even now. The fear won't leave me alone.'

There was another pause.

Sweat glistened on his forehead. Soon it would trickle down

his cheeks, on to his neck and under his shirt. The terror in his eyes was as sharp as a knife blade. He lowered his gaze to his lap, where his hands were clasped.

He was crumbling, it was merely a case of seizing the moment. And Ascalchi knew the right moment to get a witness talking: a minute too late and it would be difficult to get the desired result.

'Are you afraid because you've been threatened, Ortu? Is that what you're trying to tell me?'

Ascalchi had reverted to the man's surname.

'No. That's not what I meant, Superintendent, sir. I know how certain things work and no threats were necessary. My wife and I are separated. I have two sons and I have to pay child maintenance every month. The judge set the rate. I can't lose my job. Help me, please ...'

He started sobbing and the first tears appeared on his face. Genuine ones. Having held them in for so long, now that he'd started it seemed his weeping would go on for ever.

Ascalchi nodded slightly, as if to show a certain degree of empathy: another interrogator's technique. Then he sat down again without taking his eyes off the other man. Years of experience had also taught him how to read body language: the movements of the face, even the almost imperceptible ones, the continuous movement of the hands ...

After a while Ricci murmured to Ortu, 'That's enough now. Act like a real man and you'll see that everything will work out. Come on, be strong!'

But panic was still visible on the witness's face.

Ascalchi was watching him, ready with the next question, but he didn't have time to ask it. Drying his tears with a crumpled tissue, Ortu broke the silence to ask the police officers exactly what they wanted to know.

'What do you mean? Haven't you understood yet? We want you to tell us everything you know, everything you saw during your shift on the night of 17 to 18 October. You went to Borgo Bellavista at least twice, at 1.45 a.m. and 3.50 a.m. We took the records from the guard post by the gate – I can show you if you want. And we've already questioned your colleague who worked the previous shift; he told us that you were half an hour late when you came to take over.' Ascalchi pulled some sheets of paper out of a folder. 'Here they are, photocopies of the records.'

'Come on, be strong!' Ricci intervened again.

'I'm afraid of losing my job. Will that happen?'

'No, not if you tell the truth.'

Italo Ortu looked up toward the ceiling as if searching for the answer there. Then he started to tell his story with an anguish that seemed genuine.

He'd seen two men moving furtively through the compound's garden during his round at 1.45 a.m. One was taller and stockier than the other. He'd been frightened because he'd heard about those dangerous Eastern European criminals who were spreading terror throughout the Tuscan countryside, ready to kill for a slice of bread.

'I was petrified; I hid behind a bush and drew my pistol. I was shaking so much that I had to hold it with both hands. I kept thinking about my children, about the fact that I might never see them again. I love them to death and they love me, too. It's obvious during my weekly visits.'

He paused in his account for a few minutes and wiped convulsively at his tears with the paper tissue. Perhaps he was angry as well as afraid. Angry at finding himself in this situation.

'Carry on!'

He had lost sight of the men but assumed that they'd gone into the Russos' house because they seemed to have been heading in that direction. They'd reappeared after a few minutes with a third person who was walking between them. Keeping within the cover of bushes and moving slowly, the security guard had followed them. In the weak light of the lamps around the swimming pool, he'd recognised the profile of the tall, thin man: it was the lawyer, Russo. Then he heard a voice and caught a few words.

'What exactly did you hear?'

'"You didn't want to tell us, you piece of shit. Even after we threatened your . . ." or something like that, Superintendent.'

'What then?'

'Then I heard a muffled shout. And nothing more. I moved away very slowly, making sure I stayed behind the bushes.'

'How long were they inside the house for?'

'I don't know. I was frozen and I couldn't think clearly. Perhaps only a few minutes, perhaps much longer. I don't know.' He broke off and began to sob, hiding his face in his hands.

Ascalchi let a few minutes pass while he made sure the written version of the statement wasn't missing any details and, most importantly, that it had recorded the witness's words and reactions faithfully, even the apparently authentic fit of weeping. They were details of no little importance, ones worth highlighting on the page: they could contribute to making the account more credible.

At the first rereading it struck Ascalchi as an honest version of events, but it raised some doubts that needed to be cleared up – and they'd have to strike while the iron was hot.

Ricci left the room and returned minutes later with two bottles of water, which he placed on the table with some plastic cups.

Italo Ortu took one. He opened it and filled a cup with a visibly shaking hand. He drank it down in one. Then he said he felt better and he was ready to continue.

Ascalchi moved on to the next question, as there were already some points that needed clarifying. 'What language were the two men speaking?'

'Italian. They weren't foreigners, if that's what you want to know.'

'Are you sure?'

'One hundred per cent, Superintendent. It was clear from the few words I heard.'

'Did they have an accent or use dialect?'

'No, I don't think so. But you have to remember that I was so scared I almost pissed myself.'

'And why did you continue to do nothing at that point? Couldn't you have used your radio to raise the alarm at your headquarters?'

'I was still too scared. I'd realised they must be powerful people to treat an important person, a lawyer like Russo, like that. And there must have been someone even more powerful behind them, protecting them. Someone even scarier.'

'Did you hear shots?'

'No.'

'Are you sure?'

'One hundred per cent sure.'

'Describe their appearance.'

'It was dark when I saw them, how am I supposed to describe them?'

'There was faint light around the swimming pool. You said so a little while ago, otherwise how would you have been able to recognise Signor Russo's profile?'

Italo Ortu seemed to be thinking, still clutching the now-disintegrated tissue in his hand. Then he explained that one of the men was tall with quite a stocky build. His face was regular, at least as far as he'd been able to see. The other man was shorter and thinner. And he might have had longer hair than his accomplice.

'Was he as short as you?'

'More or less.'

'How tall are you?'

'Just over five foot six.'

'Were they holding anything?'

'I didn't notice anything.'

'How were they dressed?'

'They might have been wearing heavy jackets.'

'They didn't have their faces covered then! Is that right?'

'Yes.'

Nobody said anything for a moment.

Then Ascalchi made Ortu repeat the whole account again, concentrating on the details. But he didn't contradict himself a single time. He repeated what he'd said word for word.

'You're coming back to Florence with us, Signor Ortu,' he said authoritatively at the end, the hint of a smile on his lips. 'If you don't come willingly, we'll be obliged to apply to the Prosecutor for a warrant to bring you forcibly. You can be certain that we won't leave the island without you.'

'You don't want to arrest me, do you?'

'No. But we need to try to put together an identikit of the two criminals.'

'Can't that be done here?'

'No. We also need to show you some photos of ex-convicts, and those are back in our office.'

Ortu seemed to think for a long moment, then he agreed in a small voice.

'But don't make me lose my job. I beg you.'

Ascalchi didn't reply, but he exchanged a look of understanding with Ricci.

They were satisfied.

Ascalchi printed the statement, read it aloud and then placed it in front of Ortu.

'We need a legible signature on every page, here,' he said, pointing to the place at the foot of the page.

Italo Ortu signed without even reading it.

Ascalchi couldn't wait to tell Ferrara the news. And to get back to Florence with useful evidence that could shine some light into the black hole in which the investigation was currently lost.

34

Florence

'I'll get her into bed sooner or later!'

Luigi Vinci had just finished admiring the backside of the waitress as she moved away having taken their order, but his thoughts had returned to the policewoman sitting opposite him.

Teresa Micalizi had arrived at the Prosecutor's Department as the place was starting to empty for the lunch hour. She had accepted his invitation, convinced by Vinci's claim that he could only see her during his break.

They were in a restaurant on the Piazza della Signoria, where the Deputy Prosecutor had a regular table booked Monday to Friday for the same time every day. By day it was mainly frequented by white-collar workers who worked in the area: bank employees and directors of insurance providers and building societies, owners of estate agencies and also a few judicial staff, given how close it was to the Prosecutor's Department and the tribunal offices at the Piazza San Firenze. In the evenings it was taken over by tourists. Huge T-bone steaks were displayed in the window like precious merchandise to entice the customers inside.

Sitting at one of the best tables, they began to discuss the case, but they stopped when the waitress returned with their dishes. A salad and a slice of beef with rocket and Grana Padano each and a carafe of house red. The woman asked whether they needed anything else, then moved away to serve other customers when they said no.

They picked up their knives and forks and leaned over their plates as they began to cut up the meat. There were a few moments of silence, interrupted only by the rattling of their cutlery and the bustle of the restaurant around them.

Sitting at the table opposite were a man and a woman, perhaps husband and wife. They had finished eating and he was reading the paper. Displaying amazingly white teeth, the woman exchanged a smile with Teresa when their eyes met for a moment then looked down as if she'd been recognised, but although Teresa returned her smile, she didn't recognise the woman's face.

'I've been told that Ascalchi's gone to Sardinia to question the security guard. Is there any news?' Vinci began once he'd finished chewing, turning the conversation back to work.

'Not yet. We're waiting to hear from him.'

'Let me know when you do, no matter what time it is. You can even call me at home.'

'Yes, sir.'

'Any other news?'

'We're working on the material that was taken from the Russos' house.'

'Update me from time to time on any developments, and don't take any independent initiatives like your boss does. I'm serious, Micalizi. Everything needs to cross my desk. Understood?'

Teresa nodded.

'Good. I'm sure we'll get along well together.'

They continued eating, then Vinci got back to work. 'Don't let yourself be influenced by those photos Ferrara was talking to me about – that material will be more effort than it's worth in a trial. It's not enough to bring a charge. Besides, who are we supposed to charge? The victim?'

'Not the victim, but the person who killed him, who Russo

was probably blackmailing. It's only a theory . . . ' Teresa took a risk.

'Leave it alone. You need to pay careful attention to questioning the family. Be tactful. Do we understand each other?'

Teresa nodded.

A moment later Vinci indicated to the waitress that they were ready to pay. Then he got up, followed by Teresa, who thanked him.

As she turned to leave, Teresa's gaze met the old woman's. She smiled at her again, while her husband remained immersed in his newspaper, as if he were in the living room at home. The two of them hadn't exchanged a single word the entire time. Perhaps they had already said everything they had to say to one another during their long years of living together. Perhaps theirs was the silence typical of those who find pleasure, and even love, just in being close to one another.

'What are you doing at the weekend, Teresa?' Vinci asked once they were outside.

'I'm going to stay with my mother in Milan and I'm taking my cat, Mimì, with me. I'll be back on Sunday evening.'

She wanted to add something more, but she held back. It wasn't appropriate to share confidences with a deputy prosecutor you were working on a case with.

But Vinci was pleased. She'd told him something personal. Perhaps he'd be able to get her into bed earlier than he'd expected. Married to a thirty-year-old woman, he'd watched her become as round as a barrel after their second child and he no longer felt any physical attraction towards her. Nothing. When he fucked her now it was almost always a case of conjugal rights, but he had to let his imagination wander in order to manage it. And of late, it had often been Teresa he'd been imagining in his arms.

Still using her first name, as they said goodbye he told her, 'I like it when you do that, Teresa.'

'What?'

'When you run your hand through your hair to tidy your fringe.'

Teresa blushed.

Then she shook his hand and walked away down the Via dei Calzaiuoli on her way back to Headquarters.

During the short walk back to his office, Vinci thought about the little list of things he aspired to and constantly daydreamed about: a second house up in the mountains, perhaps at Cortina, a fast, luxury car, a few adolescent lovers . . . Just like his boss – his role model as a man and as a prosecutor.

But first on the list would be Teresa Micalizi. It was a wager he'd made with himself.

35

3 p.m., Santa Trinita Basilica

The driver left Rizzo by the Colonna della Giustizia, the tallest and most beautiful of the city's columns, sculpted in precious granite.

There was nobody in front of the church of Santa Trinita and the police officer was surprised. He had imagined that lots of people would attend the Russos' funeral.

Piero Franceschini had carried out the autopsy on the body of Elisa Rotondi that morning. It was a fairly swift process. The bullets had been retrieved during the surgical procedures and there was absolutely no doubt as to the cause of death. In contrast with her husband, she had enjoyed excellent health and would have lived a long life had she not been murdered.

Rizzo entered the church and was struck by the scent of incense floating in the air and the solemn music coming from the organ. He proceeded along the right-hand aisle, looking around discreetly.

It was not unknown for a killer to attend his victim's funeral. Sometimes they had even left a bunch of flowers or signed the book of condolences, and that was the reason Rizzo was memorising the faces of the attendees and trying to interpret their expressions.

Then the priest, a plump, youngish man, stepped up to start the funeral service.

There were about fifty or so people in the pews. Noticeably few. Rizzo asked himself why. There were only four lawyers present, easily distinguishable by the black robes they had worn as a mark of respect for their colleague.

Donato Russo was sitting in the front row. He was wearing a dark grey suit and a black tie and hiding his grief behind a large pair of dark glasses. His daughter sat next to him and the family resemblance was obvious. Although she had inherited her father's height, the girl seemed quite delicate. She had a similar profile to his and the same colour eyes and, at that moment, the same expression of suffering. To the other side of him was his uncle, the victim's brother, with his wife and two children. He seemed distraught and he looked exhausted. Corti and his wife Rosanna sat in the second row. Behind them were the president of the Tribunal and the president of the Court of Appeal. But many seats had remained empty. There were also a few elderly ladies, who stood apart from the rest. Perhaps they were regular visitors to the church.

The priest, with his beautiful voice, gave the impression of wanting to get the mass over in a hurry, perhaps due to other commitments.

Only Antonello Corti went up to the lectern to remember his friend Amedeo and his wife. He made a brief but incisive speech. After talking about his partner's noble human qualities and great professional abilities, he asked his colleagues in attendance to uphold justice on its journey to identify the perpetrator or perpetrators of the murder and to arrive at the truth.

'I won't give up until the truth is brought to light,' he concluded.

Then they raised their voices, but only the women made the effort to sing. At last, it was time for the Eucharist.

Once the mass was over, the organ struck up its litany once

more as the mourners filed up to the coffins to say their final goodbyes.

Rizzo moved away towards the exit and after a while his gaze fell upon a man who was standing slightly apart. Short and wearing a dark-coloured hat, he had taken up position by one of the slender rectangular pillars that separated the three naves. Presumably he had arrived late. Rizzo didn't recognise him, yet his face seemed familiar. A gesture the man was making caught his attention, though: he was making the sign of the cross upside down, starting from the bottom.

The police officer waited a little longer before going outside. He wanted to observe that guy more closely.

Once the coffins had been carried out on the shoulders of the undertaker's staff, people started to leave the church a few at a time and in absolute silence, because there's nothing like death to prevent conversation. Rizzo mingled with the flow of people.

Then he saw Corti and went over to him.

'Catch these killers! His relatives and we, his friends, want justice,' the lawyer told him as soon as he reached him.

'We're doing everything we can.'

'But this isn't where you should be looking for them. Tell your chief that,' replied the other man with a look of disgust.

'Ferrara knows what he's doing,' Rizzo replied, and he moved several feet away as the bells began to toll dully. Corti continued babbling incomprehensible words. As soon as the policeman saw him move away, he looked towards the façade of the basilica, but the man who had roused his curiosity was no longer there. He waited a few moments, then he went back into the church. He walked along the central aisle, looking left and right, but he didn't see even the shadow of the unknown man. Finally he went outside and took a walk around the piazza and the adjacent streets. Nothing. The man had disappeared among the tourists. He tried one more time along the nearby Lungarno. Nothing there, either.

He decided to go back to the office, the inverted sign of the cross still in his head.

Back at the church, only the Russos' immediate family had climbed into the cars that made up the cortège. They were now following the funeral director's luxurious Mercedes towards the Trespiano Cemetery on the Via Bolognese, almost at the border between Florence and Fiesole.

Soon no one would speak of Amedeo and Elisa Russo any more, because death makes us all equals.

36

6.59 p.m., the Chief Superintendent's office

Gianni Ascalchi knocked on the door of Ferrara's office. He'd arrived at Florence's Peretola Airport on the 17.25 flight from Olbia with Ricci and Italo Ortu.

'Make yourself at home, Gianni.'

'Thanks, chief.'

Rizzo had just left the room after updating Ferrara on the funeral. He had also told him about the presence of the man in the hat who'd made the unconventional sign of the cross: he'd thought about it at length, and in the end he might have managed to identify the man's face: it could have been Cosimo Presti, the journalist.

'Right then, Gianni, any interesting news? You only hinted on the phone, but now tell me everything,' Ferrara encouraged him, impatient to know the details.

'We might have our first real clue,' replied Ascalchi, with a slight smile on his lips that changed his face completely. Then he took a seat on one of the two black chairs. He was visibly tired, but there was a spark in his eyes as he told Ferrara everything that had happened, with a precision that seemed almost obsessive at times. When he'd finished, he handed the statement to the Chief Superintendent.

Ferrara read it several times, shaking his head. He paid special attention to the words the witness had heard: 'You didn't want to tell us ... you piece of shit. Even after we threatened your ... '

'It's something,' he commented.

Perhaps that information would allow them to reconstruct the attackers' *modus operandi*. At any rate, even from those snippets of sentences, it was possible to deduce that the killers – two, as they'd surmised – were Italian and they wanted something very specific from the lawyer, Russo, who they called a 'piece of shit'.

So, had they shot the wife before they killed the husband? It seemed that way from the account. And, in that case, had they done it to make the lawyer understand that they were serious?

Provided Ortu had told the truth, it was a plausible reconstruction supported by objective facts. What was more, those words were almost identical to the ones spoken by Daniele De Robertis, suggesting there might be a link to the secrets Russo had been keeping right up until his death.

Then Ferrara was struck by a thought. They needed to consider the possibility that Ortu was an accomplice and that this was the real reason he hadn't raised the alarm during the attack or once the two men had gone away. Perhaps Ortu had been selective in what he'd told them, Ferrara reflected.

'Do you want to question him, chief?' Ascalchi asked, breaking the silence and the flow of Ferrara's thoughts.

'One moment, Gianni.'

Ferrara wanted to think a while longer. 'No,' he replied.

'No? But I brought him here. He's in the waiting room at the end of the corridor.'

'On his own?'

'Ricci's with him. What should I do?'

'Talk to him a bit more. We need to determine whether he's involved. Monitor his phone calls and see if you can find out his plans for the next few days – whether he's going back to Sardinia or intending to stay in Florence.'

'A phone tap.'

'Exactly. And we'll get hold of his telephone records, too.'

'Can I send him on his way, then?'

'Not yet. First get him to do an identikit of the two men, even a rough drawing. At least then we'll have justified the cost of bringing him back from Sardinia.'

'OK.'

'Prepare the request for the phone tap as a matter of urgency, and attach the statement you took in Sardinia and your report. The phone calls could tell us something interesting. If we manage to plant some kind of bug, perhaps in his car, that would be even better. Give the documents to Teresa when everything's ready.'

'To Teresa?'

'Yes. She'll take them to Vinci. I've made her our official liaison with the Prosecutor's Department for this case.'

Ascalchi frowned. He would have liked to go and see the Deputy Prosecutor himself, but he didn't complain. Orders weren't up for discussion. He guessed that this must be a part of some strategy. 'OK, chief,' he replied.

'Ah, Gianni, one more thing.'

Ascalchi was moving towards the door, but he stopped and turned. 'Yes?'

'Set up a team to tail him and observe his every move, at least for the first twenty-four hours. And pay a visit to the ex-wife. You might learn something about Ortu's friends and habits from her.'

'So we're going to tail him until his phones are tapped?'

'Exactly! But don't get carried away. It may be that he's telling the truth and he's got nothing to do with this, that he really was just scared.'

Alone again, Ferrara arranged the letters on his desk then closed his office door behind him as he set off home, convinced that the Prosecutor's Department wouldn't be able to

refuse them authorisation this time. This wasn't some anonymous tip-off, they needed to clarify information supplied by an
eyewitness, and this was the quickest way to do it. It would also
be in the interests of Italo Ortu himself, whose part in events
needed to be confirmed.

That was why Ferrara had decided not to question him personally. He would confront him, if necessary, after they'd carried
out these checks on him and had the results of the phone taps.

The artist from Forensics worked on the task for almost two
hours. Young and fortified by great patience, he had done
sketches that were immediately erased, drafted new lines and
then, faced with Italo Ortu's perplexity, suggested other ones. He
didn't want to give up.

In spite of giving the impression of wanting to make an effort,
the witness was struggling to provide a reliable description of the
two attackers. His memory of the two men was, for the most
part, blurry.

The technician put four drawings, all of them incomplete, in
front of him. None of them had defining characteristics. The
lines were imprecise, and so were the faces. Only the height and
build were clearly defined. He asked him which one resembled
the two criminals most closely.

Ortu leaned in close, concentrating, then shook his head and
replied, 'None of them.'

Just for the sake of being thorough, Ascalchi eventually came
up with a different approach. He showed Ortu mugshots of
some known Italian criminals, specialists in break-ins. He hadn't
done it earlier because he didn't want to influence the description
for the drawing.

Once again, the result was negative.

Then he showed him Daniele De Robertis's mugshot, but the
witness excluded it.

'He looks about the same height as the man I saw, but his

build is completely wrong. He was much stockier,' he explained.

'But you said they were wearing heavy jackets!'

'Yes, but I had the impression that he was bulky because he was well-built, not because of the heavy jacket.'

At that point the police officer decided to give up.

'Sleep on it. Perhaps you'll be able to remember the faces more clearly when your mind's fresh. If that's the case, let me know,' he added.

'I'll try.'

'You can go now. I'll arrange for a car to drop you off.'

'Thank you. And I beg you, please don't make me lose my job,' Ortu murmured in his ear, leaning close.

'Don't worry!' the police officer reassured him. He thought he saw genuine gratitude in the other man's eyes.

37

9.12 p.m., Michele Ferrara's home

It was Petra's birthday. She and her husband celebrated at home – just the two of them. They would happily have gone to Da Giovanni, their favourite restaurant on the Via del Moro, but the Chief Superintendent's work had prevented it, so Petra had set about preparing a dinner of tagliolini pasta in a wild boar sauce followed by roast lamb with artichokes. For his part, Ferrara had stopped by Caffè Gilli on his way home to buy a mimosa cake, like the ones eaten on International Women's Day. They made a toast with glasses of sparkling Ferrari wine.

A day like any other, if it hadn't been for the cake and the sparkling wine. And the envelope that he handed her afterwards.

'This is my present,' he told her.

She opened it. There were two undated aeroplane tickets, destination: St Kitts and Nevis, two islands in the Lesser Antilles in the Caribbean. She'd dreamed of visiting them for a long time, attracted by the crystal waters and the amazingly white beaches. And, most of all, by their distance from Florence. But she'd stopped hoping by this point.

'How lovely! When shall we go?'

'Soon. The weather's nice there all year round. It's always hot.

And this Sunday, we'll go to Da Giovanni,' he promised her. Petra didn't reply; she was too accustomed to missing out on their annual celebrations due to his damned work.

After dinner, he opened the sliding door on to the terrace and lit a cigar. He puffed on it several times, letting the smoke out of the crack he'd opened. Then he sat down at his desk with a glass containing two fingers of Slyrs. A gift from his German friend Karlheinz, this was the whisky he drank with his Antico Toscano from time to time. It was an extraordinary pairing in his opinion. Like red wine and a cigar.

It was one of the times of day he loved most. Free from the constant ringing of the telephone. No meetings to run off to. No commotion in the corridors with officers hurrying in and out with the day's detainees and convicts. Shouting. Swearing. Orders.

None of that.

In his mind he dived back into the case and started making notes on the key information they'd gathered so far. It was a technique he used when he needed to deal with the most complex cases. He would jot everything down on printer paper and then, over time, he'd add more and more detail until he'd drawn up a convincing portrait. An excellent way to keep all the clues in front of you and assemble and reassemble the investigation, piece by piece.

Russo Double Murder:

Date: Monday 18 October, between two and four in the morning.

Victims: Amedeo Russo, 57, and his wife Elisa Rotondi, 52.

He was hit on the back of a head with a blunt object with no corners or edges and drowned in the swimming pool.

She was seriously injured by two shots from a 7.65 calibre pistol. Shot sequence: the first hit her chest, the second hit her head from close range.

At the time of the attack she was in her bedroom watching television.

She died in hospital during her third surgical procedure on the morning of Tuesday 19 October.

Clues and useful information:

Metal fence cut with a suitable tool (not found at the scene).

Shoe prints on the ground in the garden near the swimming pool, trainers, size 8 and 9 ½.

No sign of a break-in via either the front door or the windows. The door was found ajar by Antonello Corti, who discovered the body.

Album with nine 7 × 5 colour photographs. Five show murdered women. Prostitutes.The other four appear to depict the celebration of a satanic rite. The photos feature eight hooded men in dark robes. They are around an altar on which a young, dark-skinned woman lies naked. She's stretched out, lying on her back, her legs are apart and her arms stretched up above her head (her hands and ankles are tied, perhaps with thick cord). A crucifix with an inverted Christ protrudes from her vagina.

One of the men is waving a crucifix with a headless Christ in the air. Another has a dagger or knife with a snake-shaped handle. In the next photo the same hooded man drinks from a chalice and there are several vivid red marks on the young woman's body. Blood? A SATANIC PRACTICE INVOLVING HUMAN SACRIFICE?

Motive:

Amedeo Russo may have had secrets.

Was there a dark side to his life?

Or might he have been a blackmailer?

Two sources:

1 The prisoner officer at the prison in Pisa, who heard Daniele De Robertis say to Russo: 'It's time to share your secrets.'

2 The security guard Italo Ortu, who heard one of the two killers say the following phrases in Italian with no noticeable dialect or accent: 'You didn't want to tell us . . . you piece of shit. Even after we threatened your . . . '

Suspects:

Two men wearing size 8 and size 9½ shoes.

One tall and stocky.

The other shorter (around five foot six, according to Ortu, the eyewitness).

Probably professionals.

May be acquaintances, allowed to enter the home of Amedeo Russo.

However, neither of the two seems to be Daniele De Robertis (negative response from Ortu when shown De Robertis's photo), unless the witness was misled by the heavy jacket the killer was wearing. The height, at least, seemed to be a match.

Ferrara re-read his notes, highlighting certain passages in yellow:

It's time to share your secrets.

You didn't want to tell us . . . you piece of shit. Even after we threatened your . . .

He would have liked to break those phrases into tiny pieces and look at them under a microscope. Perhaps then he'd be able to discover the true motive.

He thought some more and told himself that these expressions, coming from different sources and gathered at different points in time, definitely changed things. However thick the cloak enveloping the case might be, there had to be a tiny opening that would serve as a starting point.

The motive of the 'secrets' might be their best hope. If they could only catch him, surely Daniele De Robertis would be able to provide important information.

Ferrara highlighted the fugitive's name as well.

He sat thinking for a long time, asking himself whether the double murder could be linked to those of Sergi and the IT expert Fabio Biondi.

Then he took the holy picture of Saint Michael the Archangel out of his diary. It had been blessed and he'd been given it by a priest during a visit he and Petra had paid to the little church near the Duomo. He'd always carried it with him from that moment on, almost as if he wanted to protect himself from the evil with which his work brought him into contact.

The saint was depicted in armour, a sword in his right hand as he pinned the devil to the ground with his foot. Ferrara started to read the prayer written on the other side of the card:

O glorious Archangel St Michael, Prince of the heavenly host, defend us in battle, and in the struggle which is ours against the principalities and Powers, against the rulers of this world of darkness, against spirits of evil in high places. Fight this day the battle of the Lord, together with the holy angels, as already thou hast fought the leader of the proud angels, Lucifer, and his apostate host . . .

He put the holy picture back in his diary and drank a sip of Slyrs. Then he lit a new cigar. He got up and looked outside once he reached the sliding door. Then he began to walk up and down the living room, glancing at the grandfather clock from time to time. He was tired, but he wanted to think a bit more to try and clarify his thoughts.

It now seemed highly unlikely that the killers were members of an Eastern European gang and they needed to discard this line of inquiry definitively or it would mislead them. Instead, they had to concentrate on Florence's secret world once more, on those VIPs who, according to a journalist's informant, took part in black masses to keep boredom at bay. It was almost a trend; he had also read about it in an important national daily. Silvia De Luca, the expert on the esoteric, had told him about it, too. They were unsavoury individuals, well-known personalities and members of the haute bourgeoisie, and politicians with extremely singular tastes.

There is a moment when an investigator's intuition starts to become so strong that it turns into conviction, especially when they manage to identify a motive that, although mere theory as yet, nevertheless represents a good starting point for further inquiries.

This was one of those moments.

He was still mulling over his decision when the ringing of the telephone brought him back to reality. He went to answer it, thinking it would be someone wanting to wish his wife a happy birthday. The caller ID display showed the central line at Headquarters. The grandfather clock read 10.55 p.m.

He lifted the receiver, hoping that they weren't about to tell him about another crime.

*

'Hello?'

'Good evening Chief Superintendent, I'm sorry to disturb you at this hour ...'

'Has someone died?'

'I've got someone on the line who's insisting on speaking to you, sir. What shall I do? Should I put them through?'

'Who is it?'

'He didn't want to tell me, but I understand that he's one of your informers.'

'Put him through,' Ferrara replied, asking himself who it could be at that hour. Yes, he did have informers, but they'd never disturbed him so late at night in the peace of his own home. It must be something really important.

'Chief Superintendent Ferrara?'

'Yes, speaking.'

But the voice didn't say anything.

'Chief Superintendent, Genius has nothing to do with this business with the lawyer, Russo. Leave him alone because he wants to help you. It would save you time and energy.'

The voice was calm, as if discussing the weather forecast, but it seemed slightly artificial to Ferrara. He strained his ears, trying to make out some background noise, to hear the timbre of the voice better. 'Who are you?'

'A friend.'

'A friend? Whose friend?'

Silence.

'Hello? Hello? Are you still there? Say something!'

He'd hung up.

Ferrara stood motionless for a while with the receiver in his hand, then he slammed it down. A moment later he dialled the number for the central line. He wanted to trace the phone from which the call had been made, even though he knew that in all likelihood the man would have used a public phone box or a 'dirty' phone and they wouldn't learn anything. Of course he wouldn't have been stupid enough to use a traceable number that could lead back to him.

After speaking with Headquarters, Ferrara concentrated on the content of the phone call. It hadn't sounded like Genius's voice to him. In fact he'd been struck by a slight southern accent.

Had it been the other fugitive?

De Robertis probably suspected that the police had linked the murder of the Russos with the visit he'd received in prison.

But why had he made him call? Was it true that Genius had nothing to do with the murder, or was it merely an attempt to throw them off the scent?

His instinct wasn't any help.

Headquarters rang him back to say that the phone call hadn't been made from Tuscany but, given the hour, he'd have to wait until the next morning for details of the exact location and phone. The technician from the phone company would not be prepared to go to the office and work overtime without an injunction proving judicial authorisation.

Ferrara went back over to the sliding door and looked outside again. The sky was completely dark. There were no stars and not even a sliver of moon.

It was entirely black. Like his spirit.

He went to bed with the words of the unknown caller buzzing in his head: 'Chief Superintendent, Genius has nothing to do with this business with the lawyer, Russo. Leave him alone because he wants to help you. It would save you time and energy.'

Before he gave in to sleep, he thought again about the need to delve into the occult. A thought that brought Father Giulio Torre's name to mind.

He would call him tomorrow and arrange to meet.

He needed to hurry up and give absolute priority to this case, shelving all other investigations for the moment. The staff of the *Squadra Mobile* was being steadily reduced in size by the transfer of officers who weren't replaced by new arrivals, which meant it was impossible to pay the same attention to all their open cases. Now they had to give priority to certain cases to the detriment of others.

Unfortunately that was the way things were. And he couldn't change matters.

38

Night, Headquarters

Shut up in his office, Rizzo was busy going through the files on the prostitute murders from the nineties.

There had been five such murders in all, committed between 1992 and 1997. The archivist had brought up the relevant files, which contained records of everything: the Forensics team's analysis; details of the pathologist's findings at the crime scene; the autopsy report; and the investigation reports. All five cases remained unsolved.

And now it was almost midnight and his eyes were staring at the pictures taken by the photographer from Forensics following the discovery of the body of Rita Perfetti, aged thirty-four, killed in December 1995. These documented the surroundings and the position of the body, exactly as it had been found by the first police patrol on the scene.

The murder had taken place in an apartment on the first floor of a building in the historic city centre. Most of the building's occupants were young Italian and foreign students, who paid a low monthly rent, always cash in hand.

The body was found on the bedroom floor. It was almost completely naked, lying with the head turned to one side and the legs spread wide apart. She was wearing nothing but a light-coloured

T-shirt, which was pushed up almost to her armpits. Several stab wounds were clearly visible. The receiver of a landline telephone was visible beside the body.

'Perhaps she tried to summon help,' Rizzo said to himself, pondering this last detail. If his theory was correct, there must have been a time lapse, albeit brief, between the attack and death. Perhaps the woman had sensed she was about to be attacked. Or perhaps, after she'd been wounded, she'd managed to pick up the receiver to call for help.

The photos spoke for themselves. They detailed the position of that disfigured body. They told of the horrific wounds, the massive loss of blood. It had been an attack of unusual brutality. Whoever inflicted those wounds must have been driven by an incredible hatred of the victim.

Rizzo concentrated on the other details in the photograph and after a while he had a sudden flash of inspiration.

He took a deep breath and got up to open the window. He needed some air. After a couple of minutes he went back to his desk.

He studied the photo from Russo's album. It had struck him that some of the details were missing: the presence of the telephone and the big puddle of blood around the head, for starters. But what had really caught his attention was the T-shirt. In the photo taken by Forensics it had been pushed up to the victim's armpits; in Russo's photo it hadn't. And nowhere in the official file was there a close-up of the victim's face.

The death portrait.

The photos in Russo's album must have been taken by the killer, or by someone who was present and witnessed the crime. An accomplice. The woman had been photographed before she died, before she'd summoned her last reserves of strength to reach out for the telephone in an effort to call for help. The T-shirt must have been pushed up as she dragged herself towards the receiver.

'There's no way Russo's photos could have come from official files,' he murmured to himself.

Then he moved on to the reports on the investigations. From these he learned that Rita Perfetti was a prostitute with a fixed clientele. She hadn't had a pimp, at least not in the last few years, and hadn't been in any relationships at the time. These were all confidences shared with the police by a close friend of the victim.

From the final report he learned that the killer, who remained unknown, was suspected of having carried out a similar crime in an apartment on the Via Nazionale in 1992. There were a number of similarities. And the victim in that case had also been a prostitute.

He pulled another file towards him, determined to stay up till the small hours.

39

It was the morning of Sunday 23 February 1992.

A woman's trembling voice had called 113 to report that her neighbour had died in an apartment on the Via Nazionale, right in the city centre, just a short walk from Santa Maria Novella railway station.

She had been murdered.

The victim, Antonella Corvaglia, a thirty-eight-year-old Tuscan, was a prostitute. She was well known in the area; she loitered on the corners of the alleys around the station, picking up clients who she would then take back to her ground-floor apartment.

Rizzo took his time studying the initial report and the file with the printouts of the photographs taken when the police first arrived on the scene.

The body was on its back and half hidden by a sheet. There were deep knife wounds to the neck, which had caused a large puddle of blood on the floor. Once the sheet had been removed, it was possible to see that the body was completely naked, legs akimbo and with outstretched arms. The victim wasn't wearing underwear. She had suffered numerous stab wounds – at least thirty-five – with the fatal wounds concentrated around her neck.

Rizzo saw that there were indeed striking similarities between the murders of Rita Perfetti and Antonella Corvaglia. Not only had the victims both been prostitutes, but they'd been killed in the same way: both had been found in the privacy of their own bedrooms, naked, their genitals exposed, their legs apart and their arms outstretched; they had died as the result of stab wounds, most of which were delivered to the neck.

The underwear they had been wearing had not been found at the crime scenes and it was possible it had been taken as a form of trophy by the killer.

He turned to Amedeo Russo's album. And gave another start.

In this picture the victim had been captured completely naked and not half-covered by the sheet. Again the photo wasn't a perfect match with the official version. There was something different, something that gave him pause for thought. Something that was missing from the Forensics file.

It was the blood, which was spurting from the carotid artery. The photo must have been taken when the woman's heart was still beating and she was still alive.

Only the killer, or his accomplice, would have been able to capture that shot. Just as in the case of Rita Perfetti.

'Fuck! The camera!' he thought. During the search of the Russos' house, they hadn't checked to see if there was one on the premises.

He closed the file, slipped the album into his desk drawer and went home, tired and with his thoughts whirling non-stop.

In the darkness of his bedroom during the few hours that remained of the night, Rizzo kept seeing those images before him. He closed and opened his eyes several times to get rid of them, but in vain. Most of all it was the picture of Antonella Corvaglia that preyed on his mind. As he lay in his bed he could see the blood flow out of her throat with every beat of her heart and her pulse grow weaker and weaker as her body gradually gave up. During that brief time frame, a matter of a few seconds, the photographer had taken the photo.

But had it been the only one?

PART FOUR

A SMALL STEP FORWARD

40

London

The passengers felt the wheels vibrating as the plane touched down.

After a few seconds the captain's voice announced that they had landed at Heathrow Airport and that they'd arrived at 7.40 p.m.: exactly on time.

Richard Wilson was among the passengers.

He had left New York at eight in the morning, travelling business class. They'd summoned him for an urgent meeting without any indication why. All he knew was that it must be something drastic, because he'd only arrived in New York from Europe twenty-four hours earlier. After spending the entire flight puzzling over it, he was sure that he had done everything to the best of his abilities and that there wouldn't be any problems – at least, not for him. But then why this summons?

He was the first to disembark when the aircraft door opened. He stamped his feet a couple of times to restore the circulation in his legs, something he always did, then set off confidently towards the terminal.

He was wearing an elegant grey Armani suit, which fitted in very well with his image as a businessman. In his hand he carried a soft, black leather briefcase, his only luggage. Nearing forty, he had finely sculpted, almost aristocratic, bone structure. His blue eyes stood out in his tanned face and his wavy chestnut hair was combed back with a small amount of gel.

His expression betrayed no concern.

He was among the first in line for passport control. After they had checked his stamps and scanned his passport, he went through the metal detector then followed the green route at Customs. He had nothing to declare.

When he emerged into the Arrivals area of Terminal 1, a tall, elegant man studied him with pale eyes that seemed to shine. He made a call from his mobile. A short one.

Richard Wilson walked on, passing through the automatic doors and exiting the airport building. It had taken him less than half an hour to complete a procedure that had been known to take hours.

Outside, he was welcomed by a cool breeze as he scanned the line of waiting cars for the Jaguar that was to collect him. He saw it and went over. The windows were tinted and the young driver was wearing a spotless uniform. The rear door clicked open and Richard Wilson climbed in. The driver started the engine, placed his gloved hands on the steering wheel and drove off. He took the B470, a local road that led to the village of Cranford. He would then take the A4 to London.

Richard Wilson looked at his watch. He had time to spare. He took a mobile phone out of his briefcase and made a call. He heard it ring one, two, three times, then it went to voicemail. He left a message, explaining that he was making perfect time. As he replaced the mobile phone, a slight smile appeared on his face. But that smile died on his lips a moment later.

The car had pulled over at the side of the road without him noticing. He didn't have time to wonder why. In the same moment he sensed that something wasn't right, he received confirmation that his end was very near, just as his path as a powerful man was a single step away from an unimaginable ending. But life was strange and nobody knew this better than him.

The young man behind the wheel had turned round and was looking at him. He was holding a pistol with a silencer. With a steady hand he fired two shots at point-blank range.

Accurate ones.

Richard Wilson collapsed on the seat.

A wound had opened in the middle of his forehead and blood was dripping from it. His eyes, still wide open, were turned upwards toward the car's ceiling.

The wealthy investor with apparently infinite financial resources, in reality a high-profile drug trafficker and member of the secret lodge of the Black Rose, had died. He had gone back to hell, from whence he seemed to have arrived in order to spread death.

And his body would be difficult to find.

The car set off again at normal speed, while the silence was broken by the roar of an aeroplane taking off.

A meeting had taken place a little over twenty-four hours earlier in an eighteenth-century suite at the Russell Hotel in London, close to the financial district. The only person absent was Richard Wilson, who had been in Italy to resolve some delicate issues.

Sitting in comfortable leather armchairs, they had begun by running through the usual agenda, discussing the world's financial markets and adjusting their investment strategy. Then, prompted by recent events in Tuscany, the discussion had moved on to other topics. Unmentionable ones. In the end, they had agreed upon a new plan of action, to be implemented with immediate effect. The first step: to eliminate Richard Wilson.

The initiate had failed and was no longer considered trustworthy. Far from protecting the secrecy of the lodge, his actions had endangered it. It was to prove a fatal mistake on his part.

41

9 a.m., Wednesday 21 October, Headquarters

Donato Russo was in the *Squadra Mobile*'s waiting room, pacing back and forth across the floor, stopping in front of the window from time to time to glance outside. He couldn't wait to be summoned.

After a stressful ten minutes, an officer accompanied him to Teresa's office. The interview with Renato Russo, Amedeo's brother, had already been underway for fifteen minutes in Rizzo's office.

Donato recognised the policewoman behind the desk as soon as he entered the room. Just as he recognised the second police-woman, who was sitting in front of a computer alongside her: she was the officer who'd tried to stop him outside the hospital room where his mother lay.

'Please, make yourself comfortable,' Teresa told him, gestur-ing him to a chair and getting up to shake his hand. He shook it and sat down.

'Could you tell me the reason for this summons?' he demanded, unable to keep the note of anxiety out of his voice.

'It's routine,' the policewoman replied.

'Routine? What routine? It was the funeral yesterday! My

parents are dead. They were murdered! Why don't you leave me in peace? I'm a victim, too.'

'We wish we could, but we need to find those responsible. You want them found, don't you?'

He nodded.

'Listen,' Teresa continued, 'we need to ask you a few questions and your answers could help us direct the path of our investigation.'

'Go on, then,' he told her.

'Let's start with you. If I'm not mistaken, you're a lawyer like your father, is that correct?'

It was the standard opening for an interview and an attempt to put the person being questioned at ease.

Donato Russo informed her that he was thirty-seven years old and a widower. Officer Belli started to tap at the keyboard.

'Any children?'

'One: Flavia. She's sixteen.'

Russo explained that he worked as a lawyer in his father and Corti's firm, and he lived in his parents' old house on the Via dei Mille, which he had had remodelled.

'Now get to the point,' he added confidently, shifting in his seat. 'I haven't got time to lose. I need to go to the cemetery at Trespiano to oversee my parents' interment in the family tomb.

'We'd like to know if there's anyone you suspect.'

'Absolutely not. It must have been those foreign criminals. The Prosecutor said the same thing at his press conference. Scum like that come to Italy knowing they can get away with murder. If they committed a crime like that in their own countries, they'd spend the rest of their lives rotting in prison. Here, you can't even catch them.'

'Could you tell us whether your father had any problems at work. Were there any difficult clients, for example?'

'What are you trying to suggest? My father was well loved and respected by everyone – clients and colleagues alike.'

'Did he have any enemies? Can you recall any incidents that might help us?'

'You're on the wrong track completely!' His tone was glacial now. 'You won't get anywhere if this is the approach you're taking, you'll draw a complete blank. There have been no such incidents, either in the recent past or further back.'

'If I keep asking questions, it's because we want to discover the truth. We want to catch those responsible and, please believe me, we'll do everything in our power to put them away for a very long time.'

'I believe you, but you're going about it the wrong way. And you won't catch those killers by observing the mourners at the funeral. I saw your colleague at the church yesterday—'

'And what conclusions have you reached?'

'I've just told you: it was those foreigners who've been carrying out all the robberies. They'll be Eastern Europeans, like the press and the Prosecutor say.' He stopped, his throat dry. 'Could I have some water, please?'

Officer Belli got up and took a bottle of water from a side table. She filled a plastic cup and handed it to him. Then she returned to her seat, ready to start typing again.

After he had drunk the water, Russo took a deep breath. Staring the policewoman in the eyes, he said, 'My family have no skeletons in the closet.'

No skeletons in the closet! Teresa didn't believe it for a moment. Everyone has a dark side that they keep to themselves and don't share with anyone, not even those they love.

'One last thing . . . ' she said, drawing the interview to a close, having realised that she wasn't going to learn anything useful.

The man glared at her while, apparently oblivious to his impatience, she explained that they needed to complete an inventory of the items in the house in order to ascertain whether the killers had taken anything away. She concluded by asking whether he would be available to accompany her.

'Certainly. I know my parents' house very well. I used to go there almost every day when I wasn't in Rome. If anything's missing, I'll know.'

'Good. So, what do you say to meeting there later on?'

'After two. I have some things to do before then.'

'All right. Let's say half past two.'

'I'll be there. By the way, when will you release the house?'

'When it's no longer useful to the investigation. It's a decision that can only be made by the Deputy Prosecutor.'

Teresa got up and saw him out. They were no further forward. Clearly the son had no intention of helping them discover the truth.

'No skeletons in the closet!' was the only sentence that had stuck in the two policewomen's heads.

Shortly afterwards, they went out to get a coffee with Rizzo, who'd been interrogating Renato Russo. He hadn't had anything interesting to say either. The brothers didn't see each other much, only at Christmas. It was as if they lived on opposite sides of the world, not sixty miles apart.

Going for coffee was a ritual that Teresa and Officer Belli repeated several times a day. Their working relationship was turning into a friendship, as often happens with police officers, even those of different ranks.

It was a positive aspect of a difficult job.

The Chief Superintendent was busy when they got back to the office.

'The chief doesn't want to be disturbed,' Fanti told Rizzo and Teresa.

'Who's with him?' asked Rizzo.

'I don't know.'

'How come you don't know?'

'I didn't see them. I was working on the computer.'

Same old Fanti. He'd go to any lengths to keep Ferrara's secrets!

The Chief Superintendent had been talking to Father Torre for several minutes. The priest had studied the phenomenon of Satanism in great depth and had even written books on the subject. When the Chief Superintendent had called him that morning, the priest had set off immediately for Headquarters, realising from Ferrara's tone of voice that it must be urgent.

Ferrara took an envelope from the top drawer of his desk.

'Needless to say this is top secret, Father . . . '

'What do you mean, Chief Superintendent? You know me by now – I'm silent as the grave.'

'I apologise, but you know how it is . . . given the delicacy . . . '

'Don't worry. Tell me what it is that's bothering you.'

Ferrara spread the enlarged photos of the suspected rite side by side on the desk in front of him.

'Take a look at these, Father, and tell me what you think.'

The priest leaned forward and studied them one at a time without touching them, a grimace on his chubby face.

'It's all right to touch them – they're copies,' said Ferrara. 'The originals have been stored as evidence.'

'Thank you.'

Father Torre took his time looking at each image, shaking his head several times. Then he spoke. 'There's no doubt about it, Chief Superintendent. These photos show the celebration of a satanic rite, in all probability a sacrifice, and there are various details that prove it.'

He explained that the crucifix with the headless Christ and the dagger with the snake-shaped handle were particularly important symbols in this context: the sacrifice of a young woman to Satan.

'Along with the five-point star, the inverted cross is one of the most popular symbols in the modern Satanic cult,' he explained. 'It's an expression of the rejection of Christ, Chief Superintendent. As can clearly be seen from the photo, they've removed his head.'

Ferrara had grabbed a piece of A4 paper from the printer and was taking notes.

The priest continued his explanation: 'The crucifix placed in the woman's vagina is a gesture of provocation—'

'What about the knife?' asked Ferrara.

'It's a dagger, Chief Superintendent. And it's in the shape of a snake because it represents Satan, the "ancient serpent" of the Apocalypse. The hooded man is about to stab the young woman, a virgin destined to die. The poor girl!' The priest's face darkened.

She looked young enough to be a minor.

They were silent for several seconds, both deep in thought.

Ferrara imagined that dagger clutched in the right hand that hovered over the girl's chest. She was completely naked because – as Silvia De Luca, the expert on the esoteric had explained to him – for those worshippers she represented the altar, from which her blood flowed, warm and sweet.

'The virgin mustn't die right away. The officiant stabs her repeatedly without killing her. Then he collects the blood in a chalice and drinks it while her heart gradually stops beating. Only afterwards does he kill her in Satan's name,' Father Torre concluded, the tremor in his voice betraying his inner turmoil. He'd been particularly struck by the young victim, who looked as if she came from somewhere outside Europe, one of those girls who are exploited and abused, forced to live clandestine lives by criminals with no scruples. Victims with no names and no one prepared to look for them. Who disappear. For ever.

Father Torre looked at the four photos again, lingering for several seconds over each one. Then he said, 'The number eight is important, too.'

'The number eight?'

'Yes. As you can see, there are eight hooded men, wrapped in dark cloaks as black as night.'

'Why is that important?'

The priest explained that the figure eight was the symbol of infinity, the reflection of the spirit in creation, of the incalculable and the inexpressible. It indicated the unknown that follows God's perfection, symbolised in the Bible by the number seven.

'It's the number that incites us to search for and discover transcendence, Chief Superintendent. And, as it's an even number, it is composed of feminine energy and is passive.'

He stopped for a moment, perhaps to take a breath or perhaps to find a better way of expressing himself, as the sceptical expression that had appeared on Ferrara's face had not escaped him. He went on, 'In other words, Chief Superintendent, it's the number that symbolises death in terms of a journey. Even black, the colour of their cloaks, symbolises death. They wear red ones for rituals concerning love.'

Ferrara nodded. 'Would you like a coffee, Father?' he asked. He needed a moment to think. There was a detail that was buzzing round inside his head, but he couldn't bring it into focus.

'Thank you, I'd love one.'

Ferrara called Fanti. 'Two of your special coffees, please. Make me look good,' he told him.

While he waited, he realised what was tormenting him. Those two words, 'Great Beast', that he'd read in Genius's diary with reference to Sir George Holley.

There was one last question he needed to ask Father Torre.

'This is excellent coffee, Chief Superintendent!'

The priest had drunk the black, cream-free coffee in small sips and now he was drying his full lips on a clean white handkerchief.

'It's a secret recipe, Father,' Ferrara replied, raising his voice so that his words would reach his secretary's office. He was sure Fanti was eavesdropping.

'Do you want to ask me anything else?' said Father Torre, slipping the handkerchief into his pocket. He'd noticed that Ferrara had become thoughtful.

'Yes, there's one last thing.'

'Well, ask away!'

'One of our suspects has been referred to in a killer's diary as the Great Beast. What significance might that epithet have?'

'I take it this is in a magical context?'

'Let's assume so.'

Father Torre explained that in the book of the Apocalypse, Satan is called by that name. 'But it's also the nickname by which the Englishman Aleister Crowley, a controversial figure you've surely heard of, was known. For some, he is the founder of modern occultism. For others, he is a source of inspiration for Satanism.'

Ferrara nodded. The name was familiar. He jotted down a few words and made a mental note to reread everything he'd jotted down in the course his conversation with Silvia De Luca, the researcher into the esoteric. He thought he remembered her mentioning Crowley, too. Why hadn't he thought of it sooner? Then he asked Father Torre whether he knew anything about initiation rites.

The priest thought about it and finally answered in the affirmative. 'Not in Tuscany, though.'

'Where?'

'In the Marche. A brother who is on the front line in the fight against such sects put me in touch with a young girl who'd been a victim of Satanism.'

When she was thirteen, this young girl had been lured in by her teacher, who was the priestess of a sect. She'd manipulated the girl into believing she was the reincarnation of her daughter, who had died shortly beforehand.

'The woman made the girl drink her blood to bind her to her in an irreversible pact – and that's not all.'

Father Torre paused, the Chief Superintendent's eyes fixed on him all the while. Then, when he continued speaking, he explained that the young girl had been raped by several hooded men inside a deconsecrated church.

Hooded men again.

'What happened to this girl?' asked Ferrara.

'She's safe now, under the protection of the brothers.'

'Thank you, Father. I think I'm going to find this information you've given me very useful.'

'Not at all. Please call me whenever you need me. I'm happy to be of assistance. But let me tell you one last thing before I go, Chief Superintendent.'

'What's that?'

'Only the small fish end up in the papers.'

'You mean that the ones pulling the strings never come to light?'

'Precisely. They're important people. Men of power. They can do whatever they want.'

Ferrara got up to shake Father Torre's hand, then he accompanied him to the door.

He was still reflecting on their conversation, the correspondence between black cloaks and death and red cloaks and love, when Fanti appeared at the communicating door.

He stopped on the threshold with an envelope in his hand.

'What is it, Fanti?'

'It's from the Prosecutor's Department, chief,' replied his secretary, waving the envelope in the air. He made as if to leave, but Ferrara called him back.

'Yes, Chief Superintendent?'

'Run a search on this name, please,' he told him, handing him a green Post-it on which he'd written Aleister Crowley's name.

'On the internet?'

'Yes. You need to find out everything about him, visit every site that comes up. And print me a copy of anything interesting you find, but try to avoid duplication to save paper. If I'm not here when you finish, leave the printouts on my desk.'

Fanti nodded and hurried back to his computer.

This mania for savings would soon find them writing things by hand.

Nobody knew how to eke out paper like Fanti. He often argued with the staff in the finance office to get hold of cartridges for the printers and he sometimes even spent money from his own pocket to buy them from the shop near the Piazza San Marco.

While Fanti got busy with his research, Ferrara opened the envelope. It contained a letter from the Chief Prosecutor.

CONFIDENTIAL

To: Chief Superintendent Michele Ferrara
Head of the Florentine *Squadra Mobile*
cc: The Commissioner for Florence

Subject: Request for written explanation

In relation to a complaint received by this office, an explanation is requested of the motive behind the search of the offices of the deceased lawyer, Amedeo Russo, carried out under your own initiative.

As you were aware, you should have arranged for a warrant from a deputy prosecutor and the personal presence of one of my deputies, who could then have requested the attendance of the police.

I consider your actions to be particularly serious given your history of personal initiatives, acted upon without prior agreement from my office, recently causing me to have to reprimand you verbally.

I ask the Commissioner, to whom a copy of this letter is sent for information, to take whatever measures he deems appropriate while awaiting the conclusions of the preliminary investigations relating to the disciplinary proceedings that are already underway.

Yours faithfully,
Signor Luca Fiore
Chief Prosecutor
Florence, 20 October 2004

A complaint had been lodged, but by whom? It must have been Antonello Corti.

The Chief Superintendent left the room, heading for the second floor.

42

This time Ferrara didn't go via the secretary.

He pressed the white button by the office door and went in as soon as the green light came on to indicate that he could enter.

He was greeted by an unstoppable river of words: 'You've really done it this time . . .'

Ferrara tried to reply, but Adinolfi silenced him, shouting, 'I haven't asked you to speak!'

After a rapid movement of his shoulders, as if he wanted to shrug off a weight, he continued, 'You've got yourself into a real mess this time. After all these years of service, you still haven't grasped the fact that you have duties and that you can't just follow your head and trample all over legal procedure . . .' The Commissioner was waving his copy of Luca Fiore's letter as he spoke.

'I'll have to let the Chief of Police know. Do you have any idea of the consequences of this illegal action of yours? You'll have to stand trial for abuse of office at the very least,' he added, more red in the face than ever.

'But, Commissioner, I haven't broken any laws—' Ferrara tried in vain to defend himself. The other man cut him off again.

'Send your explanation to the Prosecutor. I don't want anything to do with this.' He slumped back in his chair, exhausted.

Heaving a sigh, he went on: 'It's a judicial issue to be resolved between you and the Prosecutor. As head of the *Squadra Mobile*, you are answerable to the Prosecutor, not me.'

'I'll take care of it.'

'And there's another thing. In the letter, the Prosecutor asks me to consider the adoption of possible initiatives while we wait for the conclusion of the criminal case. Do you know what that means?'

Ferrara remained silent.

'It means that I should suspend you, or transfer you to a different department, perhaps immigration, so that you can gain some experience in that area.'

'Do what you think best,' snapped Ferrara, and he left the room in a towering rage.

So they were going to make him fight for his dignity, both personal and professional.

For him this was a battle that was not merely righteous, but sacrosanct.

The explanations could wait, just like the response to Dentice's parliamentary question, Ferrara decided.

Having returned to his office, he closed both doors and began rummaging through his papers. In addition to Luca Fiore's letter, his mind was full of the Englishman, Aleister Crowley. That name had triggered a recollection . . .

He soon found confirmation. His memory hadn't let him down.

He spent some time studying the notes he'd written after his meeting with Silvia De Luca. The expert on esotericism had named Crowley, also known as the Great Beast, as one of the most famous occultists in history, an occultist who upheld the idea of the 'just' death of a woman in the course of the celebration of a sex-based rite. Without taking his eyes off the page, he considered the theory that Sir George Holley, another

Englishman, might claim direct descent from Crowley and thus be referred to by the same name in Daniele De Robertis's diary.

But he could also be nothing more than a follower, in thrall to Crowley's ideas, Ferrara reminded himself, trying to come up with a plausible explanation.

Moving the notes aside, he spotted some sheets of paper that Fanti must have placed on his desk while he was upstairs with the Commissioner. They were the results of the research he'd asked him to carry out.

The occultist's real name was Edward Alexander Crowley. He had been born in Warwickshire, the same county as Shakespeare, on 12 October 1875 and died on 1 December 1947. Ferrara was struck by the man's versatility: artist, poet, novelist, mountaineer, social critic, black magician and occultist.

At the age of twenty-three he had become a member of the Hermetic Order of the Golden Dawn and had consequently founded an independent branch called Argenteum Astrum . . .

Ferrara lit a cigar and took a break. His mind was starting to whirl even faster.

After a couple of puffs he continued his reading and discovered that various famous figures from the past had been bewitched by Crowley's persona. Winston Churchill and Adolf Hitler had studied his ideas, and Hitler had gone further, endorsing some of Crowley's propositions. On another of the pages Fanti had printed he read that Crowley's influence on the world of music was also notable.

Sir George Holley could well be one of his followers.

'Fanti!' he called, pausing in his reading.

'Yes, Chief Superintendent? I'm continuing the research, sir. There's still a lot of material.'

'Keep going, but could you make me a coffee first – a double espresso.'

Coffee and a Tuscan cigar. Who knew whether they really

helped with concentration, but that was what he always told himself.

After drinking the coffee in small sips, he continued reading. It seemed that Benito Mussolini had chased Crowley out of Italy because of stories of his perversion. This was back in the twenties, after the Englishman had founded an abbey in a villa in Cefalù, near Palermo. He'd named it *Thelema* (the Greek word for 'Desire' or 'Intention'), and his black magic practices there had become legendary. Apparently the Englishman had chosen to build a lighthouse in the same place, to illuminate humanity.

'A dangerous madman – in my own Sicily!' Ferrara thought to himself as he read the final lines of Crowley's biography. His last words, before falling into a coma and dying on 1 December 1947, had been: 'I am perplexed.' He had died wearing a talisman made of parchment impregnated with menstrual blood.

Perplexed?

Ferrara put the papers in his desk drawer and kept on thinking.

Now he needed to decide what to do.

43

Yorkshire, England

The bells of the nearby church chimed two in the afternoon.

A metallic grey Bentley drove through the gates to the castle and stopped in front of the huge door. The driver got out of the car. He was tall and solidly built, like a block of marble, and wore an impeccably cut dark blue wool suit. He had crew-cut grey hair and wore sunglasses.

He went over to the entrance and tugged on the bell pull with the self-assured air of someone visiting an old friend. On the ring finger of his outstretched hand, something glimmered in the sunlight. It was a ruby in a gold setting with a stylised rose engraved on the stone.

The large door slowly opened and the butler, a tall, thin man in classic black livery with white gloves, immediately withdrew at the sight of the ring, averting his gaze with a murmur of respect.

'My master is in the library, waiting for you,' he said, turning to lead the way. The guest followed, turning his gaze to the walls of the long corridor to admire the familiar works of art, which included a Picasso worth several million pounds. He was an art aficionado and visited the most prestigious art galleries whenever time allowed.

The servant stopped in front of a heavy door with a golden handle and knocked.

'Come in!' said a voice from inside.

'Your guest has arrived, sir,' the butler murmured, pulling the door ajar.

'Show him in.'

The room was large and bookshelves of splendid dark wood containing antique volumes and scientific tomes lined the walls. Two crystal chandeliers gave off a white light. In the centre of the room stood a long, rectangular table, its surface covered with brown leather. Matching antique armchairs were arranged around it.

It was an austere library, reminiscent of the décor of the most exclusive English clubs. It symbolised wealth, elegance and enviable power.

Sir George Holley, the owner of that castle near Fountains Abbey, sat in one of the armchairs, a copy of *The Times* in his hands. He was a powerful man who had never let himself be overwhelmed by ambition – unlike some of his peers, who had been reduced to poverty for their folly. No, he was shrewder, more able and more intelligent. He had always been the man with a thousand resources at his disposal, worldwide. At least until now.

Sir George had recently turned seventy-five, but he looked at least ten years younger. Tall and well groomed with white hair, his face was free of wrinkles and his hands showed no signs of ageing.

There was a sweet smell of tobacco in the room and the only sound was the ticking of a clock.

The guest in front of Sir George puffed out his chest in a manner typical of a military salute, then he took off his dark glasses and turned his gaze on the lord of the manor. 'Good day, sir,' he greeted him.

'Make yourself comfortable, Bill!'

Sir George waved him towards the chair on the other side of the table, opposite his own. He closed the paper and set it aside while the other man gracefully took his seat. Then he pressed a bell and summoned the butler, who appeared shortly afterwards carrying a silver tray. Having poured tea into two fine porcelain cups and arranged the sugar bowl and a plate of biscuits, the servant withdrew swiftly from the room.

Sir George rubbed his hands together, then picked up his cup and took a sip of the fragrant blend. It was clear from the expression on his face that he was savouring it. Then he looked at his guest.

'I think it is superfluous to tell you that the events of recent weeks have put our very existence at risk,' he began, steepling his long fingers in front of him with the air of one who is about to discourse on a particularly important issue.

He paused and took another sip of his tea. As he drank he was thinking about that Florentine investigator who was determined to make his life impossible. And not only his life. This lone police officer was proving tougher and more capable than any he'd encountered before, even among the English police force. The persistent bastard had even made it as far as his home in Tuscany, only just missing him. He needed to be taught a lesson that he would never forget.

'Thanks to Richard, a number of trails have been left that could yet lead to our discovery. It was regrettable that he had to be dispensed with, but we were left with no option. He'd made too many mistakes and chosen unreliable people,' Sir George continued.

His guest nodded.

'Given the position you hold, I want you to be the one to manage the situation and keep me informed. We must prevent them from sticking their noses into our business.'

'They've already asked for information several times, sir, but they haven't received the answers they wanted.'

'Good. I knew I could rely on you. And what of my request that you gather information on that Chief Superintendent who dared to come to my villa at San Gimignano – have you made any progress on that?'

'I have indeed.' He took an envelope from his briefcase and placed it on the table. 'I'm sure you will find much in there that will be of interest to you, Sir George.'

'Excellent!'

'And don't worry, if that fugitive should turn up here, he will be rendered neutral,' the other man continued.

Sir George nodded his approval. 'Now, listen carefully and I'll tell you what remains to be done . . . '

The man showed no flicker of emotion as the plan was laid out for him, along with his latest assignment, which he would have no option but to carry out.

'Remember, we must act with maximum speed and absolute discretion if we are to remain one step ahead of our enemies. Do you understand me?'

'You've made yourself very clear, Sir George, as always. Rest assured, I know how to get the job done.'

Then he got up, said goodbye and left.

Sir George Holley was a man accustomed to wielding power. Born into the aristocracy, he had built upon his hereditary influence and was skilled at manipulating both people and situations for his own benefit. Now he was ready to use every resource at his disposal to ensure the survival of the Black Rose, and also maintain his own power, at all costs.

Alone once more, Sir George opened the envelope his guest had left on the table and pulled out a document. It was a photocopy of Chief Superintendent Michele Ferrara's service record, which was kept in the confidential archives of the Ministry of the Interior.

A graduate in Law from the University of Catania, Ferrara

had enrolled in the police force at the age of twenty-seven after coming top in the examination to gain one of eighty-one positions to train as a chief superintendent. He had attended the training course in Rome for six months before being sent to his first operative position in Sardinia. Over the following years he had served in Calabria, Campania and Tuscany in increasingly prestigious positions.

He had been showered with awards in the course of his career: mentions in dispatches, accolades, commendations, monetary prizes.

There wasn't a single disciplinary charge against him.

An honest and tireless police officer, loved by his colleagues and almost all his superiors, except the more recent ones ...

Clearly, here was an intelligent, determined adversary, stubborn and highly resourceful.

So far as Sir George was concerned, he was also a fucking nuisance.

Who the hell did this Italian policeman think he was, trying to stand in his way, persistently interfering in the work of the Black Rose?

The future belonged to men like Sir George. He'd risen to the top and stayed there because of his ability to manipulate and instil fear, always keeping one step ahead of the judiciary and the police, even that pain Ferrara inspite of his undeniable commitment and tenacity.

If the nuisance posed by Ferrara could not be neutralised, there was only one thing for it.

He would have to be eliminated.

44

Borgo Bellavista

The police had returned to the 'house of death'.

For the residents of the compound and the surrounding area, the Russos' house had become a sombre landmark. Who knew how long it would be before they could pass by without casting a nervous glance at the scene of the tragedy, before they stopped calling it 'the house of death'. Perhaps never.

The compound was in the grip of an unnatural calm when the police officers arrived at two thirty in the afternoon. They looked around and realised that all the neighbours' doors and windows were shut tight.

There were six officers in total, including Rizzo and Teresa. After removing the police tape, they went inside the house with Donato Russo and headed straight for the office.

They found everything as it had been left on 18 October. The same muddle of papers was spread on the floor and the desk, and there were traces of graphite powder on the door, the window handles and the furniture. The house was enveloped in the mysterious silence that reigns over the scenes of the most horrific crimes.

Although visibly upset, Donato Russo moved calmly. He went through the objects one by one. When he'd finished he told them that, at first glance, it seemed nothing was missing.

'You'll need to check the documents on the floor,' Rizzo reminded him.

'But I don't know anything about my father's letters. I didn't rummage through his things, and nor did he discuss his correspondence with me,' the son objected.

'Try anyway, please.'

Rizzo gave him a pair of latex gloves and Donato patiently examined each sheet, concluding that it was all regular correspondence. Then he leaned over to look at the letters in front of the bookshelf, whose drawers had been emptied out on to the floor.

'Office stuff, family photo albums, pictures from my wedding, and my daughter Flavia's baptism and first communion,' he said.

'In your opinion, what were the criminals looking for?'

'Well . . . money, I suppose. What else would these criminals from the East look—' He didn't finish his sentence. He'd turned to look at the desk and his face suddenly froze, as if he could see his father sitting there still, his head bent over some paperwork. He couldn't wait to get out of there.

Rizzo stared at him for a moment and it seemed to him that Russo had teary eyes. 'Do you know where your father hid money and valuables?'

'Not at home – they wouldn't be here. My father didn't keep important things here.'

'Then where did he keep them?'

'In the safe at the company office.'

'We need to go down to the basement,' Rizzo said and made for the stairs, followed closely by the victim's son.

'But there's nothing here!' said Donato Russo with a start as soon as he walked in. 'There was a comp—'

'It's all right,' Rizzo cut him off. 'We've taken the computer and various other objects from the desk, including a mobile phone.'

'Why?'

'It's standard practice. We need to check the contents.'

'But it will just be my father's work. He often shut himself away down here to get some peace after dinner.'

'Can you tell us whether anything's missing other than what was on the desk?'

The man let his gaze wander, then shook his head.'

'Nothing's missing at all?'

'No.'

'Did your parents own any cameras?' asked Rizzo.

'Why do you want to know? What's that got to do with their murder?'

'I need to run a check.'

'What sort of check?'

'It's confidential.'

Donato Russo frowned. He couldn't imagine how a camera could be important. He gave it some thought and then replied, 'My parents weren't really into taking photos. Whenever we had family get-togethers it was always me or my daughter who took them.'

Having gathered up all the letters from the office, Rizzo followed them out of the front door and signalled for the police tape across the entrance to be replaced.

'Can I go now?' asked Donato Russo.

'You'll have to come into the office to witness the redaction of the report and to sign it. It's only a formality. It won't take long.'

'Is that absolutely necessary? I've got things that need to be done and I've lost enough time already.'

'If you can't come now, you can drop by another time.'

'Perhaps tomorrow, if that suits you.'

'No problem. Everything will be ready.'

'Will you be sending it to the Prosecutor's Department?'

'Yes, but not until you've signed it.'

Donato Russo nodded and strode away from the house. He was the first of the group to get into his car and drive away from the compound.

6.36 p.m., the Chief Superintendent's office

After a day of feverish activity, Rizzo was finally able to speak to Ferrara. The pair of them were sitting in the Chief Superintendent's office, discussing the photographs from Amedeo Russo's album and in particular those of Rita Perfetti and Antonella Corvaglia, the prostitutes killed in 1995 and 1992.

'I still need to check the other files, Michele, but it seems reasonable to assume that the third photo will also present differences when compared to the photos from our archives.'

'So Russo had photos of the crimes, or at least two of them, that weren't acquired through official activity.'

'That seems certain.'

'Do you think he was involved?'

'Hard to say. But even if he wasn't, they came into his possession somehow. Perhaps he was using them to blackmail someone.'

'If that's the case, the words spoken by Daniele De Robertis and the snatch of conversation Italo Ortu overheard start to add up. Russo was punished for the blackmail and the killers were searching for the photos in question.'

'But they didn't find the album.'

There was a pause. Both men were thinking.

'What's their next move going to be?' Ferrara asked.

Rizzo remained silent for several moments. 'Until we know more about them, there's no way of telling,' he concluded.

'Keep examining the files. Some other lead might crop up, something that was missed at the time.'

'I'll do it first thing this evening.'

'Thanks, Francesco.'

The Chief Superintendent glanced at the clock. 'I need to go now,' he said. 'Call me if there's any news.'

They walked out of the room together and the Chief Superintendent left Headquarters.

He was sitting in his usual place, behind a tiny desk, and there was a pipe sticking out of one corner of his mouth.

The Chief Superintendent had dropped into his friend Massimo Verga's bookshop on the Via dei Tornabuoni just ahead of closing time. He'd been let in by Massimo's long-time employee, Rita Senesi, who'd sent him up to the mezzanine level with a smile and a nod of the head.

'Well, well, well, look who's turned up!' exclaimed Massimo when Ferrara appeared in the doorway. Books were piled on every surface, even on the floor and the chairs. Balancing the pipe in the ashtray, Massimo got up to embrace him.

The bookseller was Ferrara's closest friend. Back in the summer of 2001, the Chief Superintendent had even put his career on the line for him after Verga disappeared under mysterious circumstances, along with his lover, the owner of an art gallery in Forte dei Marmi. The two of them had been hunted by the police on suspicion of having killed his lover's husband, a Florentine PR man who had died in suspicious circumstances at his wife's villa, but thanks to his friend's efforts it had all turned out all right for Massimo.

Michele and Massimo had first met while attending secondary school in their hometown, Catania. After a long interval, they had found each other again in Florence, where Massimo had opened his bookshop.

'You're getting fat,' said Ferrara, nodding at his friend's prominent stomach.

'You're right, Michele, but you know how much I enjoy my food and I haven't been very active for a while.'

'Don't tell me you spend all your time in this hole!'

'Why don't you tell me what brings you here at this hour?' Massimo asked, changing the subject. He cleared a chair, dumping the books on top of a pile that was already on the floor.

'Have a seat,' he said, gesturing towards the chair. 'You know you can smoke in here, don't you?'

Ferrara pulled a cigar out of his case and lit it while Massimo picked up his pipe again.

'Come on then, tell me!'

'Have you heard anything about the Russo murder?' Ferrara asked, well aware that Massimo's bookshop was an important gathering place for the people of Florence. Some arranged to meet in a basement room there from time to time to discuss literature and both local and national politics.

'Nothing. It's as if nothing had happened in this city. Life in those circles carries on as normal. Besides, as you well know, it's not the first time something like this has happened.'

'Not even a passing comment?'

'Nothing. But tell me, Michele . . . ' he stopped for a moment, looking his friend straight in the eye, 'how can you hope to get anywhere with this? Aren't you tired of it yet? Haven't you understood, you blessed fool, that there are mysteries that can never be solved and that it's useless to keep trying?'

'You think the murder of the Russos is destined to end up as one of the cold cases . . . another of the city's mysteries?'

Verga nodded.

Ferrara was certain that his friend knew more than he was telling. 'Why do you say that these cases will never be solved?'

'I'll tell you – but let me have a puff on my pipe first.'

After relighting it, Verga inhaled deeply and the air was rapidly filled with smoke. As he smoked he got up and closed the door. Once back behind his desk, he began to speak again.

'Amedeo Russo used to come into the bookshop,' Massimo began, and he went on to tell how the lawyer had recently asked him to track down a copy of a rare French-language book on esotericism. The bookseller had managed to get hold of a photo-copied version through a colleague in Paris.

'I rang to let him know and he turned up here less than half an hour later to collect it.'

'Did you ask him what he wanted it for?'

'No, he told me of his own accord that it was in relation to a legal case he was studying. I thought it must be one he was working on.'

'Did you keep a record of the title?'

'I got myself a copy at the same time. I wanted to read it out of curiosity. It's a shocking book.'

'Why?'

'At a certain point it says that, according to the teachings of a noble Florentine who lived in the eighteenth and nineteenth centuries, for a true sacrifice to Satan, it's necessary to kill somebody.'

'In the same way that Crowley, the occultist, claimed that the death of a woman in the course of a sexual ritual was "just"?'

'I can see you've done your research. But this book goes on to talk about the sacrifice of a couple.'

'Could you lend me the book?'

'Yes. I've underlined the most interesting parts. Remember to give it back afterwards.' He opened one of the drawers of his desk, took it out and flipped through it. He found the relevant page and marked it with a Post-it, then he handed it to Ferrara.

Ferrara studied the cover. In the centre was a picture of a cross and a flower. He read a few words: *Alchimie – Hermetisme et Ordres Initiatiques.*

'And be careful! Don't go walking into a minefield because you'll find you're on your own – I know the way your superiors work. Think of Petra, and be careful,' Verga told him, handing him an envelope in which to put his copy. Then they embraced and the Chief Superintendent left.

Since it was late by this time, he headed home rather than

returning to the office. After dinner he would try to translate the underlined passages with the help of Google: Chief Super-intendent Ferrara didn't speak French. He might not achieve the world's most faithful translation, but he should be able to get the gist of it.

During the brief walk, one of Massimo's statements echoed in his mind: 'according to the teachings of a noble Florentine who lived in the eighteenth and nineteenth centuries'. Was this a pact between Florence and the Devil that had its roots in those centuries?

What about England? And the teachings of the Englishman, Crowley?

Was the high command of evil in Tuscany – or was it actually in the United Kingdom?

45

Another positive match.

Rizzo found it in the file on the murder of a woman who had been killed during the summer of 1996 not far from Antonella Corvaglia's home. The murder took place in an apartment building frequented by prostitutes and ex-prostitutes; it hadn't been the woman's home but a soulless workplace.

Her name was Barbara Cardella. Although she didn't look that old, she was over fifty when she died. In her younger days she had sold herself on the paths of the Parco Delle Cascine, but in recent years she had received her few remaining clients, the loyal regulars, at that apartment.

As usual, Rizzo had begun by reading the initial report and carefully examining the photos taken by the Forensics team.

The woman was lying on the floor in the bedroom. She had her legs spread wide and she was wearing a dressing gown. There were no obvious wounds on the body. Bulging eyes, a protruding tongue and blood coming from the nose seemed to suggest strangulation was the cause of death. And then there was the bruising beneath her chin.

The apartment was tidy, apart from the bedroom, where drawers had been pulled out and their contents tipped on to the floor. The front door showed no sign of having been forced, so the victim must have known her killer.

So this time the killer hadn't used a knife or taken her under-wear away with him, Rizzo observed, before moving on to read the investigative reports.

Then he began on the witness interrogations. A number of witnesses had been questioned, including a neighbour. The woman had started by complaining that this prostitute killer was making it hard for her to earn a living. Nobody wanted to pro-tect call girls of a certain age any more; the pimps preferred young girls, ideally foreigners from Albania or Senegal. Those girls brought in a lot of money without causing any problems.

Then she recounted a conversation she'd had with the deceased the previous evening. Barbara had stopped to talk to her outside the apartment building and mentioned that she wanted to stop working. The neighbour couldn't be entirely sure of the motive behind this decision, but she had the feeling it was because Bar-bara had been threatened by someone.

Even more interesting was the interview with a man who'd been in a romantic relationship with the dead woman. Barbara had told him some weeks earlier that if anything bad ever hap-pened to her, he should go and find a man's attaché case that was hidden in the storage room. According to him, it was a safe place because robbers would hardly be likely to break into an old house where a prostitute lived.

Could it have been a robbery on commission that went wrong? Rizzo wondered. Since the killer hadn't inflicted knife wounds on the body and it was likely he had taken valuable items, Rizzo was inclined to view this crime as falling into a different category to the other two.

He soon changed his mind when he examined the photo in Russo's album. Whereas in Russo's photo blood seemed to be dripping from the woman's nose, in the one taken by Forensics it was obvious the blood had stopped flowing a while ago.

Once again the photo in Russo's album had been taken before the police arrived on the scene.

It was past midnight and the Superintendent was asking himself a lot of questions.

What was in the mysterious attaché case? Valuables? Money? Jewellery?

Before closing the file, he read an article from a daily newspaper that he'd found amongst a batch of press cuttings. The journalist suggested that one person was responsible for the crimes involving Florentine prostitutes – and not just Florentine ones. According to him, the same person had also struck in the Veneto region. In his opinion, a serial killer was waging a campaign against prostitutes, driven by a desire to clean up the world. An avenger.

Rizzo stared at the byline.

The author of the article was Cosimo Presti.

He set the cutting aside so he could make a copy to attach to the report he was writing for the Chief Superintendent.

Maybe it had been Presti at the funeral!

He ran an Internet search for other articles, but there wasn't much: a few lines for each murder, but only in the local press. In each piece it said that there were no suspects, and there were no references to a possible serial killer. Cosimo Presti had apparently come up with that theory all by himself.

Was it all a con? Was he trying to throw people off the scent? Could it be that he was a Satanist? Or did he just know more than his colleagues?

And if so, how?

There were no new findings in the investigation for the next three days.

The police officers' spirits were not improved by the criticism levelled at them by the media. They accused the *Squadra Mobile* of being incapable and of having no chance of capturing the dangerous Eastern European criminals who had caused such panic.

The financial checks on Amedeo Russo and his clients had

offered no new leads. They'd come up with no suspicious individuals who might have had a motive to kill the Russos.

Nothing.

Both Italo Ortu's landline and mobile phone had been tapped since the afternoon of Thursday 21 October. Vinci had agreed to the request and provided an urgent warrant during another lunch meeting with Teresa, which had pleased the policewoman. She had, however, been struck by one of the Deputy Prosecutor's comments, although she hadn't quite understood what he was referring to. As he was saying goodbye to her, the Deputy Prosecutor had looked her in the eyes and said, 'One should never turn one's back on certain opportunities.'

Thus far the phone tap hadn't yielded any interesting conversations. Italu Ortu had returned to Sardinia, so the landline for his home in Florence had remained silent. He had made a few calls from his mobile, but they were all to relatives. The staff at Police Headquarters in Oristano, who had been drafted in to help, had tailed him since his arrival at the airport in Olbia, but they hadn't witnessed anything worth reporting. The man had gone straight to his village. Apart from a few evenings playing cards in a bar on the village square, he hadn't left the house. None of his companions had a record. They worked for the forestry service, the police, or in local businesses.

Thanks to his wife's friend, Rizzo had managed to get hold of the Russos' telephone records, both for the landline and the mobile with the missing SIM card. The SIM had been active and working up until the night of the crime. In fact, its last recorded activity had been at 1.36 a.m. on the night of 18 October. There had been a very brief call, barely nine seconds long, from a mobile phone with an international 0049 prefix. A German number.

It could be an important lead. Ferrara and Rizzo suspected that the killers had made that call, which might explain why there were no signs of forced entry. They had alerted Interpol, hoping to find out who the number belonged to. Presumably the caller must have been someone known to the victim, or perhaps they had identified themselves by giving a name known to Russo or his wife.

Several of the numbers that appeared on the telephone records had yet to be identified. Venturi and Fanti had split the task between them to speed up the process.

The Chief Superintendent had also been busy tracking down a phone number. He'd found out that the call referring to Genius that Headquarters had put through to him at home late on Wednesday evening had been made from a public telephone box located in the train station at Como.

Despite the progress they'd made, they were no closer to solving the double murder. It was beginning to look like a perfect crime.

But Ferrara didn't want to think like that. He had always maintained that the perfect crime didn't exist. In fact, he was a firm believer in the saying that to err is human. A killer, no matter how skilful they might be, would slip up somewhere along the line, just as the police themselves inevitably made mistakes. Had he and his men made any? He had reviewed the action they had taken so far several times and it seemed to him that everything had been done rigorously, even if there were a few 'buts'. Yes, his officers had done everything within their power, *but* how much more would they have achieved if the Prosecutor's Department had approved all their requests, including the one to tap the telephone lines belonging to the law firm and the Cortis' home?

The Chief Superintendent had also rummaged through his files in search of documents from old investigations. Among other things, he had found the list of the lodges of Florence which he'd been sent several years earlier by Raffaello Petrini, a friend in the Prosecutor's Department in Bologna, who had carried out a difficult investigation involving deviant masonic lodges. Running down the list of members, Ferrara hadn't been at all surprised to find the names Amedeo Russo and Antonello Corti. Many prominent doctors, architects and engineers also featured. It was another of those powerful groups that had survived the judicial system's periodic crackdowns.

But there was nothing that could be linked to the crime.

The Chief Superintendent spent those three days reviewing his notes on the murder of Antonio Sergi and the death of Fabio Biondi, updating them with the latest findings.

Night of 31 August to 1 September 2004

Location: Lake Bracciano

Victim: Antonio Sergi

Cause of death: Strangulation

Clues or useful leads: He was collaborating with the Secret Service, on whose behalf he had infiltrated an international criminal organisation. Among his papers were references to 'the Archivist', who 'worked from home'.

Responsibility for the investigation lies with the Civitavecchia Prosecutor's Department.

Suspects: persons as yet unknown

Night of 4–5 September 2004

Location: the Isolotto district of Florence

Victim: Fabio Biondi

Arson attack on his apartment.

Clues or useful leads: Testimony from the victim's aunt and a friend, Alba Cechi. The latter had been told a secret by Biondi: he was keeping something important in his safe.

Documents found in the safe: photocopies labelled 'confidential' containing references to cases that were either already closed or still open. A folder labelled THE BLACK ROSE, containing sheets of paper stamped 'Top Secret'. A file.

Fabio Biondi must also have been working for the Secret Service, one of those specialists who get brought on board from time to time.

Suspects: whoever killed Sergi must have known about Biondi's role, or have extracted this information from Sergi before his death.

Ferrara had concluded bitterly that the investigation to catch Genius had distracted him from taking the case of Fabio Biondi, which was, in all probability, connected to Sergi's, any further. He had attached these notes to his ones on the Russo double murder and he intended to get in touch with the Deputy Prosecutor in Civitavecchia to find out how their investigations were going.

His review of the earlier cases didn't stop him chewing over the Russo case. There were two things in particular that he kept coming back to.

The first of these was Amedeo Russo's photo album. He agreed entirely with Rizzo's conclusion that the photos of Rita Perfetti and Antonella Corvaglia had been taken during the murder, so Amedeo Russo would not have been able to obtain them through legal channels.

But if not through legal channels, how had he come by those photos? Was he the photographer? Or had someone given the photos to him? And if so, why?

The same questions applied to the close-up of Barbara Cardella, the victim who'd been strangled rather than stabbed. And then there was the mystery of the attaché case stolen from the store room in the building where she was killed. What was in the case? Was it taken by the killer?

About the only thing they could be certain of was the fact that the photographs had been placed in the album by Russo. His fingerprints were all over them. No trace of anyone else's prints.

Another dead end.

Then his thoughts turned to the other photos, the ones of the Satanic rite. Rizzo hadn't found anything in the *Squadra Mobile's* archives. He wanted to ask the Prosecutor's Department for authorisation to examine the files on cases with a link to Satanism – if there had ever been any such cases. Based on experience, this permission would prove difficult to secure, at least in Florence.

The Chief Superintendent knew of some cases that had caused a considerable stir, but they had been linked to other cities. The investigations had only been able to gather scattered pieces, insufficient to provide a complete picture. Satanism was a hidden world; one that outsiders struggled to see in context.

The second thing he kept coming back to was the book he'd borrowed from Massimo Verga. The highlighted passages, once translated into Italian, had confirmed what his friend had told him. Basically it was an essay on the use of human sacrifice to honour Satan.

It wasn't proof of anything. There was nothing to conclusively link this Satanic activity with the Russo double murder. However, there were material leads that carried a certain weight in the reconstruction of events and in the search for those responsible.

Although it remained unclear whether Amedeo Russo was a killer, an accomplice, or, more likely, a blackmailer, Ferrara couldn't help feeling they'd taken a small step towards identifying a possible motive.

46

Borgo Bellavista was invaded by hordes of curious onlookers during those three days, and they weren't all locals. Some of them even brought their children. They parked in front of the gates and peered through the railings to stare open-mouthed at the house where the double murder had taken place. They even took souvenir photos, as if they didn't have anything better to do. These were the horror tourists, prepared to travel hundreds of miles to visit the scenes of crimes.

It was a new fashion and a very sad one.

Those same three days saw the Flying Squad rapid response team, whose four or five patrols monitored the whole of Florence and its immediate surrounding area twenty-four-seven, summoned to a rather serious incident.

It was Sunday 24 October, an otherwise peaceful day. Even the football match between Fiorentina and Roma, two teams who'd always had a strong historic rivalry, passed without incident. Then, shortly after nine in the evening, a call came through to emergency services. In an agitated voice, an anonymous female caller told the police operator she had heard disturbing sounds from the apartment of one Edoardo Degli Aldobrandi who lived in a building on the Viale Italia, near the theatre.

'That lecher can't be allowed to carry on! There are young

boys, continually coming and going, even at night. I can hear them pleading and weeping.'

The Operations Room sent a squad car. A few minutes later, Inspector Trovato – a veteran who still found himself reduced to donning his uniform due to staff shortages – arrived on the scene. He rang the bell several times without receiving a reply and was about to get back into the car when he heard a sliding door opening. A woman appeared on a balcony and indicated the top floor: Degli Aldobrandi lived there. Then she signalled to Trovato that she had opened the front door for him.

It took several rings of the doorbell outside his flat before Edoardo Degli Aldobrandi appeared. He looked to be in his fifties, and when he opened the door he was tying the cord on his red silk dressing gown, as if he'd just put it on.

'What do you want?' he asked, clearly irritated by the intrusion.

'Are you Signor Degli Aldobrandi?'

'I am the Marquis Edoardo Degli Aldobrandi,' replied the man, fixing the police officer with a harsh glare.

'Is anyone else at home?'

'Why do you care? What do you want?'

'I asked you a question, sir, and I'd be grateful for a response.'

'I'll be making a complaint to the Commissioner and to the Prosecutor's Department tomorrow morning. You can't carry out raids like this.'

Just then Trovato noticed a shadow at the doorway of a room leading off the passage. 'We need to check,' he said, not intimidated in the least, and he planted his foot in the doorway to make sure the Marquis couldn't slam it in his face.

'Check? What do you need to check? I'm the Marquis Degli Aldobrandi and it's my taxes that pay your salary. If you don't leave this minute, I'll report you to the Prosecutor's Department for housebreaking.'

'Step aside, sir,' replied Trovato impatiently, shooing the man away from the doorway with a quick movement of his arm.

The two police officers finally made it through the door.

Ignoring the homeowner's threats, Inspector Trovato went straight towards the place where he'd spotted the shadow. It was the doorway leading into the bedroom.

The room was in semi-darkness, barely lit by the faint pink glow of a lamp on the bedside table.

There was no one in sight. The bed, a double, was unmade. Trovato spotted a video camera pointed at the pillows. After checking in the wardrobe and behind the curtains, he knelt down beside the bed. He saw a shadow crawling in the darkness. A pair of frightened eyes. Bare feet.

'Police! Come out of there!' he shouted, his hand moving to his holster. Then he stretched out his free hand, grabbed a young girl's ankle and pulled her out. She was completely naked and looked to be about thirteen years old. Trovato heard her moan something in an incomprehensible language. In the same instant, he realised that a young boy had popped out from under the covers. He was naked, too. At first glance, he appeared to be the same age as the girl, with a similar mixed-race complexion. He spoke to the girl in a threatening tone. She broke off whatever she'd been saying so suddenly it was if she'd been struck dumb. Then she bent down and began pulling an old pair of jeans and a T-shirt out from under the bed.

Degli Aldobrandi appeared in the doorway and began to shout, 'This is my house – I'm going to report you! You can't just come in here like this!'

'Is that a threat?' asked the officer who was standing beside him.

'It's a warning.'

'These are minors,' interrupted the Inspector.

'It's my house. You're violating my privacy, it's a crime.'

'And you've committed crimes, too. Now hurry up and get dressed, you're coming to Headquarters with us.'

'I'll make a phone call and this will all be cleared up.'

'No phone calls for now,' replied Trovato, snatching the cordless phone from the Marquis's hands. 'And get dressed, you two,' he added, turning to the children.

The two adolescents, who appeared to be of Indian origin, refused to say a word. Based on anthropometric checks, it turned out that they were both fourteen, the boy almost fifteen.

The Deputy Prosecutor on duty, Erminia Cosenza, didn't authorise the arrest of Degli Aldobrandi, nor did she allow them to seal the apartment off, but she asked for it to be searched immediately, so Inspector Trovato went back with two patrols. First and foremost, they needed to identify who had been exploiting the two minors.

While the Marquis remained at Headquarters, one of his nieces, an attractive woman in her thirties, agreed to accompany the police to witness the search. It took them several hours to complete the task: the apartment comprised nine rooms, all of them spacious and full of furniture. Ostentatious luxury was everywhere.

Once they had completed the search of the lounge and the bedroom, where they seized the video camera and several videotapes, they moved on to the attic, which served as a storage space. There they found numerous objects of interest, stacked on metal shelves or on the floor. One bookcase was full of wooden boxes that contained erotic magazines, some of them collectors' items. Inspector Trovato noted with amazement that books of a pornographic nature were arranged side by side with those on religious themes.

He also discovered a variety of specialist sex toys, most likely bought from abroad, and women's clothing, including bras in a variety of sizes, knickers and nylon stockings. And then there were shoe boxes full of videotapes and photographs in both black and white and colour. Many of them had been taken with a Polaroid and depicted scenes from orgies. A rectangular box that had once been white emerged from a chest. Inside was a black hooded cloak. In another box the same size was a second hooded cloak, this one red.

That attic was quite the treasure trove.

PART FIVE

AN UNMISSABLE
OPPORTUNITY

47

Monday 25 October

Chief Superintendent Ferrara looked at the clock. It was quarter to eight. He opened the envelope labelled CONFIDENTIAL. DELIVERED BY HAND which Fanti had left on his desk.

He had learned from his secretary that a police officer from the Civitavecchia commissariat had left it with the security guard.

He read the only sheet of paper it contained.

Subject: Criminal investigation no. 2709/04

Request for collaboration with regard to the murder of Antonio Sergi, Inspector with the State Police, whose body was discovered at Lake Bracciano on 1 September 2004.

To the Chief Superintendent of the *Squadra Mobile*
Care of Police Headquarters
2 Via Zara
50129 Florence

Facts have emerged in connection with the above-mentioned murder that link the victim to a certain Fabio Biondi, who died following an arson attack on his home in Florence on the night of the 4-5 September 2004.

In particular, Sergi's mobile telephone records have revealed that there was contact between the two men, with some calls made only a few days before his death.

On this basis we ask for information on:

The status of the investigation into the death of Fabio Biondi; a full report on Biondi: marital status, activities, any criminal history, friendships, acquaintances, anything you might find in the course of your investigation relating to incidents at checkpoints or involving stop-and-search procedures in public places. We are particularly interested in the nature of his relationship with Inspector Sergi and would appreciate any other useful information.

Please consider this a matter of urgency,

Kind regards,

Signor Enrico Impallomeni

Deputy Prosecutor

Civitavecchia, 23 October 2004

Impallomeni had pre-empted him! Ferrara called Rizzo to let him know about the letter.

'Francesco, prepare a note with all the information we've gathered on Fabio Biondi and then take it in person to Deputy Prosecutor Impallomeni.'

'Should I also mention the fact that Sergi was working with the Secret Service?'

'Yes, and tell them about the references to the Black Rose in the documents we found in Biondi's safe, too. Even though the Prosecutor's Department here in Florence isn't doing anything, with luck, Impallomeni will. We need to work with him.'

Rizzo nodded. 'Great idea,' he said.

Perhaps this Deputy Prosecutor would give them a hand without realising it, thought the Chief Superintendent as his colleague left the room, the letter in his hand.

Then he summoned Ascalchi and reminded him to go and have a chat with Italo Ortu's wife: 'Perhaps we'll manage to rock the boat a bit and finally learn something interesting . . . '

Trovato came in a few minutes later. He wanted to talk to Ferrara about the previous day's operation, which had only been concluded shortly before dawn.

'We've catalogued all the material we seized and we've charged Edoardo Degli Aldobrandi with sexual offences against minors,' the Inspector told him.

'Why didn't you arrest him?'

'Signora Cosenza, the Deputy Prosecutor, insisted that he should be released on bail. She didn't think there was any risk of flight or tampering with the evidence, and he doesn't have a previous record.'

The Chief Superintendent scowled. 'Where's the material?' he asked.

'In my office.'

'Have you gone through it?'

'Only superficially, to complete the report on the items seized.'

'I'll send my secretary to collect it. We'll take over from here.'

It was standard procedure. The Flying Squad carried out the initial intervention and paperwork, then the investigators from the *Squadra Mobile* took over. Mostly it was all mundane stuff – petty theft, drunken brawls, pickpockets and bag-snatching incidents – but from what he'd heard, Ferrara thought this case might be something out of the ordinary.

48

The Rifredi district, Florence

Lorenza Cossu lived in a fairly modest apartment building that had been built in the seventies. It was in Rifredi, the city's most north-westerly district, a long way from the historic centre.

The history of Rifredi was linked to the Church of Santo Stefano in Pane, which had been the parish of Giulio Facibeni, who was famous for giving help and protection to children persecuted by the Nazis during the Second World War. Nowadays its focal point is the Piazza Dalmazia, where it's still possible to find independent retailers who resist the invasion of the supermarket chains that have destroyed the identity of the historic shopping area.

Pino Ricci parked on the side of the road opposite the building's entrance. A group of schoolchildren with backpacks were passing by, laughing at one of their number who was making witty comments; perhaps too witty for youngsters of ten or twelve, but such are the times we live in.

'Wait here for me,' Ascalchi told him before getting out of the unmarked Fiat Punto. He crossed the street and went through the building's open front door. He found himself in a narrow, rather run-down hallway which reeked of lemon detergent. On one of the walls were various items of graffiti written in black marker: SHITTY CITY, I LOVE LEO, LONG LIVE THE MONSTER. He scowled with disgust as he read these last words. Florence would struggle to rid itself its label as the City of the Monster or Monsters, such was the fascination of evil, impossible to erase after those terrible murders in the seventies and eighties. He glanced along the rickety mail boxes, barely managing to decipher the surname he was looking for.

He stopped in front of the door of the first apartment on the ground floor and rang the bell. The chime echoed inside, and this was followed by the sound of steps coming closer. He imagined a suspicious eye pressed against the spyhole, then came the sound of the key in the lock and the door opened. A woman with the puffy, red-veined face typical of alcoholics appeared in the doorway. She seemed tired and was of indeterminate age. She was wearing a black T-shirt under a rather scruffy, faded pink dressing gown and on her feet were a pair of wooden clogs. Her fat ankles were covered by socks that seemed an attempt to coordinate with the rest of the outfit, but these were completely discoloured, too.

'What do you want?' she demanded.

Ascalchi stared at her for a moment. 'Are you Signora Cossu?'

The woman hesitated, studying him for a moment.

'Yes, I am,' she replied, standing as still as if someone were pointing a pistol at her head. Subtle lines wrinkled the skin around her lips, most likely the effect of years and years of cigarettes.

The police officer introduced himself, pulling his police ID out of his jacket pocket. 'I'm Superintendent Ascalchi from the *Squadra Mobile.*'

She looked him in the face, her expression wary.

'I'm here about your ex-husband . . . '

Lorenza Cossu raised a hand to her forehead and leaned her right shoulder against the door.

'What's that waste of space done—' She stopped short, biting her lip and blinking. She seemed confused.

Ascalchi put his ID card away, slipping it into the same pocket he'd taken it out of.

'I'd like to ask you a few questions. I won't keep you any longer than necessary.'

'Please, come in.'

The woman moved aside to let him pass. They went through the hall and entered a rather bare room. There was a large television standing in one corner, turned on for the moment. A little girl of five, or maybe six, was sitting on the lemon-scented floor. She had her legs crossed and was holding a rag doll. Music was blasting out from another room.

'Go and tell your brother to turn that radio down,' the woman told the little girl. Then she turned back to the police officer and invited him to take a seat.

Ascalchi sat in an armchair. It was old but comfortable. Signora Cossu, on the other hand, perched on the small sofa. She picked up the remote and turned off the TV. The blonde presenter dressed in a chef's outfit had been leaning over a plate of chicory risotto, the umpteenth recipe suggested to the enthusiastic television audience. Signora Cossu put her right hand on a crocheted doily arranged on the armrest and began to move her feet nervously.

'I'm listening,' she said, once they were alone.

Ascalchi pulled out his notebook and rummaged in his pocket.

'Has Italo been in some kind of trouble? I don't work – I wouldn't know what to do without the money he gives me,' said the woman, seeing that the police officer was taking some time to find a pen.

'One moment, signora. You're being interviewed as a person who might have information of interest to our investigation.'

'What information?'

'Please, let me do this in an orderly fashion.'

She looked at him, perplexed.

'Are you in contact with your ex-husband?' the policeman asked.

'Once a week. He comes here to see the children. But why do you want to know? Has he done something?'

Ascalchi shook his head. 'No,' he replied.

'He hasn't hurt anyone, by any chance?' Her eyes had become bright.

Ascalchi was about to reply when he heard shouting.

'I've told you that I don't want you in my room. Go away!'

Shortly afterwards a young boy of eleven or twelve came into the room. He was shouting at the top of his voice and dragging his sister behind him. Her face was screwed up and she was crying.

'You mustn't send her into my bedroom, Mum! How many times do I have to tell you?'

The woman snorted angrily. 'Stop that, Carletto!' she shouted back.

Ascalchi decided to intervene. 'You're squeezing her wrist too tight, let her go!'

'And who the fuck are you?' asked the boy, glaring at him.

The police officer noticed the strong resemblance to his father. 'You're hurting her, let her go,' he insisted, making as if to get up, while the little girl stared at him with gentle eyes.

Their mother got involved. 'Hey, I know how to look after my children myself.'

It didn't look that way.

'Let her go! And go back to your room,' the woman ordered her son, springing to her feet. The boy suddenly gave up the fight. He went down the corridor and, as soon as he'd closed his door behind him, turned the music down.

The little girl calmed down immediately and Ascalchi guessed that these shouting matches must be a regular occurrence.

'Excuse me a minute. I'm going to take her to my mother's.

She lives upstairs,' said the woman, and, taking her daughter by the hand, she made for the door.

She came back barely five minutes later, dabbing with a tissue at the sweat that had gathered on her forehead. She sat down on the sofa again.

'Are you too hot?' Ascalchi asked her.

'Those children!' she sighed, ignoring the question. Then she leaned over the coffee table, took a cigarette out of the packet and lit it, inhaling deeply. She blew out a cloud of smoke that looked a bit like a cloud of steam. Maybe she was trying to relax.

'Would you like a cigarette too, officer?'

'No, thank you. I don't smoke any more. It's a terrible vice.'

Ascalchi would have like to add that smoking kills. It caused tumours like the one he'd been diagnosed with. But he didn't. He needed to get this job done and he couldn't let himself waste any more time. He did give the half-empty packet a disapproving look, though.

His disapproval was wasted on the lady of the house. She continued exhaling smoke until it began to fill the room. She watched it curiously without saying a word.

It was the police officer who broke the silence. 'Now, signora, let's carry on with our conversation.' They had effectively stopped mid-question. She looked down and finally put the cigarette in the ashtray.

'No, signora, your husband hasn't done anything serious. You needn't worry.'

The woman's expression seemed to soften. The lines between her eyebrows gradually faded. 'Well then, why have you come here, officer? Why this interview?' she asked, picking up the cigarette again and raising it to her lips.

Ascalchi asked her whether Italo Ortu had any additional

income. After all, he had to pay for the running of two house-holds and, as everyone knows, children are expensive.

'Additional income? What do you mean by additional? He's a security guard. He does an honest job and often works nights to earn a bit more,' she replied.

'Of course, but are you aware of anything else? Who knows, a second job, perhaps? Some cash-in-hand work?'

'No, absolutely not. Why are you asking me all these questions?'

The vertical lines between her eyebrows had reappeared.

Ascalchi lowered his voice. 'People who don't do their jobs properly can also be arrested,' he said, staring at her.

She jumped to her feet and dropped the cigarette. She picked it up from the coffee table, took a last puff and then angrily stamped it out on the floor.

'I've had enough of that son of a bitch. I don't know anything about his life any more and I'm not interested. I've no idea what the hell he might have done. If he hasn't done his job, that's his business.'

'Please sit down, Signora Cossu. Don't get worked up. I'm not accusing him of anything, I just want to try and understand what kind of guy your ex-husband is.'

'Are you here in connection with the crime at Borgo Bellavista? I know he was working in that area.'

'Exactly! That's why I'm here. Based on appearances, he wasn't doing his job, but I can't tell you anything else at the moment.'

'Are you suggesting that he's implicated?'

'No, don't misunderstand me.'

'Then make sure you explain more clearly.'

Ascalchi paused before replying, taking time to think. The woman stared him in the eye, waiting to hear what he had to say.

'I thought you might have noticed something strange in your ex-husband's behaviour recently, some kind of change ...

having more money to spare, perhaps ... that's all. I'm not accusing him of anything in particular.'

She nodded. Her eyes betrayed her fatigue, and perhaps something else, too: her fear of losing the support to which she was entitled. She took another cigarette out of the packet, lit it and blew a cloud of smoke towards the ceiling.

'I can't help you. I haven't lived with him for years, and when he comes here for a few hours he always seems the same: very affectionate with the children. As for money, even when we were together he never told me anything about it.'

'And how did he behave towards you?'

The woman raised her eyes to the ceiling then replied, 'He hates me.'

'Why?'

'We were always fighting.'

There was a long silence.

'What did you fight over?'

'He used to drink. He would come home drunk and hit me. He'd go berserk. He even joined Alcoholics Anonymous, but he would always start drinking and beating me again after a while. It was torture. I hit the bottle too in the end, and just as badly. It's the myrtle liqueur from my home town that's helped me through, but now my liver's shot to bits.'

So she *was* a drinker!

'Does he have any friends?'

Absolute silence once again. She blew out another cloud of smoke. Then she put the cigarette down and it burned slowly.

'Does he have any friends?' Ascalchi asked again.

'I don't want Italo to lose his job like his brother did.'

'His brother?'

'Yes, Rocco.'

'Tell me what happened.'

'You have to promise me that our conversation will remain secret.'

Ascalchi put his pen down. 'I give you my word of honour.' He felt his mobile phone vibrate in his trouser pocket and put his hand over it to muffle the sound, which was like a swarm of insects. 'Trust me!'

'In 1992, Rocco lost his job as a security guard,' the woman began.

'Why?'

'One moment.' She got up and took a cork-coated bottle and two glasses from a drinks cabinet. 'Can I offer you some myrtle liqueur?'

'Thank you.'

She filled the two glasses and handed one to the police officer. She lifted hers to her lips and downed it in one, then lit another cigarette. She smoked like a chimney!

Ascalchi, who had only accepted the liqueur out of politeness, barely sipped it and tried not to cough. He wasn't used to drinking alcohol without eating a substantial meal first.

'We can carry on now,' she said, after taking a series of drags on her cigarette.

She explained that in the eighties Rocco and Italo had lived with their family in Turin where their father worked as a labourer for Fiat and their mother worked as a seamstress for several businesses. Their father was a hard worker and had managed to get his eldest son, Rocco, taken on by a firm of security guards which had the contract for the Fiat plant at Mirafiori, the biggest industrial complex in Italy.

'But Rocco had other interests—' She was cut short by a violent coughing fit. She jumped up and went into the kitchen to get a bottle of water and took a long swallow.

'Do you want some?'

'No, thank you.'

She stubbed out her cigarette, which had burned down to the filter.

'What sort of interests?' Ascalchi asked her.

'Magic.' She looked the police officer right in the eye, as if she wanted to see what effect that word had on him.

'Magic?'

'Yes. Have you heard of Satan's Faithful?'

Ascalchi shook his head. 'No, the name means nothing to me.'

She explained that Rocco had formed a sect that went by that name. They were convinced that the devil was in money, orgasm and thousands of other things. The only way to join was by swearing a pact with your own blood, a pact that couldn't be broken. Once you were a member, there was no turning back.

She then explained that at the end of the eighties the group had come to the attention of the Carabinieri. Their investigations had gone on for a couple of years, then they moved in and arrested Rocco and several other members.

'They were charged with a number of serious offences, the worst of which was probably sexual assault against minors. In the end they were all acquitted due to lack of evidence, but Rocco's employer fired him. That was in 1992.'

'What does he do for a living now?'

'He's a magician.'

'In Turin?'

'No, in Bologna, or rather the surrounding area. After all that nasty business he moved to where some of his followers live.'

'And what about Italo?'

'Italo had nothing to do with any of that back then.'

Back then!

'And now?'

'I don't know whether or not he's in touch with his brother now.'

Ascalchi wondered why the woman had told him about her former brother-in-law's problems. He wanted to know more, but this magic stuff was a closed book to him.

'Thank you for your time,' he told her. Then he looked at the notebook. The page was almost completely blank. He'd only written down the general details of the witness and the house. He closed it and put it back in his jacket pocket, along with his pen. He got up and, after giving her his business card, shook her hand.

'Call me if you think of anything,' he told her.

'I've already told you all I have to tell you. And remember, you gave me your word of honour.'

'Don't worry!'

Ascalchi moved towards the door as she lit her umpteenth cigarette. She was standing up, looking out of the window.

Once outside, the police officer heard the music blasting out again. It must be like this every day. He was sure the woman couldn't be happy living like that. He thought he heard another coughing fit.

Life wasn't like the movies, not everyone got to be part of a wonderful love story. Signora Lorenza Cossu, with her wrecked lungs, made him sad.

He was immersed in his bitter reflections when he realised that his phone had started ringing again.

It was the Chief Superintendent.

'Gianni, why didn't you answer before?'

Shit, it had been him calling!

Ascalchi told Ferrara what Lorenza Cossu had told him.

'What's your impression of her?'

He would have liked to say that she had seemed a complete drunkard, that he'd seen her knocking back myrtle liqueur as if it were water, despite the early hour, and that she smoked like a chimney. Instead he just said that she was a woman who was suffering and that her ex-husband must have caused her all kinds of trouble.

'Go to Bologna and get some information on this Rocco from the head of the *Squadra Mobile*. Give him my regards, he's a friend of mine,' Ferrara ordered him.

'All right.'

'Keep me posted – and turn up the ring tone on your mobile!'

The Chief Superintendent hung up as his secretary put his head round the door to announce a visitor.

An unexpected one.

Veronica Borghini, the Russos' fashion-stylist neighbour, was in the waiting room. She was about five foot seven and slim with short, ash-blond hair. She had an amazing tan and was wearing a beautifully made cream trouser suit, a white T-shirt and high heels and sunglasses and carrying a Louis Vuitton bag. She didn't look much over thirty.

'Ask her to wait and call Venturi for me. Tell him to bring the emails he found,' Ferrara ordered.

While examining the computer that they'd found in the Russos' cellar, Venturi had been struck by some emails addressed to 'Veri'. It turned out that 'Veri' was Veronica Borghini, the neighbour they hadn't been able to interview yet. Following that discovery, the Chief Superintendent had wondered whether she might have been Russo's lover.

Perhaps that was why the Russos slept in separate bedrooms . . .

'Was it you who summoned her here?' the Chief Superintendent asked as the Inspector entered the room.

'No, chief.'

What a strange coincidence!

'What exactly do the emails say?'

Venturi handed him a sheet of paper from the folder he was carrying.

'This is one of the most recent, chief. It's dated 15 October, barely three days before the double murder.'

Veri, can I still call you 'my darling'? I can't stand your frequent absences and your projects abroad that keep us separated any more. I suffer, but I know I love you. I'll love you until the end of my days. The distance between us, and your possible unfaithfulness, scare me. I need to talk to you. Something unthinkable has happened and I want you here by my side. I love you! I love you! I love you!

Your Amedeo

'Well done, Signor Lawyer!'

It was the letter of a suffering lover, but also of someone scared by something unexpected.

'Guess how old Veronica is, chief.'

Ferrara scowled but didn't reply.

'Thirty-six, and she's divorced.'

'What did he write to her in the other emails?'

'More or less the same thing. He must have been very ... attached to her.'

'And what did Borghini write in reply?'

'We haven't found any emails in reply.'

'He could have deleted them.'

'It's possible. But we'd need to get an international warrant before we could try to recover them from the server.'

The Chief Superintendent nodded. He knew the procedure and he was aware how long it could take to obtain authorisation.

'It's also possible that Russo read them on another computer, perhaps the one at the office, and, feeling safer there, might not have deleted them.'

Ferrara nodded again. It was feasible. Lucrezia, the secretary, had told him that someone had checked Russo's computer during the search supervised by the Deputy Prosecutor. Perhaps Teresa would be able to learn something from Vinci.

Ferrara gave him back the sheet of paper.

'Let's question her now.'

If that woman knew something, she needed to talk.

But what if she was involved, too? Surely not.

273

That theory had the potential to destroy the jigsaw that he was slowly putting together, piece by piece, in his mind.

Tread softly, Ferrara told himself and he got up to go and meet Veronica Borghini.

'Please make yourself comfortable, signora.'

'Elegant' was the first adjective that came to mind as he looked at her.

The Chief Superintendent held out his hand and she shook it and then went and sat down in the only empty chair facing the desk without taking off her sunglasses. Venturi was sitting in the other and she gave him a distracted glance. She crossed her shapely legs, her hands clutching the bag she held on her lap.

'I'm sorry I couldn't come sooner, but I only got back from presenting a new collection for next season in Paris yesterday. I knew you were trying to find me, so here I am,' she said, before the Chief Superintendent had time to ask his first question. Her tone was confident, self-assured. And she'd looked the police officer in the eye as she spoke.

'Who told you?'

'Signora Corti.'

'We've spoken to all the victims' neighbours. We'd like to ask you a few questions, too,' he explained.

'Go ahead, Chief Superintendent. I was shocked at the news. We were all sure that nothing bad could happen in our little gated community, especially not a murder.' She took off her sunglasses and placed them on the desk. She had light blue eyes and not a single line or wrinkle, although this may have been due to an injection or two, or some touching up by the plastic surgeon.

'Two murders,' Ferrara reminded her.

'Of course, his wife, too.'

'Did you know Signor and Signora Russo?'

It might have seemed a silly question since they lived in the same compound, but the Chief Superintendent wanted to put her at ease.

'Certainly. There aren't many of us and we all know each other, even if we don't all socialise. We just say hello or good evening on the rare occasions we bump into one another.' The woman was direct and concise and seemed very sure of herself. 'My schedule didn't coincide with the Russos' – and not with anyone else's either, if I'm honest,' she explained.

'Did you have any kind of relationship with the lawyer?'

She looked at him questioningly. 'I'm sorry. What sort of relationship?'

'A professional one.'

'What do you mean?'

'Any legal business?'

'Oh! There was one case.'

'What was that?'

'He represented me during my divorce from my ex-husband – a jealous, violent man.'

'And were you satisfied with Signor Russo's work?'

'He provided top-class representation. He worked extraordinarily hard.'

'When did your divorce come through?'

'It was finalised at the start of last summer.'

There was a long silence.

The Chief Superintendent wondered whether to get straight to the point and ask about the emails, but his instinct told him not to rush things. Perhaps some discreet investigation might uncover further ulterior motives to justify a second round of questioning. He wanted to know more about her. About the Russos. And also about this jealous, violent ex-husband.

Veronica Borghini's gaze wandered around the room as if searching for a point to fix on. Her eyes settled on Ferrara once, and then only briefly. She was waiting for the next question and after a while she glanced at the gold Rolex she wore on her wrist.

'What's your ex-husband's name?'

'Why do you want to know? That's all over now.'

'Just so we have all the relevant details.'

She didn't object. The name Gennaro Renzi didn't mean anything to Ferrara.

'What does he do?'

'He's in manufacturing.'

'Which industry?'

'Silk. He's got a factory in Prato.'

'Do you know whether Signor Russo was a member of a masonic lodge?' Ferrara risked asking the question.

'But Chief Superintendent, masonry is secret! How would I know?'

'Were there any rumours around the compound?'

'I've already told you, I'm not close to my neighbours. Besides, what's that got to do with his death?'

'Nothing. It was mainly curiosity; we've heard a few rumours and I wanted to see whether any had reached you,' the Chief Superintendent tried to bluff.

'I don't know anything about it,' she replied curtly.

'All right, signora, you can go, but I think we'll need to see each other again.'

'Why?'

'To take a formal statement. All the other residents of Borgo Bellavista have given one. I realise you don't have time now and I don't want to keep you.'

'A statement?'

'Yes, we need to interview you as a person who may have information of interest to our investigation.'

'But I don't know anything!'

'It's merely a formality.'

'I'm at your disposal, but bear in mind that I'm extremely busy and I'm only in Florence for one week. I leave for New York on Sunday evening.'

'Absolutely. I'll call you in before Sunday.'

Veronica Borghini got up. She shook hands with the Chief Superintendent and Venturi and left the room. She had slim thighs.

As soon as the door closed behind her, Ferrara ordered the Inspector to send an urgent request to tap the woman's phone lines.

'Attach the emails and a brief summary of today's conversation,' he told him.

He was curious to see whether the Prosecutor's Department would put another spanner in the works.

49

Bologna

'Make sure the Police Vehicle sign is clearly visible, Pino. You never know!'

They had just parked the car in one of the spaces reserved for police vehicles in the Piazza Galileo Galilei in front of Police Headquarters in Bologna.

Ricci made sure the sign was clearly visible through the windscreen and followed Ascalchi, who was walking towards the main entrance under the colonnade.

They had driven past the two towers that were the symbol of the city shortly before they arrived. 'Aren't they beautiful!' Ascalchi had exclaimed in admiration when the Asinelli and the Garisenda towers, named after the families who'd had them built, came into view.

'They look like they're about to fall over, a bit like the Leaning Tower of Pisa!' Ricci had commented. 'It would be a real shame if that were to happen.'

'Oh, they won't fall. They've survived wars and the passing of the centuries,' Ascalchi replied.

'Why did they build them so tall?'

'As a show of power, my dear Pino. They were a symbol of

the importance of the richest families of the age when they were built, sometime around 1100, if I'm not mistaken.'

'Ah, power! Like the Twin Towers in Manhattan, which crumbled as if they were made of flour,' sighed Ricci in a sad voice, thinking of all the innocent lives wiped away on 11 September 2001.

As they went into the public waiting room, they passed a disheartened Senegalese couple who'd probably been waiting for several hours from the look of them. Ascalchi and Ricci went over to the reception desk, which was manned by two uniformed officers. One was talking on the telephone and the other was sorting through some papers. Ascalchi introduced himself, saying that he'd come from Florence and needed to speak to the Head of the *Squadra Mobile*.

'Do you have an appointment?'

'Yes, I called a couple of hours ago. He's expecting me.'

The officer got up and invited them to follow him, leading them through a labyrinth of corridors until they reached the offices of the *Squadra Mobile*.

'Wait here.'

Ascalchi and Ricci sat down.

The officer returned a few minutes later. 'He's dealing with an emergency and asked if you could wait.'

It was almost ten minutes before Alessandro Polito, Head of the *Squadra Mobile*, appeared. 'Come into my office,' he invited them with a smile.

Before listening to the reason for their visit, Polito reminisced about a previous collaboration between his team and the Florentine *Squadra Mobile*, back in 1999, after two girls, Cinzia Roberti and Valentina Preti, had been brutally murdered in Bologna.

'You should have seen them. They're the kind of images that remain burnt into your eyes forever,' he said. Apparently, when he'd arrived at the crime scene, they'd found the smaller girl lying beside her friend in a lake of blood with a horrific wound in her back. Their bodies had been butchered.

Ascalchi scowled in disgust. 'Did you catch the killers?'

'Yes, thanks to the collaboration between our offices. And your chief, Ferrara.'

'Who were they?'

'There was only one – a serial killer who was originally from Calabria and went by the name of Mike Ross.'

Ascalchi had joined the *Squadra Mobile* a few months after the double murder and was unfamiliar with the story, but Ricci remembered hearing about the case: 'Wasn't he the guy who was pretending to be an American?'

'That's the one. But now let's get down to work. Tell me why my old friend Ferrara has sent you to visit me.'

Ascalchi told him about their current investigation and the story Lorenza Cossu had told them about Rocco Ortu. 'We'd like information on this person. It sounds as though he's working as a magician here in Bologna, or in the surrounding area.'

Polito didn't need to look up the file. He knew about Ortu and his previous activities in Turin. The Turinese Police Headquarters had sent him a copy of all their files on Satan's Faithful.

'He's a strange guy. He walks around in sandals and an orange tunic, even in winter, in spite of the cold and the snow,' he told them.

'Eccentric.'

'Fairly. We've investigated him a couple of times and even used phone taps, but unfortunately we haven't gathered enough material to bring him to trial.'

'Can we see the file?' asked Ascalchi. 'We might find something referring to his brother, Italo – it's him that we're interested in, in relation to our case.'

'No problem.'

Polito picked up the phone and ordered the archivist to bring him all the paperwork.

'Would you like a coffee while we wait?' he offered. 'Not one of those ones from the machine, I'll take you to a bar near here.'

'Thanks!' they replied in chorus. The prospect of drinking proper coffee in a bar was a well-earned treat.

50

Donato Russo's home, Florence

It was ten past four in the afternoon when Donato Russo returned home to find his daughter wasn't there.

He stuck his head into her bedroom with its yellow walls and floral curtains, but there was no sign of Flavia or the backpack she used for school. After taking several days off for the period of mourning, she had returned to lessons at the Santissima Annunziata State High School near the Villa del Poggio Imperiale, a popular school among the haute bourgeoisie who valued top-class education and cultural instruction. It was one of the first girls schools in Europe, the brainchild of the Marquis Gino Capponi and opened by the Grand Duke Ferdinando in 1823.

Flavia studied the *Liceo classico europeo* syllabus. A model student, she was admired by her classmates for her beauty and her brains. Only one or two, who felt they were in competition with her, hated her and spread unpleasant rumours about her, claiming that she exploited her family's good connections and was too easy with boys and things like that. Unfortunately that was the way of the world. In reality, Flavia was a calm girl, radiant and full of life; she had an infectious laugh that made everyone smile, but when she was sad she knew how to hide it.

'Where the hell has she got to? And why hasn't she called me? I'll give her hell when she shows up,' Donato told himself, trying to hide the anxiety that had overwhelmed him.

As usual, he'd dropped her off at school this morning on his way to work. Flavia made her own way home, almost always by bus, though occasionally on the back of a friend's moped. She'd never been this late before, and especially not without telling him.

He called her on her mobile, but after the first ring the metallic voice cut in and announced that the phone was either switched off or unavailable. He tried again a few minutes later, but he got the same response. He waited an hour, repeatedly telling himself that no, nothing could have happened to her and that he was worrying for no reason. Then he picked up the phone book and looked up the numbers of her closest school friends, guessing she must have gone home with one of them. She wouldn't have simply disappeared without telling anyone or leaving a message, he reassured himself as he wrote the phone numbers down on a scrap of paper.

Then he made three phone calls. All three friends told him the same thing: They'd gone their separate ways at the school gates. Flavia, still sad because of what had happened to her grandparents, had decided not to hang out with them. The last they saw of her, she was walking alone along the Viale del Poggio Imperiale, heading for the bus stop at the Porta Romana. It had been ten past one, or quarter past at the latest.

Anxiety gave way to fear.

He felt a tightness in his chest. He had brought Flavia up alone since she'd been four years old. His wife had fallen prey to an incurable illness after barely five years of happy marriage and had died in a prestigious Swiss hospital. Not even those high-profile surgeons had been able to save her, and he had returned to Florence with his young wife in one of the aeroplane's refrigerated containers.

It hadn't been easy living alone with Flavia, but with the help of her grandparents he'd managed pretty well. He'd had a few romantic relationships, but nothing that had lasted because Flavia had reacted badly to them. The worst had been when he'd introduced her to a woman with whom he planned to live. His daughter had opposed it and forced him to give her up.

Could there be a boy involved? She had never mentioned a boy to her father and they told each other everything. Even her friends, her closest friends, had ruled it out when he asked them about it on the phone.

Could she have had an accident?

He dialled the emergency numbers for the city's hospitals. They all replied in the negative: no sixteen-year-old girls and nobody by the name of Flavia Russo had been brought in. He tried calling her mobile again, but got the same reply as before. It was turned off or unavailable. He felt as if he was suffocating as he repeated, 'Where's she gone? Why hasn't she been in touch?'

The sudden ringing of the telephone at 5.45 p.m. echoed like a gunshot. His heart pounding in his chest, he ran into the kitchen.

His phone lay there on the table where he'd left it.

The number on the screen was Flavia's. Donato Russo answered breathlessly just before it went to voicemail.

He didn't have time to speak before the voice of an adult male, deep and cold, told him, 'Be careful what you do and say, otherwise—'

'Who are you?' Russo interrupted. It was a voice he didn't recognise. A voice that didn't have a typical Florentine accent.

'Let me speak!' the man ordered him. 'There are several of us. And, if you don't do as we tell you, there will be consequences.'

'Listen to me—'

'Daddy!'

The phone was passed from hand to hand.

Just that one word. And a couple of sobs. A small gasp.

'Flavia! . . . Flavia! . . . Flavia . . .'

After several seconds he heard the man's voice again.

'Do you understand now? We've got your Flavia and we'll leave her alone as long as you do as you're told. You'll hear from us soon and we'll tell you what you need to do. In the meantime if you want your daughter back at home safe and sound, don't do anything stupid like go to the police. If you do, we'll kill her.'

'Hello? Hello?'

Nothing.

They'd hung up.

He stared at the display for some time, his daughter's voice and the sound of her breathing still in his ears. Then he opened the folder listing the last calls received. He wasn't mistaken. They had called from Flavia's phone.

He waited for the phone to ring again.

It remained silent.

Donato slumped into a chair, his head in his hands. He started to sweat. They'd killed his parents and now they'd kidnapped his daughter. His only daughter. Who could hate his family enough to commit murder and to kidnap Flavia? he asked himself, his throat dry with anguish. Who was trying to punish his family, taking everything away from him? Who wanted to destroy him, and why?

Overcome with panic, he tried to order his thoughts, then he was struck by a doubt: if the killers were those Eastern European criminals like everyone seemed to think, why had they taken Flavia? Perhaps there was something more important in it for them. Something he was unaware of. To reassure himself, he told himself that they must have taken her by mistake and they'd let her go as soon as they realised their error.

Still clutching the telephone, he tried to recall the conversation.

'You'll hear from us soon and we'll tell you what you need to do,' the unknown man had told him.

The fear in Flavia's voice echoed in his head.

But what did they want him to do? He wanted to scream, to hurl the phone away. But, with an effort, he controlled himself and tried to think things through. He could come up with only two options.

The first: to call the police.

He could report her missing, but without mentioning the phone call. However, given the huge number of teenagers who ran away from home and then came back of their own accord within a short space of time, the police might let the first twenty-four hours pass without doing anything.

It would be a different matter if he told them about the threats he'd received.

But where could they look for her? There were so many places you could hide a sixteen-year-old. Thousands and thousands, surely. And even more if they were to kill her and make her body disappear. He felt a shiver run down his back at the thought of it.

The second option: to wait for the kidnappers' next move.

He would decide whether or not to contact Police Headquarters afterwards. Maybe that woman who'd questioned him – perhaps a policewoman would act with greater caution.

Good sense, and, most of all, a father's love, encouraged him to go for the second option. He started to pace up and down the hallway.

'You'll hear from us soon!'

Distraught, he went into the living room and slumped into an armchair. He closed his eyes as if in doing so he could ease the pain that was creeping through his bones. He remembered his father's stories about the Sardinian kidnappers who had operated in Tuscany during the seventies and eighties, and the rumours about their missing victims having been fed to pigs. Gradually he slipped into sleep.

He saw Flavia, shouting desperately for help, flailing in the mud and shit, the pigs moving in, ready to devour her. He woke up with a start, sweat pouring off him, telling himself over and over again that no, he wouldn't let that happen, he would do anything and more to bring his little girl back home.

This reality, unimaginable until a short while earlier, made him certain of one thing. All his dreams as a parent were on the verge of destruction. Along with his aspirations of becoming a successful lawyer, like his father had been, and his paternal grandfather before him. The perfect future he'd planned was suddenly fading away.

From that moment on his life would be filled with pain and misery.

He stopped thinking and sat staring blankly into space.

Half an hour later the intercom bleeped, but Donato Russo didn't hear it. He was in Flavia's room, where he had just finished examining her computer, hoping to find some emails between her and her friends. He wanted to know if his daughter had told them about anything strange or suspicious that had happened recently. Nothing, he found nothing.

He started looking at the objects that filled Flavia's world: posters of singers, her clothes arranged neatly in the wardrobe, the copy of *Harry Potter and the Order of the Phoenix* left on her bedside table.

Another bleep. Somebody had pressed the button on the intercom by the front door a second time.

This time he heard it and got up from the small armchair, his legs trembling, barely able to support his weight as he made his way along the corridor that lead to the front door.

'Who is it?' he asked.

'The police.'

His mouth went dry and he felt light-headed. In a daze, he pressed the buzzer to open the door. 'They've come to tell me they've found the body,' he thought as he waited for them to come up. 'They'll ask me to take a seat and then they'll tell me that Flavia's dead, that they've found her body in a lay-by on the autostrada or in a clearing in the woods.'

After a few moments a uniformed police officer arrived at the door holding a document. 'Are you Donato Russo, the lawyer?'

'Yes, I am. Tell me, has something hap—'

'Superintendent Rizzo, the Deputy Head of the *Squadra Mobile*, has sent me with the statement for you to sign.'

Relief surged through him. He asked the man in and, with a trembling hand, signed the papers without reading them. He gave them straight back.

'Please pass on my apologies to the Chief Superintendent. I was supposed to drop by Headquarters, but with all these things to do . . . ' he was saying.

'Don't worry. Superintendent Rizzo sends his regards and his thanks for your help.'

Donato saw the officer out and closed the door to the apartment again. Only then did he allow himself to take several deep breaths.

Fuck! If the kidnappers found out that the police had been at the house, they'd think he had reported the kidnapping.

He started trembling violently at the thought.

As soon as he got back to Headquarters, Ascalchi went to brief the Chief Superintendent on the investigations the Bologna police had carried out into Rocco Ortu.

The 'magician'.

The case history file he'd been given inlcuded a copy of Ortu's criminal record. There were several crimes listed, including a couple of livestock thefts from when he had lived with his grandparents in Sardinia as a youngster; sheep-rustling was endemic on the island. Then, there were the crimes he'd committed in Turin, although he'd been acquitted of the charges.

'What about his brother Italo?'

'No mention.'

'Is he married? Does he have children?'

'No, or at least, not according to the file. From what we understand, he lives in a commune, or something of the kind.'

'In Bologna?'

'No, in the countryside.'

'Where?'

'At Sasso Marconi, in the Apennines.'

'What sort of commune is it?'

'Some kind of sect.'

'You should go and have a look around.'

'We'll go tomorrow. Ricci's got an informer in the area. Well, he was actually one of Sergi's guys, but Rizzo's met him too and he went to a few of their meetings.

'Go and find him.'

'It won't be hard.'

'Why?'

Ascalchi smiled.

'Is something funny?'

'Yes, chief.'

He explained that he'd learned from Rizzo that the man, who had married a local woman, had been arrested for libelling a trade union in Bologna, but that he'd been released after barely two days in prison.

'A lack of specific, serious and connected evidence?'

'No, chief.' Ascalchi burst out laughing.

'Come on, let me in on the joke. What happened?'

'There wasn't a cell or a toilet that could accommodate him – he weighs over thirty stone!' Ascalchi burst out laughing again, deforming his facial features even further.

For the first time in days, Ferrara let himself go, though he couldn't say whether it was Ascalchi's story that made him laugh or the expression on his friend's face.

'Go and pay him a visit tomorrow,' Ferrara replied, becoming serious again.

'Ricci knows where to find him.'

Still smiling, Ascalchi left the room. A moment later Ferrara heard him start laughing again.

51

Flavia woke up.

For a moment she thought she was dreaming.

She opened her eyes but she couldn't see anything. The room was in semi-darkness with only a dim light in the corner to her right. She blinked but couldn't bring any objects into focus. There was a constant pounding in her head and it was impossible to think straight. It took a few moments before she realised that she was on a mattress on the floor. She took a deep breath to try and stop the panic. Breathing out slowly, she strained her ears, trying to hear something, but the only sound she could hear was her own breathing, which was becoming more and more wheezy. She realised she was cold. She closed her eyes again.

The memories exploded in her mind like lightning flashing against a black sky.

She was on her way home after class, walking down from Poggio Imperiale to catch the bus at the Porta Romana. A man had grabbed her by the arm and forced her into a van that looked like an ambulance. He was wearing a white paramedic's uniform. She had seen some cars travelling along the road in the opposite direction, but none of the drivers had seemed interested in what was happening. The man had jabbed a needle in her arm, and before she could scream a hand had covered her mouth.

She didn't remember anything else.

Overwhelmed by fear, she thought of her grandparents, murdered in their home.

'Now it's my turn,' she told herself. 'Why? What have I done?'

Her heart began to beat faster and faster. She realised that her bladder was full to bursting. Perhaps from the cold, or perhaps from fear, she began to tremble. In despair, she cried out for her father, then gave a hysterical sob as the faint echo of 'Daddy' faded into the darkness and urine trickled on to the floor.

Why? Why? Why?

She had no idea how long she'd been in this place. Telling herself she'd have to find a way to get out of there, she slipped into sleep.

The eye that had been watching her through the hole in the opposite wall moved away. The kidnapper had other things to do.

He had found Donato Russo's weak spot. Now the time had come to exploit it.

It was the most anxious night of Donato Russo's life.

Unable even to doze, he tossed and turned between the sheets. After a while he glanced at the clock on the bedside table: 3.20 a.m. He had thought it was at least five or six o'clock. And he recalled the words his grandfather used to say: the night never ends. It was true; there was no peace. He was consumed with guilt for not having collected Flavia from school. But how could he have known this would happen? There had been no warning signs, nothing to suggest she was in danger.

'Stop torturing yourself,' he told himself, knowing that there was nothing for him to do now but wait – and pray that they wouldn't hurt Flavia. He got up, went into the bathroom and looked at himself in the mirror. He barely recognised his own reflection. His eyes were ringed by dark circles. His skin was grey. And his cheeks were hollower than they had ever been, even at his parents' funeral.

Then he went into the living room. He flopped down on to the sofa next to the side table where the telephone sat, defiantly silent. He waited there for the arrival of the first light of dawn in an unnatural silence, his gaze fixed on the telephone.

And his anxiety increased with every minute, accentuating his solitude and his powerlessness.

52

5.30 *a.m., Tuesday 26 October, Piazza San Marco*

Luigi Ciuffi left the house at ten past five that Tuesday morning. The air was cool and the city was calm, but it would soon be awake, if still drowsy. The streets were lit by the faint glow of the street lamps and the dark sky was devoid of stars. It was his favourite time of day, perhaps because it reminded him of the times when, as a student, he would leave the house at dawn after drinking a couple of egg yolks to run along the Lungomare Caracciolo, from Mergellina to the Piazza Vittoria and around the Napoli Gardens. Far from the city's dangers, he had enjoyed the solitude.

As he walked, he felt confident of uncovering some important clue that would kick-start the investigation.

As he turned right at the traffic lights, leaving the Via Nazionale for the Via XXVII April, he spotted two women in short skirts in a bar. Prostitutes at the end of a night's work, he thought. He looked at his watch and carried on walking. A little way further on he saw a female tramp digging through a dustbin. He shook his head and quickened his pace.

In less than two minutes he arrived at the Piazza San Marco where a gigantic bronze statue of General Manfredo Fanti, the work of the sculptor Papi, stood on a pedestal with inscriptions in bronze relief.

As he drew closer, he spotted Felice Contini. The informant. He had called him from the office the previous evening to arrange a meeting for 5.30 a.m. the next day.

A bar on the corner of the Via Cavour was already open. One of the Flying Squad's patrol cars was parked outside and the two uniformed officers could be seen sitting at the bar alongside the handful of patrons who were having a coffee before heading into work.

'Good morning, Superintendent,' Contini greeted him. He had slipped behind the statue on the side that faced the entrance to the church and was peering around furtively, as if afraid he might be seen talking to the police.

'You've chosen a good time, haven't you!'

'I've made you get up early, but you won't regret it.'

'Talk!'

'Amedeo Russo was blackmailing someone.'

'Who?'

'Someone with several skeletons in the closet.'

'Who?'

'Someone who liked young flesh for their parties.'

'And how was Russo blackmailing them?'

'He had proof. Incriminating material.'

'What sort of material?'

'Now you're asking too much. I can tell you that Russo liked young flesh, too, but he'd distanced himself a bit recently. That's what's being said in certain circles.'

The paedophilic ones!

'Minors, then?'

'Yes, under fourteen, sixteen at the most.'

'Who provided them?'

'I don't know that. It's a secret world.'

Of course, but Contini was one of those bastards who traded naked photos of little girls.

'Italians? Foreigners?'

The man shook his head in denial. 'I don't know. But you should try the Africans,' he added.

'Be more specific.'

'The Nigerians.'

Ciuffi nodded. The *Squadra Mobile* had recently identified a couple of Nigerian women, both former prostitutes, who ran a child prostitution ring from their apartment. During the investigation, one of the victims had told them that she'd been sold by her own parents when she was barely thirteen. They'd delivered her to a woman who was connected to the traffickers; she'd been transported across the deserts of Nigeria and Libya to a kind of receiving centre on the Libyan coast, where they'd put her on a boat to Lampedusa.

Once in Italy, she was told she would have to pay fifty or sixty thousand euros to free herself from slavery. Prostitution alone would never raise that kind of money; in order to pay them off she would be forced to take advantage of her young compatriots, sell them into slavery too. It was an endless chain, which, in her case, was broken by the intervention of the police. They got her into a centre for women rescued from the streets, where hopefully she could start to build a new life for herself.

That investigation had shown that Nigerian organised crime might be a new phenomenon, but it seemed to be thriving in Florence.

'Give me a name, Contini!'

The informant looked around.

Across the square, the two police officers were just leaving the bar. Felice Contini looked at them with suspicious eyes. First one, then the other. He had the impression that the fatter one had been part of the patrol that had taken him to Headquarters the day before. He studied the officer while he stood still on the pavement and shook himself to straighten his uniform jacket. Then he watched him until he got into the passenger side of the car. His colleague was already at the wheel.

'Fuck!' exclaimed Contini, returning to the shelter of the statue.

'What is it?'

The informant explained that he was afraid of being recognised. 'We need to split up, Chief Superintendent.'

'No, give me a name! I want it now. You've made me come here, and at this hour . . . '

The police car was slowly pulling away.

'Fuck it, give me a name, Contini!'

'Oba.'

'What did you say?'

'O-B-A,' Contini spelled it out.

Still at walking pace, the patrol car was making a tour of the square as Contini and Ciuffi ducked behind the statue so as not to be seen.

'Tell me who that is and where they live! You know incomplete information isn't worth a damn to me.'

'She lives outside the historic centre.'

'Where?'

'Outside.'

'Where exactly?'

'In a house she owns on the Via Pisana, opposite a shop selling computers and televisions. Near a supermarket.'

The Flying Squad patrol had by this time completed their circuit of the square and were heading down the Via Cavour towards the Duomo. The two police officers would soon be reprising their battle against the bag snatchers. It was the most common crime in the city centre and was almost always committed by the same suspects.

'Are you sure about that?'

'Fuck it! I'm sure,' replied Contini disrespectfully. 'I don't tell fairy stories. What I say is the truth. I've kept my promise, but don't come looking for me any more!'

'Thanks, Contini,' said Ciuffi. 'We understand each other.'

'And obviously I haven't told you anything and I don't want to have anything to do with this business. Those are powerful people.'

Powerful and perverted!

'Don't worry. One last thing: where do they hold these parties with their "young flesh"?'

'That's asking too much. Do you want to get me killed? Ask Oba. She's one of the ones who provide the minors.'

Ciuffi didn't push it.

'Tell your chief, Ferrara, that Contini is a man of his word. And that I don't have anything to do with those murders. They're out of my league. It's useless hauling me into Headquarters. Doing that only humiliates me and puts my life at risk.'

'Don't worry. Let me know if you have any other information.'

'Forget about me, Superintendent. And be careful – Oba practises black magic. She's a truly dangerous woman. If someone finds out I've been talking, I'm a dead man. Those people don't mess around – not the Nigerians or the people they do business with. And there's a lot of unrest in the city since your raid on the Marquis Degli Aldobrandi's home.' A shadow of fear crossed his face.

Ciuffi would have liked to ask him what he knew about the Marquis, but Contini was hurrying off down the street. He was certain the informant knew more than he'd revealed and wished there were some way to get him to talk. Still, at least he'd given them something.

Reviewing their conversation, Ciuffi told himself that the mingling of black magic with prostitution was nothing new. He knew from previous investigations that the 'mamans' kept their girls in line either through violence or through magic. If the victims were disobedient, the 'maman' would threaten to cast spells or conduct voodoo rituals against them and against their families. Such threats terrified the girls far more than any physical punishment they might inflict.

Ciuffi himself felt a tremor of fear, but it wasn't the threat of black magic that worried him so much as the prospect of going up against the invisible ones. He didn't know who this Marquis Degli Aldobrandi was, but he was bound to be part of that circle of powerful untouchables. Yet the informant had mentioned a raid – surely he would have heard if that were the case? No, it must have been the Carabinieri.

He glanced at his watch. It was still early. He would have plenty of time to think, have a hot shower and eat breakfast with his family.

And then he would go and see Ferrara.

Making his way to the office shortly before eight, Luigi Ciuffi thought back to the first time he'd seen Contini.

Ciuffi and his men had raided Contini's apartment as part of an anti-drugs operation. They'd seized an illegally owned pistol that had been hidden in the toilet cistern, along with a bit of grass and a couple of lines of cocaine – for personal use, according to Contini. And then they'd found the shoebox full of photos of naked boys and girls, some of them very young, in provocative poses. The discovery had led them to believe that the man was part of a paedophile ring.

He thought back over the interrogation that had taken place, and he heard once more the words with which they'd come to an agreement at the end of the conversation.

'A deal that's good for you and for me, too,' he'd told Contini.

'And what's that?'

'I'll only charge you for the pistol. Once you get out of jail, you have to keep me informed of what's happening on the streets. You'll give me the names and addresses of the pushers and you'll tell me what they're dealing. In return, I'll pretend there were no photos, for now, and I'll also pay you back later on.'

'You mean you want me to be a spy?'

'You'll make a friend.'

'I promise I'll get in touch if there's anything to tell,' were Contini's last words before he was transferred to the prison at Solliciano.

He'd been released after serving a couple of years but had never been in touch. Ciuffi hadn't set eyes on him again until he was brought in as part of the round-up following the murder of the Russos.

But that morning he might just have delivered on his promise.

8.15 a.m., the Chief Superintendent's office

Luigi Ciuffi was in for a surprise when he opened the door.

It was a scene of complete mayhem – which was highly unusual for that hour of the morning. The chaos had nothing to do with the presence of his colleagues Rizzo, Venturi, Ascalchi, Ricci, Micalizi and even Fanti. It was due to the piles of boxes on the floor, which Fanti was busily emptying and arranging the contents on a table and a desk borrowed from another office for the occasion.

He approached Ferrara's desk with a questioning raise of his eyebrow.

'One of the Flying Squad patrols seized all this material on Sunday,' explained the Chief Superintendent. Then he told him about the raid on the Marquis Degli Aldobrandi's apartment.

Aha, that was the raid Contini had mentioned!

'Anything interesting?'

'It looks like it. Fanti and Officer Belli have been cataloguing the material since it was brought in. I've had them cart it up here so I can examine it personally.'

Having learned the details of the operation lead by Inspector Trovato, Ciuffi commented, 'This case makes me think of the one involving that girl we found half-dead on the edge of the woods above Scandicci a few summers ago. Do you remember?'

The Chief Superintendent nodded. The girl, who they had named Stella, had been the victim of some powerful paedophiles. That was back in August 2001.

'I've got some news, chief,' Ciuffi said, then he recounted the conversation he'd had with Felice Contini word for word, starting with the phone call he'd received from the informer the previous evening. The thing that had struck him most had been the reference to the Marquis. He told Ferrara the exact words Contini used: 'There's a lot of unrest in the city since your raid on the Marquis Degli Aldobrandi's home.'

Those words set the Chief Superintendent thinking. Without realising it, Inspector Trovato might have stumbled upon something even more serious than the items seized from the Marquis's luxurious home. This could be tied into one of the darkest and most inadmissible of the city's mysteries.

Ferrara got up and went to rifle through the papers that he was storing in the mobile bookshelf. He unlocked the bottom door, pulled out a folder and began to flick through it until he found the document he was looking for. It was a report by his colleagues from the SCO and the anti-drugs team in Rome. In cooperation with Interpol, they had established the existence of a Nigerian criminal association in Italy, organised over various levels. Ferrara sat down and began to read, lingering over the segments where the various roles within the organisation were described:

The 'connection man' is the one who organises the journeys and sources the documents necessary to leave the country illegally;

The 'trolley' is the one who accompanies the youngsters to their destination;

The 'head mamans' are those who manage the prostitutes within

*a precise system of territorial subdivision of each city, especially in
northern and central Italy;*

*The 'mamans' are the ones who are responsible for controlling the
prostitutes on a lower level, in addition to being the owners of several girls.*

'Luigi, this Oba could be the head maman,' Ferrara said, after
setting the papers aside. 'We need to identify her and pay her a
visit, perhaps even tonight,' he added, thinking it would be best
to strike fast in order to take advantage of this information.

Ciuffi nodded.

'Establish the identity of everyone you find and have them
brought in to our offices. Seize everything that could be useful,
every piece of paper you find with something written on it,' he
went on.

Ciuffi couldn't wait to get started. 'I'll take care of it, chief.
We'll bring in every last scrap,' he reassured him with a slight
smile.

'And we'll do this off our own bat.'

'Shouldn't I request a search warrant from the Prosecutor's
Department?'

'No. Get someone from the Immigration Office involved –
that way we can carry out our raid under the guise of a routine
check on illegal immigrants.'

'Perfect, chief!'

'Then we need to find out where these parties take place. See
if you can find Contini again, get his back against the wall. He
must know more.'

'He said we're putting his life at risk. He'll never agree to talk.'

'Insist.'

'OK.'

Ciuffi left the chief's office raring to get started. As always.
After all, it was a case of catching criminals.

53

Sasso Marconi

Sasso Marconi is a town in the Emilian Apennines about ten miles from Bologna. It is the hometown of Guglielmo Marconi, the famous physicist and inventor, whose remains rest in his paternal home of Villa Griffone.

Ascalchi and Ricci left the A1 autostrada shortly after eleven in the morning and made their way towards the town. They were heading for a tavern near the central square that was managed by their informer. Leaving their pool car near the Carabinieri barracks, they set off on foot.

'There it is – that's the place,' said Ricci.

A short, heavy-set man in his fifties was standing outside, writing the menu on a blackboard. The set lunch comprised pasta with beans, pork chops and a quarter-bottle of the house red wine for nine euros.

'That's good value,' commented Ascalchi, greeting the man.

'You're too early,' the man replied. 'The kitchen doesn't open until half past twelve.'

The dining room, all dark wood with a low-beamed ceiling, was in darkness. The air smelled of wine and garlic. The main room was deserted but a couple of the tables had been set. Behind the bar, a fat woman with dark, messy hair was wiping her hands on a rag. She looked up when she heard them arrive.

'Can I help you?' she asked.

'Something to drink, please. We'll sit there,' replied Ricci, nodding to his right. He'd just spotted the man they were looking for.

'Make yourselves comfortable. My husband or I will be with you shortly.'

'Thank you.'

They sat at the table next to the informant. He was a mound of flesh, enormous and solid. There was a half-empty carafe of wine and a full glass in front of him.

'Hello, Tommaso!' Ricci greeted him with a smile.

The man returned the greeting, but his eyes remained hard, his forehead furrowed. 'It's a while since we've seen each other,' he said. 'Where's Sergi, Florence's answer to Serpico? Why hasn't he come?'

The two policeman exchanged a look. Surely he must have heard the news? But when Ricci told him about finding their colleague's body, his shock and sadness seemed genuine. He explained that he no longer watched television and didn't read the newspapers as he hadn't had a proper home for almost a year.

'Why not?' Ricci asked him.

'I couldn't pay the rent and the landlord threw me out. The bar doesn't make much money and the town is only busy in the summer months. My money has to support my brother's family too.'

He told how the bailiff had showed up one morning, accompanied by two carabinieri, and forcibly removed him from his home. He'd been living in a caravan on the outskirts of town ever since. Isolated from the rest of the world, except for the odd visit to the bar. These days he only came in to have lunch.

'My wife left me. She felt the cold,' he added, his eyes bright with sadness, or perhaps alcohol.

'I'm sorry,' replied Ricci.

'What brings you here?' asked Tommaso.

Just then the woman from the bar arrived. 'What can I get you?'

'A carafe of red wine,' replied Ascalchi.

'A litre?'

'No, half.'

The woman went away with a scowl.

'She's my sister-in-law,' smiled Tommaso.

'Rocco Ortu. That's who's brought us here,' said Ricci.

The fat man picked up his glass, which was almost invisible in his enormous hand, and drained it in one mouthful. Then he put it back on the table and wiped his mouth with the back of his hand. He was about to speak, but he saw his sister-in-law returning with the carafe on a tray. 'One moment,' he murmured, giving them a wink.

After placing the wine on the table, the woman went back to the bar. The police officers filled their glasses and raised them in a toast.

'To Serpico, a real cop! An old-school cop!' said the big man, beating Ricci to it.

'To our colleague!' the two police officers replied.

'I don't know anyone called Rocco Ortu,' Tommaso told them. 'What does he work as?'

'Nothing. We're told he lives in a commune and is a pretty eccentric guy. He wears an orange tunic even in wint—'

'The magician!' said Tommaso, cutting him off. 'The guy's a fool. He lives out in the middle of nowhere; we rarely see him around here.'

'Is he on his own when you see him?'

'No. He's always with some young woman or other, often a girl with long hair who walks barefoot, even in the winter. But why are you interested in him?'

Ascalchi and Ricci exchanged a look. It was Ricci who spoke.

He told Tommaso about the double murder at Borgo Bellavista and explained that they suspected that Rocco's brother, a security guard who'd been on duty on the night in question, might be involved.

Tommaso filled his glass and tossed the wine back. The two policemen drank a sip.

'What are the victims' names?'

'Amedeo Russo and his wife, Elisa.'

'I don't know them,' said Tommaso impassively. Then he picked up his glass again and emptied it. He put it roughly on to the table. 'But I could tell you something interesting that might please your chief. By the way, is it still Ferrara?'

'Yes, why?'

'Haven't they got rid of him yet?'

'What do you mean?'

'It was "on the cards",' he raised his hands with fingers curved to indicate quotation marks. 'Or so I've heard.'

'Tell us more!' Rizzo encouraged him.

'And you'll be able to help me?'

'What sort of help do you need?'

'To find a house, here or nearby. I want to get my wife back.'

'I can't promise you anything, but if what you tell us proves useful, I'm sure the Chief Superintendent will be able to sort something out.'

Some clients had entered the bar. One of them came to sit in the same part of the bar as them, although he was two tables away.

'Stay and have something to eat, that way we can talk more easily,' Tommaso suggested.

Ascalchi and Rizzo looked at one another, then Ascalchi agreed. 'All right.'

The man spoke for almost two hours straight.

When he finished, the two police officers said goodbye and promised that they would be in touch to help him resolve his personal problems.

Full of energy, they got in the car and set off at top speed. Ascalchi waited until they were out of town before speaking. 'Shit, Pino, you go looking for one thing and you find something completely different!'

'That's what always happened with Serpico,' replied Ricci. 'He was forever wearing down the tyres, driving hundreds of miles, and wrecking the soles of his shoes, but he always found something.'

They hadn't learned anything about Rocco Ortu, nor about Amedeo Russo, but they had discovered some potentially explosive information.

And now they couldn't wait to tell the Chief Superintendent.

54

Vinci was on the telephone when Teresa found him.

He nodded for her to sit down. Once he'd finished his conversation, the policewoman handed him the folder containing the request to tap Veronica Borghini's phone before he had a chance to speak. Vinci flicked through it rapidly without lingering over any of the attached documents. Then he looked up and stared at her for a long moment.

'Let's go and get something to drink,' he said, getting up.

When they reached the Piazza della Repubblica, Vinci suggested going further afield instead of heading into one of their regular haunts. 'How about Il Revoire in the Piazza della Signoria?' he asked her. Without waiting for her answer, he continued, 'Did you go to Milan?'

'No.'

'Why not?'

'I had to work. I'll go next weekend.'

'That's going to be tough if you follow your boss's example.'

'No, I'm going to go this time.'

'We'll see. But if you do stay in Florence, I can offer you an alternative for Sunday morning. We could play tennis.'

Teresa remained silent.

'Don't you like tennis?'

'I've never played.'

'Try it and you'll be hooked. I'll teach you.'

'But I don't have the right clothes.'

'We'll buy them on Saturday.'

Silence.

'Well, what do you say?'

'I'll see.'

In the meantime they'd arrived at Il Revoire, where Vinci chose a small table set slightly apart. They ordered two house *aperitivi* from the waiter.

Teresa didn't give Vinci time to speak. Sensing that he was eager to return to the subject of the weekend, she headed him off by asking, 'What do you think of the contents of the request? The woman was Russo's lover.'

'It's always work, work, work. Take a break.'

'It's important. I care about this investigation.'

The waiter placed their drinks and a couple of small dishes containing olives and salted crackers on the table.

'To my new tennis partner,' said Vinci, lifting his glass in a toast. He took the first sip and continued talking, ignoring what Teresa had told him. 'There's something I'd really like . . . '

She stared at him.

'I'd like us to become proper friends.'

Teresa blushed. She was tempted to retort that she was just a policewoman who was working with the Prosecutor's Department, but she stopped herself.

'Don't you want to?'

'But . . . '

'No buts. Let's start with the tennis.'

Teresa felt so uncomfortable that she couldn't wait to get away. At long last Vinci paid at the till and they set off along the Via dei Calzaiuoli. When they reached the Coin department store, she asked when he would be able to let her have the authorisation, emphasising the urgency.

'I don't know. Fiore might not agree.'

'Why not?'

'He doesn't like digging in certain places.'

'But—'

'There's something you need to know, Teresa, and I'm going to tell you because your friendship is important to me. But you must promise you'll keep it to yourself.'

The policewoman nodded.

Vinci stopped and put an arm around her shoulders. He leaned so close to her he was almost touching her left ear, murmuring: 'Fiore isn't an independent man.'

A confused expression appeared on Teresa's face.

'Don't you understand?'

She shook her head. Vinci moved away and held his hands in front of his abdomen, miming a small apron.

'Is he a mason?'

'Well done! I can see you've understood.'

They walked on and Teresa said goodbye in front of the entrance to the Prosecutor's Department.

Luca Fiore was a mason and not an independent man. This was the last thing they needed!

The Chief Superintendent was not in the best of moods and the news his team brought him wasn't about to change that. In fact, Ferrara was sure that these new discoveries would make the investigation even more complicated.

He received the first piece of news from Ascalchi and Ricci on their return from Sasso Marconi.

During the two hours when Tommaso had spoken like a river in full spate, he had revealed the existence of a house, known as 'the House of the Roses', where bizarre parties took place featuring frenetic sex, often with minors. A house that held all the dirty secrets of its frequent visitors: people of a certain calibre, able to do as they pleased and live out their fantasies, even if those fantasies involved murder. The guests always arrived with a black hood over their heads so as not to be recognised. They looked like executioners.

And that wasn't all.

Tommaso had also told them that the owner enjoyed protection at the highest level, even from the offices of the judiciary, so much so that when anonymous letters denouncing him were received, they went straight into the wastepaper basket.

'Did he give you any names?' asked the Chief Superintendent.

'No. He swore he didn't know any.'

'And where is this house?'

'He doesn't know, but from what he's heard it could be somewhere near Chianti,' replied Ascalchi again.

The Chief Superintendent lit a half-smoked cigar and took a few puffs. Then he held it between his lips. 'Anything else?' he asked.

'Nothing, except that, according to Tommaso, investigations into corruption and misuse of public money are also being buried.'

The Chief Superintendent didn't ask for details. It was nothing new. He was well aware that investigations into this kind of crime in Florence never got off the ground, unlike in other cities. Here there would be no *Mani Pulite* drive of the kind that had brought down the First Republic in Milan. No, in Florence it was as if the politicians were a race apart.

Teresa gave him the second piece of news. Having thought long and hard, the police officer had decided she shouldn't leave her chief in the dark. She should tell him what Vinci had told her in confidence.

She'd gone into his office with Rizzo, in whom she'd already confided. The Chief Superintendent listened to Teresa and then turned to Rizzo. 'It's pointless deluding ourselves, Francesco. As long as Fiore's in office, we're never going to get anything out of the Prosecutor's Department.'

The other man nodded vigorously. 'This would explain why some of our investigations have stalled or been buried.'

'I've always said that civil servants, particularly those who have certain responsibilities, shouldn't serve in the cities where they have strong ties and bonds of friendship. Their decision-making can too easily be influenced.'

'Especially if they happen to have skeletons in their closets.'

'Exactly. They're vulnerable to blackmail.'

'How are we supposed to move forward?' Rizzo asked, sounding dejected.

Ferrara took his time answering; he was trying to form a plan of action in his mind.

'We've got a card we can play. It might be the only one, though,' he replied eventually.

And he explained that they needed to exploit the fact that Impallomeni, the Deputy Prosecutor in Civitavecchia, had an interest in their investigation, and ask him to provide them with the warrants they needed for the investigation into Antonio Sergi's murder.

It could be their last hope of uncovering the truth.

PART SIX

DEVELOPMENTS

55

Borgo Bellavista

Veronica Borghini was home alone, but she wouldn't be for long.

While she waited, she imagined their meeting. The thought excited her to the point where her heart was pounding in her chest, as it always did on such occasions. They hadn't seen each other since she'd returned to Florence. She opened one of the drawers in the walk-in wardrobe and deliberated before opting for a transparent baby-doll. She took it out and looked at it for a moment before putting it on. She opened another drawer that contained the sort of items one might expect to find in a high-class prostitute's closet – not that she was a member of that profession – but after pondering for a while, she closed it. This wasn't the evening for that sort of thing.

She stretched out on the bed, took a transparent ziplock bag from the bedside table, opened it and held a pinch of powder in front of her nose. One, two, three snorts in a row.

Now all she had to do was wait. The fragrance of fresh flowers was in the air, along with the voice of Lucio Dalla, one of her favourite singers. A romantic atmosphere, exactly the way she liked it.

Veronica was an extraordinarily beautiful woman who had

made many men lose their heads. Even within that gated community. The man she was waiting for had first taken a fancy to her back when they attended the same middle school. Their paths had then diverged, only to meet again fatally all those years later.

When he came in she got up, smiling at him. She stretched out her arms in an explicit invitation which he accepted, running his tongue across her shoulders and up her neck to arrive at her lips. It was a long, passionate kiss. As she worked her way down his firm, handsome chest with its curly hair, she whispered to him how much she'd wanted this moment.

'If you only knew how much I've missed you,' he replied afterwards with a groan. He held her tightly to him, kissing and caressing her. Finally he undressed, folding his suit and placing it on a chair.

'I'd like to be tied up tonight.'

He nodded.

She went over to the walk-in wardrobe and took out a pair of handcuffs and placed them on the bedside table.

Donato, her secret lover, was the only one with whom she was able to satisfy her most secret vices. They made love, first tenderly, while she moved with an apparently innate sensuality and then forcefully, with greater passion. Then Veronica took the handcuffs and slipped them on. He attached them to the head of the bed.

And the sex was frenetic.

Afterwards, as they lay in exhausted abandonment between the sheets, she told him that the police had sent her another summons for the following day, at three in the afternoon. As she spoke she played with a paper tissue, tearing it into tiny pieces. She was nervous. She was not at all happy about that official summons.

'They want to question you, the same way they have everyone else,' he said, as if it were nothing to worry about.

'But I went in of my own accord only yesterday, just like you told me to do.'

'Did they take a statement?'

'No.'

'Then that's what they need to do now.'

'What should I do?'

'Turn up and tell them what you know.'

As he left the house, Donato Russo was debating whether he should have confided in her about Flavia. He'd parked around the corner from the entrance to the compound, and during the short walk to his car he hesitated a couple of times, thinking about turning back. His hand was on the door handle when he finally made the decision that yes, he did need to talk to someone about it.

But as he released the handle, ready to retrace his steps, he felt a hand on his shoulder.

There were two of them, their faces covered by balaclavas and latex gloves on their hands. The taller man was holding a pistol with a long, black barrel.

As soon as he saw them in front of him, Donato Russo's blood ran cold in his veins. He knew there was no point trying to escape; there was no way the gunman could miss at such close range.

'Who are you? And what do you want from me?' he asked, leaning against the car door for support.

'Don't ask stupid questions,' the shorter man replied. 'We want to let you know that you shouldn't be afraid for your daughter. Stay calm and do as you're told, then you'll be able to see her again soon.'

'Just tell me what you want me to do!'

'We want the films and photos your father had. Otherwise you and your daughter will end up the same way as your parents.'

'But I don't know what you're talking about.'

'Find them. Soon.'

'What films, what photos?'

'The ones Fiorenzo Muti gave your father.'

'Fiorenzo Muti?'

'Yes, him – the one who should've removed every trace, including the bodies.'

'Then why don't you ask him—'

'What? Are you pretending you don't know? It won't help. Fiorenzo is dead.'

'I want proof that you have my daughter, that she's alive.'

'You'll have it soon, sooner than you can imagine. In the meantime you've got other things to worry about. You need to get going, and make sure you stay away from the police. Understood?'

'Yes.'

'You've got until Sunday. Monday morning will be too late if you want to see your daughter again. Now get in your car and get out of here.'

The two strangers had disappeared by the time Donato Russo started the motor. He put the car into first gear, his hands shaking on the wheel. He drove with a single thought in his mind: he needed to bring Flavia home. He needed to find what those criminals were looking for. There was nothing left for him to do but obey and hope.

At least now he understood what had happened to Flavia, why they'd taken her.

What he didn't understand was how his father had come to be mixed up in this affair. If it turned out he'd been engaged in criminal activity, then his son's life would be ruined too.

Donato had given up all thought of confiding in anyone else. Nobody could help him with this, it was something he would have to face by himself.

By the time he got home, he'd had an idea. He would start by looking up all the files relating to Fiorenzo Muti.

Perhaps he would find some clue in there.

56

~ ⑤)

Night of Tuesday 26 to Wednesday 27 October

It was almost two in the morning when the patrol cars crossed the Indiano bridge at the far west end of the Parco delle Cascine, named after the pagoda-shaped monument to the Indian prince Rajaram Chuttraputti who had died in Florence on his way home from London. After the cremation, in accordance with Hindu teachings, his ashes were scattered at the confluence of two rivers: the Arno and the Mugnone.

There weren't many cars around at that time of night. Just a few young people on their way home or heading to a nightclub.

They turned left along the Via Pisana. After half a mile the drivers pulled over. This was where Oba lived. The house Felice Contini had told them about had been located that afternoon.

The workers of the Florentine Environment Department were in the process of cleaning the street. It was the one day of the week when people were not allowed to park their cars there, the penalty being forcible removal and the payment of an exorbitant fine. It was almost legalised extortion.

The front door was simply pulled to.

Ciuffi, Ascalchi and Ricci were the first in and went up the stairs. They found a man dozing on a chair in front of the door. They weren't sure he was Nigerian, but he was definitely

African. Hearing them arrive, he opened one eye. Ciuffi showed him his police ID and told him to open the door because they needed to talk to Oba. The man gave him a questioning look.

'Move it!' barked Ricci, grabbing him by the arm.

The man pulled his arm free and reluctantly opened the door, leading the way.

In front of them was a corridor as long as a train carriage with various rooms opening off it. The doors were all open wide. Peering inside, the police officers could see dormitories with women stretched out on the floor and lines of laundry hung out to dry. The air smelled of a mixture of sweat, dust and unidentifiable odours. Once they reached the end of the corridor, the African man got ready to knock on a door, the only one that was closed, but Ricci blocked his hand.

'Get out of the way,' he ordered, pushing him against the wall. 'What's your name?'

'Amir.'

Ricci turned the handle and went in with his pistol in his hand. Ciuffi followed while Ascalchi remained in the doorway to keep an eye on Amir. Their colleagues had taken up positions throughout the building, some in front of the entrance, some covering the doors to the main rooms, ready for the order to proceed with the search.

The room was in semi-darkness. Candles and cups containing burning oil stood on the worn, grubby terracotta tiled floor. The policeman flicked the switch to his right and the central ceiling light came on.

'What the fuck are you doing here?' shouted a woman, her head half-hidden by a red quilt. Her dark eyes, two burning pinpricks, were hostile. She stirred, pushing her hair back. At the same moment another head appeared beside her, that of a young girl with extremely black skin.

Ricci went over while Ciuffi looked around him. There were

votive statues arranged on the bedside tables. Strange masks. Feathers. Twigs. And a number of other unknown objects. There was a peculiar smell in the air.

'Put that pistol away! Who are you?' the woman asked again, as she stirred, revealing a face that, in the light, was covered in scars.

'Police! Get up, Oba! We need to talk,' replied Ciuffi, showing his badge.

'What the fuck do you want?'

'We're investigating a murder.'

'A murder?'

'Yes.'

'What's that got to do with me?' The woman sat up and put her feet on the floor, having pulled the covers over the girl's face. 'Why would I know anything about a murder?' she asked again.

'The victim liked young girls. And you were the one who provided him with them,' replied Ciuffi.

'Who told you that?'

'It doesn't matter who told me.'

'You're on the wrong track, policeman.'

'We're going to put your business under the microscope, Oba.'

'You can't search my house without showing me the decree from the judge first. I know your laws.'

'We don't need a warrant. We want to know who these women are, where they're from, whether they've got permission to stay in the country, why the young girls are so far from their families. Your dirty business is finished!'

This time the woman had no comeback. She got out of bed, completely naked, took a black dressing gown from a chair and wrapped it round her stocky body.

'Let's go to the kitchen so we can talk,' she said.

'At last,' said Ciuffi. 'You're starting to see sense.'

As she led the way along the corridor, Ciuffi ignored the frightened women peering out of their dormitories.

He was ready to close his eyes to that evil in order to defeat an even worse one.

He'd been mistaken.

Oba had no intention of cooperating with the police or even negotiating a deal with them. She just wanted to know the details of this murder they were investigating.

Ciuffi limited himself to explaining that they were looking into several murders, including that of a colleague, and they'd discovered that juvenile prostitution was connected to the case in some way.

'I don't know anything,' replied Oba when Ciuffi fell silent. 'Now go away, otherwise I'll have to call my friends. They're important people, they'll squash you like ants.'

'Important people?'

'Exactly. You're just a little nobody.'

Ricci was about to spring forward and give her a slap, but Ciuffi stopped him with a look. The woman, meanwhile, had moved towards the telephone on the sideboard. When she lifted the receiver, the policeman moved like lightning and snatched it from her hand.

'I need to make a phone call,' protested Oba.

'Not now. We're going to search the apartment. Sit down!' Ciuffi ordered her.

The woman suddenly launched herself at him and tried to hit him in the face. He dodged her and, with Ricci's help, hand-cuffed her to the gas pipe.

'Don't cause any more trouble, you ugly witch!'

Ciuffi gave the order for the search to begin.

The Nigerian criminal underworld had proved to be one of the hardest to penetrate, which gave them all the more reason to search every last inch of that house.

*

'What's your problem?'

They'd returned to Headquarters and Ricci had seized Amir and pinned him against the door of a metal locker in what had been Serpico's office. Oba was in a different office with Ciuffi and Ascalchi.

'It's time to tell the truth. You need to come clean, otherwise I'll do you some damage,' continued the policeman, beside himself with anger.

'You're crazy!'

Ricci pressed the man even harder against the locker.

'I'm not joking. My best friend was killed. This was his office. And this is where I want to hear the truth,' he replied through lips that trembled with rage, veins pulsing at his temples. '*You* were the ones who provided the girls for those rites. We have proof.'

A number of objects seized during the raid had been arranged on the desk. Diaries. Notes. Addresses. Amulets. Hair. Candles. Needles of different shapes and sizes. Many of these objects were from Nigeria, where it was said the most powerful witches in the world lived. And then there were the videos, the most compromising items they'd found on the premises. They showed young girls being raped, tortured and, in all probability, killed. There was a market for such videos and a secret international network of paedophiles to distribute them. According to a press cutting they found in a drawer, similar films had been seized during a recent police raid in London. Ciuffi wondered how many of the girls in those films had disappeared, never to be seen again.

Of the various notes, one – handwritten and unsigned – seemed particularly significant: *Don't forget that the big party is drawing near and we are awaiting the gift for the priestess.*

'We'll be able to lock you up with what we've got here, Amir,' continued the policeman without releasing his grip. 'If you want to stay a free man, you'd better start talking.'

His threat had the desired effect. A look of terror on his face, Amir pleaded, 'Let me go! I'll tell you everything I know.'

Ricci pointed to a chair, told him to sit down. Then he took the seat opposite.

'Go on then: talk!'

57

The eastern ring road, Milan

Salvatore Santachiara was known as Turi *'u smilzu*, Skinny Turi, to his friends.

He was almost six foot seven and extremely thin. Though he'd only recently turned twenty-four, he'd been driving like a maniac long before he was old enough to have a licence. Some people, his closest friends, had nicknamed him *'u curriduri*, the Racing Driver.

That night he was driving along the ring road at top speed, overtaking an endless line of lorries. There wasn't much traffic at that hour, and he considered the overtaking lane to be his alone. He needed to get to the centre of Milan for a little job that was going to earn him points within the *family*. Though he didn't yet know all the details, he was certain this was his big chance, the one he'd been waiting for.

Alfio, his older brother, had gone out on a limb to get him this opportunity and he didn't want to disappoint. As he always had done in the past. All he had to do was take the envelope that they'd given him and stick it in a postbox. And that would be the start of a closer link with the *family*.

He'd just passed a service area when he saw the blue lights of a police car in the rear-view mirror. It too was in the overtaking lane. He put his foot down on the accelerator, thinking he might be able to outrun it. It had been stupid to steal an Alfa Romeo Giulietta, he should have looked for a Porsche or a Ferrari rather than taking the first car he'd found.

If the theft hadn't been reported yet, he should get away with a speeding ticket. But he instinctively took his right hand off the wheel, removed the envelope from the glove compartment and slipped it under the mat on the floor.

He turned up the radio. It was tuned to 103.3 and Isoradio was on air giving advice to drivers.

Who the hell gave a fuck!

He would have liked to change the station, find some decent music, but he decided against it. He needed to concentrate.

The patrol car overtook him and the policeman in the passenger seat signalled to him to pull over on to the hard shoulder. He obeyed, waiting for the officers to get out of their car, but they stayed where they were. Shit, they were running a check on the number plate!

When they did approach, one came to the driver's window and the other took the passenger's side. Turi's eyes slid from one to the other.

'Good evening, or rather good morning, given the time,' he said to the one who'd stopped by his window.

'Get out of the car!' the officer ordered, his hand on the butt of his pistol. Turi obeyed. 'Licence and documents!'

He pulled his licence out of his wallet. It was German and valid in all European countries. Alfio had got it for him when they were working in an Italian restaurant in Wiesbaden. It was one of the places where his brother had invested the illegal capital he'd earned through drug trafficking and extortion rackets. It showed Turi's photo, but the personal details were someone else's.

'The vehicle documents are in the glove compartment,' he said.

'Where?' The policeman bent over to get them.

Turi didn't reply.

He took off running, threw himself over the safety barrier and then down the embankment, ignoring the pistol shots the second officer had fired into the air. As soon as he landed, he leapt to his feet and ran until he reached some bushes where he could hide.

He was in deep shit now. Even if he managed to get away from the police, how would he explain this to Alfio – and more importantly to the *family*?

'If you lose the envelope, you'll be fucked. In fact, we'll both be fucked,' his brother had warned him.

Turi saw torch beams moving towards him, though they were still some distance away. He tried to hide himself deeper among the foliage. Then he heard the police officers talking to each other, though he couldn't make out what they were saying. They sounded excited though.

Had they called for reinforcements? He was fucked!

He moved forward on all fours.

The darkness was on his side, perhaps he might make it.

58

Wednesday 27 October

It was the middle of the night. He felt a prick in his arm and he woke up. Itchy. 'Petra,' he murmured. He reached out his hand, but he couldn't find her. He was alone in the bed. He looked towards the door and caught sight of a shadow disappearing. The sound of steps. Petra must have got up to get a glass of water or use the bathroom. He turned on the lamp on the bedside table and noticed a line of blood coming from a small hole in his arm. There were other noises, coming from the hall this time. He turned off the light and got up, but his legs gave way. He got up again, rubbing his arm, as his throat became drier and drier. Someone was laughing, but it didn't sound like Petra. He reached the hall and looked more carefully. Someone was dragging Petra, his Petra, by the arm and she was reaching out a hand towards him but she couldn't reach him. When she was on the threshold he realised that the stairs were in darkness. His legs gave way again. He tried in vain to get up. His vision clouded. He thought he saw an inverted crucifix hanging on the door, right next to the brass plaque with his surname on it. Then his eyes closed and he didn't see anything else. His breathing had slowed. He thought he heard a voice coming up from the stairwell and it was saying, 'We'll sacrifice her.' He

couldn't breathe and was unable to move. No . . . no . . . no . . . Petra
no . . .

Everything turned black.

'Wake up!' Petra's voice. 'Michele!'

She was shaking him gently, but he was struggling to return to the real word, still wrapped up in his nightmare. Then, when he broke free after a few moments, he found himself in his bed and smelled the aroma of coffee. He looked instinctively at his arm and saw no trace of blood. No, there was no hole.

'What are you looking for?'

'Nothing, Petra.'

'It's almost eight and the office have been trying to get hold of you.'

'Who?'

'Ciuffi.'

'Did he leave a message?'

'Only that there's news.'

'It's late, damn it!'

'I wanted to let you sleep. You were tired – you've been tossing and turning all night, as if you were having the most terrible nightmare.'

He shook his head, unable to speak. Then he jumped out of bed and hugged her tightly.

'You're not on your own, Michele. I'll always be there for you and we'll get through this, too, you'll see. I'm sure it must be awful for you.'

Her eyes were like windows to her heart. He saw the concern there and kissed her on the lips. 'You've always given me the strength to overcome every obstacle,' he told her.

He didn't know what would become of him without Petra.

She was a real treasure. No, not just a treasure, his true love.

Once the shadows of the night had dissolved in his wife's embrace, Ferrara felt ready to face the new day. He put on a pale grey suit and phoned his colleague. That was how he learned the news.

It was one of the few mornings when he didn't eat breakfast at home. He drank a cup of coffee, a bitter one, then he hurried in to Headquarters.

9.05 a.m., the Chief Superintendent's office

Don't forget that the big party is drawing near and we are awaiting the gift for the priestess.

After a detailed briefing on the previous night's operation, Ciuffi showed the Chief Superintendent the note found at Oba's house. Ferrara examined it carefully. It had been handwritten in black ink with a fountain pen.

'Oba's got something to do with the rituals. There's no doubt about it,' commented Ferrara. 'Have you found anything that links her to the Marquis Degli Aldobrandi?'

Ciuffi shook his head. 'Not yet, but there are letters and documents that are still being translated.' And he added that, in the opinion of one of the officers from Immigration, they might have been written in Hausa.

'We need to nominate a backup from the judiciary police, or even ask the consulate for a suggestion.'

'Will do, chief,' replied Ciuffi.

'And this Amir, what did he have to say for himself?' asked Ferrara.

'He's still with Ascalchi and Ricci. He speaks and then he clams up, as if he's afraid. He's confirmed his compatriots' participation at some parties, but he doesn't want to say where and, so far, he's trying to keep Oba's name out of it.'

'There's no way she's not involved!' objected the Chief Superintendent.

'I think the same – that's why Pino is still working on Amir.'

'Good, keep me posted. And when we're done, arrest them all for criminal conspiracy, human trafficking, illegal immigration, abuse of minors, sexual violence . . . '

'It'll be my pleasure.'

'Get hold of Contini too.'

'Will do. I reckon he'll have lots to tell me.'

Alone again, the Chief Superintendent read some of the articles that Fanti had downloaded from the Internet, starting with the press cutting that had been found at Oba's house, reporting the seizure of films destined for London paedophiles.

In spite of many years of close contact with evil, Ferrara experienced a hitherto unknown feeling of horror that morning. He discovered that in 1990 Scotland Yard had set up a special team to investigate pornographic 'snuff' videos, which showed victims being tortured to death. The English police had discovered that at least twenty children who'd disappeared without a trace in the preceding seven years had been tortured and raped in the course of satanic rituals. The stories they'd uncovered were beyond belief: children and teenagers offered to the priests of a sect and their followers; foetuses forcibly extracted from the wombs of underage mothers and then burnt to death; tombs profaned by night; cannibalism and mysterious rites.

Shocked by what he'd read, the Chief Superintendent summoned Rizzo and briefed him on the Scotland Yard cases. His deputy could tell how upset he was just by looking at him.

'We have to go to London, Francesco. It's vital that we examine the documents from those investigations, even though the events they refer to occurred over ten years ago. There's always the chance that there might be something more recent, possibly connected to our investigation.'

'I agree, Michele.'

'Prepare a detailed report for the Prosecutor's Department in Civitavecchia and deliver it in person to Deputy Prosecutor Impallomeni, along with our response regarding the Fabio Biondi case.'

'The notes on Biondi are ready, so as soon as I've completed the report I'll go and see him,' said Rizzo, energised at the prospect. 'I'm sure I can make a convincing case for extending the investigations.'

An anonymous envelope.

It had been left in the postbox at the entrance and Fanti had placed it in full view, next to the articles downloaded from the Internet. The envelope was addressed to Ferrara and the address had been written using a stencil. He put on a pair of latex gloves and opened it. Inside was a single sheet of paper folded into quarters.

On the paper were a few lines of writing, also written with the aid of a stencil.

> You've got the film now and you won't sleep for many nights. You will be disturbed by the things you know, which you will want to talk to me about. If someone said the word 'magic' to me, I would say: you are the right person.

It was a challenge. The author of the letter was testing Ferrara.

But who was this mysterious individual? And what task did he have in mind for 'the right person'? Was he supposed to investigate the world of sorcery?

And what did he mean by 'You've got the film now'?

Ferrara looked at the envelope. It was white, nondescript, widely available. Stamped and labelled as having been sent from Florence.

He summoned Fanti. 'Have you checked the video tapes and DVDs Inspector Trovato seized from the Marquis Degli Aldobrandi's home?'

'I'm working on it with Officer Belli.'

'Found anything interesting yet?'

'So far they've been films of places, mostly abroad, and pornographic films, some of them involving minors. The men's faces are never shown.'

'Keep going – and keep me posted. Make this your number one priority!'

Fanti almost ran out of the room in his eagerness to comply.

It was shortly before midday when Fabrizio Maiolino, the director of the Milanese traffic police, rang Ferrara to tell him what had happened during the night on the eastern ring road.

'The car had been stolen from a motel car park outside Bologna a couple of hours earlier,' he explained. 'And the German driver's licence the driver showed us turned out to be fake.' The original licence had been stolen from Frankfurt am Main in Germany and then doctored by replacing the photograph.

From the photograph, and the fingerprints found in the car, they'd identified the fugitive as twenty-four-year-old Salvatore Santachiara, originally from Bagheria in Sicily, with previous convictions for theft.

'We suspect that he's a foot soldier for one of the Cosa Nostra organisations. His brother, Alfio Santachiara, has convictions for associating with the Mafia. He emigrated to Germany several years ago, but it looks as though he's still affiliated to a *family* from Palermo – at least, that's what his online communications indicate,' Maiolino continued.

Ferrara was just wondering what any of this had to do with his office when the traffic cop pre-empted his question. 'I'm informing you because my men found an envelope addressed to an individual in Florence. It was hidden under the carpet in the footwell. The address was typed and inside there was note and a Polaroid of a frightened-looking young girl sitting on a chair in front of an unpainted wall. Everything suggests that this is a kidnapping—'

'But nobody's been kidnapped here, certainly not a young girl,' Ferrara interrupted. 'Who's it addressed to?'

'Donato Russo, 1236 Viale Volta, 50129, Florence.'

The Chief Superintendent was silenced for a moment. Then he asked, 'What does the note say?'

'One moment while I find the photocopy. The Forensics team are running tests on the original.'

Ferrara made some notes while he waited.

'Ready, Michele?'

'Yes, I'm here.'

'Well then, here's what it says: "Here is the proof you asked for. Now get to work. As we've already told you, you've got until Sunday if you want to see your daughter again."'

Ferrara transcribed the sentences, then he reread them to make sure he hadn't skipped any words. 'Send me a photocopy of the note and a copy of the photo please, Fabrizio.'

'I'll send a patrol to deliver it. You'll have it this afternoon.'

He put the phone down and looked at his notes. The detail about the driving licence having been stolen in Frankfurt Am Main intrigued him. The telephone call received by the Russos at 1.36 a.m. on the night of the crime had been made from a mobile phone with a German prefix, though they had yet to trace the owner.

Were these coincidences?

And what about the kidnapping of Flavia Russo?

The mystery was becoming more and more intriguing.

59

3 p.m., Headquarters

'Let's get started with the statement,' said the Chief Superintendent as soon as Veronica Borghini sat down in front of him,
looking elegant in a white trouser suit. 'As I mentioned earlier, we
are interviewing you as a person who may have information
useful to our investigation,' he clarified, turning to a stratagem
that was often used, even when information had come to light
that could be classified as evidence.

Under Italian law, a person who may have information useful
to an investigation doesn't have the right to a lawyer, nor do they
have the right to know what information the police hold on
them. In practice, the witness is, in some ways, more exposed
than someone under investigation or who has been implicated,
since the latter have the option to refuse to answer. The witness,
on the other hand, must supply truthful answers and confess
everything they know. If they don't, their statement may be
deemed false or reticent, leaving them open to a charge of aiding
and abetting in the eyes of the judiciary, or the prosecutor could
accuse them of making a false declaration, which carries a
penalty of up to four years' imprisonment.

Venturi positioned his fingers on the computer keyboard,
ready to type.

'Your complete personal information, address and profession, please,' Ferrara began.

'Veronica Borghini, born Fiesole on 8 August 1968, currently resident in Borgo Bellavista; profession: stylist.'

'Let me remind you of the facts, signora,' continued the Chief Superintendent. Having stated that the purpose of the investigation was to identify those responsible for the murder of Amedeo Russo and his wife, he repeated what she had told him about having entered into a professional relationship with the lawyer on the occasion of her divorce from her ex-husband.

The witness seemed nervous: she kept shifting in her seat and her eyes were fixed on her Gucci bag. As she had done during her previous visit, she held the bag on her lap.

'With this in mind, I would like you disclose the true nature of your relationship with the lawyer Amedeo Russo.'

'But I've already told you, Chief Superintendent. Russo's law firm dealt with my divorce.'

The law firm!

'No, signora. There was something else between you and Amedeo Russo. Something much more personal.'

The woman stared at her bag in silence, the only sound came from her fingers tapping nervously on the desk. The varnish on her nails was blood red.

'Don't make me read the letters out, signora. I would be grateful if you would tell me the truth,' said Ferrara. 'And may I remind you that, if you were to lie, you could find yourself charged with aiding and abetting, with all the legal consequences that entails.'

'I'd like some water, please.'

The Chief Superintendent called his secretary. A few moments later, Fanti came in with a bottle and two plastic cups. He placed the tray on the desk and disappeared without saying a word.

She drank a sip of water then looked the Chief Superintendent in the eye while she continued to reflect on his words: 'Don't make me read the letters out ... you could find yourself charged with aiding and abetting ... '

'What letters do you mean?'

'Do you think that we have time to waste, signora? Among the material seized from the Russo home in the course of our investigation, we recovered some very significant correspondence addressed to you. Need I say more, or are you prepared to admit that you know which letters I'm talking about?'

'Amedeo Russo was in love with me, but I didn't return his affections,' she replied, looking down at her legs.

'There, that's more like it. Explain the nature of your relationship, please.'

'It's private, Chief Superintendent. It has absolutely no bearing on your investigation.'

'That's for us to decide, along with the Deputy Prosecutor.'

'I understand that it's your job, but it's not nice to see your private life exposed for all to see.'

'What's this "for all to see"? This is an official police inquiry; the information is required for documents required by the Minister.'

'Yes, OK. And it will be passed to the lawyers. And then the journalists will get their hands on it, and, eventually, it will be on everyone's lips. I wouldn't be the first to see their privacy invaded.'

'I can assure you that absolute discretion will be maintained on the part of my office.'

Silence fell once more. It was suddenly broken by the ringing of the telephone.

Ferrara lifted the receiver. It was the Commissioner and the tone of his voice didn't bode at all well.

'I'll be right there,' he replied. 'Excuse me one moment,' he said, turning to Veronica Borghini before leaving the room.

*

He returned ten minutes later, a grim look on his face.

Someone knew that he'd summoned Veronica Borghini to his office and they'd been putting pressure on the Commissioner, who was apoplectic as usual: 'What do you expect her to know about the murders? She's a busy woman with an important job and her friendships are absolutely above suspicion. Hurry up and let her go,' Adinolfi had thundered.

'Now, signora, let's continue with our conversation,' said Ferrara.

'Yes, Chief Superintendent. The truth is I did have a romantic relationship with Amedeo Russo, but after six months I decided to break it off.'

'Why?'

She looked up, then straight back down. She was obviously struggling.

'Why?' Ferrara insisted.

'It wasn't working for me.'

'What do you mean? You no longer had feelings for him?'

'It's difficult to explain,' she replied after a pause of several seconds.

'Try, signora!'

'Amedeo had some strange . . . habits . . . I hope you've understood me.'

'No. What kind of habits?'

A new silence. Shorter.

'Sexual requests, Chief Superintendent, to which I couldn't accede. He even went so far as to suggest a foursome. At that point I dumped him.'

'How did he respond?'

'He reacted badly, and even started to harass me. He flooded me with emails and notes that he would leave in my letterbox. I wanted to report him for stalking, but I decided against it. I didn't want the hassle, and I especially wanted to avoid the gossip I knew it would cause.'

'Do you know the names of the other couple willing to take part in a foursome?'

'No, absolutely not! He didn't tell me, and nor did I ask him. I didn't want to meet them. The very thought of it disgusted me.'

What if Amedeo Russo had had the Cortis in mind?

'Would you make sure to contact me, signora, in the event you realise there's some detail you've forgotten to mention?'

'Certainly, but I'm sure I haven't overlooked anything.'

The Chief Superintendent brought the statement to a close, printed it, reread it and handed it to the witness. He tried to imagine Amedeo Russo's secret life as he watched the woman while she leaned over the desk to add her signature to the document.

A crack had opened in the façade.

Not only had Russo been a great lawyer, he'd been a genuine pervert, too.

60

The Civitavecchia Prosecutor's Department occupied a building near the military academy.

While the Chief Superintendent finished questioning Veronica Borghini, Rizzo was being shown into the Deputy Prosecutor's office. He had called that morning to make an appointment for four in the afternoon, hoping the Deputy Prosecutor would have more time to talk at that hour of the day. During their brief telephone conversation he'd been pleased to discover that, unlike the vast majority of his colleagues, Enrico Impallomeni didn't seem overly formal.

The Deputy Prosecutor's office was light and spacious. The furniture was modern: a desk made of light-coloured wood with a computer and printer, some chairs and a perfectly ordered bookcase. To one side was a waiting area where the police officer had been invited to make himself comfortable.

Enrico Impallomeni wasn't yet forty. He was short and thin with an open face, which was rendered more mature by his reddish beard. Originally from Rome, he had worked his way up through the ranks of the Prosecutor's Department at Trapani in Sicily before being promoted and transferred to his current post.

Rizzo told him what was known about the death of Fabio Biondi, handing him the report he had prepared.

'This story of the Black Rose is interesting,' commented the Deputy Prosecutor. 'I think you're right: we need to assume that the deaths of Sergi and Biondi are connected.'

Rizzo then explained to Impallomeni that they were also turning to him with regard to the investigation into the Russo murders. He was tempted to mention the difficulties thrown up by the Prosecutor's Department in Florence, but he discarded the idea. Although Impallomeni had shown willingness in their dealings so far, he couldn't be sure that he wouldn't close ranks and side with his fellow prosecutors rather than the police. Rizzo therefore confined himself to explaining how the *Squadra Mobile* intended to proceed with the investigation.

'No problem,' said Impallomeni when he'd finished. 'I'll give you the warrants, including the international request to England. Will you be dealing with it personally?'

'Yes.'

The Deputy Prosecutor went to sit at his desk. For a moment he sat back in his chair and took a deep breath.

Then the computer began to whir.

Back in Florence, the Chief Superintendent was accepting delivery of the much-anticipated parcel from Milan.

'A traffic police patrol brought it,' his secretary told him as he placed it on the desk. Then he cleared his throat. 'Chief, Belli and I have got something we'd like to show you.'

'Come back in five minutes. I want to have a look at this first,' Ferrara replied, opening the envelope and pulling out the documents his colleague Maiolino had told him about.

After studying the photograph and note, he rang Rizzo on his mobile. His deputy answered on the first ring. 'Where are you, Francesco?'

'At Impallomeni's office. He's giving me the warrants.'

'All of them?'

'Yes.'

'Excellent. But listen, you also need to ask him for authorisation to tap Donato Russo's phone and acquire his call records,' he instructed, briefing him on the latest developments. 'I'll get Teresa to give you the numbers shortly.'

'Perfect.'

Now it was Fanti's turn.

'Well then, what have you found?'

'Something interesting,' his secretary began. Beside him, Belli nodded in agreement.

'Tell me more.'

'You need to see this tape,' said Fanti. 'There was a scrap of paper inside the case with "My Mass" written on it.'

'My Mass?'

'Exactly, chief.'

'Let's have a look then.'

The video began with a panoramic shot of what looked like the saloon on a ship. The passengers were standing in the corner of the bar or in line by the self-service buffet. Then there was a shot taken through a porthole: in the distance were chalk cliffs that rose precipitously above the sea.

'The white cliffs of Dover!' Ferrara said to himself.

This was followed by footage of red double-decker London buses, seen through the windscreen of a moving vehicle. A man on a bicycle drew level with the vehicle as it slowed at traffic lights, and a group of school children wearing backpacks crossed the road ahead of the car in uniforms consisting of grey skirts or trousers and blue shirts. The camera followed them and for a moment it was possible to make out the tax disc in the bottom corner of the windscreen on the driver's side.

It was an Italian car and a left-hand drive!

Then the images on the screen became blurry and the Chief Superintendent thought the film was finished. He was about to ask Fanti to turn it off, when the screen filled with colour once more and an old man with an imposing and well-groomed countenance appeared. He was sitting at a table in a room with floral curtains; beyond the open the window a green lawn seemed to continue as far as the eye could see. The man's right elbow was on the table and he was staring into the camera and stroking his chin. In front of him was a glass containing a dark liquid, that might have been beer. A chalice, apparently containing wine, made a brief appearance.

When the film cut to footage of a church, Ferrara began to watch more carefully.

A young-looking woman was stretched out on the altar. She was naked, her body like a marble statue. When the lens zoomed in her face, two dark eyes were clearly visible. Red candles were lit around her.

Hooded figures slowly began to draw near. They were all wearing red robes. Ferrara heard Father Torre's voice in his head, explaining the significance of the colour: red meant 'love'. He had scarcely finished the thought when the video cut to what appeared to be a genuine rather than staged orgy.

Finally, the pieces of the puzzle were starting to come together. As soon as Fanti turned off the television, Ferrara said, 'Get Inspector Trovato to go to Edoardo Degli Aldobrandi's home tomorrow morning and summon him to my office.'

'For what time, chief?'

'Straight away. I want him here first thing.'

When Ferrara got home, he was still thinking about the anonymous letter: *You've got the film now and you won't sleep for many nights. You will be disturbed by the things you know, which you will want to talk to me about. If someone said the word 'magic' to me, I would say: you are the right person.*

Was Edoardo Degli Aldobrandi's video the film in question? If so, the letter must have been sent by someone very well informed – or perhaps personally involved.

An informer?

61

Wiesbaden, Germany

Wiesbaden is the city of thermal baths and casinos.

It had recently seen pizzerias and Italian restaurants sprouting like fungi, a common occurrence in many German towns. What was suspicious was that the vast majority were the fruit of the investment of illicit capital earned through drugs trafficking and, in the eighties and nineties, also from the ransoms paid for the release of hostages kidnapped in various regions throughout Italy.

One of these restaurants within walking distance of the casino was owned by Alfio Santachiara. The staff were all Sicilian. Santachiara knew perfectly well that German law didn't yet recognise the crime of Mafia-related criminal conspiracy, any more than there was a law against laundering dirty money. Therefore, although they might be considered suspect, neither his belongings nor his properties could be confiscated. He also knew that the country's police were determined to keep their eyes closed. In fact, they officially denied the presence of the Mafia within their territory. This was an enormous mistake, since in reality the Sicilian Mafia and, more importantly, the Calabrian 'Ndrangheta had been well-established there for some time, finding a true paradise in Germany, which guaranteed a façade of complete legality.

Alfio Santachiara wasn't paying his usual attention to the activity in the restaurant that evening. His mind was elsewhere. He sat at the same table the whole time, the one nearest the till. He was alone and there was a bottle of wine in front of him. He would take a sip from time to time, looking around him.

He was tormented by the thought of having made an extremely serious error in recommending his brother for the job of 'postman'. Salvatore had disappeared and hadn't been in touch with anyone, not even him. Worse still, he was being hunted by the Italian police. Eventually the investigation would be extended to the international level, and in particular Germany. Right there, where Alfio lived.

After the restaurant had closed and all the staff had gone home he closed the till then went into the kitchen to check everything was in its place. He pressed the light switch but the light didn't come on. A moment later he was stunned by a violent blow to the head. He fell to the floor with a groan and he was quickly turned face down and his hands and feet were bound.

'Let me go, you sons of bitches!' he muttered. His attackers hoisted him up, dragged him into a corner of the kitchen and laid him out on a table. They turned on the light and Alfio Santachiara found himself looking into three unfamiliar faces. But they were definitely southerners, like him. Yes, that much was clear. Just as it was clear that his brother must have got himself into some really deep shit this time.

'What do you want?' he asked.

'Your brother, the Racing Driver, where the fuck is he?' one of them asked in Sicilian.

'I don't know. I haven't heard from him,' Alfio replied in the same language.

'Where is he?' the tallest of the three repeated in a cold voice.

'I don't know, I swear on the Virgin,' replied Alfio, his heart in his mouth.

It was the truth.

While two of the attackers positioned themselves on either side of the table, the third came closer and put a mask on him that left only his mouth and nose uncovered. The man forced open his lips and slipped a funnel between them. One of them pinched his nose shut and the other climbed on top of him, sitting on his legs to keep him pinned to the table. Then the third man began to tip water from a plastic bottle into the funnel. Slowly.

'This is called a Sant'Antonio, but you already know that. It's what the police back in Palermo used to do to make their informants spill the beans,' said the same voice. 'They used salt water from the sea, but this works too.'

Alfio Santachiara was suffocating. His chest heaved again and again but he couldn't bring all that water up. Desperate for oxygen, he struggled to free himself, but his efforts were in vain. He was overcome with panic and realised he was about to die, right there in the kitchen of his restaurant, where fish specialities from his native Sicily were prepared each day. Dishes of shellfish, followed by sea bass, gilthead bream, mussels and authentic Sicilian swordfish – caught in the Strait of Messina, not the Japanese kind.

He barely noticed when they took the mask off him.

He vomited.

'I'll ask you one last time: where is your brother?'

'I don't know. It's the truth. Let me go and I'll find out and let you know,' he stammered.

'You're the lowest of the low and unworthy to belong to the *family*. You're so ready to turn traitor, you'd even betray your own brother,' said another of his attackers.

They put the mask on him again and rammed the funnel back into his mouth. Alfio tried to speak, to say something more, to beg, to plead, but the flow of water had begun again. Panic became terror.

And he thought he was dying.

For real this time.

62

Wednesday 28 October, the home of Edoardo Degli Aldobrandi

Inspector Trovato rang the doorbell of the Marquis's apartment at a few minutes after eight in the morning.

Despite repeated attempts, there was no response. He went down to the floor below and the door opened wide before he had a chance to press the doorbell. The woman who'd called the police on the evening of the raid appeared.

'I saw you arrive,' she said.

'Do you know whether the Marquis is at home?'

'I haven't seen him since Sunday evening, or heard any of the usual noises. There's been no coming and going either.'

'Any idea where he might have gone?'

'No. If you ask me, he's hidden himself away – can't bear to be seen because of the shame.'

'Thank you, signora.'

As soon as he was back in the car, Inspector Trovato rang Ferrara.

'Track down the niece who attended the search. Maybe she'll know where her uncle is,' the Chief Superintendent told him.

Trovato called his own office to get the woman's address.

She lived in the Via della Vigna Nuova, one of Florence's main fashion streets, just a few minutes away from the Marquis's home.

The Inspector was back outside Edoardo Degli Aldobrandi's door half an hour later, accompanied by the niece. He rang the bell several times but there was no reply. At that point the young woman pulled a bunch of keys out of her handbag.

'We'll open the door with these,' she said as she put one into the keyhole. 'My uncle gave them to me in case I needed them, especially in the summer when he goes away on holiday.'

They went into the apartment.

'Uncle, Uncle!' she shouted in a worried voice.

There was no reply.

There was nobody in the bedroom and the bed had been made.

The niece opened the bathroom door. An ear-piercing shriek startled the inspector, who'd been checking the other rooms. He ran to her.

He was hit by a sickening odour, bitter-sweet and rotten. He covered his nose and mouth with his hand.

The young woman was stretched out on the floor. She'd fainted.

He saw the Marquis Degli Aldobrandi in the empty bath. He was naked and his face was swollen and pale as a ghost. Some flies were resting on his mouth whilst others buzzed around in the air that stank of decomposition. There were deep black cuts along his left arm and the blood had pooled on the carpet. A kitchen knife lay beside the body.

It looked as though Edoardo Degli Aldobrandi had killed himself after being released by the police at dawn on Monday.

The Inspector lifted the young woman off the ground, took her into the bedroom and laid her carefully on the bed.

Then he made two phone calls.

One to 118.

The other to Ferrara.

The niece was feeling better and she was now sitting on a stool in the kitchen. Inspector Trovato sat opposite her, his notebook open.

When the Chief Superintendent arrived she was murmuring, 'Poor Uncle Edoardo. Why did you do it?'

'Good day,' Ferrara greeted her.

The young woman returned his greeting as the Inspector jumped to his feet.

'This is Chief Superintendent Ferrara, the Head of the *Squadra Mobile*,' he said, addressing the woman.

'How are you feeling?' Ferrara asked her.

'I'm recovering.'

'The medic who responded to the 118 call has seen her. He gave her an injection and didn't think it necessary to take her to the hospital,' Trovato chimed in.

'Do you feel up to answering some questions?' asked the Chief Superintendent.

The young woman nodded. 'Go ahead.'

'What's your name?'

'Virginia Degli Aldobrandi. Edoardo is my father's brother.'

'Her father's already been informed. He'll be catching the first available flight,' added the Inspector.

'Where is he?'

'In Geneva. He's an ambassador.'

'Was your uncle married?'

'Divorced. His wife left him after barely a year of marriage.'

'Any children?'

'None.'

'Has he ever behaved in such a way as to indicate that he had suicidal tendencies?'

'No, never, but he seemed very upset on Monday morning

when I told him how the search went. He'd never imagined that something like this could happen to him. It was as though his whole world had come crashing down on top of him.'

'I'm sorry to tell you this, signora, but we found two young illegal immigrants hiding under his bed. I don't think he can have been unaware of the risks he was taking . . . '

'I know. It was a vice of my uncle's. All the family knew, but there was nothing we could do about it. It was like an illness. That's why we didn't really get along. My father was extremely angry.'

'Did your uncle have any friends? Acquaintances?'

'None that I know of. Perhaps you should ask my father.'

'Did he travel abroad?'

'He went to Thailand last summer. He would go there every two or three years for at least a month at a time.'

'What about within in Europe?'

'He'd go to England. He had a number of friends there.'

'Do you know them?'

'No. He would tell us he was going, but he never said anything else.'

'So you don't know who they are?'

'No, but my father might know them.'

'Was your uncle interested in esotericism?'

'I'm sorry, but again I don't know.'

'Thank you. Inspector Trovato will draw up a statement detailing what you've told us. That way you won't have to come down to Headquarters.'

The Chief Superintendent got up and headed to the bath-room.

Francesco Leone, the pathologist on duty, had just finished the external inspection of the body, which was now stretched out on the floor. He was taking off his protective mask and latex gloves.

'It's suicide. There's no doubt about it,' he declared as soon as Ferrara joined him. 'And death occurred sometime on Monday evening or night,' he added, inwardly congratulating himself on anticipating the Chief Superintendent's next question.

Ferrara, however, had an entirely different question in mind:

Was it possible the Marquis would turn out to be the key to this investigation?

63

'Chief Superintendent!'

Ferrara had just reached the pool car when he heard his name being called. He turned and immediately recognised the man looking for him. It was the journalist Cosimo Presti, who was standing behind two cars parked at an angle.

'What are you doing? Are you hiding?' he asked the reporter once he reached him.

'I wasn't hiding. I happened to be passing and I recognised you.'

'What do you want?'

'I'd like to talk about the lawyer, Russo, and other things that are likely to be of interest to you.'

'Come and find me at the office if you know something.'

'Perhaps you've misunderstood me, or maybe I haven't been clear enough: I'm offering you a deal.'

'A deal? What are you talking about?'

'An exchange of information.'

The Chief Superintendent's gaze went from quizzical to cutting. He'd never liked Presti, and he didn't have time for his nonsense now. 'What information? Get to the point, Presti.'

'You help me, I help you. I've got contacts in the Prosecutor's Department – I could tell you what I find out. I get the impression you're not held in very high regard by my friend Luca Fiore.

In return, you give me information about the investigations. I've got a new gig with a weekly paper and I could use an exclusive to build up my reputation, make a good impression with the boss.'

'But I could read this information of yours in the papers anyway,' objected Ferrara.

The journalist shook his head. 'Not everything makes it into print. But I know some things that could be very important for you. And what's more, my dear Chief Superintendent, I'll give you a preview.'

'Of what?'

'I'm writing a book and—'

Ferrara cut him off. 'I've absolutely no interest in your book or your literary ambitions. You've got the wrong guy – carry on turning to your friend Luca Fiore for information.'

'But the Prosecutor doesn't have all the information. You don't tell him everything you know, do you?'

'Get out of here, Presti. Don't try and hinder my work. I won't report you this time, I'll pretend I didn't see you, but be warned, what you've just done is called "incitement". Incitement to commit a crime. The secrets of an investigation can never be revealed.'

Ferrara opened the car door and got in. Presti came over and leaned towards the window.

'You'll regret this, Chief Superintendent,' he threatened as the car began to move.

Ferrara heard his words clearly in spite of the closed window.

'Sleazebag!' he muttered.

'What did that man want?' asked the driver.

'He's just some tramp. Let's get back to the office!'

You're not held in very high regard by my friend Luca Fiore.

Certain episodes were beginning to make sense to Ferrara. One of them was recent: during the investigation into the murder of Senator Enrico Costanza he'd submitted an application to the

Prosecutor's Department for authorisation to acquire the call records and set up a tap on Cosimo Presti's phone lines. The Senator had been seen dining with the journalist at one of the restaurants at the Hotel Villa Medici in Porta a Prato just hours before he was killed at his villa, but in spite of that Ferrara's request for authorisation had been denied.

And now here was Presti, loitering outside the home of the Marquis Degli Aldobrandi immediately after the body was discovered. How had he known the police were there?

There had been a number of occasions in the past when Presti had been spotted at a crime scene by the first patrol car to arrive. It was well known that journalists monitored police radio frequencies, and usually a crowd of them would gather like vultures, so nobody paid him much attention.

Now, however it sounded as though Presti had an advantage over his fellow journalists. For he enjoyed the complicity of an institutional 'canary' – an excellent 'canary', too, given that it was the head of the Prosecutor's Department.

What was in it for Fiore though? Ferrara tried to think of a reasonable answer.

Did Luca Fiore have any skeletons in the closet? Perhaps Presti knew about them and was blackmailing the Prosecutor to extort information from him. Was that why every attempt to investigate him was blocked?

Then another thought struck him.

What if it had been Fiore himself who asked Cosimo Presti to make Ferrara that offer . . . ?

PART SEVEN

HONOURING THE DEAD

64

The offices of the Russo and Corti legal practice

Donato didn't find anything useful in Fiorenzo Muti's file.

Lucrezia, the secretary, had provided him with the paperwork relating to Muti's many crimes, which ranged from rape to sexual assault to assault against minors to the double murder of a couple surprised in the woods in the middle of a tryst.

Amedeo Russo had managed to secure his acquittal for the latter crime, albeit by dubious methods. It was a professional success which had increased the lawyer's fame.

Donato Russo did, however, find something in the safe.

It was the first time it had been opened since his father's murder. He was convinced it was the only place he might find what he was looking for, and he wasn't mistaken.

He noticed an envelope with a wax seal sitting on top of some documents. It was addressed to him. He pulled it out and immediately recognised his father's handwriting. With a lump in his throat, he began to read.

My precious son,
 If you're reading these few lines, it means that what I would never ever have imagined has actually happened.
 It's just after two in the morning and, having

thought about this for a long time, I've decided to write this to charge you with a specific and delicate task.

Go to the Banco Nazionale del Lavoro in the Piazza della Repubblica and open the safety deposit box that's in my name. I've made sure you-know-who is authorised to give you access. Forgive me for not speaking to you about this. The key is here in the envelope. You will find material that I beg you not to examine. You will need to destroy it. Immediately. And I mean immediately. I beg you, for the good of all of you and so that my memory is not besmirched.

I have loved you very much and I wish you all the luck in the world and, most of all, the best possible health. And the same to my little Flavia, my darling granddaughter.

Forgive me,

Your loving father

Florence, 28 September 2004

Donato read his father's letter again with tears in his eyes. He looked at the date and realised it had been written barely twenty days before he was killed.

What could have happened to make his father so frightened?

He was at the BNL half an hour later. He introduced himself to the manager, a middle-aged man, who examined his documents and then led the way. They took the lift down to the basement, where a security guard stood sentry. A member of staff in suit and tie sitting behind a desk made Donato sign a register before accompanying him to the safes. Amedeo Russo's was number 804 and was one of the largest.

The man took out a rectangular box and carried it into a small room with a leather chair. 'I'll wait for you outside,' he said in a brusque voice.

In the box was a diary and some DVDs. Donato counted eight of them. A date was written on each of them in black felt-tip. The diary was from 1998 and contained only the odd note here and there. He put everything in his briefcase and the bank's employee accompanied him to the exit.

He went straight home, his father's words resounding in his head. *You will need to destroy it. Immediately. And I mean immediately. I beg you, for the good of all of you and so that my memory is not besmirched.*

65

Donato Russo hadn't noticed anything strange during the journey from the office to the bank and from the bank to his home. He had walked briskly with his gaze fixed straight ahead. Most importantly, he hadn't noticed the Franciscan monk with the thick white beard who hadn't let him out of his sight for a moment.

The monk had lingered under the portico while he was in the bank, moving to and fro between the newspaper kiosk and Piazza della Repubblica without ever losing sight of his objective. Once the monk had seen Donato Russo leave and turn his rapid steps towards home, he'd continued to follow him discreetly. His instinct told him he'd hit the bull's eye. Bang on again. He was a true master of disguise, and on this occasion he had also changed the colour of his eyes to green, thanks to his new contact lenses.

Now all he had to do was wait for Donato's next move. That would require a new appearance. He got into a van and when he got out he was the perfect tourist. Wearing worn jeans, a leather jacket, a reddish beard and big sunglasses, he wandered nonchalantly along the pavement of the Viale dei Mille, past the building where Donato Russo lived.

He was ready. As always.

*

Donato Russo knew that he couldn't respect his father's wishes. Perhaps he would have done if Flavia hadn't been involved, but now he was desperate to understand what had happened, what he needed to do and who he was dealing with.

He put the first DVD into his computer.

A beautiful girl, perhaps a model, with short, blonde hair appeared on the screen. She was completely naked. There was a man, shot from behind, sitting on the edge of the bed.

'You're amazing, sweetheart . . . '

'I'm going to start undressing you, we're going to play a new game this time,' she whispered in a slight foreign accent.

'What do you want to do, sweetheart?'

'It's a surprise. You have to trust me.'

'You know I like to play games.'

The young woman opened the drawer of the bedside table and took out a case.

'The House of the Roses really does think of everything,' he said. The recording finished with those words.

He watched the film a second time. The voices weren't at all familiar, and nor was the physique of the man, who was rather short. Surely it couldn't have been his father.

He moved on to the other DVDs and became more and more disturbed. The women's faces changed but the men were always shown from behind and the content never varied. His father had kept a complete sexual archive in that safe.

When Donato had finished he switched off the computer and opened the diary from 1998.

A list of names caught his attention. He recognised some of them: politician friends of his father's. But there was one that struck him in particular. He flicked through a few more pages and found a second list, a series of dates this time, which didn't tell him anything.

It was explosive material and in any other circumstances he would have respected his father's wishes and destroyed it. But

Flavia's life was at stake. He had no alternative: he would have to give this to the kidnappers.

There was nothing to be done but wait for them to get in touch again. Perhaps they would come looking for him like they had the first time, on his way back from Veronica's house.

He would go to her house every evening. At least until Sunday, the day of the ultimatum.

He would bring Flavia home!

66

Why had he killed himself? Out of shame, or because he was afraid of being implicated in other, more serious, events?

After leaving the Marquis's home, the Chief Superintendent had returned to his office, wondering about the motives behind such an act.

He recalled what Contini had told Ciuffi: 'There's a lot of unrest in the city after your raid on the Marquis Degli Aldobrandi's home.'

Perhaps Rizzo would have been able to help him unravel the knot, but he'd left for London that morning, taking the warrant provided by Deputy Prosecutor Impallomeni with him.

He summoned Teresa to see if there was anything new from Donato Russo's telephones, which had been under surveillance since the previous evening.

'There still haven't been any calls, chief,' replied the policewoman.

'And how's the tailing going?'

'He went to the BNL in Piazza della Repubblica and then home from there, which is where he is now.'

'Did they notice anything strange?'

'Nothing.'

'OK, Teresa. We're not letting him out of our sight.'

'Absolutely not.'

Teresa had received a phone call mid-morning that had left her very thoughtful, so she had taken advantage of her conversation with Ferrara to talk to him about it: Vinci had summoned her urgently. The Deputy Prosecutor's voice hadn't seemed warm and friendly like it had on other occasions. Had something happened? The Chief Superintendent had advised her to say that he was the one responsible if Vinci accused her of anything.

'Update me as soon as you get back to the office, Teresa.'

'Of course, chief, I'll let you know the moment I'm back.'

Vinci was waiting for her on the pavement in front of the Prosecutor's Department. He was pacing nervously up and down and he started towards her as soon as he saw her.

'Come with me, Superintendent,' he invited her in a formal tone.

They crossed the Piazza della Repubblica in silence and continued along the Via del Corso. They reached the area near Dante's house and went into a building to their right. These were the offices of the presiding judge and had once been the seat of the magistrate's court before it had been abolished. They went up a room on the first floor with no one else in it.

'Sit down, Superintendent,' he ordered in the same glacial tone.

She obeyed, slumping into a seat with a fake leather cover that was rumpled in more than one place, while Vinci made himself comfortable behind a dusty desk and began to drum the fingers of both hands.

'I've put my trust in the wrong person,' he began, his face becoming darker and darker. 'It was a gross error of judgement and I've got proof of it.'

Proof?

'What's happened?' asked Teresa nervously.

'You're asking me? Don't you know? Are you trying to make fun of me as well now?'

She shook her head. 'I would never do that.'

'Are you trying to tell me that you know nothing about the kidnapping of Donato Russo's daughter?'

Silence fell.

'The Chief Prosecutor in Milan told Fiore. He said the traffic police had informed your boss, the Chief Superintendent. Him again! All that man ever does is cause trouble.'

'It was a regular inter-office communication. We knew you'd be informed by your Milanese colleagues. It's procedure.'

'What procedure? Ferrara's procedure?'

'He would have got in touch with you. I'm sure of it.'

'Are you defending him now?'

'He doesn't need me to defend him.'

'This morning I arranged for the telephone company to be called to have Donato Russo's telephone lines put under surveillance. My secretary was told that they'd been put under surveillance yesterday evening, in accordance with an urgent warrant issued by the Prosecutor's Department in Civitavecchia,' ranted Vinci. 'There's a name for that sort of behaviour – disloyalty. Or, better still, betrayal!'

Teresa maintained a stony silence.

Vinci got up and began to walk backwards and forwards. He stopped in front of the window for a long moment, his back to the policewoman. When he turned, his words came out as a low hiss: 'You can go now, Superintendent, and you should know that you're in serious shit this time. And forget what I told you the other day – it was a lie, a complete lie.'

Teresa didn't reply. She had understood. She got up and left the room with a curt 'good day'.

67

The Chief Superintendent's office

The meeting began at 3.30 p.m. on the dot.

The *Squadra Mobile* and the Forensics team had left the Marquis's home some time earlier and returned to their respective offices.

They had barely settled themselves round the table when the Chief Superintendent began to speak. 'We've had yet another revelation.' He let his gaze run over all those around the meeting table to underline the importance of this. 'Whatever the motive for his suicide may have been, based upon the material seized from his apartment Edoardo Degli Aldobrandi was a person of great interest in our investigation. That's why Francesco has gone to London.'

He paused briefly then continued, 'We need to take our investigation to the next level, since it seems our case has become even more complicated. It's time to get the facts in order. So we're going to go over everything – from the beginning.'

He reviewed the Russo murders in a succinct, dynamic style. It was always a good idea to repeat such things so that not even the smallest detail was lost. Then he concentrated on the lawyer's 'secrets', another important element which from now on could be considered important in relation to the motive. He reviewed the evidence: the testimony of the prison guard, that of Italo Ortu, the information Felice Contini had given them and the album seized from the victim's home with those disturbing images of the murdered prostitutes and the satanic rite, those death portraits that seemed to beg for justice.

Everything tallied.

'And now we need to add the kidnapping of Flavia, Amedeo Russo's only grandchild. It appears to be an attempt to get the photos they couldn't find. That's why they're blackmailing Donato Russo. The envelope seized by the Milanese traffic police implies that they have made contact with him. At this point Donato Russo is the key to shining a light on the murder of his parents,' Ferrara continued.

Ascalchi, Ciuffi and Venturi nodded vigorously.

'Teresa?' Ferrara looked at her, concerned. 'You seem distracted. Don't worry about what Vinci said. The best way for us to respond to his threats is with facts. Those are our strength.'

'Yes, chief, the facts.' The policewoman smiled, albeit a little uncertainly. 'I agree with everything you say, it's just that—'

'I told you not to worry about what Vinci said.'

Teresa smiled at him with more conviction.

'Good! Let's go and get a coffee before we move on to the question of the Nigerians.'

In the meantime the Surveillance Room at Headquarters hadn't registered anything new from Donato Russo's telephones.

No contact with the kidnappers and no conversations referring to his daughter's kidnap. Only routine phone calls to his uncle and the firm's offices. But a call from one of Flavia's school friends asking for news was just coming in.

'She's with our relatives at Livorno. She needs rest and something to take her mind off all the sadness,' Russo had told her.

At 4.07 p.m. an extremely brief direct call to a mobile phone was recorded. The mobile belonged to Veronica Borghini.

'Expect me this evening, Veri,' Donato Russo had told her.

'I will, darling. With the usual anticipation . . .'

The Chief Superintendent had no sooner arrived back in the office than Fanti told him about the phone call.

'Well, there's a surprise! And if it hadn't been for the Prosecutor's Department in Civitavecchia, we'd still be in the dark,' he said, thinking about the request for a warrant to tap Signora Borghini's phones which was still lying unauthorised on Vinci's desk. 'First we find out she was Amedeo Russo's lover, now it turns out she's involved with Donato. Tell the officers not to let him out of their sight for a single moment and to log exactly how much time he spends at Borghini's house.'

While Fanti returned to his office to make the phone call, Ferrara summoned the team into his office for a briefing. He began by reminding them that even though they hadn't been able find conclusive evidence to link the Nigerian woman, Oba, to the current investigation, there was still illegal activity that needed to be stopped. 'We should be able to get some help with that in England. Scotland Yard's investigation into those minors who disappeared without trace after being sexually abused may throw up some leads that will be useful to us. I'm also hoping they can shed some light on the material seized from Edoardo Degli Aldobrandi.'

Though there were many points that still needed clarifying, the 'MY MASS' video they'd found in the Marquis's apartment meant that they at last had some solid evidence to support their hypotheses.

'Francesco's going to see if the English can identify the man featured in the video,' Ferrara told them. 'If they can, it might just crack this case wide open.'

68

Yorkshire, England

Sir George Holley was lifting the telephone receiver to his ear when a sudden thunderclap made him jump. He looked out of the window of his study as the darkness of the countryside was illuminated by a flash of lightning. The weather conditions were doing nothing to dispel his unease. The news Bill had given him earlier had sent him into a mood as dark as the thunderclouds that filled the sky.

By the time he hung up, his displeasure had turned to rage. That imbecile Richard Wilson and his mistakes had set in motion a domino effect. Everything he'd worked to build was now in danger of collapsing around him. His business empire, the Lodge, even his own life were now in jeopardy. And despite the measures he had put in place to guard against further damage, a Florentine policeman by the name of Francesco Rizzo had just arrived in London, armed with 'potentially explosive' information – but Holley's spies were so fucking inept they couldn't even tell him what that information might be.

Gordon Taylor looked like a mastiff.

He was tall and solidly built with wavy grey hair. That day he was wearing a pair of dark trousers and a crew-neck sweater made from Shetland wool. His melancholy expression and the web of lines on his face were a legacy of the thirty-odd years he'd spent on the force.

A tri-coloured white, black and tan English Setter was curled up at Taylor's feet. He studied their Italian guest with a gaze as melancholy as Taylor's.

Having arrived at Scotland Yard, Rizzo had discovered that the principal architect of the 1990 operation on 'snuff' videos was now retired. To his relief, a phone call had secured him an audience with the former Detective Chief Inspector.

Perhaps there's some truth in the saying that dogs resemble their owners, thought Rizzo as he took a seat opposite the British policeman in the living room of his home in Smithfield, near the famous meat market.

Taylor took a Dunhill out of a packet and lit it. He offered one to Rizzo, who accepted.

'So, Superintendent Rizzo, how can I help you?'

Rizzo spent the next half hour unravelling the complex investigative knot of the previous months for his colleague. The Englishman listened attentively, then, when Rizzo concluded his account, he took out a new cigarette and put it between his lips without lighting it. Taylor remained like that for several minutes, the cigarette unlit, shaking his head as he tried to process the information.

Finally he spoke: 'It's going to be difficult to prove that all these investigations are connected.'

'I know. We'll need irrefutable evidence to get a conviction.'

'It's almost impossible to acquire irrefutable evidence where occultism and perverts are involved.'

Rizzo nodded disconsolately. He couldn't accept the idea of throwing in the towel, especially after he'd come this far.

'Would you like a cup of tea?' said Taylor, getting up from his armchair. The English Setter got up too, ready to follow its master into the kitchen.

'I'd love one, thank you,' replied Rizzo, amused by the dog's devotion.

A few minutes later Gordon Taylor returned with a loaded tray. He poured the tea, handed a cup to his guest and then sat down. The dog stared at him as if he were waiting for him to give him something then rested his muzzle on Taylor's leg.

'No, there's nothing for you, Jack,' he said, stroking the dog's head. Then, after taking a sip of his tea, the Englishman looked up at Rizzo.

'I think that the murders you've told me about might just be the key that opens the door to a secret world where ritual murder is routinely practiced ... ' He paused to light a cigarette while Rizzo stared at him curiously. 'Anyone who tries to penetrate that world is signing their own death warrant. They'll do anything to protect their secrets.'

'Are you referring to a deviant masonic sect, by any chance?'

The other man nodded. 'We spent years trying to penetrate their wall of secrecy, but every time we thought we were getting close they shut us down. All I can tell you is that there are a lot of them and they are extremely powerful. They will stop at nothing to protect their identities, and they can rely on friends in high places, even among the government, the judiciary and the police force itself. Éminences grises, acting on behalf of the sect members, guarding their secrets.

Éminences grises! It was the same the whole world over.

'Have you carried out a lot of these investigations then?'

A banal question, perhaps, but Rizzo wanted to keep him talking so that he could learn as much as possible.

'Yes, but they got the better of us every single time. Justice and, ultimately, civilised society have been defeated.' Sadness tinged with regret clouded the Englishman's features. 'You know ...' he took a deep drag on his cigarette, studying the bluish cloud that curled towards the ceiling for a moment ' ... history repeats itself, years or even centuries later. To understand certain cases it's sometimes necessary to study similar crimes from the past.'

'This sect has been established in England a long time then?'

'Certain lodges, like the Golden Dawn, began here – one of its branches subsequently spread to Florence. Crowley – the Great Beast 666 – was English. Have you heard of him?'

'Yes.'

'The first true modern serial killer was English.'

'Jack the Ripper.'

'Precisely.' Taylor stubbed out his cigarette. 'Has it struck you that there are parallels between the murder of this couple that you're investigating and the Monster of Florence?'

Rizzo nodded.

'We followed that case. In fact we even made our own contribution, although unfortunately it turned out to be fruitless.'

'I knew the FBI were involved, but not Scotland Yard.'

'Yes, us too. A piece of fabric found in a suspect's house was sent to us a for a DNA test. The Italian authorities didn't have the technology to carry out such tests back in the eighties. As I recall, the suspect wasn't a native of Tuscany ... ' His brow furrowed as he tried to recall more details, but the name eluded him. 'Anyway, you see my point: history is full of cases with strong similarities to the one you're working on. And then of course there's the long-standing connection between Florence and London – a pact with the Devil, sealed in blood, its roots reaching back through the centuries.'

Rizzo knew that the English had enjoyed a long-standing love affair with Tuscany, and Florence in particular, but this was the first he'd heard of a blood pact with Satan.

His face must have betrayed his incredulity.

'You don't seem convinced,' said Taylor.

'I don't know. These cases you're talking about, they could just be coincidences. I mean, I don't normally believe in coincidences, but—'

'They're not coincidences. Study the past and I guarantee you'll see what I'm talking about.'

Rizzo decided to bring the conversation back to the present. Even though he thought some of the Englishman's ideas were far-fetched, he'd come to the conclusion that he could be trusted. 'Does the name Sir George Holley mean anything to you?' he asked.

The expression of genial interest on the Englishman's face suddenly disappeared. He got to his feet abruptly. 'Wait here a moment. I need to check something.' Followed once again by the dog, he disappeared into the other room.

A few minutes later he reappeared. 'Something's come up. Can you come back another time?'

'When?'

'Ring me tomorrow.'

And with that Gordon Taylor ushered Rizzo out of his house, closing the door firmly behind him.

Alone again, Gordon Taylor poured himself a second cup of tea and sat down to think back over his conversation with the Italian. He'd taken a liking to Rizzo, recognising a kindred spirit. Listening to his account of the investigation that had been taking place in Florence, he'd been reminded of himself as a younger man, confronted by horrific crimes yet unable to bring the perpetrators to justice. He had been reminded of his old boss, too. Sir Edward Brown had been relentless in his pursuit of those responsible. Then, a couple of months before he was due to retire, he'd been found dead in a hotel in the Balearics. According to the authorities, Sir Edward had taken his own life.

Taylor had never accepted that suicide verdict. It was completely out of character for the man he'd worked with all those years to do such a thing. But although he'd been certain it was a case of murder disguised as suicide, no one would listen to him.

Wearily he got up, went into his study and removed a wooden case from the bottom drawer of his desk. He slipped the key into the lock and opened it, then took out a couple of sheets of paper and read them for the hundredth time.

Dear Gordon,

I have arranged for this letter to be delivered to you in the event of my death. I rather doubt, given the nature of our recent investigations, that it will have been due to natural causes.

You know as well as I that for some years now the most heinous crimes have gone unpunished because the men responsible occupy positions of power and influence. Far from upholding the law, they subvert it in order to engage in their vile rituals and depraved practices. They abuse the trust invested in them, they rape and mutilate and murder innocent victims, and they do it with impunity. They are a canker at the heart of society, but such is their power, every attempt to expose this evil is suppressed, all evidence destroyed.

After launching investigation after investigation, only to see my efforts thwarted, I came to the conclusion that my one hope of building a successful case against them would be to resort to subterfuge. I turned to conducting my inquiries in secret, and when damning evidence came my way, I did not declare it. Piece by piece, I hid it away where they could not get their hands on it, in readiness for the moment when the right conditions would prevail for justice to be done.

My great fear, however, is that I will be eliminated before that day arrives. Hence this letter. You, Gordon, are my insurance policy, the one person I can trust to act in the event that I am no longer able to.

No doubt you are eager to learn where this hoard of evidence is. But before I tell you, I must issue a word of caution: do not act in haste. Whatever the circumstances of my death, do not attempt to avenge me by exposing these hard-won secrets, for you will only jeopardise your own life and any prospect of achieving justice. If you reveal them to our colleagues in the force there's a danger the ensuing investigation will be suppressed, just as our investigations were. I don't think I need to tell you that the judiciary cannot be trusted, and neither can the politicians.

I therefore offer you two suggestions: either find an independent newspaper or broadcaster you can rely on, or seek out an ally within one of the European police forces – ideally the Belgian or Italian force, since there are specific references in the hoard that may be of interest to them.

When the time comes and you are ready to act, go to Church Wood and look up that old friend I introduced you to when you came to stay at the manor. He will guide you to an outbuilding where you will find a trapdoor concealed beneath several bales of hay. It leads to a basement that is full of junk accumulated by my parents over the years. Look carefully and you will recognise an item of mine. I advise you to remember my personal details, because they will serve you well.

Take care, my friend. I wish you good fortune.

Yours,

Edward

Taylor refolded the sheets of paper and put them back in their place, carefully locking the box and returning it to the drawer. Then he looked up to find Jack watching him. The dog began to wag his tail, a reminder that it was time for their afternoon walk.

'Do you know what I should do?' Gordon Taylor asked, stroking the dog's head.

Jack barked.

'Quite right, Jack. There's a lot resting on this; instead of rushing into a decision, I should sleep on it. In the meantime, let's take our walk, shall we?'

69

The home of Veronica Borghini, Florence

As he climbed the step to the front door, Donato Russo had the distinct impression that there was someone behind him. When he turned his head, his impression became certainty.

A tall man, his face hidden by a balaclava, grabbed him by the neck. A second masked man materialised alongside him and taped his mouth shut with duct tape.

'Give me the keys and don't put up a fight,' one of them muttered in his ear.

Shaking, Donato Russo nodded towards his right-hand trouser pocket. The man took the key and opened the door. They went inside. Then they moved silently through the darkness until they came to the bedroom.

Veronica was stretched out half-naked on the bed, illuminated by the red glow of a bedside lamp. The second masked man leapt forward, covering her mouth with a gloved hand and cutting off her scream.

'Don't make a sound or I'll kill you!' he snarled.

Then he removed his hand and applied duct tape to her mouth.

'Put some clothes on, you slut,' he told her. He followed her to the wardrobe and made her put on a black silk dressing gown, leering as he watched her wrap it around her body and tie the cord. Then he tied her to a chair with another strip of tape, leaning in close to tell her all the things he'd like to do to her.

In the meantime, the hooded man had led Donato Russo into another room. Once there he took the tape off his mouth.

'Now we can talk,' he said.

'Please don't hurt us, I beg you,' Russo whispered in a small voice.

'Did you find what we asked for?'

'Yes.'

'We saw you go to the bank today. We know what time you went in, how long you stayed inside and what time you left. Did you find what you were looking for?'

'Yes.'

'And where have you put it?'

'I want my daughter back before I give it to you. Safe and sound.'

The man didn't reply. He put the tape back over Donato's mouth and tied him to a chair. He needed to make a phone call from a secure mobile phone.

The police surveillance team who'd been monitoring Donato Russo's arrival at his girlfriend's house through infra-red binoculars, observed the attack and got straight on to Headquarters. The Chief Superintendent gave the order to wait for reinforcements and to intervene only in an emergency. Then he summoned Teresa and Venturi and set off at breakneck speed for Borgo Bellavista.

They pulled up a short distance from the entrance to the gated compound to wait for reinforcements in the shape of Ciuffi and an NOCS special response team. It was agonising, sitting there doing nothing, wondering what was going on inside the house, but Ferrara was gambling on the criminals keeping Donato Russo alive until they had the photographs.

Ordinarily, the Chief Superintendent wasn't a risk taker when people's lives were at stake, but he calculated the risk would only be increased if they went in now, without backup.

No, better by far to trust his instincts.

'Your daughter will be here soon,' said the masked man. Then he slipped the pistol out of the waistband of his trousers and loaded a round.

Donato Russo was convinced this would be the last night of his life. He knew too much. The names of the politicians and their vices. Their dirty secrets. But the only thing that mattered was Flavia. If it was true that she was alive, that was all he cared about.

Half an hour later the silence of the countryside was broken by the rumbling of a car's engine. It was a Fiat Panda four-by-four.

The two police officers who were watching the turn-off for the private road that led to the compound radioed that it had gone past. Aside from the driver, there appeared to be no one else inside.

'We mustn't be seen!' said Ferrara, ordering everyone to remain out of sight.

The car slowed down as it approached the compound. Then, one hundred metres from the entrance, the driver hit the brakes and threw the vehicle into reverse.

He must have seen something to alert him to the police presence.

The Chief Superintendent radioed the team watching the turn-off and they emerged from their hiding place to signal to the driver to stop. He leapt from the vehicle and tried to flee, but was soon caught. They found a pistol with the registration number filed off in the waistband of his trousers. An illegal weapon.

A more important discovery was waiting for them when they opened the boot.

There was Flavia, curled up like a puppy. Her hands and feet were bound and she had a gag over her mouth. Though they tried to be as gentle as they could, when they lifted her out she whimpered and screwed up her eyes in pain. A police officer undid the gag so that she could breathe, and held her while she retched into the gutter. Then Flavia burst into tears of relief.

The Chief Superintendent knew that the two criminals inside the house would soon be wondering where their accomplice had got to. His failure to arrive could send them into panic, which could prove fatal for Donato Russo and Veronica Borghini.

He had two options: wait for the NOCS team or go in now, without backup. Ferrara rang Ciuffi and asked when the specialist team would arrive. Then he consulted with Ascalchi, Venturi and Teresa.

They needed to make a decision; they were running out of time.

Inside the house the hooded man was pacing backwards and forwards, glancing at his wristwatch and muttering under his breath.

Veronica was terrified. Her head was spinning and she felt as if she was going to be sick. She used her eyes to beg her captor to take the tape off her mouth. The man let himself be persuaded.

'I need the toilet,' she said in a small voice.

He untied her and marched her to the bathroom, then leaned against the doorframe, watching. 'Hurry up!' he barked. 'Otherwise I'll take you back again.'

'At least turn around,' she pleaded. 'I can't go with you watching.'

The man laughed. 'Don't even think about it!' He pushed

himself away from the door. 'Come on, gorgeous, let's get those panties off, eh?'

With one hand he reached under her dressing gown and tore off her underwear. His other hand was fumbling with the zip on his trousers. He couldn't hold back. Seeing her half-naked and terrified had turned him on, and now he was going to fuck this slut, just the way he'd been fantasising about from the moment he saw her on the bed.

Her eyes dark with fear, Veronica begged him, 'Please, don't—'

'Shut up, slut, or I'll dismember that hot little body of yours!' He spun her round so that she was forced to bend over the sink, then he penetrated her. Gripping her hips tightly, he thrust into her again and again, with such force that she felt herself tearing inside. Unable to hold back, she let out a scream.

The other criminal was turning toward the sound of the scream when he heard a noise at the front door. Hurriedly turning out the light, he dropped to his haunches, using the chair to which he'd tied Donato Russo as a shield.

When he saw the police coming in, he came out of his crouching position.

'No!' yelled Ferrara, his torch beam finding the hooded man.

Bullets sliced through the darkness. There was a thud as the criminal dropped his sixteen-round automatic pistol and collapsed against the wall, then he slid to the ground.

'Fuck off,' murmured the injured man when the Chief Superintendent leaned over him. 'Go to hell, you piece of sh—'

Those were his last words.

Then he closed his eyes.

Forever.

When the lights came on, Teresa was stretched out on the floor. Her shoulder, arm and leg felt wet. It didn't take her long to realise that she wasn't damp with sweat but soaked in her own blood. The air was saturated with the bitter smell of gunpowder, which was creeping into her nostrils.

Ferrara looked like he was about to shout, but his voice was stifled by dismay. He knelt down beside her to check the extent of her injuries. Teresa's head was bleeding too.

'Call an ambulance,' he ordered.

'Two ambulances,' Ascalchi's voice was like an echo. Donato Russo had also been hit.

At the first sound of gunfire, the other kidnapper had climbed out of the bathroom window. There was no one watching that part of the house. He tore off the mask that had been covering his face and set off running as fast as he could into the woods.

Veronica was on her knees on the bathroom floor, doubled over with pain. 'Fucking bastard,' she sobbed, over and over.

When the police broke down the door and tried to help her up, she stretched out an arm, pointing to the open window. 'That way.'

By this time Ciuffi and the reinforcements had arrived. Pino Ricci set off in pursuit of the rapist, yelling for his colleagues to spread out and cover all exits. They couldn't let him escape.

Attracted by the shots, the residents of the compound had gathered in front of Veronica Borghini's house. Pale and scared, they huddled together, talking in low voices. Antonello Corti was among them, his face livid. He tried to approach the house, but a uniformed officer waved him away.

Suddenly all that could be heard was the wail of sirens as the ambulances and other emergency services rushed to the scene.

'Oh God, please let her make it!' the Chief Superintendent kept repeating, clutching Teresa's hand as he sat beside her stretcher in the back of the ambulance.

It seemed to take forever, but finally they made it to the hospital at Ponte a Niccheri.

'We're here,' he murmured to her as they wheeled her through the entrance. Her eyes were closed; she didn't hear him. She had lost consciousness and the darkness had swallowed her up.

The darkness.

Flavia had climbed into the second ambulance with her father, stroking his face as the paramedics attended to the bullet wound in his leg. Donato Russo didn't seem to hear them when they told him it wasn't very deep and should heal within a few days; he was too busy hugging his daughter.

For Teresa the prognosis was not so good. She was rushed straight into surgery, her condition critical, while the Chief Superintendent paced the corridor like a caged lion.

70

Friday 29 October

It was almost five in the morning and the Chief Superintendent, who had returned to the office several hours ago, had just finished watching the last of the eight DVDs removed from Donato Russo's home. He had been joined by Deputy Prosecutor Impallomeni, who had set off from Civitavecchia the moment he received word of events in Florence, intent on hearing the full details and ready to authorise the next steps of the ongoing investigations. Like Ferrara's old friend Anna Giulietti, he was a deputy prosecutor you could count on.

The DVDs all followed the same pattern, though the participants varied. The men had all been filmed with their backs to the camera. One man was filmed screwing three young girls: the eldest might have been sixteen, or seventeen at the most. The youngest looked to be ten or eleven.

Ferrara and Impallomeni exchanged a look of disgust when they saw the images from the last two films: a girl, probably a minor, was stretched out on the bed wearing nothing but a pair of blood-red panties, a colour that stood out against her black skin. Her thin wrists were secured to the wrought-iron bedstead. There was no sound on the video; the action played out in an eerie silence.

To begin with, her movements didn't give the impression that she was scared. If anything, she seemed to consider it a game. Then a man stepped into view, wearing a sadomasochistic outfit: a leather bodice and fishnet tights. On his head was a hood. In his right hand he was holding a wad of cotton, which he pressed against the girl's nose. The man kept a hand around her throat during the entire sexual act, clearly to increase his own pleasure. When he reared up he squeezed even harder, so that the girl began to thrash around underneath him. The more she struggled, the more aroused he became. Then she fell still. The man calmly raised himself off her body and began to use his left hand to masturbate, spurting sperm over what was now a corpse.

Disturbed, Ferrara put the final DVD. The opening sequence showed a scene that was familiar to him: figures approaching a chapel set in a garden. This was followed by a shot featuring hooded figures around an altar on which lay a dark-skinned young woman, her hands and feet tied. They began to enact a ritual during which one of the adherents waved a crucifix with an upside down Christ in the air, while another brandished a dagger with a handle in the shape of a snake. Yet another thrust a crucifix into her vagina. The man with the dagger plunged it into the woman's body. A chalice was placed so as to catch her blood. When it was full, the hooded figures passed it from hand to hand, taking it in turns to drink.

In every respect, the DVD matched the photographs in Amedeo Russo's album. Presumably the photographs were screen captures from the DVD footage.

There was, however, one crucial difference between the photos in the album and the DVD. In the film version, the men had been shown walking through the garden towards the chapel without their hoods. Some had been photographed from behind and others in profile, but two of them were instantly recognisable to Ferrara: Cosimo Presti and Luca Fiore.

The Chief Superintendent made a note of the time code for each DVD and the date on which the recording was made. In every case they had been made between midnight and three in the morning.

Under Impallomeni's watchful gaze, he then skimmed through Amedeo Russo's diary until he found the list of the names that matched the individuals in the videos.

Among them was the Honourable Orazio Dentice – the politician who had accused the *Squadra Mobile* of 'chasing shadows' in an interview with *La Nazione* at the time of the Roma stabbing. And then he'd tabled a parliamentary question.

The Commissioner was still waiting for the information he'd requested from Ferrara in response to that parliamentary question.

Well, here it was: the information he wanted. This explained everything.

The list included the names of pillars of the community, considered beyond reproach. The DVDs proved they were anything but.

For the Chief Superintendent the most shocking discovery was Luca Fiore's participation in the video showing scenes of human sacrifice. It was dated 1981.

His intuition hadn't let him down. Luca Fiore's double life had made him susceptible to blackmail.

Ferrara felt a weight bearing down on him at the thought of the scandal that was about to erupt – a scandal of immense proportions, unprecedented in Tuscany and perhaps in Italy. He knew he could expect a concerted attempt at a cover-up; there were vested interests who would try to suffocate the investigation by any means at their disposal, legal or illegal. If they succeeded, the truth might never be known. The Chief Superintendent couldn't help wondering whether, ultimately, he'd be the only one determined to uncover the truth at all costs. The prospect was not an encouraging one.

He was conferring with Impallomeni, trying to agree a strategy for confronting the situation, when two officers led a handcuffed man into the room. He was over six foot tall with an athletic physique. The officers explained that this was the criminal who had fled Veronica Borghini's house. They had tracked him down to an abandoned cave at Maiano.

Ferrara recognised him as soon as he saw him.

It was Genius.

Daniele De Robertis had grazes on his face and hands from the fight he'd put up, resisting arrest. A tough guy, right to the end.

His eyes met the Chief Superintendent's, then he turned and gave Impallomeni a questioning look.

'This is the Deputy Prosecutor from Civitavecchia,' said Ferrara. Then he added, 'Genius, the moment to talk has arrived.'

'Where's my friend, Pasquale?'

'He died when we returned fire after he seriously wounded one of my colleagues. Donato Russo was shot, too, but only superficially.'

Genius curled up in a ball, the news hitting him like a blow to the stomach.

The Deputy Prosecutor gave Ferrara a nod, then got up and left the room. He realised that this was a conversation best left to the police, at least to start with.

'Pasquale Nigro, your accomplice from Palermo who was bringing Russo's daughter to you, is still being questioned,' said the Chief Superintendent. He'd emphasised the *still* to make it clear that they were learning a lot, but Genius merely scowled.

What did he care if the guy spilled his guts to the police? He was just a nobody, a foot soldier. Pasquale, on the other hand, was perhaps the first true friend he'd ever had. And now he was dead, all because he'd been trying to help him.

As soon as they sent him back to prison, Genius would be dead too. He wouldn't stand a chance once he was deprived of the protection of Salvino Lo Cascio's *family*.

His gaze took in the pile of DVDs on the desk, then he looked the policeman in the eye. 'You're a brave man, Chief Superintendent. I didn't think you'd get this far. Most of your colleagues would have allowed themselves to be stopped, but you've persisted.'

He paused for a moment. He'd been of the opinion that everyone who knew anything would be killed, and that included the Chief Superintendent, but maybe he'd underestimated him. Perhaps if he put his trust in this policeman he could still have his revenge, even if he wouldn't be able to exact retribution in person.

'I think you're right,' he said, nodding to himself. 'The moment to talk has arrived.'

'Good,' said Ferrara, waving for him to take a seat.

'I tried to point you in the right direction from the start,' Genius began after making himself comfortable on one of the two seats. 'I got Pasquale to call you . . . '

Aha! The phone call!

' . . . sent you that note. So you know quite a lot of it already, but now you're going to learn the whole story – maybe more than you want to know.'

And maybe less. Genius had every intention of keeping the *family* who had done so much for him out of the story.

In the three hours that followed, Ferrara listened while Genius talked.

About the House of the Roses, a place of sadistic perversion.

About the international organisation that had infiltrated governments and police forces.

The Chief Superintendent transcribed every last detail into a voluntary statement by the detainee – a procedure allowed by law, which permitted him to listen to Daniele De Robertis without a lawyer present.

Because Genius hated lawyers.

He wanted nothing to do with them.

So it was one-on-one: just the Chief Superintendent and the detainee.

And under the rules governing voluntary statements, Ferrara was prohibited from asking a single question. So there could be no interrogation, no opportunity to steer the detainee to provide information on a particular event or person. It was all down to Daniele De Robertis to decide what he felt he ought to say.

But one after the other the pieces of the puzzle fell into place, fitting together perfectly, until it was complete. And at last the Great Beast, Sir George Holley, was revealed. A criminal with blue blood and a dark heart. He was the head of the Black Rose sect. The list of crimes he had committed ran to several pages; in addition to participating in the ritual sacrifice of a number of women and children, he had ordered the murders of Antonio Sergi and Fabio Biondi.

When Genius had finished talking and the statement was complete, Ferrara arranged for him to be taken to a secret safe house.

Adrenaline coursing through his veins, the Chief Superintendent waited until he was alone before ringing Rizzo in London to tell him about Genius's capture and statement, and pass on a warning: he should be wary in his dealings with Scotland Yard.

And he passed on the name that Genius had given him.

71

Parco delle Cascine

That night, while the operation at Borgo Bellavista was taking place, the Carabinieri had received a 112 call from a woman asking them to send a patrol car to the Parco delle Cascine. She'd told them she was at the pyramid on the Viale degli Olmi, which had been built by the Florentine architect Giuseppe Manetti in the seventeen hundreds for use as an ice-house.

The Carabinieri found no trace of the woman when they arrived, but there was an aluminium box sitting in front of the Fountain of Narcissus, the sandstone fountain which bears an inscription in honour of the famous English poet Percy Bysshe Shelley. Unsuspecting, they went over to it. Inside was a heart, covered in blood, and a piece of paper with Ferrara's name on it.

The pathologist's tests revealed the heart to be of animal origin. It would have been considered a prank, if not for the reference to the Chief Superintendent. The Carabinieri called in an expert on the esoteric who told them about a ritual whereby a heart was left out in the open in this manner to kill an enemy. As the heart was slowly devoured by animals, the intended victim would die an agonising death.

Nigerian beliefs!

Instead of going to Scotland Yard, Rizzo telephoned Gordon Taylor and asked if he could call on him. Taylor suggested that he come straight over.

They settled themselves in the same room as the previous day, but this time there were no leisurely cups of tea or cigarettes on offer. As soon as Rizzo was seated, the Englishman reached for the wooden box that was sitting on the table in front of him.

'There's something you need to read,' he said, reaching into the box and removing Sir Edward Brown's letter. 'Your English is excellent, but let me know if you have difficulty with any of the words.'

Rizzo took the sheet of paper and read it.

'What was in this hoard?' he asked when he'd finished.

'I haven't seen it yet. You've read what Sir Edward had to say about finding an ally – well, I tried, but . . . ' He stopped and looked at Rizzo ' . . . I didn't have one until now. We can go today, if that's all right with you.'

'Of course – and thank you for trusting me. But first I need to tell you about a phone call I had earlier this morning, from my boss . . . '

Rizzo quickly ran through the latest developments in the case. Then he repeated the warning Genius had issued with regard to Scotland Yard: that they should be wary of an individual named Sir Bill Evans.

'But he's the new chief – Sir Edward's successor,' said the Englishman, shaking his head in stunned disbelief before galvanising himself into action. 'This is all the more reason for us to get going – we can talk on the way.'

While Taylor drove, he told Rizzo how Sir Edward Brown had been forced to resign after his investigation into the pornographic 'snuff' videos implicated some important figures in London society.

'Everything came to a standstill on the investigation after that. I put it down to the fact that nobody else had all the details – Sir Edward wasn't a great one for committing things to paper, though at the time I wasn't aware that was a deliberate strategy on his part – so his successor would've had to start from scratch. But of course he didn't. And now we know why.'

'Some things are the same the whole world over!' commented Rizzo, and he described how the Head of the State police had tried to have Ferrara transferred to put a stop to his investigations into the Monster of Florence. He'd had to go through two legal appeals before he could return as head of the *Squadra Mobile*. 'Thank God it didn't end in a fake suicide in our case!'

'Indeed,' said Taylor. 'I should like to meet Chief Superintendent Michele Ferrara one day.'

72

The House of the Roses

After spending the morning in Ferrara's office, Deputy Prosecutor Impallomeni had prepared the documentation required to
gather evidence for the ongoing investigation. Top of the list –
given what Genius had told them about the House of the Roses,
the villa in San Gimignano owned by Sir George Holley – was a
warrant to search the premises.

At ten past five that afternoon, Ferrara pulled up outside
the imposing wrought-iron gates with three entwined black
roses that had haunted his dreams for so long. He was accompanied by a small army of police officers and Forensics
technicians.

The Chief Superintendent pressed the buzzer on the video
intercom several times.

'Who is it?' The voice from the intercom sounded elderly.

'Police!'

'One moment. I need to make a phone call.'

'Open this gate now!'

There was no reply.

Ferrara gave the order to climb the gate.

Pino Ricci was the first one over, immediately followed by
Ascalchi. They ran to the front door where they found a man in

his seventies with a mobile phone in his hand. Ricci took it from him.

'But what are—'

'Shut it!' Ascalchi told him, showing his police ID. He spoke into the phone: 'Hello?'

Nothing.

There was no one at the other end. Ricci hung up.

'Open the gate!' Ascalchi ordered the man, who was then led into a room for questioning.

He told them he was Sir George Holley's caretaker, and his name was Oreste Binci. It turned out he was also the maternal uncle of Fiorenzo Muti – Amedeo Russo's infamous client.

The search began.

It would take several hours given the number of rooms and outbuildings, not to mention the huge landscaped garden.

They would turn the whole thing upside down, no matter how long it took. When it came to searches, Ferrara went by the dictum that you knew what time you were starting but you never knew when you'd finish, especially when everything needed to be inspected so very carefully.

Kent, England

The village of Church Wood was situated deep in the Kent countryside, a ninety-minute drive from London which the two men spent swapping anecdotes about their most rewarding cases while Jack dozed on the backseat.

Taylor had only been there once before, but identified the manor house that had been Sir Edward's home without difficulty. The 'old friend' referred to in the letter lived in an annex just across the courtyard from the main house.

The elderly man who opened the door recognised Gordon Taylor at once.

'He said you'd be coming,' he told him as he shook his hand.

Then he noticed Rizzo and gave Taylor a questioning look. 'Who's this?' he asked sharply.

'He's a colleague from Italy. A police officer, like Edward,' Taylor reassured him.

The old man didn't seem too happy about having a stranger along, but he beckoned for them to follow him through a gate and along a slightly overgrown path to an old brick building with a tin roof. 'This is it,' said the man.

Taylor handed him Jack's lead and asked if he'd mind watching him while they went inside. Then they stepped into the dim interior and immediately began moving aside bales of straw until they exposed the trap door.

'Looks like an old air-raid shelter,' said Taylor, leading the way down the steps. His torch illuminated piles of boxes and discarded junk. He quickly spotted the battered briefcase Edward had used for work lying in a corner.

'Aren't you going to open it?' said Rizzo.

'Not here.'

They made their way back up the steps with the briefcase, and then, after thanking the old man and collecting Jack, went outside to the car.

Taylor drove for ten minutes or so, then parked in a layby. He picked up the briefcase. It was secured with a combination lock.

'Remember my personal details,' his friend had advised him.

He put in the day, month and the last two digits of the year Edward had been born.

The lock opened.

Inside were sheets of paper and photographs. Taylor flicked through the material, then handed the photos to Rizzo, who instantly recognised the one with Sir George Holley's name written on the back. He knew that face: it was the man with the glass of beer who'd featured in the video labelled MY MASS, seized from Edoardo Degli Aldobrandi's apartment.

'I think it would be best if you took this briefcase to Florence,' said Taylor. 'Given what your boss learned about Sir Bill Evans, the sooner you can get it out of the country the better.'

Rizzo was in full agreement. 'I'll take the next flight.'

73

The secret places

The search at San Gimignano was still underway.

The Forensics team had come armed with a vast array of equipment, including a Geodar. When they used it to survey the section of the garden surrounding an old deconsecrated chapel, they found that the earth had been disturbed. There were no trees nearby, so it wasn't caused by roots spreading underground. No, this was man's hand at work, not nature's.

They brought in mini Bobcat diggers, which were now moving the earth under the light of powerful lamps while Ciuffi stood by, overseeing the operation.

Inside the house itself, the Chief Superintendent was summoned by a shout from one of the officers who'd been searching the basement. He hurried down the stairs into a vast area where enormous vats of wine were stacked from the stone floor all the way to the vaulted ceilings. The search team were gathered in one corner: they'd found a recessed button in a niche, and when they'd pressed it, a hidden doorway had opened.

It was a secret passage.

Using torches to light their way, they went down stairs that had been worn uneven through use. Ahead of them were more tunnels leading to smaller spaces. It was a labyrinth.

They paused when the tunnel led them to an open space with an iron cross embedded in the ground and a painting of a shell on one of the walls. Below the shell, on the bare floor beside a battery-powered air-quality indicator, was an old chest secured with a rusty padlock.

'Break the lock!' ordered the Chief Superintendent.

Ricci broke it off with a single kick. Inside was a notebook containing page after page of writing. It was a list: names, addresses – not just in Italy but worldwide, dates of birth and another number that Ferrara couldn't fathom at first, until he flicked back to the beginning and realised the list had been compiled in chronological order according to these final numbers. It seemed likely that they referred to the date each individual had joined the lodge of the Black Rose, and, given the place where the list had been found, it couldn't mean much else.

Ferrara was about to place the book back in the chest when Officer Perrotta came running in, breathless with excitement. A secret compartment had been discovered behind a large mirror in one of the bedrooms. 'You need to come and see, chief.'

As they turned in the direction of the stairs, Ricci pressed the PLAY button on a stereo they'd found. The notes of a Bach sonata spread through the room, creating an eerie echo throughout the cellar.

The Chief Superintendent followed Perrotta through the house, the music still playing in the background. He was almost at the door to the bedroom where the secret compartment had been found when his mobile phone rang. He looked at the display: Rizzo. He answered, his heart skipping a beat. He had a strange premonition.

'What is it, Francesco?'

Rizzo told him about the trip to Kent and the briefcase, then reported that he would shortly be boarding a flight to Rome – there weren't any direct flights to Florence.

'I'll send someone to pick you up from Fiumicino airport,' replied Ferrara. 'Have a good journey and be careful.'

'Don't worry, Michele.'

The secret compartment behind the mirror held a video camera and a metal rack full of videos and DVDs along one of the walls. The camera was situated so that it could film what was happening in the bedroom. Ferrara recognised the room as the one that had featured in the videos Russo had stashed away.

The House of the Roses' secret room.

Was it the only one, or were there others?

The Chief Superintendent urged the officers to keep searching, then he dialled the direct line to his office. Impallomeni, who had remained at Headquarters to wait for news, answered in person.

Ferrara told him about the latest developments.

'My congratulations to you and your men,' replied the Deputy Prosecutor. 'I'll join you right away,' he concluded.

'I'll be expecting you.'

Ferrara hung up thinking that once again his instinct had led him true. Here at last was a Deputy Prosecutor who knew how to work alongside the police.

Out in the garden, the Bobcat digger had been busily excavating a trench. At a depth of just over one metre a black plastic bag had been unearthed. Inside were human remains, along with an inverted crucifix and a dagger with a serpent-shaped handle.

The Chief Superintendent made his way over and gave the order to label the remains. The knife was identical to the one in Amedeo Russo's photo album. So was the crucifix. Could these be the remains of the young dark-skinned girl who'd been sacrificed to Satan?

'Carry on!' he ordered. 'We're not leaving until we've checked every last inch of this garden.'

He moved away a few metres, taking stock. It was beginning to look as though they had found the lair of the Great Beast. It was in this very villa that the gatherings of the Black Rose sect had taken place. It was here, not in England, that powerful men had come together. Politicians, civil servants, businessmen, even some celebrities. Their names were all accurately recorded in the book stored in the chest.

Ferrara was certain that the human remains they'd found wouldn't be the only ones. But how many other victims would go undiscovered? It was inevitable when an investigation had to contend with murder on such a massive scale

Within the hour, two further sacks were uncovered in the presence of the Deputy Prosecutor. These too contained human remains and the identical two items: a crucifix and a dagger.

The searched continued for several more hours. The police officers lost all sense of time and, on leaving the villa with the material they'd seized and the custodian in handcuffs, they were amazed to realise that the dawn of a new day was breaking on the horizon.

74

Monday 1 November

The police spent the next forty-eight hours watching the video-tapes and DVDs recovered from the villa.

They had only managed to identify a handful of the women from the films. However, they were able to confirm that the African girls had indeed been provided by Oba, as proved by a sheet of paper found amongst the seized papers which featured her name and address.

They weren't professional prostitutes, but aspiring models and actresses seeking their fortunes. Or rather, girls hoping to get a job in return for sexual favours. They had been the ones to satisfy these men's perverted pleasures. They had been the ones to enliven these monsters' nights.

The identity of those responsible was no longer a secret known only to sect members. Through a macabre coincidence it was 1 November, All Saints Day, when the dead are remembered. Operation Honour The Dead was launched that same day. It was a police operation of historic scale.

The first person Ferrara handcuffed was Luca Fiore. He arrested him personally, as he left his house on his way to pay the traditional visit to the family tomb. He wanted to save him the humiliation of being arrested in front of his employees on a workday.

The warrant for his arrest had been signed by Enrico Impallomeni, who had not been the least bit intimidated by the scale of the investigation – proof that yes, you could still have faith in the judiciary.

Fortunately the bad apples were destined to meet an ignominious end sooner or later.

In England, Sir George Holley and Sir Bill Evans, the head of Scotland Yard, were among those arrested, thanks to the evidence painstakingly gathered by Sir Edward Brown.

Gordon Taylor rang Rizzo to congratulate him. He was delighted he had managed to achieve justice for his old chief and friend, something he'd feared would never happen in his lifetime.

An emotional Rizzo invited him to Florence for the approaching Christmas holidays. 'And bring Jack with you! Imagine the walks we can go on in our beautiful countryside,' he told him before he hung up.

EPILOGUE

Florence, Ponte a Niccheri Hospital, 3 November 2004

The Chief Superintendent walked through the hospital doors with a bunch of roses in one hand and a couple of newspapers in the other.

He went to the room where Teresa Micalizi still lay.

They let him in at reception even though it was outside visiting hours. When he knocked gently at the door, the policewoman's mother came to open it. She hadn't left her daughter's side for a single moment. She was waiting for her to be discharged so she could take her home to Milan.

Teresa smiled when she saw him come in, her eyes shining. As soon as the Chief Superintendent came over to the bed to stroke her cheek, she thanked him for everything he had done, and especially for gaining permission from the hospital authorities for her mother to stay in her room.

'It was the least I could do, Teresa,' Ferrara replied.

'No, you've done a lot, chief.'

Her mother had taken the bunch of flowers and was busy arranging them in a glass vase.

'I brought these for you. You can read them in peace later on,' said Ferrara, showing her the papers and putting them on her bedside table.

'No, I want to read them now,' she replied, curious.

Ferrara handed her *The Times*.

The headline on the front page announced: HEAD OF SCOT-LAND YARD AND SIR GEORGE HOLLEY ARRESTED. HISTORIC MURDERS COME TO LIGHT.

In one of the photos Sir George Holley was immortalised leaving through the front door of his castle. He was wearing a dark hat and gold-rimmed glasses. He was flanked by two agents from Interpol.

The Times paid tribute to the Italian police for their decisive contribution to the effort to bring such dangerous criminals to justice; criminals who'd been above suspicion until that moment. And, furthermore, for enabling them to shine a light on the murder of a number of young Britons who had been lost without a trace.

'I'll treasure this,' said Teresa.

'They'll discharge you soon.'

'I know, the doctor told me this morning. I might be out of here next week.'

'And you'll be coming with me,' interrupted her mother.

'Yes.'

The Chief Superintendent said goodbye and left the room.

She was a brave police officer. He wished her every happiness.